The Clockwork Dagger

The Clockwork Dagger

Beth Cato

HarperCollins books may be purchased for educational, business, or sales promotional use. For information please e-mail the Special Markets Department at SPsales@harpercollins.com.

FIRST EDITION

Designed by Paula Szafranski

Library of Congress Cataloging-in-Publication Data has been applied for.

ISBN 978-0-06-231384-3

14 15 16 17 18 OV/RRD 10 9 8 7 6 5 4 3 2 1

To Jason. Because.

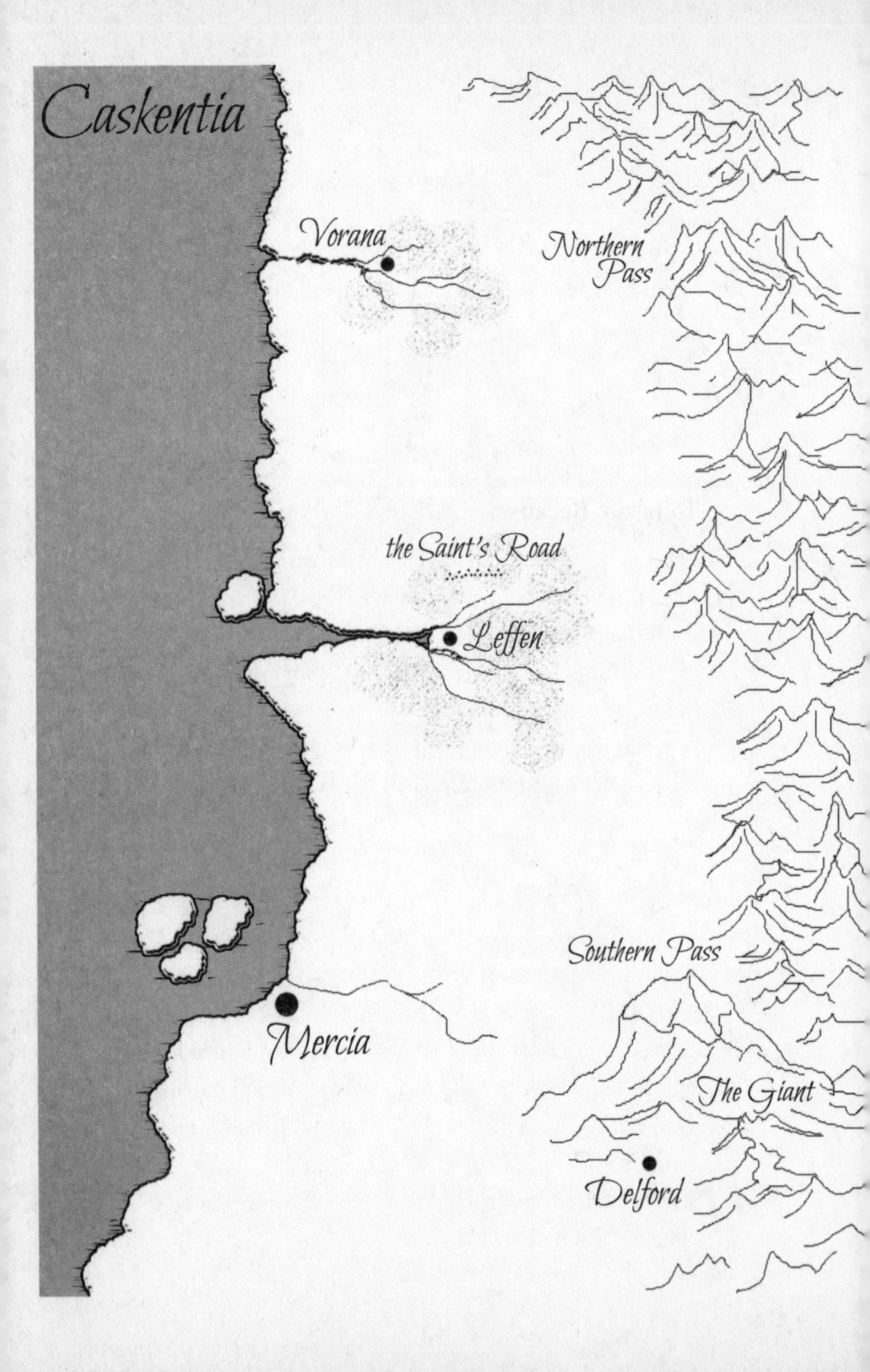
Caskentia
Vorana
Northern Pass
the Saint's Road
Leffen
Southern Pass
Mercia
The Giant
Delford

Chapter 1

Octavia Leander's journey to her new source of employment was to be guided by three essential rules: that she hide her occupation, lest others take advantage; that she be frugal with her coin and avoid any indulgences that come with newfound independence; and that she shun the presence of men, as nothing useful or proper could possibly happen in their company.

Not ten feet from being let out of her carriage, Octavia was prepared to shatter Miss Percival's most strongly advised first rule.

The dog was but a puppy, round tummy swaying and tail wagging. It had whirled in the middle of the busy roadway and then chased after a chugging steam car. Along the elevated wooden boardwalk on the other side of the road, a little girl cried, tears leaving clean streaks in the gray filth of her face. A broken leash draped from her hand. Even through the port-side din of bells and motors and murmuring humanity, Octavia could hear the joyful barks of the puppy.

She also heard the sharp crunch and the guttural howl.

Seconds later, the klaxons and discordant notes of fresh trauma rang faintly in her ears.

Urgent healings of dogs and other small creatures, such as children, only invited grief. Miss Percival's advice echoed in her mind. *You are a businesswoman, not a charity worker.*

Those canine notes of pain pierced through any armor offered by rationality.

"Fiddlesticks," Octavia muttered beneath her breath.

She glanced both ways. It was a busy avenue four lanes thick, the traffic a mixture of horses, steam cabriolets, and automated cycles, all of them stirring up a thick cloud of dust. The fumes stung her nose and burned in her eyes. She could no longer see the dog. No matter; the cry of fresh blood would call her forth. Octavia set her satchel atop her rolling case and strapped the two together, then pulled forth her parasol. She flared it open to reveal cloth of a brilliant blue with a white lace trim. Stabbing the parasol forward as a bright shield, she stepped into traffic.

A chorus of steam horns, like maddened geese, deafened her. A workman leaned out of his lorry and swore. Octavia refused to meet his eye. The wails of the body in need guided her around the backside of a cabriolet. She spied the filthy lump of mutt just ahead, not far from the fidgeting hooves of a drayman's carriage.

"By Kethan's bastards! Are you mad?" snarled the driver from his high seat. His body's song burbled sour notes of infection.

Octavia didn't deem him worthy of reply. In a graceful gesture, she shut the parasol and hooked it on her luggage strap. She snapped off her gloves and tucked them into a satchel pocket, then scooped up the fat pup. It whined and tried to struggle, the cries of its blood louder than the vocalizations. The dog's side was caved in and bore the distinct narrow track of an automated cycle. Tucking the puppy against her hip, she strode toward the walkway, her suitcase bouncing with each rut. A few more horns blared, and then the rattle of traffic resumed.

On the boardwalk again, the reality of what she had done caused her knees to quiver. *The puppy needed me, but I didn't need to nearly kill myself in the process. Lady, what was I thinking?*

Now here she was, burdened by luggage with a dying puppy on her hip, soiling her best new dress. Only new dress, actually. It was a good thing the cloth was a deep burgundy.

However foolish Octavia's actions, Miss Percival's first rule of travel still held true. Octavia couldn't advertise the fact that she was a medician.

Shops and strolling merchants lined the boardwalk. Pedestrians swerved around Octavia and didn't otherwise react to her presence, as though well-dressed young ladies often hauled about bleeding animals. So many bodies in proximity left her addled by the mad chorus of their bodies' songs.

Her one certainty: the puppy was dying.

She glanced both ways and spied the dark recesses of an alley. Tugging her bags behind her, she found shelter in the shadows.

The space was tight, not ten steps across, with buildings towering high above. Rubbish bins and refuse blocked the way almost entirely. By the smell of the place, this was where chamber pots were dumped. Hardly a hygienic environment, but she had little choice. At least it was quiet.

Almost camouflaged by rotting bundles, a decomposing body sat in a collapsed heap. The faded green clothes were standard Caskentian army attire. The posture reminded her of a child's doll. The spine and head bowed forward to touch the lap, the legs and arms sprawled as if boneless. There was also a literal lack of bone—the legs were missing from the knees downward, maggot-smothered flesh exposed to the air. This had been a double amputee, a soldier. Whether he died by starvation or more insidious means, someone had stripped him of his mechanical legs and undoubtedly sold them for scrap. His soul had long since departed; there was no music, no hum.

The puppy squirmed against her. Urgency pushed her forward to the discarded chassis of a wagon.

She heaved her case up into the flatbed. The wood seemed relatively clean even if damp. Octavia set down the limp pup. She passed her hands over the extended staff of her umbrella. The fresh blood on her hands dried and fell away as dust. The copper of the staff was naturally antimicrobial, and radiant enchantments to kill zymes and eliminate excess body fluids took care of the rest. Her skin sanitized, she unstrapped her satchel.

Casting a glance to the windows above, she muttered, "Do you know the risk I'm taking, little pup? People are desperate, and angry, and I have so few herbs. I shouldn't do this."

Her fingers didn't hesitate as she opened her bag to reveal clear jars with contents ranging from vivid purple to sandy brown to powder white. She knew each jar by location, smell, and sound, by how the contents spoke to her. A formal diagnosis wasn't necessary; she knew she needed Bartholomew's tincture and pampria to mend bone, flesh, and organ.

There were many herbs with natural healing properties that could be used in common doctoring, the stuff any illiterate goodwife could do, but only certain herbs could be utilized by the Lady with a medician as conduit.

With a flick of her wrist, Octavia opened the necessary jars. She undid the drawstring of the honeyflower pouch and scooped enough to spread it in a circle around the still puppy. Magical heat crackled beneath her fingertips as she touched the circle. The Lady was listening.

This was where it could be tricky. Would the dog understand what she asked of it and grant her permission to heal?

"Pray, by the Lady let me mend thy ills," murmured Octavia, bringing her gold-tinted fingers to rest on the puppy's head. The animal whined. She sensed the way easing, the conduit opening. Discordant music flared in her ears even louder than before. She hadn't healed a trauma this severe since armistice.

Armistice—whatever that meant. As if the fighting between Caskentia and the Waste ever truly stopped. *I can't stop the conflict, but I can mend this dog. That is something. To that sobbing little girl, it may be everything.*

First, to knit the bones that crushed against the poor beast's lungs. She pinched out the soft white powder of Bartholomew's tincture and tossed it over the bloody mess of the dog's ribs. The enchanted herb was absorbed in an instant. The puppy grunted, releasing a sharp breath. The off-key tubas within the music went mute.

Next for the organs and flesh. She pinched pampria from its jar and extended her hand over the puppy. The image of the creature filled her mind, of how it had looked pleasant, plump, and intact only minutes before. The presence of the Lady flowed over Octavia, warm and heavy, as the coarse red herb drifted to the dog below. Soft light traced the puppy's body then faded to nothing.

The music altered to follow the rhythm of a heartbeat, the body of instruments almost synchronized. Octavia unstoppered a final jar. Using a small spoon, she dipped out a few globules of soaked Linsom berries. They were absorbed in an instant as new lines of red, healed skin emerged beneath the crust of blood. No fur, but that would grow back in time.

"Thank you, Lady, for extending your branches." Octavia bowed her head as a sense of sadness weighed on her again. *Profoundly blessed by the Lady; profoundly isolated by most everyone else.* Five minutes spared for this healing. Other girls might have prayed for an hour for the same results, and none could hear the song of a body outside of an active circle.

She brushed her hands against the soft grains of honeyflower. The music vanished, the circle broken. The healed puppy emitted only the faintest of tones, all in tune and easy to ignore. She pushed the evidence of the honeyflower into the slats of the wagon bed.

The puppy craned its head as if to examine itself, tail already thudding a steady beat. Octavia smiled. Under normal circumstances, she would remove the blood and leave her patient looking as good as new. Here, it was best for the dog to appear unhealed and graced with a light wound.

Out of curiosity, Octavia peeked beneath the tail. A young boy-pup. Perhaps that explained his lack of judgment. She snorted and shook her head. *As if I was any smarter as I bounded into the street.*

She packed up to leave. A sudden ache in her left forearm caused her to pause. "Lady, already? It's only been a few days," she murmured.

With another glance up and down the alley, she unbuttoned her sleeve at the wrist and pulled it halfway to her elbow. She unwound the inch-wide bandage to reveal the plug of cantham wax over her wound. The wax sealed the incision, but also prevented it from healing.

Octavia peeled back the wax. Blood immediately welled along the fingernail-size cut, and she angled her arm so it dripped between the wagon slats to the dirt below. The pressure in her arm eased, blood slowing, as a single blade of grass thrust up through the gap in the wood. Her offering was accepted. Quickly, she reapplied the wax and wrapped the bandage, then grabbed the puppy before he made a mad dash for freedom.

"Let's go find your owner," she said, standing with the wiggling puppy cradled against her hip again.

The decomposing body still slouched amidst the trash. She paused to stare. The bustling street was no more than a dozen feet away.

"I'm sorry," she whispered, pressing a fist to her chest. Sorry he had died like this; sorry that the alley vermin would steal away his flesh until there was no more. "Lady, I pray you granted him mercy in those final moments."

She walked on. If anything, her experience in the war had taught her to acknowledge the dead and not linger, or the countless corpses would consume her days.

Octavia crossed the street at the corner. The merchants along that side of the road looked to be shut down, and the shade of the walkway had become a lane of shanties. Most of the occupants seemed to be women and children, some of them gathered around a horse trough to scrub their threadbare clothes against slatted washing boards.

Ten years ago, I was like them. Orphaned. Hungry. The days a blur of sadness, cold, and the overwhelming discordance of humanity in ill health—until Miss Percival saved me.

A disruptive hum rang in Octavia's ears, though not as loud as the fresh blood of trauma. The notes came as no surprise. Sniffing, she detected the heady sweetness that was the signature of pox, as bodies exuded fluid from countless pores.

I don't have enough herbs to save them all. If I stop, if I try, they will riot. They will tear me apart with their need. Lady, help me.

Tears beaded her lashes. Stiff-legged, she wound through refugees tainted with imminent death, and finally spied the girl who had held the dog's leash.

The child's face was still streaked clean with tears. Her jaw dropped at the sight of the puppy. "You found him!"

The puppy wiggled as Octavia handed him over. Warm coziness filled her chest. She had done the right thing, even with the risk considered.

A rail-thin woman stood behind the girl. "You thank the lady," she said, her face hawkish and severe. "You thank her for saving you from that beating your pa woulda given once he got back."

The girl lowered in a clumsy curtsy. "Oh, thank you, ma'am," she said. "Now we won't go hungry tonight and Pa won't beat me or nothing." Her eyes shone, bright and happy.

Octavia's smile froze on her face. She thought to reply, and instead bobbed her head and backed away. *I'm a fool.* A puppy that plump couldn't be a pet. The dog probably weighed almost as much as the child. It had undoubtedly been stolen to serve as their dinner.

The wheels of her case thudded on the uneven boards. She then realized the intensity of the gazes on her, her new dress, the bags hauled behind her.

It's not as if Octavia had much in the way of material goods either; she barely had enough coins for her trip. It would be a blessing to arrive in Leffen in several days, where money promised by Miss Percival waited for her in an account. Even so, Octavia had far more to her name than this sorry lot.

She crossed the street again, her pace brisk. The attention of the refugees weighed on her.

At the next street corner, she reached for the watch at her waist and fumbled open the case. It was ten till ten. Her eyes widened. Her airship left at the half hour.

She glanced back a final time. The two sides of the street seemed to exist across a great divide, but she heard the people's songs. Everyone suffered. Too many stomachs groaned, too many agonies went untreated.

Lady, help them. I can't. She steeled herself and turned away.

Octavia entered the flow of hurried pedestrians, her eyes on the bulge of airship balloons visible between the high-peaked roofs.

The heavy, cloying odor of enchanted aether hovered over the docks as heavily as the dust. Men were everywhere, yelling, walking, driving lorries. A few scattered women seemed out of place, too colorful against the drabness of sooty work clothes and suited businessmen.

Octavia paused along the walkway, gasping for breath as she stared up at the boarding masts. There had to be at least thirty of them, each resembling a lighthouse made of battered chrome. Few towers hosted airships. No surprise there. The Caskentian government had seized or declared privateer the best airships for use during the war. However, that still left a solid half mile of airships and masts.

The first mast had been altered to resemble a giant clock. She gave it a double take, just to ascertain the time again, and noted thick black bundles attached at each quarter hour. A sign in the center of the clock's face read WASTE *NOT* in elegant calligraphy. She took in the size of the bundles, and the rough shape. The lowest one, suspended beneath the 6, had been shredded at the bottom, revealing skeletal feet.

The bundles were bodies, convicted collaborators of the Waste. No one else gave the clock a second glance. A few children played in its shadow.

"Oh Lady," she murmured. Displays of the executed were common at the front. The bodies of deserters would be strung on poles along an avenue. It was for morale, or so commanders said. Morale. It was for fear, fear to force their unwilling conscripts to stay. The same reason these bodies existed, suspended on time itself.

How many of these dead were truly Wasters? Few or none, likely. True Wasters were survivalists, hunters. They wouldn't be caught so easily, nor would they give up on their war, no matter what the armistice declared.

Wasters wanted independence, and claimed it was Caskentia's fault their land was blighted nothingness. As if Caskentia were to blame for the high peaks of the Pinnacles and the rain shadow on the other side! The Wasters' demands were endless: for their blighted land to officially be known as the Dallows, rights to irrigate from the mountains, etc.—and most ludicrous of all, a cure to the magicked curse on their prairie.

Caskentia couldn't even cure itself. Its currency was worthless, its populace starving. The Queen, her council, and Daggers stayed locked away in the palace, safe and secure, as hunger and disease continued to slaughter the people.

Octavia bent to her satchel and tugged out her boarding pass. Her eyes scanned both sides. A most unfeminine growl escaped her throat and she was half inclined to ball up the pamphlet in frustration. It didn't list a mast number.

Cities. Stinky, confusing, crowded, dead bodies all about. Lady, help me escape this accursed place.

"Oy, you need a porter?" piped up a voice. She smelled the boy before she saw him—he was dust personified, a golem of old in the form of a prepubescent child. She couldn't even discern his hair color under the muck.

"Oh, thank you. I'm looking for the *Argus*. Can you perhaps show the way?"

He thrust out a grubby palm. She stared into it, blinking. Was he supposed to take her by the hand? It seemed strangely intimate.

His hand jerked back. "Hey, what's yer game?" he snarled.

"My game?"

"What, you think I be doin' this for free?" His expression turned outright feral, dark eyes glittering against his browned face.

"Oh," Octavia said quietly as the boy shoved his way back into the crowds. She had so little money that even if she had known his desire, she might have resisted. Her light breakfast soured in her stomach. So far, her first morning of independence had been one disaster after another.

She continued onward, her case rolling with rhythmic ka-thunks along the wooden boardwalk. Her head craned and eyes narrowed, she could make out some of the craft names high upon their hulls. Some were wooden constructs, like a seafaring vessel, with the balloon suspended above; others had the craft built into the balloon itself. Was "balloon" even the proper term? Octavia didn't know. She knew very little, apparently. Miss Percival had bought the ticket and hadn't told her exactly what sort of ship she would spend the week on.

"I should have asked," she muttered. She should've asked many things, but Miss Percival likely wouldn't have answered, anyway.

Sadness stabbed at her chest again.

If she missed her flight, what would happen? Could she get a refund? She didn't have enough money for another airship booking. Perhaps barely enough for a hotel.

After a few more days, I won't need to fuss about cities or worry about finances, not for a long time. Delford will be a quiet village, peaceful. They need me. After I aid their recovery from the Waster poisoning, it'll be a place where birdsong is louder than the klaxons of bodies in agony.

"Pardon me, m'lady, but you seem lost." A musical, deep baritone caused her to turn. A man stood inches away in steward's garb. His crimson jacket was right at her eye level, with double rows of gold buttons fitted across a rather broad chest. It looked reminiscent of an old military uniform, complete with glimmering epaulets. However, the attire had been in use for some years. White threadbare streaks radiated from the buttons, and the epaulets had only haphazard gold fringe. All that, she absorbed in an instant.

Then she looked up at his face.

His skin was the color of nutmeg, unblemished and tight. The skin color denoted him as Tamaran, from that nation of science and logic far to the south. But most of all, his hair drew her eye. Drawn into a leather queue, his thick mane had the texture of a black silk kerchief balled in a fist and set to dry. It lay against his shoulder like a cat's poufy tail. She could imagine the texture of the rippling kinky strands beneath her fingers.

"Oh." With a start, she realized she was gawking as if she hadn't seen a man before. She had seen plenty, and naked at that. Albeit the copious amounts of blood and gore were a sufficient turnoff. "Oh, um, I'm looking for the *Argus*. If you can help, I do have a copper."

Oh, you ninny. She would have withheld her coin from a beggar child yet volunteered it to the first man who smiled her way.

Such a pleasant smile it was, too—brilliant white against his darker skin. He even had all his front teeth. "Do not trouble yourself. I am going that way as well." He jutted out an elbow.

Now this was a proper gentleman, complete with a lilting Mercian accent. Octavia hooked her arm around his.

"Shall I take your bags?" he asked.

Her smile froze on her face. "Oh, no. I'm quite fine,

thank you." *Too many lives depend on that satchel. Touch it, and you'll get a faceful of capsicum.*

He bowed his head in acknowledgment as they began to walk. She had the urge to close her eyes and listen to the soft music of the man beside her. He was healthy, his body fairly quiet. And yet . . . something was missing.

All medicians—even Miss Percival—required a circle to hear the music of a body in need. At the academy, it hadn't taken Octavia long to realize how profoundly different she was, and how others responded to those differences.

This man was different from most of the others around, too. Half of his right leg was gone.

His knee was intact, but below that, his body was silent. There were physical signs as well—the mechanical extension was heavier than flesh, and he compensated with the slightest tilt of his torso and drag of his leg. The fact that he didn't limp was noteworthy. Whoever designed the leg had the light hand of a master.

"Have you been in the city long?" asked her cicerone.

"No. Only a half hour or so, and I'm quite ready to leave. I much prefer the country."

He glanced both ways and led her into the avenue. "This is nothing compared to Mercia. Have you been there, m'lady?"

"No, sir. I'll visit there by airship this week." *A night in Mercia will be enough. I can say I've been there and never return.*

He grunted. "'Tis a beautiful place in many ways, especially along the bay and the palace quarter, but the quagmire of exhaust and humanity corrodes the spirit with utter swiftness."

She cast curious eyes on him. "That's quite poetic." *And exactly how I feel.*

"Is that such a surprise, for a man in my position to manage a few pretty words?" A gap in his coat revealed itself along a shoulder seam, showing a flash of a lighter red satin lining. He regarded her solemnly, head tilted to one side. "Forgive my forwardness, but 'tis dangerous for a lady to travel alone, especially to Mercia. You truly intend to travel by airship, by yourself?"

Oh, no. He did not go there.

Octavia stopped in her tracks, finger pointed toward his chest. "Please, don't tell me you are one of those men who believes women should be treated like porcelain roses, brought down for an occasional dusting and public display." She'd had enough of that pompous attitude from men at the front. If she could patch a ruptured bowel, she could walk across a street by herself, thank you very much. "I may need help navigating this strange city, but I am quite capable of making this journey on my own."

He raised both hands in supplication. "If you are a rose, m'lady, 'tis to your advantage to have thorns." She had expected more bluster, or chagrin. Instead, his words were sober and his gaze even. "Some lives attract more danger than others. This North Country around Vorana—I confess, I have visited here only for port calls, but it strikes me as a pleasant place, one worth staying in."

Oh Lady, if only I could. "If you're not willing to help me, sir, then I'll continue on my own."

"No. Forgive me for speaking out of turn. I will escort

you, and gladly. I am simply—I am simply weary of people being hurt by Mercia and its ways."

She inclined her head to indicate agreement, but didn't hold his arm quite so close.

They approached a mooring tower, its sides bearing a painted ad for Royal-Tea with its mimicry of the crown logo as depicted on coins. Swirling calligraphy boasted FOR VITALITY! FOR HEALTH! FOR CROWN! along with the smiling face of a towheaded girl, a can of the tea held at her cheek.

"This is the *Argus*." He motioned toward the airship attached to the tower of tea advertisements.

Octavia had seen a good many dirigibles at camp, but never up close. The balloon extended for some seventy-five feet, the cloth dulled silver. Only the pilot's nest peeped from the front; the rest of the cabin was within the hull. The lower part of the balloon was lined with windows and fluttering crimson swags cut in long triangles. The scent of dust was pushed aside by the increasingly heavy odor of aether-enchanted helium. By the intensity, she surmised some aether magi were at work nearby.

"The ship is rather . . . " She searched for a polite word.

"Dingy?" There was that grin again. Pale, icy blue eyes seemed to twinkle. That eye color was most definitely not a stock hereditary feature of Tamarania. Nor was the twinkling.

"I hoped for a more courteous adjective," Octavia said.

"Most anything docked here could be described in a less courteous way. All of these airships are over forty years old. I believe the *Argus* was acquired by the military for use as a transport in the last war."

"It's a wonder the vessel was returned, considering . . . " *How the military treats the expendable.* Not a thought to finish out loud.

Miss Percival's face flashed in her mind, so recently aged and wrinkled, her head bowed over financial figures at lamplight. Caskentia hadn't paid the academy for its services at the front. Miss Percival would do most anything to keep the school open and the girls in good care.

Octavia looked past her guide to the base of the tower. "I see the ticket agent there. My gratitude to you, sir . . . ? I don't believe I ever heard your name."

"I had not given it, m'lady. The name is Alonzo Garret." He bowed again, that magnificent hair draping forward.

Icy horror clenched her in place. A Tamaran, and so few of them lived this far north. The last name of Garret.

"Of relation to the General Solomon Garret?" she said, doing her utmost to keep her tone mild.

He stood tall again. Something had stiffened in his face, his eyes now unwilling to meet hers. "Very few people make note of that name these days, m'lady, after the heroism of the recent war. Solomon Garret was my father."

"Thank you again," she murmured. She yanked her suitcase along the cobbles of the port, walking toward the ticket line with all the world blurred around her.

His father. Of course. No wonder he had been knowledgeable of airships.

She had just spoken with the son of the man who killed her parents.

Chapter 2

Octavia's gloved hands fidgeted on the handle of her suitcase as she waited in line. *General Garret. Fire. The frenzied song of raw bodies and blood. The suck of mud against my bare feet.*

Her stomach roiled. She stared up at the battered and abused cylinder of the mooring tower. Leaving behind her old life and enduring the turmoil of the city had already made her anxious as a suckling foal separated from its mother, and now this revelation.

Inhale. Exhale, breathe out the nightmares, just as Miss Percival always taught me. I can do this. I must do this.

Several men waited in line ahead of her, their suits wearing a thin layer of brown grime. The man in front had a small mechanical lizard perched on the brim of his hat. By its lack of movement, she assumed it was nonfunctioning until a tiny copper-pink tongue tested the air. The lizard's beady eyes roved about and seemed to focus their dead gaze on her.

During the second war, when Octavia was but a girl, the Wasters had infiltrated the coast with refitted airships of unparalleled swiftness. They bombed cities—Mercia in particular—and exercised finesse in doing so at night and zipping away without interception.

General Garret, he was a hero then. He created a small two-person craft he dubbed the "buzzer" with which he could overtake an airship and penetrate its hide with a harpoon. It all worked quite well until that night over Octavia's own village. The Wasters' airship had been a hydrogen mix and caught aflame as it crashed, taking down Garret's buzzer and killing hundreds of people.

The truth was, if Garret hadn't caused the crash of the *Alexandria,* the Wasters could very well have killed Octavia and her family that same night. She really shouldn't hold it against the general's son, and yet that name and her grief were seared together in her memory.

The airship's conflagration roared, but the brief, intense cries of blood from my home, from my neighbors, were louder yet. All I could do was stand there ankle-deep in the muck of the field, eyes aching from heat and tears and the brilliant crimson of the flames.

She let her eyes half close as she inhaled and exhaled, breathing out the terror.

I am past all that. Today I'm traveling to my new life. I will visit Vorana, Leffen, Mercia, and then Delford. The people there need me. I'm a tool of the Lady. I can cure their rashes and virulent tumors. I can make a home and establish roots as deep as the Lady's Tree.

I'll belong somewhere again. She managed a tepid, hopeful smile as the panic faded.

"Next!" called the ticket agent.

Octavia blinked. No one stood ahead of her.

"Name?" The man's upper lip was sparsely adorned with whiskers, his cheeks marred by pale divots from pox. He was lucky. He'd be immune as the disease spread anew.

Like other Percival girls, Octavia had worked with dairy cattle at the academy and developed an immunity through early exposure to cowpox. Science and doctoring had its uses, but she felt far more comfortable when relying on the Lady.

"I'm Miss Octavia Leander," she said, setting her boarding pass on the ledge. His eyes slid over her for a split second as he grabbed the papers. His attention on her boarding pass was just as fleeting.

"Everything's in order." He stamped three sheets in sequence and passed one back to her. She tucked it into her satchel pocket again. He handed over a key; it was an antique-looking thing, all knobs and ornate curves and patina. He motioned to her right. "Leave your bags with the steward and take the lift up. Follow the signs. You have bunk 3A on deck A. Have a pleasant flight to Mercia aboard . . ." He glanced to one side. "The *Argus*."

"Thank you." She tucked the room key into her satchel.

Rounding the tower, she found a man in attire similar to Alonzo Garret's. However, this man was so short that the top of his head just reached the level of her bosom. If not for his perfectly coiffed beard, she would have thought him an adolescent.

"I can take your bags, m'lady," he said, his voice soft enough to be mistaken for a girl's. His gaze stayed on her face, much to her relief.

"No, thank you," she said, teeth grinding. *I'm a woman, not an invalid.*

"It's his job to carry your bags," said a masculine voice. It was the man who had stood in front of her in line. A tailored suit fit his narrow form and flared at the hips, the cloth pin-striped gray on satiny black. His bowler hat rested at a jaunty angle. Clean prints from his fingers were visible on the filthy brim.

"I'm quite capable, thank you," she said.

"I don't believe I have introduced myself," said the man. His black mustache was as thick as a sausage and wiggled as he spoke. "I am Mr. Drury." He bowed with an elegant flare, hat doffed. "I trust you'll be on this airship for the entire journey to Mercia?"

"Yes," she said. Her fingers found the knob of her umbrella and fidgeted with the smoothed wood. The little steward hauled luggage around the curve of the tower.

Mr. Drury's face brightened. "How wonderful! Have you traveled by airship before?"

"No." She stared at the lift doors, willing the blasted thing to come along and save her from this small talk.

"Oh, you will find it is a most glorious way to travel. You see, I'm a salesman for Royal-Tea, and frequent airships and rails." He flicked a wrist toward the signs on the tower above and then brought his hand down on her upper arm, squeezing as if to test her muscles. Octavia's jaw dropped in shock as she jerked back. Mr. Drury offered a playful wink in response. "Have you, by any chance, tried Royal-Tea?"

"No!"

"Oh, I can remedy that. I brought along several cases and have offered them to the commissary staff aboard this vessel. It's my sincere hope that you'll open a can and see why Royal-Tea has become the most popular ready-made virgin drink in all of Caskentia."

"I would rather not."

"Perhaps I can find a way to change your mind?" His voice was mild, but she couldn't suppress a strange chill.

"I don't drink or eat from cans, if given any choice. I've seen the dangers of ptomaine poisoning." The lift approached with a mighty rumble.

"Ah, poison." He looked almost amused. "An understandable concern. However, I must boast that Royal-Tea has had no incidents of ptomaine. We heat our cans, utilizing the latest scientific advancements from the south. Royal-Tea is designed to benefit health—in fact, we guarantee it!"

The lift doors parted. No one else stood inside. Octavia rolled her case in and turned to face the opening. Mr. Drury sidled in beside her just as the doors closed as tightly as the royal vault. She squelched her sudden alarm. It was a short ride. Surely he wasn't foolish enough to try anything.

"My dear lady, I don't believe I caught your name?" The floor lurched as the lift began its ascent with the slow grind of gears. *Too slow.*

"Miss Leander."

"A beautiful woman should not be alone in a city such as this."

"I can manage on my own, Mr. Drury."

"Modesty suits you." The metal floor rumbled.

"You're being terribly forward, sir." She sidestepped away, trying to make the movement nonchalant. Her right-hand fingers slipped from her suitcase handle to the concealed pocket at her waist and its tiny flute of capsicum. A single puff of ground peppers would leave him blind and in agony for the better part of an hour—and perhaps have the same effect on her as well, considering their close, confined quarters.

"Most women here," he said, disdain in his tone, "would have gladly surrendered their bags to the porter. You didn't. That says much of your strength."

Was that why he took liberties with her person, groping her arm? "I'm a farm girl. This is naught to me."

There was something calculating in his eyes. Octavia was reminded of older men as they played a match of Warriors, studying the triangular game board for long minutes as they positioned their mechanical battle beasts. Mr. Drury looked at her as if she were a rival mecha on the precipice's brink.

She clutched the capsicum flute in her fist, her sweaty skin slick against the metal.

The doors popped open. A gush of aether stung her nose, but she didn't take her gaze from Mr. Drury. She didn't dare.

"Oh, there you are, m'lady. I have been looking all over for you." She recognized the voice, that accented baritone.

Him again? She shuddered.

Mr. Garret entered, his heavy boots echoing in the

metal chamber. His broad shoulders provided a barrier between her and Mr. Drury. "Come along," he said, taking her elbow as he had before. His intense gaze met hers, his head barely nodding as if to signal her.

Mr. Garret knew exactly what he was doing. Because of Mr. Garret's father, her parents were dead. Indignation flared—who was this man, to presume to rescue her? But his expression was of kindness, the very opposite of Mr. Drury's cool calculation. She felt her hackles lower.

"Oh, thank you, sir," she said, forcing her voice calm. She wheeled her case in front of them, the metal and wood wheels roaring on the coarse deck. Wind blasted her face, and her hand instantly reached to check her headband.

"M'lady, I hope to speak to you again on board. Don't forget my offer of tea!" Mr. Drury flashed another salesman's smile as he edged past them and up the ramp into the airship.

Mr. Garret leaned closer. "Did he accost you?"

"I'm unharmed, but he was . . . strange. Far too forward." She released a shuddering breath. Mr. Garret had been forward as well, but in a very different way. That had to count for something.

Mr. Garret pulled back and glowered up at the airship. "I am glad you are well, and I assure you, I will keep my eye on him aboard. You may put away the pepper pipe now, unless you wish to practice it on me."

Octavia stared at the three-inch flute in her hand, remembering it was there, then tucked it back into the pleats of her dress. "The *Argus* is your ship, sir? Mr. Garret?"

"'Tis my employer. Since we will be traveling together, may I inquire about your name?"

A strong gust of wind almost bowled her backward. They were quite high—perhaps higher than she had ever been on an open railing. The metal deck encircled the top of the mooring tower and revealed a panorama of Vorana with its high-peaked roofs and toothpick-thin streets. A sliver of blue glimmered beyond the buildings: the estuary that led to the sea. If she turned and looked to the north, she could probably see the woods and the meadows that trailed toward home.

No, not home, but I'll have Delford soon enough.

She focused her gaze on Mr. Garret. He remained quiet, no doubt awaiting her reply. "Octavia Leander."

He angled out his elbow toward her. Behind them, the elevator clicked and rumbled as it descended. "Well, Miss Leander, allow me the pleasure of escorting you inside without further unpleasantness."

Unable to speak, she curtsied her approval. Walking by her side, he led her up the ramp and within the shadowed underbelly of the airship.

THE PASSAGE NARROWED AND forced them to walk hip to hip. Embedded glowstones edged the metal floor on each side and illuminated red mahogany walls similar in color to her hair. The odor of aether faded, replaced by slight staleness and strong garlic.

Mr. Garret sniffed. "The kitchens are just ahead. Lunch will be served soon after we alight."

The ramp ahead sloped upward. Overhead, she heard footsteps and deep, muffled voices. "Tell me, Mr. Garret, what's your occupation on board?"

"I am a steward, like the little fellow at the base of the tower."

She studied him out of the corner of her eye. A steward. Many women wouldn't curtsy to a servant like him, or engage him in a casual conversation as she was doing now.

He's been nothing but respectable to me—far more than most. His surname may be Garret, but there's more to him than that.

"That man . . . I don't want my room anywhere near his."

"'Tis not likely. We try to book solo women and married couples along the same wing, and men on the other. However, this is a small craft with only twelve double-berth cabins, and there are several common areas where you may encounter him again."

"I'll defend myself if necessary."

"I hope it will not come to that, m'lady."

Oh Lady, so do I.

A doorway ahead was labeled with various signs. On either side were two staircases leading up, shaped in an inverted *V*. Mr. Garrett pointed to the hallway ahead. "This floor features the lavatories and showers. The smoking room is the most popular social setting aboard. Everyone dines upstairs in the promenade. Your room is also on the deck above."

Octavia unstrapped her satchel and tossed it across her shoulder like a bandolier, parasol clattering against the wall. He said nothing as she hauled the suitcase up the stairs. Her breath huffed. By the time she reached the top, her arm ached slightly, and it was a relief to set down the case and pull out the handle again.

Signs pointed toward the promenade on one side and the cabins on the other. A cage against the wall held a fluttering mass of mechanical birds. The paint on their wings had chipped and let various shades of metal shine through. En masse, they clicked and whirred and tweeted, the sound echoing slightly.

"Do you recall your berth number?" Mr. Garret asked.

"Three-A."

"This way, then." He took her on the left fork. The short hallway consisted of six doors with barely any space between. The two of them standing together with her luggage made the space claustrophobic. Mr. Garret knocked on the door for 3. Octavia heard the clatter of a lock and the door cracked open.

"Pardon me," said Mr. Garret, bowing. "I have brought your roommate, a Miss Octavia Leander?"

"Oh, certainly! Goodness gracious." The door widened to reveal a thick figure in a screaming purple dress. Her silvered blond hair featured a broad blue streak that started at her forehead and swirled into a plump bun pinned atop her head. In truth, everything about her could be described as plump. Her cheeks and jowls were heavy and rounded, and even her fingers on the door resembled puffy pastries.

But Octavia had a hard time looking at anything other than the woman's hair. It was . . . bold, to say the least.

Dyeing in streaks like that had been a Mercian fad years before, and was currently about as en vogue as riding a swaybacked horse.

"I'm Viola Stout," the woman said, bobbing her head. Garish blue eye shadow matched the streak in her hair. "Here. Do come in! I am delighted to make your acquaintance. Absolutely delighted."

"Oh. Uh, thank you." Octavia offered a warm smile. Mrs. Stout's name struck her as allegorical to her very body type, like a character in a religious tract.

Mr. Garret backed away, barely squeezing around the suitcase. "I must return to my duties, Miss Leander. I trust you are well now?"

"Yes, thank you, Mr. Garret. I'm much obliged for your assistance."

With a final little bow, he walked away in commanding strides.

"Goodness, I don't think I've seen a Tamaran in years. Such a nice walk he has. Mmm-hmm, yes. Fitted uniform pants are such glorious, underappreciated attire," said Mrs. Stout, fanning herself for a moment. "Well! Come inside, child. I fear it's rather cozy."

Cozy was an understatement. The room seemed to be little more than a six-by-seven-foot rectangle. A padded bench jutted out with a large silver object lying flat against the wall above it. On the far wall, a sink showed a few splashes of water still on the aluminum surface, a small mirror on an arm to one side. Across from the bench, a few curtains denoted what must be a closet. No wonder Mr.

Garret had emphasized the promenade and smoke room for socializing.

"Now, now, it won't be that uncomfortable," said Mrs. Stout, clucking her tongue.

"Was my expression so obvious?" asked Octavia.

"Well, it is a bit of a shock on your first excursion. This lower bunk is yours. When we're ready for sleep, we signal a steward and he makes up our beds." She motioned to a pull cord and then to the large silver rectangle flush with the wall. That had to be the upper bunk. "Is there anything you need to hang in the closet?"

"Oh. No. Not right away, certainly." Octavia hadn't given thought to how Miss Percival's advice on secrecy extended to the packing of her garments. Her warded medician uniform was folded atop her other clothes in her suitcase. "I assume they bring a ladder to access that bunk?"

"Yes, that will all come in the evening, along with the pillows, bedding, and tenting for privacy." Mrs. Stout edged over to sit on the bed. She held up a small paperbound book—a pulp mystery novel, its cover depicting a terrified woman fleeing from a tall figure in a pointed brown hood. "I hope you don't mind that I've been sitting here. I had hoped to meet my roommate in privacy, rather than guessing who you would be amongst the other ladies. You never know the sorts you'll meet on an airship." She punctuated the statement with a regal sniff.

"No, no, that's fine. I'd rather make your acquaintance without others prying." Others, meaning Mr. Drury. She sat down beside Mrs. Stout. The bed seemed quite firm, not even squeaking beneath their weight. She glanced up. The ladder would have to be a solid five feet in height. Mrs. Stout showed no outward health issues, nor did her body reveal any unusual musical tones. She seemed quite healthy for someone about a half century in age.

"Mrs. Stout, would you prefer the lower bunk? I'm quite fine with climbing to the upper bed."

A dazzling smile caused Mrs. Stout's cheeks to round like risen muffins. "Oh. Truly? It would be easier on me. As my dear husband liked to say, I'm in good enough shape to be requisitioned by the government, but I can still be a bit unsteady at times. You're an absolute sweetheart for thinking of my comforts! If you don't mind me asking, how old are you, child?"

"Twenty-two."

"Goodness. My two children are barely older than you. Now, how was your ride into Vorana today? Is the North Road as rough as always?"

Octavia stilled. "How did you know I came in on the North Road?"

Mrs. Stout made a dismissive flick of her wrist. "I saw you riding into town."

My carriage was enclosed. She regarded her new roommate with leery eyes, suddenly reminded of her troubled encounter with Mr. Drury. "The North Road isn't a pleasant ride in a wagon, but that sort of motion doesn't usually disturb me."

"Ah, that old road never changes. As I always say, 'Adversity steels the will, and the stomach. Only some stomachs have an easier time of it than others.' "

It was a saying Miss Percival had been known to quote as well, and Octavia had never heard it elsewhere. Perhaps it was a generational thing, as the two women were likely close in age. Or perhaps there was something more to this Mrs. Stout.

"Are you from Vorana?" asked Octavia.

"No. Nearer the coast, actually. Haven't been here in years." Mrs. Stout's smile dimmed. "So, child, how—"

A loud bell rang from somewhere in the hallway. A sudden lurch knocked Octavia sideways, half sprawled in Mrs. Stout's plush, purple lap. Chuckling, the older woman set Octavia upright and patted her hand. "That's just the takeoff, dear. Normally there's a bit more of a gap between the warning bell and that first lurch. Quite hasty of them. That does mean, however, if you wish to see the city we must get to the promenade straightaway."

"Oh, yes! I would love to see the view." Octavia bounded to her feet, catching herself against the wall for balance. She edged her suitcase into the tight confines of the closet and then hoisted her satchel onto her shoulder again. She didn't place any faith in a room key.

Mrs. Stout shook her head, grinning. A wisp of silver hair draped along her cheek. "Ah, to be young and on an adventure! Come along. I believe the library side will offer the best view."

Chapter 3

As they walked down the hallway, the craft made another small lurch. This time, Octavia was ready and braced herself against the wall. "Does the airship always bounce around so much?"

"Takeoffs and landings have the most careening," said Mrs. Stout. "Once we're in the air, it tends to be quite smooth."

They passed the staircase and mechanical birds and through another door. Octavia paused in shock. After the cavelike labyrinth she had encountered thus far, she hadn't expected the promenade to consist of sterile panels and round white tables. Glittering chandeliers swayed slightly and made no sound; the crystals and glassware had been spaced so they did not strike. The clink of goblets and muffled laughter completed the scene. A liveried steward rushed past them with a tray of wineglasses.

A mechanical band sat in the middle of the room, motionless and quiet, burnished nickel skin a contrast to the glaring whiteness of the walls and tables. The four figures looked downright primitive in construction; it's a wonder they hadn't been scrapped in the war. The flutist had to be little more than skin, gears, and automated bellows.

"I like to consider myself an accomplished traveler," continued Mrs. Stout. "My husband often journeyed for business, and after the children were grown, I accompanied him. Airship travel isn't quite what it was before the recent war, but this seems to be a decent craft."

Long rows of windows flanked the promenade and angled out at forty-five degrees. As she approached, Octavia could see the blur of buildings below and the fair blue of the sky. Tucked against the wall were several shelves of books and padded lounge chairs. A woman in a periwinkle shift sat in one of the chairs, a child on her lap. The babe couldn't have been more than two, his face beet red and dark eyes too large. He had the drawn look of one accustomed to eating little, as did his mother. A rag doll of a mechanical man lay at the mother's feet.

"Our airship is already angled south toward Leffen," Mrs. Stout said as she leaned forward against the glass, her bosom like a mighty cushion.

A few windows were open. Cool, refreshing air gushed against Octavia's face. Strands of hair tickled her cheeks and nose. No matter how she fussed with her headbands, she could never contain her crazed hair for long. The window felt chilled through her gloves as she leaned forward. The peaked roofs already looked smaller, like a confectioner's village at Winter Solstice, the red tiles shining beneath the sun. The mooring towers were barely in sight at the lower right. The tethered airships reminded her of a beached whale she'd seen as a girl, bobbing and struggling to return where it belonged. Long puffs of steam trailed from smokestacks. A few sails on naval vessels marked the far edge of Vorana. Beyond that, the wide mouth of the river looked more white than blue in the midday light. The ocean was a sliver at the horizon.

Beautiful. So beautiful. A view like this made the anxiety of Vorana worthwhile. The words of her father came to mind and how he regarded the airship flights he'd taken as a young soldier, back in the first war: *When up on high and looking down, I was reminded of how small I am in the scheme of the world. No more than a speck in God's eye, but what a brilliant speck I shall be!*

Father had always been something of a poet, reading old tomes of verses by the light of an oil lamp. Mother would shake her head with a slight roll of her eyes as Father muttered poems to himself, but she didn't mind, not really.

"Here, let's read this one," said the mother in the chair. The child fussed, and Octavia cringed. Crying children made her think of dying children. "It's the tale of the missing princess. Oh, this was one of Mummy's favorites, too. 'King Kethan ruled Caskentia and everyone was happy. They had meat for supper every day. But over the mountains, there were bad men. Terrible men. They did not like King Kethan. They sneaked over the mountains and to Mercia. They crept into the palace. The princess was sleeping in her bed.' Look, isn't she pretty?"

Mrs. Stout laid a hand on Octavia's forearm. "Come, come. The other side will show more of a view inland." The song of her body remained stable, but a sheen of sweat glistened across her skin. *Odd, considering the chill air, but she is at the time of life when such sweats occur.*

As they walked across the promenade, the mother's story continued: "'The princess screamed! She did not want to go with the bad men. Her guards arrived. The bad men used the princess as a shield, and oh, she is shot! Her blood stains the floor and cries for justice, for her countrymen to avenge her! The bad men carry her away . . .'"

"I haven't heard that tale since I was a girl," Octavia said.

Miss Percival didn't keep storybooks around unless they involved herb lore or something of educational use. Besides, the girls were all intimately aware of the reasons for Caskentia's wars with the Waste. They all knew of the princess who had been kidnapped in their grandparents' time, and whose loss began the cycle of conflict. One that became worse that next year when Wasters sent infernal magi into Mercia and left half the city in cinders.

"It's a story that plays wells to patriotic sentiments," said Mrs. Stout with a dainty sniff.

The neutrality of the answer surprised Octavia. *Does she actually sympathize with the Waste? Or did her husband?* Mrs. Stout had taken care to not mention his employment or home. Actually, she hadn't said outright that he was dead.

The more she spoke to Mrs. Stout, the more curious she became.

Three men and a woman chatted along the windows on

the dining room side of the airship. The men wore badges on their heart pockets and sleeves, designating them as members of some academic league. They looked strangely young to Octavia, though she had to be only five or so years older. *The war. It aged me, aged all of us.* Judging by their high giggles and staggered movements, they were well into the drink before they had even boarded. The woman was draped on a man's arm, glittery baubles dangling low from neck to hip and accentuating a waistless dress.

The little steward approached Octavia with a bow. "Ladies, may I get you something to drink? A tonic, perhaps? Aerated water? Royal-Tea?"

The very mention of the tea drink soured her taste buds. "An aerated water, thank you," said Octavia.

"I'll do without right now, thank you kindly," said Mrs. Stout.

He bowed again. "If you change your mind, I'll be serving here until supper time. You can also ring me from your room. I'm called Little Daveo." He hurried away, his short legs agile as he dodged tables and drinking men.

"With my aptitude on the marksmanship test, the old man said I could very well qualify for the rank of Clockwork Dagger soon out of the academy." The young man spoke loudly, his accent Mercian.

"A Clockwork Dagger!" The woman practically cooed. "Do you think you'll have to kill people?"

Octavia resisted the urge to recoil in disgust.

"If I must, in defense of the Queen," he said with melodramatic gravitas.

"How long do qualifications take?" asked another man. "I thought they preferred veterans from the war, officers."

"They do. But exceptions are made for those with certain skills. Quick language acquisition, marksmanship, a knack for poison"—the woman gasped—"anything that will provide an edge over the Waste. Only the best qualify for such an elite guard." His smug smile included himself as such, of course.

Mrs. Stout looked as if she had swallowed a slug. "Listen to that poppycock," she muttered, leaning closer to Octavia. "He doesn't have a callus on his hands, and he thinks he can be a spy? He hasn't known a day of work in his life. Footle and hogwash!"

Octavia scrutinized the braggart as best she could at their distance. Mrs. Stout was right—the man's hand on his glass was plush and pink. The woman had an exceptional eye.

"The term 'Clockwork Dagger' has never made sense to me," murmured Octavia. "Daggers are antiquated, not clockwork."

"It's a figurative term, really. A 'dagger' is an older name for an assassin. Caskentia trains their agents, winds them up like a clockwork toy, and sends them off to do whatever needs doing."

"Killing people."

"Not always. Information is the game, these days. Knowing what the Wasters are doing. Knowing what new innovation will emerge from the south. I daresay, they would know the color of the Queen's corset hour by hour."

Octavia glanced sidelong at her roommate. "You are a fount of knowledge, Mrs. Stout."

Mrs. Stout's lips pressed together primly as she stared at the other passengers. "You learn a lot, when you've lived as long as I have."

Little Daveo returned, passing a flute of aerated water to Octavia. The water fizzled against her lips as the bubbles tickled her nose. She stepped closer to the windows. From this side, the rolling green contours of the valley spread out before her. Reinforced irrigation canals looked so straight and smooth they had to be the work of geologica magi. Probably fifty miles away, the forested foothills stood in bold contrast to the gray Pinnacles capped in white. Such deceptive beauty.

From here, there's no trace of the young boys who froze solid during midnight watches, the avalanches that swallowed entire brigades. Those mounds of ash, almost indistinguishable from the snow, that consisted of cremated bodies and amputated limbs.

She gulped down more water, as if to wash the memory away.

By the windows, one of the young men barked in a laugh. "Did you see that?" The others murmured and leaned closer. Curious, Octavia leaned against her own window just as a small, moss-green body thudded against the glass.

She screamed, stumbling backward. As she shoved her drink onto the nearest table, her fingers grappled for the capsicum flute.

The body on the window rotated and formed an *X* shape. Long bat wings flared from its arms, its three-fingered hands twitching. The face resembled a pug dog, the snout compressed and flaring. It was beyond hideous. Dark round eyes studied her through the window, one eye encircled by pale scars and what appeared to be stitch marks.

"Is that—is that a gremlin?" Octavia asked. Her heart fluttered like butterfly wings in a windstorm.

"It most certainly is." Mrs. Stout had shown no alarm at the curiosity, only frowning. "Harmless little creatures, really. Well, unless you're wearing silver."

Self-conscious, Octavia looked at the others. They all laughed together, but not at her. The woman wore wine down the front of her glittery dress. Little Daveo was already there with rags in hand to clean up the floor.

"There's rarely only one gremlin, though," said Mrs. Stout. "Most often it means we're flying through a flock—"

A flutter of green filled the windows. More screams came from the other side of the ship. Octavia turned to see the toddler in a mad dash, his face whitened with terror, his mother in quick pursuit.

One of the young men called to a compatriot, "Go down to the smoking room! Tell the others to come up for some fun."

Fun? What could possibly be fun about these strange little creatures flying around outside?

"Miss Leander, I do believe we should retire to our room for now," said Mrs. Stout, clutching her arm.

"Why? I don't under—"

Green flashed through the air not five feet away. One of the men laughed as he staggered in pursuit, a chair in his hands. Her gaze went to the open windows. Little green bodies flooded the gap. Those dark eyes studied the room, heads cocked in jerky little movements, like a bird or a construct. More wings filled the air. A woman screamed. Glass shattered. Heavy, metallic thuds drew her attention to the young man with the chair. He was bludgeoning the gremlin. Music of blood crackled in Octavia's ears, the sound inhuman and discordant, and then it quieted. The man dropped the chair and held up the limp body. The thing couldn't have been more than a foot in diameter. It oozed strangely dark blood, its extremities dangling like a slack marionette.

Around her, blood screamed more loudly than laughter and the crunch of chairs and whatever other weapons the drunken gang had grabbed. Little Daveo, his face flushed, rushed to a bell along the wall.

"Just shut the windows and we'll take care of them!" he shouted.

"And you'll end all the fun!" cried a man.

"Damned flying rats," yelled another man. "Think you can bring Caskentia down more, eh? I'll show you . . ."

The young woman screamed shrilly and then the sound was choked off. A gremlin, no larger than an ottoman, had gripped her necklaces and hoisted her upward with impossible strength. The woman's slippered feet dangled above the ground. The man beside her managed to force her head down, allowing the necklaces to fly freely into the gremlin's grip. Its toothy smile of triumph sent a chill through Octavia.

Everything seemed to take place in a matter of seconds.

Mrs. Stout shouted something that was lost in the din. Octavia looked for others in need and only saw gremlins swirling about, clattering on windows. They wanted out. No one else wore silver. A man attacked a gremlin from behind, crushing it with a well-aimed kick.

As horrible and hideous as the creatures might be, they had the clear disadvantage. This was a slaughter.

Octavia dove for a tray left abandoned on a table. Her satchel bounced heavily against her hip. The nearest man was hunched over as he stomped the gremlin to death. She smashed the tray against the side of the man's head. He crashed to the ground, dazed.

Beady black eyes blinked at her from a puddle of blood and crushed green flesh. Before she could even step forward, its shrill music faded.

"Kethan's bastards, what was that for?" snarled the man as he bounded to his feet. His body's song was steady yet sluggish with inebriation.

"You drunken josser! Just let the creature out! That's all it wants. It didn't even steal any silver." She held up the tray again as a threat.

"Bah. It's just a bit of fun," he said, rubbing his ear.

"Your concept of fun is like kicking fresh cow patties." She almost convulsed in rage. He had no sense that these were living beings—even worse, he probably didn't care. His ilk gallivanted off to war, expecting the joy of a fox hunt.

"The little beasties will come in here and rob the ship blind," he said. "They'll jack any piece of silver not bolted down. And they're chimeras. Bloody constructs. They're not *natural*."

Gremlins were chimeras? "Even as creatures of science, they still live and breathe and bleed."

"I doubt you'll make any converts in this lot," said Mrs. Stout, her breath huffing.

"These bucks don't need conversion. They need common sense," she said, moving forward, prepared to deliver more sense in the form of a heavy wooden tray.

Airborne gremlins still darted throughout the room. More people had flooded the promenade, but the creatures proved agile enough to dodge most attacks. A harsh, alien scream sounded, the sudden music piercing. Several men in crimson garb dashed by.

Octavia waded into the scrum. She knocked one man away from a gremlin, and in surprise he shoved her back. "You're a woman!" he said, his jaw slack.

"And you're a fool," she snapped.

Stewards herded people toward the berthing. Mrs. Stout was engaged in an animated conversation with Little Daveo. Glass crunched underfoot, and Octavia studied the wreck of the room. Stains of alcohol and blood spattered the floor, green lumps of flesh strewn about.

One of the stewards had a writhing burlap bag in hand and a thick club in the other.

She advanced on him. "Can't you just let them go free?"

He studied her up and down, his expression more weary than anything. "Can't, m'lady. Have to search them for missing jewelry and items from the ship. Gremlins are sneaky buggers. Worry not, we'll take care of it quiet like. If you're missing anything—"

"No, they stole nothing from me." She turned away to get her bearings as discordant, terrible notes rang in her ears. It didn't matter that scientists cobbled gremlins together in some laboratory—their death songs sounded the same as any other being under the Lady's care.

A heavy thud and squawk sounded behind her, the steward's bat finding another target. Octavia ached to melt into the floor and cover her ears. She couldn't tolerate this. She still had the tray in hand.

I can attack the steward, get the bag—and then what? These people won't grant me peace to heal the gremlins, and the steward isn't the most guilty party in the room.

As she turned away, she noted a small green lump in a library chair. The gremlin was mostly obscured by an open book, one leathery triangle of wing in contrast to the bright red upholstery. Octavia walked in that direction in a slow and controlled fashion. No one seemed to be looking her way. She sat down on the chair, angling her hips to shelter the creature. She heaved her satchel onto her lap and let that block out the world even more.

Even before lifting the book, she knew this one was uninjured, his song soft as a hum and quickened by anxiety. She set aside the children's book about the missing princess and gasped. This gremlin was half the size of the others. *A mere baby.* He whimpered and looked up at her. His long, tapered ears quivered. As hideous as he was, her spirit was moved.

"Shush, shush, little one. I won't let you come to harm."

He quieted, as if comforted. She looked toward the windows. Several stewards were close by, already cleaning the carpet. They would order her out at any moment. The men would be on her before she could unlatch a window, of that she had no doubt.

"Miss Leander, are you all right?" Mrs. Stout's face was flushed, her fists trembling at her rounded hips. "I have filed a complaint and will take it to the captain himself. Those ruffians! Making sport like that! Oh. My goodness. That thing is scarcely bigger than a kitten."

"We can't let them kill him," Octavia whispered. An older man in crisp red attire was headed their way.

"Surely you're not suggesting . . . oh. You are."

"Please, Mrs. Stout. You said yourself that these creatures are harmless."

"Surely you sensed—saw—that girl who was almost choked to death."

Sensed? Only Miss Percival and the other girls knew of Octavia's heightened abilities. There was no way for Mrs. Stout to be privy to such knowledge. Adrenaline fluttered through Octavia's veins, but she chose to disregard the slip.

"It wanted her necklace, not to cause harm. The men aboard this ship certainly didn't display such mercy. Please, Mrs. Stout."

Mrs. Stout sighed and nodded brusquely. "Very well. Take it to our berths. We can sneak it out tonight," she whispered. She turned on her heel. "Oh, Captain! I must speak with you about this appalling matter." She practically pounced on the man, her body as formidable as a wall.

Octavia opened the middle pocket of her satchel, revealing the white of her medician blanket. "Come along now," she said, scooping up the creature. He weighed as much as two chicken eggs. The gremlin's eyes were dark and solemn as she snapped the flap shut.

Octavia escaped the room. In the open space above the stairs, she found the dandies in a mob. Considering how she had just bashed many of them with a tray, she wasn't surprised at their glowers and commentary as she hurried past.

"Upstart—"

"Meddlesome git—"

"Someone ought to teach her—"

Breathless, she fumbled out her key and opened the door, ducking inside. As she turned, a piece of paper on the sink caught her eye. As she drew closer, she noted it was a napkin.

IF YOU CONTINUE TO DELFORD, YOU WILL DIE.

The words were bold and blocky, stealing the breath from her lungs. It wasn't from the other men, not that fast. Whoever wrote this knew what she was, where she was going. What did this mean? Why would she die?

"I'm just a medician," she whispered, and knew the words for false as soon as they escaped her lips. She had never been "just a medician."

Whatever the note meant, it didn't need to be seen by Mrs. Stout. Her fingers trembling, she set her satchel on the floor and pulled out the gremlin. He quivered in her palm, his squashed nose sniffing the air. Just as Octavia crammed the note into her satchel, Mrs. Stout burst into the room.

"There!" she said with a huff. "How is the creature?"

"Well." Octavia managed a shaky smile as the gremlin scurried up her arm to the shoulder, wings tickling against her sleeves. She glanced around the room and couldn't spy any other threats. *Die. Why would I die? How do they know where I'm going?*

"Good. I gave that captain a piece of my mind, I'll tell you! His ear will be burning for hours. Give me space to get to the closet, child."

Stooping down, the older woman pulled out a brown suitcase in full leather. The corners showed softness from wear, but the craftsmanship was obvious. Mrs. Stout came from some money. She opened the case and tugged something from the base. Metal clinked. The gremlin made a sound akin to a purr as his long ears perked up.

Mrs. Stout held a small metal cage, folded down. With a few snaps it assumed its full size of about a foot in diameter. "In Leffen I intended to buy a new mecha bird. The best mechanists in the kingdom are there! I saw no point in buying a new cage when I already had one at home, so I brought this along. Do you think it's too small?"

"It looks about right to me," said Octavia, welcoming any distraction from her new anxieties. Even more, the gremlin was eager. He sprang from her shoulder and glided to Mrs. Stout's lap with the softest flutter of wings. "The cage is silver. They do have a fixation for the metal, don't they?"

"They hoard silver, but fancy all things metal, really. Finding a gremlins' nest is like a dragon's cave of old, mounded high with everything from wedding rings to engine casings from steam cabriolets."

"A man out there said these were chimeras." Octavia studied the gremlin, as if she could discern seams or mismatched flesh.

"Yes, creations out of Tamarania. It's not enough for scientists to twiddle with machines; no, they must alter living beings as well." Mrs. Stout huffed in disagreement. "Of course, there are some who say their presence in Caskentia is to undermine us."

"How's that?"

"Oh, there are *books* on the subject," Mrs. Stout said sagely, as if that made it true. Her eyes sparkled as she leaned forward with a storyteller's eagerness. "In the south, men can speak with gremlins, work with them. Here, they are mischief makers. Thieves. Some suspect that gremlins are here to ensure we cannot develop our technology, that gremlins steal everything and haul it south so those nations remain superior."

"That's footle. Anyone with sense knows Caskentia undermines itself sufficiently and doesn't require any outside interference."

"True. Nothing's been the same since the days of King Kethan." Sadness weighed on Mrs. Stout's words, but then, she was old enough to actually remember those golden years. "Most gremlin flocks live near cities, just as we found this mob today. Makes scavenging easier for them, I imagine, though you never see them inside a city. Even gremlins have standards!"

A dislike of cities. Something we have in common.

The gremlin took to the air and alighted on Octavia's lap. With an eye on his catlike mouth, she slowly stroked his head. Soft folds at the base of the ears reminded her of worn leather. The gremlin butted his head against her, chittering, and folded his body in a meditative Al Cala posture like a small child. Octavia sucked in a breath, caught by memory.

For years, when loneliness overwhelmed her, Octavia would retreat to the academy's upstairs office and crawl beneath Miss Percival's desk. Above her, Miss Percival's pen scratched on paper. Octavia bowed in Al Cala, forehead to the ground, breathing, taking in the mere closeness of another body.

"Is it the fire tonight?" Miss Percival would ask after a time, knowing of the nightmares that plagued Octavia.

"Yes," she sometimes said, or "No. The others . . ." *Won't talk to me. Say I'm too good for them. That obviously the Lady is the only friend I need.*

If it was the latter, Miss Percival's hand would work beneath the desk to rest on Octavia's shoulder. "It was the same for me."

No, it wasn't. Miss Percival couldn't hear a song outside of an enchanted circle; Octavia knew that—she had tested it with small injuries. Miss Percival was none the wiser, gifted as she was.

As Octavia crouched beneath the desk, she knew the

anxiety in her mentor's blood, the drawn-out notes of weariness and the rat-tat-tat of the constant terror that a thousand more things must be done before sleep. Sometimes the song was accompanied by the agonized resonant drum of a migraine, or the quiver of knees and hands cramped after hours of harvesting.

"Let your breath be the wind in the Lady's branches, Octavia. Give her your sorrow, your guilt."

They breathed together. In those moments, Miss Percival's song hummed in solace.

They had outgrown that ritual years ago. Judging by Miss Percival's strained song in recent months, not even Al Cala granted her respite these days.

But this gremlin—this creature cobbled together of various parts—meditated in a perfect Al Cala pose. Tears filled Octavia's eyes as she pressed a hand to the gremlin's back, just as Miss Percival once soothed her.

Do you grieve for those who died? Are you afraid to be caged within these walls, the way I feel amongst city streets?

It would be impossible to keep the creature hidden the entire trip. She knew that, and yet she couldn't withhold her fondness for this little gremlin the same color as spring leaves. *Leaf. The perfect name for a gremlin.* Mrs. Stout would never approve of the attachment it implied, so Octavia kept it to herself. Her fingers trailed down Leaf's spine to the small nub of his tail.

A bell rang out in the hall. "Come now, little one, and try out the cage," Octavia said.

To her shock, the gremlin flew right inside the silver-barred cube. Mrs. Stout did the latch. Leaf had barely enough room to spread his wings, but he didn't seem perturbed by his new confines.

"Well! The creature learned what a cage was right away," said Mrs. Stout. "My oh my. I wonder what else we could teach him?"

"Yes. There's something special about him." *Leaf.* The name fit the chimera well. He was an aberration without a true place in this world, just like her.

"I SUSPECT THIS MAY be horse, not beef, but it's cooked too long to tell." Mrs. Stout's nostrils flared as she sniffed at her supper stew. "Well, meat is meat!"

I couldn't eat flame-cooked meat for years after I moved to the academy. Couldn't even be in its presence without retching.

Octavia let a lump of gristle roll over the back of her spoon. "I suppose." The afternoon had passed in blissful peace as they taught Leaf the names of some twenty objects, but now darkness had fallen beyond the promenade's windows.

"You're fussing, not eating." Mrs. Stout pointed her spoon accusingly. "Our gremlin is caged and safe. Soon enough he'll be free, and you will have nothing to worry about!"

Today has been one new worry after another.

"Oh." Mrs. Stout's eyes widened as she looked across the room. She reached to her lap and, to Octavia's surprise, pulled out a small notebook and nubby pencil. She began to scribble, her tongue jabbing at her red-painted lip.

"What are you doing, Mrs. Stout?"

"I am a keen observer of humanity. That woman over there, her dress is coarse, like a pony in winter. I must record that imagery. It's perfect."

"You're a poet?" Octavia leaned forward with eagerness. The mechanical band played softly in the background, the sound of the mandolin soothing like a body in good health.

Mrs. Stout tilted her head, her expression mildly aghast. "Goodness, no. Though I do write. On occasion." Her scrutinizing gaze traveled elsewhere, and her pencil scratched more words on paper. Octavia noted their fellow diners made no move to socialize. Apparently, one doesn't make friends by assaulting fellow passengers with a serving tray.

Their soup bowls were empty when Mr. Garret approached and leaned over the table, his hands hovering near their dishes.

"There has been a disturbance in your room," he said, his voice low. "People complained of noise. I had seen you both at supper, so I unlocked the door, expecting a burglar."

The two women shared an expression of white-faced dread.

"Mr. Garret, I can explain—" Octavia began.

"I know what happened earlier and I can guess what happened now." His tone was mild, not indignant as she expected. "How long did you plan to keep the beastie?"

"Only until tonight," Mrs. Stout said. Octavia felt a wave of sadness at the words.

"If people already suspect something about our room, is there someplace where no one will find him?" Octavia asked. "Until we can free him, of course."

Mr. Garret considered her. "The cargo hold should do until the promenade empties about midnight. No one will hear him there. He'll be safe, Miss Leander."

Octavia released a deep breath. "Thank you for your assistance, Mr. Garret. And your humanity." *Each time I meet this man, I like him a little more.*

"Bludgeoning a defenseless creature is no sport, m'lady." His words reflected his Tamaran heritage: all logic and clear morality, even as his lilting accent was pure Mercian. For the first time, Octavia wondered what it would be like to settle in Tamarania, a city-state known for sparse crime, pacifism, and street-corner philosophers.

Mrs. Stout dabbed her lips with a napkin. "If we must wait until late for our clandestine activities, I do believe I'll retire to bed."

"Your cots can certainly be set up now, m'ladies," Mr. Garret said in a louder voice, backing up. They followed him from the promenade as Octavia scrutinized him.

Romantic entanglements, however brief, were dangerous. She knew that from the medical wards and the heartbreaks she'd witnessed time and again. A girl would heal a soldier. Enjoy his company. Think cozy what-ifs. He returns to duty. Dies in some terrible, instantaneous way.

I'll know Mr. Garret for only a few days. I'm not some flibbertigibbet out for a fling. Our relationship is temporary. Professional.

Though Mrs. Stout is right. His uniform pants do fit in an extremely flattering way.

She was so busy looking down that she almost walked

into him as he stopped at their room. A self-conscious flush warmed her cheeks as she fumbled for her key.

She entered first. The thin bunk mattress was flipped onto the floor. A splash of water across the sink revealed that the tap had been running. A handle along the wall had been flipped down, revealing a small foldout writing surface. In the midst of the maelstrom sat Leaf. His ears perked up at the sight of Octavia and he launched himself at her shoulder, squawking.

"Shush, shush," she said, nudging aside the open cage so she could squeeze beside the sink. She noted the undone padlock and scanned the floor. There was no sign of the key that had been left hooked atop the cage. Perhaps Leaf was too intelligent for his own good.

Mrs. Stout and Mr. Garret entered, and he shut the door behind him. Standing there, they occupied almost all the space in the room.

"This is what we will do," Mr. Garret said, then paused, his brows lowered in thought. "I will escort Miss Leander into the cargo hold. Mrs. Stout, I hate to leave this mess for you—"

"Tosh and fiddlesticks." Mrs. Stout flicked her hand, then smoothed the blue streak in her hair. "I'm not an invalid. I can tidy things and then call a steward to ready our beds."

"What of you, Mr. Garret?" Octavia asked. "Yet again, you go beyond the duties of your station to assist me."

"Doing what is right is often an unpopular choice. That said, I am not often popular." He softened the words with an almost bashful shrug.

Octavia pressed her fingers to her mouth as if she could hide her smile. "Oh. Perhaps that's why we get along so well, Mr. Garret."

Amusement glittered in his eyes. "Perhaps, m'lady. Now, can you cage the beastie?"

"Certainly." Octavia made a kissing noise to attract the gremlin's attention. He remained precariously balanced on her shoulder, his wing like a fan by her ear. "Into the cage and quiet, little one. We must take you someplace safe."

Leaf chittered and half slid down the slope of Octavia's breasts. He glided into the cage at her feet.

"Oh my. Whatever happened to my key?" asked Mrs. Stout. "Surely he didn't eat it?"

"I have a spare lock in my quarters," said Mr. Garret.

Octavia refastened the ineffective latch and grabbed two towels from the rack. Overlapping each other, the two cloths covered the cage perfectly. She adjusted the satchel strap on her shoulder as she stood upright again.

"People will assume there's a bird under here. I hope," said Octavia. She hoisted up the cage and checked the towels again. "That's not an unusual thing on board, is it?"

Mr. Garret shook his head, his expression one of composed amusement. Perhaps that was all this was to him—a diversion to liven up a monotonous day. He was a general's son. He may be a steward now, but certainly he'd been raised in the high society of Mercia.

Maybe I'm a mere country curiosity to him, but it's only fair. I find him equally intriguing.

Most everyone else still ate dinner in the promenade.

Mr. Garret walked at a brisk pace downstairs to deck B and along a corridor. The clatter of pans and the heavy scent of stew revealed the kitchen on the left. He opened the "Crew Only" door, and with a quick finger to his lips, led her down another hallway. Gaping doors showed berthing stacked three beds high, the wood panels torn from the wall to reveal steel. Another door opened, and the warm light of the hallways vanished in an instant.

Dim rows of glowstones illuminated a gloomy cavern suited for hibernation, the space perhaps fifteen feet in length. A musty stink pervaded along with the heavy rumble of machinery. As her eyes adjusted, she made out a few tall stacks of boxes covered with blankets and strapped to the walls.

"You risk too much in bringing me here," Octavia whispered. Instead of being fearful, she felt an excited tingle of secrecy set her body alight.

"You risk yourself." Mr. Garret frowned, shaking his head. "You are too trusting of me, m'lady. If most men took you to a place like this . . ."

You've already proven you're not most men. "So what are your motives, Mr. Garret?"

"You recognized my surname, did you not?" he asked. She nodded as she set down the cage and tossed the towels aside. Leaf's black eyes glistened in the dimness, but the rest of his green skin seemed to blend with the shadows. "Then you know that my father was not . . . regarded well for his style of command."

"I know he invented the buzzer, and about how he

died." She paused, surprised. "I never thought of it that way, but it is unusual for a general to die in such a manner."

"Soldiers are considered expendable, not generals." His deep voice softened. "But for missions of particular danger, he knew the buzzer best, and took the risk himself."

He's as haunted by the crash of the Alexandria *as I am.* Octavia had been the only survivor from her village. She had never known another person who suffered—who even remembered—the events of that night.

"I'm sorry," she whispered.

Mr. Garret met her eyes, gaze fierce. "Too many have died these recent years. I am weary of men being regarded as wood for a fire, and I will not see gremlins treated as such either."

"You fought at the front." *That's where he lost his leg.*

He looked away. His answer needed no words. She felt the profound urge to hug him, to tell him she understood about the death of his father, about the horrors of war, but she couldn't quite move. Awkwardness thickened the air.

Leaf trilled, the sound so sudden and silly that Octavia couldn't help but laugh. A smile warmed Mr. Garret's face.

"Ah, we cannot forget about the beastie. Move the cage into the shadows here." The cage rattled as Octavia shuffled it over a few feet. "Later, the smoke room will be busy, but the kitchen will not be. Duck in there, if you must. If a crewman catches you in the hallway, you can play as innocent and lost."

She arched an eyebrow. "You think they'll believe that?"

"That you are innocent, or lost?" The white of his teeth shone in the thin light.

"Did I come across as either earlier?"

"Indeed. And I think you can play the part again."

She gasped in mock indignation. "Play the part! Which one? Mr. Garret, are you insinuating that I'm not innocent? Must I remind you that I'm carrying capsicum, and not afraid to use it?"

The darkness hid it well, but she was certain he blushed deeply. "I certainly do not wish to get on your bad side, Miss Leander."

"You're a wise man." *And a collection of other positive adjectives.* "I . . . I do believe you said something about getting a lock for his cage?"

He nodded. "Yes, of course. My berthing is close by. I will return as soon as I can." He slipped away, the door shutting behind him with a soft click.

Alone in the darkness, Octavia backed up until her heels found the curved steel of the wall. "Oh, goodness. What am I doing, Leaf?" she whispered. "I only said farewell to Miss Percival this morning, and that was hard enough. She didn't even hug me good-bye. She's always been rather stoic, but not with me, not until these past few months." The lingering hurt stung her eyes. "And now I meet this Mr. Garret. I'm only going to know him for a few days, and then I'll never see him again. Rather like you, I suppose."

The gremlin chirped in return.

"You silly thing. My heart must be made of silver, the

way you've stolen it." She lowered her satchel to the floor as she stared at the door.

Octavia waited. And waited. She angled her watch toward the light as the minutes passed.

"It's as though Mr. Garret's been swallowed up by a geologica sinkhole. I can't leave you here, Leaf, not without a good lock on your cage. I hope Mrs. Stout has gone on to sleep and isn't fretting."

She shuffled her feet and kicked something solid. Crouching down, she found a hard ninety-degree angle of polished wood. A frame? Curious, she lifted it into the light, and found herself staring Queen Evandia in the eye. Octavia snorted.

"How appropriate, to find you skulking about in a place like this." She blew a raspberry at the Queen's face.

It was an older portrait, showing Evandia as young and haughty. Prim, painted lips, eyes lined by kohl and crimson. Streaks of red livened the black updo of her hair—that trendy dye alone showed the portrait's age. The canvas reeked of urine. Deep slash marks almost bisected the image, chin downward dangling like degloved skin. The work of soldiers, perhaps. Angry, starving soldiers, unpaid in months like Miss Percival. Or grieving family. Or hungry civilians, or the jobless, the sick . . . Well, that narrowed down the possible culprits to the majority of Caskentia.

It was funny, in a terrible way. Queen Evandia was so rarely seen in public due to the threat of the Waste. Now her own people would riot and lynch her on sight. Maybe that's one reason why the war dragged on—Caskentia had

someone to fight other than itself. A dozen corrupt, bickering municipalities; the city of Mercia with its half million; the palace, a world unto itself. One could argue that Evandia didn't really rule at all. She was simply . . . there. Governing the palace, while the rest of the kingdom succumbed to verdigris and rot.

"I'm sorry you'll have to be left here in such poor company," Octavia said to Leaf. The gremlin emitted a soft screech. "Yes, my sentiments exactly."

The cargo access door opened again with a burst of light. She cowered behind the boxes, willing Leaf to silence with a hand on his cage.

"Miss Leander?" Mr. Garret's voice was low.

She emerged from her hiding place, her eyes still dazzled by the brightness. "I'm over here," she said, stepping forward. The door shut, reducing the glare, and she could see Mr. Garret's face sag in relief.

"My apologies. My absence had been noted and I was required to clean up in the promenade. I hope you were not overly vexed. Here is the lock."

She stroked the lock with her thumb, absorbing the lingering warmth of Mr. Garret's body, and then fastened the metal onto the cage. She tucked the key into her satchel, knowing better than to leave it in reach of the gremlin again.

"I'll be back soon," she whispered to Leaf. He trilled a soft farewell.

"Come. I will walk you back to your room," said Mr. Garret.

The kitchen had quieted, the smell of food replaced by the fresh odor of soap and lemons. As they passed the smoke room, a deep masculine laugh carried through the walls. Her hand felt strangely empty as she traveled up the stairs. Already, she missed Leaf's companionship.

Please, Lady, let him stay safe there.

They reached the top of the stairs. Sudden and discordant music froze her in place, her hand gripping the rail.

"Miss Leander?" Mr. Garret stopped and turned, his expression quizzical.

She pushed past him, following a mad cacophony only she could hear. Bleating trumpets and crazed drums competed for dominance. Nothing spoke louder than blood, and this symphony of agony originated behind her very own door.

"Oh, Mrs. Stout," she whispered.

Chapter 4

Octavia grabbed the doorknob. It was locked as securely as the Caskentian royal vault. Her hand dove into the satchel pocket, numb and fumbling.

"Miss Leander?" asked Mr. Garret.

"She's dying." Octavia stabbed the key into the lock and jerked the knob. It spasmed open. Absolute darkness filled the room, but she didn't need light to see. Shrill flutes and wild drums originated from the bottom bunk. She staggered forward and dropped to one knee, doffing the satchel strap from her shoulder. Mr. Garret's feet were heavy on the floor behind her. The light clicked on.

Crimson pooled beneath the cot. Both beds had been assembled, a steel ladder leading to the top. A black canvas tent surrounded both bunks. The bottom bed was zipped shut, slash marks sagging open.

"My God," said Mr. Garret. The door shut behind him.

That was meant to be my bed.

Someone had carried through with the threat from the note. Why? Why her, why this? The shrillness of the blood in her ears grounded her, forcing her through shock to the duty at hand.

Octavia unfastened the middle segment of her satchel. Shoving her bag away, she stood and fluffed out her medician blanket. At seven feet by three feet, it filled up the entire floor space with some folding at the edges. In the middle lay the circle—an oval, really—woven of copper thread and honeyflower stems, which created a permanent healing surface bound to the cloth.

Octavia tore open the tent flaps, her breath catching at the sight of Mrs. Stout. The woman was as pale as death, a blue undertone to her skin. The human body contained some six quarts of blood, and Mrs. Stout's volume screamed like a thousand starving cats.

"What can I do?" asked Mr. Garret.

"Lift her at the shoulders." He deftly stepped around Octavia, taking care not to place his feet within the sanctity of the circle. They set Mrs. Stout on the blanket. Octavia's fingers brushed the copper weave of the circle. A spark crackled in the air as the enchantment activated.

Mrs. Stout's night shift was more red than white. Her large breasts lay like mashed rounds of bread at each armpit. Through the jelling blood, Octavia judged the stab wounds to be in the upper quadrant of the abdomen, most likely striking the kidneys.

Whoever did this knew exactly how to kill.

The discordant music wailed as it began to fade. Mrs. Stout's soul was slipping away.

Octavia grabbed Mrs. Stout's hand. "Pray, by the Lady

let me mend thy ills." For several long seconds, Octavia didn't breathe, the very air still in anticipation. The access came with a slight pop, the music louder again due to the circle, but still far too faint.

Octavia brushed her hands over her concealed wand in her parasol. The puppy that morning had required no more than a pinch of pampria; now she scooped up a full palm.

"Lady, hear me. Mend the body of this kind soul. Lady, be with us . . ." The ground red leaves fluttered through the air and vanished. A strangled gasp escaped Mrs. Stout's throat. Octavia bent over her and turned Mrs. Stout's head to the side just in time. The acidic stench of the vomit didn't distract Octavia from the prayer repeated beneath her tongue.

Falling back to her haunches, she reached for the jar of heskool root. The boiled roots were soft beneath her fingers, the chunks fibrous like jerky. She flicked three pieces against Mrs. Stout's skin. The marching-band rhythm of the heart's drum immediately steadied.

Lady, thank you, thank you. She added a sprinkle of bellywood bark to counter any infection from lingering zymes, and a glob of Linsom berries to mend the skin. The clamor dulled. Mrs. Stout's chest rose and dipped. Octavia allowed herself to sag onto her knuckles, loosened strands of hair snagging on her eyelashes. The wax-sealed incision on her forearm tingled, as if to remind her of its presence.

"That was amazing," whispered Mr. Garret. "Never have I seen a healing so fast."

Octavia recoiled. She had broken Miss Percival's most

vital rule for this journey, and in a spectacular way. Mrs. Stout may have somehow guessed at what she was, but Mr. Garret had absolute proof.

Her fingers trembled as she packed her jars. The pampria was half full, enough for two or three trauma cases as bad as Mrs. Stout's—certainly not adequate to start her practice. *Without the Lady's herbs, I'll be almost useless in Delford. Doctoring can only do so much for poison cases as bad as theirs. It would take months to grow pampria until it's ripe enough to harvest. There may be an apothecary in Leffen, but it would be far too overpriced, and I barely have the funds for my journey.*

She brushed her fingers against Mrs. Stout's arm, now warm to the touch. She was grateful to be able to save her friend, but the consequences were dire.

"You are a medician," Mr. Garret said in a gentle tone, probing.

"Yes." She didn't look at him. "I was trained at Miss Percival's academy."

"I know of it. One of the most reputed medician schools in the kingdom. Your skill—'tis as though your Lady's hand rests directly on you. I had the brief acquaintance of a medician. He was not as attuned."

"Ah. When you lost your leg."

Mr. Garret sucked in a breath. "How . . . ?"

"I know these things."

"As you knew of her injury before opening the door. You *are* unusually attuned."

"So I've been told." *Again, and again, and again.* She bowed her head. "Thank you, Lady, for extending your branches." She brushed her fingers against the copper circle. With an electric snap, the invisible seal broke.

He cleared his throat. "Perhaps it would help you to know I guessed at your occupation, even before this unfortunate event."

She spun to look at him. "How? When?"

"Your attachment to your satchel. Only a medician or a banker would refuse to hand over a bag, and a banker would not travel alone."

I can mend a gunshot wound to the gut in two minutes, but my lack of social graces can damn me just as fast.

"Do not worry. I tend to be more observant than most," he said. "Besides, your skill in wielding dining trays did wonders for your reputation."

She laughed, the sound verging on hysterical. "Well, at least some good came of that."

"How long will she lie here like this, Miss Leander? And this blanket—where is the blood?"

Octavia stroked at the blanket, the fabric soft as silk. "The Lady will keep her unconscious for a few hours, most likely. The crisis is past, but her body is still mending. As for the fluids, the blanket absorbs them. It's part of the enchantment. My full uniform has similar wards."

"Amazing," he murmured. "I know so little of the Lady and the Tree. You do not hear of it as a modern practice except among medicians. Not that I am slighting it, of course." She nodded to show no offense was taken. "During my other experience with a medician, I was not quite . . . of mind to pay attention to such details."

"Oh, that's quite common. Amputation is a trauma not just of the body, but of the soul. The spirit is left incomplete."

"Indeed." He studied her. "I know some regard magic as being a particular sort of science, not requiring any sort of presence or God. I am a practical man of battlefield faith, but there is obviously something to the Lady and I am curious about her nature. Pardon, I do not mean to sound judgmental, merely ignorant."

"Ignorance is remedied easily enough." She softened her words with a smile. "The Lady was a woman and mother and of great faith in God. In times of sorrow, like now, her husband and children succumbed to illness. However, she used the wisdom gleaned from their deaths to go forth and help others. She traveled beyond the Waste, healing. Some stories say the Waste was a land of plenty then, or just starting to die. It depends on the telling. She saw more pain and suffering than most people could withstand, yet she endured. At the end of her life, she begged God that she still be able to heal. She was planted in the ground and grew as a tree bound to the very soul of the earth.

"The Lady is the mother of all children, the shade on a sunny day, the balm for any wound." Octavia stopped with a bashful shrug. "The Tree is somewhere beyond the Waste and said to be higher than the Pinnacles. Her seeds bring back the decayed dead, her leaves revive the recently departed, and other parts of the tree are also powerful curatives."

"Has anyone actually seen the Tree? In recent times, I mean."

"With their eyes? No. We all yearn to see the actual Tree, wherever it is." Grand understatement, that, but one simply didn't speak of such things, not even to other medicians.

She rested a hand on Mrs. Stout's arm. "Berth 3A was mine," she whispered. "This was meant for me."

"Yes." Mr. Garret's growl caused her to raise her head.

"Do you think it's because of what happened earlier with the gremlins? Or Mr. Drury . . ."

"Any fool can bludgeon a small, cornered beastie to death. Stabbings that precise speak of more expertise."

"Then Mr. Drury—"

"I do not know about him, but this seems strangely out of proportion. Has he approached you since this morning?"

"No, but there was a note left in my room earlier, threatening my life if I continue to my destination. Someone had access to my room then, and again later, to attack Mrs. Stout."

"Hmm. Perhaps there is wisdom to the suggestion. Have you considered returning to the academy?"

"No." *I'm not welcome.*

"If someone is trying to kill you—"

"I cannot go back."

He was quiet for a long moment. "Mrs. Stout may have seen her attacker and can tell us more."

"Perhaps, though many people don't remember the moments before near-death. It's a blessing, really." She frowned. "I do need to clean up this blood before she awakens. What can be done about the bedding and carpet?"

"I will tend to it. You see a bit of everything on these ships." Mr. Garret stood and unsnapped the canvas from the support poles around the bunk.

"Truly? You see that many attempted murders and medicians failing in their attempts to travel incognito?"

"I referred more to unusual stains and matters of laundry. As for your efforts to travel incognito, I can assure you, your presence has created an unusual fuss on board ship. You are the focus of gossip right now."

She harrumphed beneath her breath. "I might find that flattering if my friend hadn't nearly died." Tears flooded her eyes. "This is . . . we can't keep this a secret, not because of me. There's still a murderer on board."

Mr. Garret folded the tenting and set it on the floor. He began to lift the sodden mattress and Octavia shook her head. "Wait a moment," she said. "This won't dry it to the center, but it will help." She unholstered her parasol and held the stick over the blood. Immediately the outer layer began to pale, the desiccated blood falling away in thick flakes like curling candle wax. His eyes widened.

"I never guessed that your medician wand was hidden there."

"Good. I might keep some secrets from you yet."

"As to the killer aboard . . ." Mr. Garret sobered. "Captain Hue is a good sort, really, but he has absolute faith in the Caskentian government. He would moor us at the nearest tower and turn the investigation over to local militia."

Octavia slumped over, one hand to her forehead. "Oh

dear. All our suspects are wealthy. They would buy off the local officials and be on their merry way within minutes."

"You are sadly astute in the workings of the modern world."

"You haven't seen how Caskentia has treated the academy. If not for the working farm, all of the girls would starve. The cattle and the spring tulips bring in more than our healing has in years." She shut her mouth with a click of her teeth. Miss Percival would swat her backside if she heard Octavia babble about privy details like that.

Mr. Garret nodded as he balled up the mattress and linens. "I will take these downstairs and return."

"I'll clean up Mrs. Stout while you're away, but . . ." Memory made her bite her lower lip. "Whoever did this had a key. The door was locked when we arrived."

He looked at the door, frowning. "Perhaps they stole her key, or a master. I will be very, very fast."

"You can't guard me night and day, Mr. Garret. I can take care of myself." She motioned to the capsicum flute hidden at her torso, rather proud of how she hid the tremble of her hand.

"I will do my utmost to keep you alive." Mr. Garret's icy blue eyes appraised her for a moment and then he was gone.

Odd. I'm usually the one who fights to keep people alive.

Octavia locked the door; at the very least, it would slow down an intruder. She dug into the closet and pulled out Mrs. Stout's case. The flap was unzipped with clothing dangling out. She froze. Mrs. Stout wasn't the sort to leave her luggage in that state.

The underclothes and dresses were a tangle, but she managed to find a spare nightdress and bloomers and set them aside. She reached for her own bag and found it in similar condition. Everything was unfolded and ransacked, though nothing appeared to be missing. Was this a robbery, or made to look like one? Maybe the murderer had been so confident he had the right bunk, he hadn't bothered to check. A few quick stabs in the dark and the deed was done.

Mrs. Stout remained asleep within the circle. Octavia tapped the copper threads. The warmth of magic thrummed against her fingers. "Lady, release thy burden on gravity and grant me time to cleanse thy charge," she whispered, concentrating on Mrs. Stout.

The older woman's body rose, her gown haphazard and stiff with blood. At about two feet in height, Mrs. Stout stopped, her body ramrod straight and supine. Octavia cleansed her with a rag enchanted like the medician blanket. She was halfway done dressing Mrs. Stout when a light knock echoed through the door.

"Miss Leander?" asked Mr. Garret.

"Give me a moment." She hurriedly did most of the buttons and looked between Mrs. Stout and the cot. It would take one small nudge to push Mrs. Stout out of the circle and onto the bed. The ability to float a patient was rare; at the academy, only Miss Percival could channel that much power from the Lady. To float a person beyond the circle—to sense anything beyond those limits—was supposedly impossible. It would certainly be convenient to move Mrs. Stout now, but Octavia wasn't foolish enough to do it and invite that kind of scrutiny.

Amusing as it would be to see Mr. Garret's reaction to such a feat of strength.

She lowered Mrs. Stout to the blanket and tapped the circle to disengage it. The heat of the Lady's presence withdrew like fireplace warmth sucked away by an open window in winter.

Upon confirming Mr. Garret's identity through the peephole, she let him in. "We need to lift her onto the bed," Octavia said as he set down the new linens. He immediately positioned himself at Mrs. Stout's shoulders.

Together, they grunted and lifted Mrs. Stout to the lower cot. Octavia nodded to Mr. Garret. "Thank you. And thank you for respecting my strength."

"We already lifted her together once, Miss Leander."

"Yes, but . . ." She shook her head, almost dazed. *I'm so used to fighting over such issues, I don't know what to make of it when I'm respected.*

Mrs. Stout's nightgown still gaped open and showed the planes of her chest, her unsupported breasts spread out and flat. Octavia spied another blemish and did a quick swipe with her rag. The mark didn't move. She leaned forward to examine it more closely.

"Is something the matter?" asked Mr. Garret.

"No. I thought I missed something, but she has a princess scar, that's all."

"A princess scar?"

"That's what medicians call it when a person has an

injury to the chest, like the missing princess in the stories. In the war, we often saw bayonet wounds or shrapnel." She held a fist to her own chest, just above the sternum, then looked back at Mrs. Stout. "By the smallness of the scar, this is probably a bullet . . . wound." Octavia stopped.

Mrs. Stout's silvered blond hair, minus the blue streak. Her age. The location and type of the wound. *It's a coincidence. It must be.* She glanced back at Mr. Garret. His honeyed skin seemed strangely blanched, the muscles in his face turned to stone.

Mr. Garret shook his head, his thick queue of hair whipping side to side. "The odds of such a thing . . . 'Tis simply not possible."

"Mrs. Stout? The missing princess?" Octavia stared at her slumbering friend.

Chapter 5

How many women of that age would bear such a particular injury? And Mrs. Stout certainly didn't have the look of a princess. Well, what Octavia would imagine by reading the stories. Any illustration of young Princess Allendia depicted her as an angelic vision of blond curls and wide blue eyes.

There was no physical comparison to be made to the current royal family. Not a year after the princess's kidnapping, the rest of her family was killed in an attack by infernal magi from the Waste. Distant cousins assumed the throne and made Mercia what it was today: a city of curfews and crime, powerful wards surrounding the city and preventing the entrance of any infernals. Queen Evandia and her children stayed sequestered in the palace for their own safety.

Surely Mrs. Stout—this plump, pleasant woman—wasn't the reason for fifty years of intermittent conflict?

Octavia sank into the carpet, her legs suddenly boneless.

"The princess was said to have a magic-inlaid tattoo between the toes of her right foot," said Mr. Garret.

"Oh my. You really . . . you really want me to check?" she asked faintly. "The stories never mentioned that."

"'Tis not public knowledge, but something known to those who work with the family."

"And what will we do if it's there?"

He closed his eyes, his expression pained. "No one would want her alive. Queen Evandia would see her as a direct threat. Others would use her as a rallying point for a civil war, elevate her as the true heir, here to re-create the Gilded Age we knew during the reigns of her father and grandfather. And the Wasters . . ."

There was no need to say what the Wasters would do. Their motivation to kidnap the princess had been straightforward: marry her to the son of their grand potentate and use the ancient royal lineage of Caskentia to found their own dynasty, their own Gilded Age.

Kidnapping and rape were well in character for those men beyond the mountains. Subsequent generations of Wasters had continued those dark methods in their fight for independence. Octavia still recalled the cacophony, both in music and digestive agony, of a thousand soldiers at the northern pass as they died in their own cots, victims of toxic zymes planted within the water.

Feeling half ill and eager to prove Mr. Garret wrong, she shuffled to Mrs. Stout's feet. There was no aura of magic, no spark, but such tattoos were meant to be subtle. Valuable horses or house pets were marked in such a way in case of theft; she had never heard of the technique being used on a child.

Opening herself to the Lady, she brushed her pointer finger between each white and wrinkled toe. Beside the pinkie, three pinprick-size moles lay in a line.

At her touch, the sudden buzz was slight, like the split-second vibration of a bee passing by her ear. Then came the burning. The heat crept up her finger, testing her endurance, testing her skill. Any lesser magus would shriek and pull away; an untalented person would feel nothing at all. Octavia breathed through the pain, remaining stoic, and the heat withdrew like a tide.

She had passed the test.

"This is the Princess Allendia, true daughter of King Kethan and Queen Varya." The voice was raspy, the magic in vapors after so many years. "Guard her well, fair magus, and treat her as your liege."

This must be a sham.

Mrs. Stout could not be the princess. But why construct this enchantment so long ago if she wasn't really Princess Allendia?

"Is that it?" asked Mr. Garret. "Did you get any response?"

She didn't hesitate. "It's nothing." It was bad enough that Mr. Garret knew Octavia's secrets. At the very least, Mrs. Stout's identity could remain in doubt.

He frowned, brows knitting together. "It looks like a tattoo."

"Well, fifty years without maintenance will erode most enchantments. Maybe something was once there, or maybe it's a peculiar birthmark and this is all footle."

He continued to study her, and Octavia looked at Mrs. Stout instead, fearing he would see through her deceit. Could this truly be the princess? The daughter of King Kethan, a man her parents spoke of with a reverence otherwise reserved for God?

There must be some other reason, some justification.

Octavia finished buttoning Mrs. Stout's gown and grabbed the fresh sheet from the floor. How would Mrs. Stout react when she knew they suspected?

A heavy hand lay on Octavia's shoulders. Mr. Garret's hands were broad and strong, his fingernails groomed with care. "I will keep your secrets," he said, his voice soft and lilting. Everything he said was a poem. "I vow that to you upon my life."

She felt a twinge of guilt at holding back information. "If Mrs. Stout is really . . . you know who, I doubt your assurances will hold weight. A woman in her position doesn't stay alive by having others know her true identity."

His hand lifted from her shoulder. "I agree." They sat there in uncomfortable silence. She fidgeted with the sheet on Mrs. Stout.

"I should finish cleaning in here," he finally said.

"Yes." Octavia didn't look at him.

Octavia and Mr. Garret exchanged few other words as he tacked a fresh carpet into the floor. When they set Mrs. Stout onto her fully remade bed, she quivered in her sleep. Her consciousness was rising.

"Thank you for your assistance, Mr. Garret," Octavia whispered at the door.

He offered her a short bow. His crimson uniform looked even more worn and rumpled after a full day of wear, but his eyes were keen. "I will monitor matters lest you be disturbed again."

"Thank you," she repeated.

She latched the door shut and then eyed the room. Any substantial furniture was bolted to the walls, so she grabbed their heavy baggage and stacked it against the door. Octavia plucked the pillow from her bunk and dropped it on the floor. The new carpet reeked of bleach and mustiness, the pile chilly from wherever it had been stored. She lay down with the light still on and glaring. From her vantage point on the floor, she could see Mrs. Stout's pasty arm dangling over the edge of the cot. It twitched on occasion, loose flesh jiggling at the elbow.

Octavia unlaced her boots and pulled down her threadbare stockings. Tucking her feet together, sole to sole, she angled her knees out in the diamond Al Cala position. She placed her hands together against her lower belly and inhaled to fill her lungs.

The chaos of the city, the search for the airship, Mr. Drury. Sweet little Leaf, the lone survivor of his flock. Mrs. Stout. Tears burned her eyes, and she breathed out, expelling the full burden of air along with her anxieties of the day. She closed her eyes, the world within her eyelids lit by the moon.

The Lady's Tree, taller than any mountain. Its bark green with algae, its branches burdened by vines and a hundred kinds of life. Waterfalls trickle through wide gaps in the bark; goats and deer bound up the slopes to hide within the thick brush.

"You know the sorrow of a woman's heart," Octavia whispered, the words slurred with tiredness. "Be with me, Lady." She breathed in again, her vision homing in on a single branch, a single leaf. She imagined the scent in her nostrils, musty and verdant. The single leaf, green and five-pointed, bobbed on its twig. As if she flew, Octavia reached out her hands to cup the leaf as it fell. It only wobbled on the twig, a single drop of dew coursing along the membranes and falling to her hands. Coolness and peace tingled from her palm and prickled the hairs on her arms, swirling in her chest. Pleasant pressure weighed against her like a stack of five quilts on the coldest winter's eve.

Octavia's soul radiated its thanks to the Lady as her body drifted to slumber.

THE SHRILLNESS OF A bell jarred her awake. Octavia bolted to sit upright, heart racing. Oh. She lay on the floor. The light was on. Muffled voices and reverberations from footsteps thudded through the flooring. Morning, already? Her fingers fumbled for her watch and she squinted bleary-eyed at the numbers upon the face. Exactly seven. Her eyes widened as memories of the previous evening flooded her mind. *Mrs. Stout.*

Mrs. Stout lay there with chapped lips agape like a fish. Her eyes were wide with shock, her silvery brow furrowed.

"What . . . ?" Mrs. Stout asked, the word slurred.

"Move slowly, Mrs. Stout. You endured a terrible trauma last night." Octavia braced her hands against Mrs. Stout's shoulders to force her down.

"I . . . oh." She pressed a trembling fist to her chest, to where the scar lay. "I dreamed . . . I thought it was memory."

"During a healing, it's common to flash back to early memories of pain," Octavia said. "I once knew a young man who lost part of his leg on the field, but when he awoke from surgery, he insisted that it was only broken. In his mind, he had returned to a childhood incident when he had fallen from a tree and broken that same leg." She shrugged. "Perhaps that's the Lady's way. There's some comfort in the familiar, even in pain."

"The Lady." Mrs. Stout licked her dry lips.

Octavia filled a small cup at the tap and assisted Mrs. Stout in sitting up to drink. "I'm a medician." She lowered her voice to imply secrecy.

"I know." Mrs. Stout leaned back against the wall.

"Do you remember anything about what happened when you retired to bed last night?"

Mrs. Stout opened one eye. "You're not going to ask how I knew, or when?"

"You mentioned my sensing abilities earlier, and I wondered what may have given me away." She paused, recalling Mr. Garret's aggravating statement. "Was it my satchel?"

"No." A smile softened her face. "But to answer your first question, I remember going to bed last night. I remember worrying over you and that little gremlin of ours, but you seemed in good hands with that steward."

Octavia's breath caught. Leaf! With Mrs. Stout's attack and the ensuing cleanup, she had forgotten all about him.

"Our cots were set up," Mrs. Stout continued, "I went to sleep. Then . . . footsteps. I thought you were back, and then there was pain. Such terrible pain." She pressed a fist to her chest again, shuddering. "I tried to scream. I know I did. But all I remember is blackness and . . . and memory . . . and then . . . It became cozy, soothing. What happened, Miss Leander?"

"You were attacked. Most brutally." She helped Mrs. Stout drink again. "Someone stabbed you. When we came in, you were near death."

"We?"

"Yes. Myself and Mr. Garret. The steward."

"Oh." Mrs. Stout frowned into space.

"We . . . cleaned up. We deemed it best to keep this attack a secret for now, but if you disagree—"

"No. I do not."

Octavia's tongue floundered in her mouth. She had to bring this up. She had to know, and yet . . . "I . . . we . . . couldn't help but notice your scar. On your chest."

Mrs. Stout's eyes flared open. "You . . . what?"

"It's probably nothing. Just a scar. We know that."

"You . . . and that steward?" Mrs. Stout glared toward the door. If she were an infernal, that entire wall would be a molten heap.

"It's okay, Mrs. Stout, really. Just say it's balderdash. A coincidence."

The older woman seemed to shrivel against the wall, both hands pressed to her face. "Lies. Do you have any idea how sick I am of lies and subterfuge? It's all good and well when reading a copper novel, but when it's your own life, it becomes so old and tiresome."

Octavia's tongue felt as dry as cotton. "You . . . what are you saying, Mrs. Stout?"

"I don't mind *you* knowing. I owe you my life, and you're one of Nelly's girls. But for a man to know, a servant . . . God, do you know how those people gossip?" Her skin resembled vellum, translucent and frail. Octavia offered her a drink and Mrs. Stout jerked her head in refusal.

"Mr. Garret has an appalling way of finding out these things," Octavia said. "He knows I'm a medician traveling incognito as well, but he doesn't know that the enchanted tattoo on your foot—"

"The enchanted what?"

"You have magic inlaid on a mark between your toes. I imagine it was done when you were quite young. It . . . it states who you are."

Mrs. Stout's throat creaked like an old door. "Oh my goodness. I didn't know. All these years, it would have been that easily revealed?"

"Well, no. How many magi have probed between your toes?" Octavia asked. Mrs. Stout managed an anemic smile. "You knew what I was and that I'm a Percival girl and Nelly . . . that's Miss Percival's true first name, but no one ever calls her that."

"Most people haven't known her for over fifty years either. I knew her when she was Nelly Winters, before she became headmistress and adopted the name Percival. She asked me to be here on the *Argus,* you see. Sent me a letter.

Offered her condolences on my husband's death, and said that she had a new girl about to set out in the world. Her most brilliant student, though rather sheltered. She knows I love to travel. I volunteered to ride along, watch out for you."

"Miss Percival actually asked this of you?" Awe softened Octavia's voice. *She cares! She just didn't know how to show it.* "But . . . I've never known of any other girls . . . I mean to say, we're all rather sheltered in regard to society. Have you done this before?"

"Never." Mrs. Stout chortled. "Are you flattered, or aghast?"

"Which should I be?" Octavia shook her head in a daze. "I know yesterday I fumbled around a bit, but surely I don't need a babysitter for the full trip."

"Now, now, child. Don't look at it in such a severe light. I'm sure Nelly regarded this as a healing journey for both of us. I've been lost since Donovan died. This gives me an excuse to get out of the house. My daughter lives near Mercia and she's pregnant with my first grandbabe. This is the perfect excuse to drop by and see her! And what I told you yesterday was the truth. I was like a lost puppy during my first few journeys by airship. I don't think Nelly has been airborne in her life, so I doubt she could teach you much of it."

"No. I don't think she has either. Miss Percival has no fondness for machines, how they've driven people from faith to science. But now, if she knew you fifty years ago, that means . . . she knows who you are?"

Mrs. Stout sobered again. "Until today, she was the only

living person who did. Back in the day . . . she was the one who healed me." Her fingers splayed against her chest. "I was near death, hiding in the brush. Those Wasters hunting for me, even as my father's soldiers hunted them. A wagon drove by with the Miss Percival of that time, and Nelly. They had worked on some special case together down in Mercia and were heading back north. They found me. Miss Percival whipped those horses into a froth while Nelly stayed in the back, working on me."

"Your condition must have been very grave to leave a scar like that. Miss Percival is a very gifted healer." *The best I've ever known.*

"She was also a mere ten years of age." Mrs. Stout's face crinkled in amusement at Octavia's gasp. "We were the same age, the two of us. She did what she could, though her skills and herbs had their limits. My recovery was long, not because of what my body endured, but here." She tapped her temple. "I was . . . they were going to smuggle me from the academy and back to Mercia when . . ."

The fire-bombing of the palace. "I'm so sorry."

"I'd say I'm over it, but . . ."

"I understand." *All too well.*

"That's my sordid story. I stayed at the academy for years, but the Lady and her Tree were not for me." She shook her head, loosened blue hair bobbing against her forehead. "I met Donovan when he brought his father for a healing. Forty years pass in a blink when you manage a business and children." She frowned. "Now, what was it you asked me again?"

Octavia smiled in apology. "Restoration does that to

the mind. It's hard to focus. And I asked you if Miss Percival knew who you were, and you answered me."

"Yes, well, and the old Miss Percival knew, of course, and I told Donovan before we married. Scariest night of my adult life, saying those words to him."

"Your children don't know?"

Mrs. Stout shook her head. "No. That's what scares me now, if the truth comes out. I'm old. If I die, well, I die. But my children, their children . . ." Fear crept into her eyes. Octavia squeezed her hand. "It's not just about our lives. It's about Caskentia. Evandia . . . dear God, look how she's mucked up everything! If she had even more power, I dread to think what would happen."

"More power? How . . . ?"

"The vault." Her voice lowered to a hoarse whisper. "The access is magicked to my bloodline, through my father. Evandia and her lot . . . there are things in there that aren't to see the light of day."

Octavia stared, blinking. The royal vault? It was treated as a joke, to say something was locked as secure as the royal vault. It was said to be the only thing standing after the Wasters fire-bombed the palace.

"Are . . . you talking about weapons? Things that can be used against the Waste?"

"Yes." Mrs. Stout's lips were thin and pale. "Books. Artifacts. I was but a slip of a girl, of course, so I only understood so much. But there are . . . what would you say if I told you I had seen parts of the Tree? The real Tree?"

Octavia's jaw fell slack. "What?"

Smugness touched Mrs. Stout's expression, and awe. "I've seen them. Touched them. A leaf of the Tree—said to bring back the dead, you know. A seed—Father wouldn't let me near that. It sat up on a pedestal. A branch, long as most tree trunks, its bark green and alive. To this day I remember the smell of the thing, all musty like fresh rain. It'd been locked in there for God knows how long—centuries, certainly—without any dirt, light, or water."

I'd do most anything to see those relics with my own eyes, and to think they're in Mercia, mere days away! For that, I'd brave the horrors of the city.

Octavia brought her hands to her chest in a gesture of respect, to which Mrs. Stout blew a raspberry.

"Child, really. There's no need of that."

"Yes, there is! So few people know about the Lady these days. If they could—"

"No." Mrs. Stout's voice was sharp. Octavia reared back in surprise. "Bringing people to your faith would be a glorious thing, I understand that well. But there's a reason those artifacts are locked away, child. And I'm telling you, just as I told Nelly when she was your age, that there was something dark about that place. When my father walked me through, he pointed to books of ancient magi, the swords and wands of a past age, even bullets of particular enchantment. But then he motioned to those pieces of the Tree and said, 'And these are the most dangerous of the lot.'"

"That's ludicrous! To say the Lady—"

"Your Lady is the protector of the living, yes? She's powerful?"

"Of course she is, but—"

"If she controls life, then what can she do with death?"

"I . . ." Octavia didn't know how to rebut that.

"Those bits of the Tree scared me. Even though they smelled of dirt and rain, I could feel their power. They crackled like a lightning storm, as if they were angry to be there. Maybe that's why I never had promise as a Percival girl. I never had any issues with being around medicians, mind you, or their healing, but something about the Lady herself . . . perhaps she's too mighty for my liking."

The Lady should be mighty. "Queen Evandia can't access the vault?"

"No. She's kin through my mother. No one can get in but me and mine. That door is sealed with the life's blood of a Clockwork Dagger–sworn magus. It's the sort of enchantment that won't wear off in time. I'm a key, child. What would Caskentia do with the contents of the vault?" She lowered her voice to a shaky whisper. "What would the Waste do? You have to promise me, Miss Leander." Mrs. Stout's hand grasped hers, suddenly strong and desperate. "If you are with me and I'm betrayed, you must . . ." With her free hand, she slashed across her neck.

"Never!" *That's melodramatic, even for a woman with a blue streak in her hair.* "I couldn't do that. Don't even think about such things, Mrs. Stout. Your secret is safe."

"Is it?" Mrs. Stout's bloodshot eyes narrowed and she glared toward the door.

Chapter 6

Despite solid hours of sleep, Octavia staggered down the quiet hallway. Perhaps she should have kept her mouth shut and acted like they hadn't seen Mrs. Stout's scar at all. *Mrs. Stout . . . the princess, grown into a flamboyant enigma with bright blue hair.*

Octavia felt an excited tingle at the very thought of her roommate; in truth, she was more awed that Mrs. Stout had been graced with the presence of the Tree than that she was the fabled lost princess.

She heard the cacophony as she hopped down the last few steps onto deck B. She stopped, one hand on the wall. The sound wasn't the wild thunder of instruments that warned her of Mrs. Stout's perilous condition, but something milder, made more potent by the numbers of the suffering. Steps hurried, she rounded the small hallway into the tiled privy.

The wailing symphony of bodies in agony was accompanied by a chorus of groans, retches, and other bombastic intestinal functions. Her hand reached for her satchel and she forced her fingers into a fist. This was probably influenza spread through the confined quarters aboard the airship. Not dire. It'd pass on its own within a few days.

A man stampeded past, almost shoving her aside in his urgency. She retreated to the corridor. *How widespread is this illness? If I set a patient in a circle . . .*

No, no, no. I'm a businesswoman, not a charity worker. I can't save everyone. She forced herself to walk away, both hands brushing against the parasol handle strapped to her bag. Her priority needed to be breakfast for herself and Mrs. Stout, and then to sneak food to Leaf.

Head down in focus, she walked smack-dab into Mr. Garret.

The steward hop-stepped with the agility of a dancer. Octavia, however, lacked that grace. She flopped backward, tailbone and pride painfully meeting the worn carpet. Clutched with her left arm, her satchel swayed and landed in her lap. The well-packed jars didn't so much as jingle.

"Miss Leander!" Mr. Garret extended a hand. "I am terribly sorry—"

"It was my fault, I wasn't looking—"

"I visited your quarters and was told you came down here. We have something of a situation aboard ship."

"This situation involves the people in the privy?" she asked, and he nodded. "When did these symptoms begin, Mr. Garret?"

"The past hour. Thus far, I count six men, including one of our crew."

"Did all of them eat breakfast this morning?"

"Some did, but many were up quite late. All of the affected were guests of the smoking room last night."

Octavia's head jerked up. "Is that so?"

"Miss Leander." He lowered his voice. "The sick crewman is Captain Hue. If the copilot comes down ill as well, we may be forced to make an emergency landing."

An emergency landing. No mooring tower.

The conflagration of the village. The Alexandria, *a deflating oval as it scraped the night sky with flames. Screams—Mother—Father. The crackle of flames in their bodies' songs—*

A strong hand clutched her arm, anchoring her to reality. "Miss Leander? Are you well?"

No. I'll never be well in that regard. She caught a whiff of his scent, reminiscent of cinnamon, and breathed in deeper. "Was anyone ill when they came aboard?"

"No. Anyone with obvious signs of illness is denied entry. We dare not risk a contagion like pox."

She gnawed on her lower lip. "Some zymes can remain dormant for days or weeks without causing outward symptoms, but for so many to get sick at once, it sounds like some kind of contamination. It could be an accident, or . . ."

It's like the poisoning at the northern pass. But why would Wasters—so soon after armistice—bother with a small, ramshackle airship like this? They favor showy productions. Mass casualties. Widespread terror. This is too meager in scope.

"What should we do, m'lady?" Mr. Garret looked on her with absolute trust.

Fiddlesticks. "Do you have a list of the ill passengers?"

"Yes. What do—"

"As you noted last night, my presence creates an unusual fuss on board. I'm about to create a further fuss within the smoke room. Are you available to join me?"

A smile, albeit weary, warmed Mr. Garret's face. "If you are about to be meddlesome, Miss Leander, then it will be my pleasure to join you."

TO ENTER THE SMOKING room, they passed through a small air lock. The door sucked shut behind them, a vent clacking in the ceiling above. "'Tis a characteristic of hydrogen-aether airships," Mr. Garret said, proceeding through the next door. "Of course, this is a helium model, so it does not have those same flammability issues."

Flammability issues. Hydrogen vessels. No, she would not think on such things, not now. Not with the captain and others ill. Her legs quivered, and she steadied herself on the wall.

The smoking room was dark, darker than even the paneled corridors and rooms of the outer ship. The cold gray steel of the walls was exposed, spaced metal sconces breaking the stark monotony. The bar sat immediately to her right, its backdrop of glistening green and amber bottles. A magicked lighter on the counter practically buzzed with the potency of its enchantment. She pursed her lips, pausing. It was old infernal magi work, and the enchantment wasn't confined to spark-lighting cigarettes and cigars; no, it encouraged people to utilize it. *Good for business, bad for lungs.*

On the other side of the room was a Warriors table. The metal pyramid was scraped and dented with several bolts missing. The warriors themselves—fighting mechanicals the size of mice—rested in an obscene tangle at the base of the board.

Mr. Garret rapped his knuckles on the hard wood of the bar. "Vincan, you around?"

A long, hoarse groan emanated from the other side of the stanchion. It was the sound one expected from a bear awakening from hibernation, a warning to skedaddle quickly lest one become a spring breakfast. A hulk of a man rose, his jaw stretched in a yawn so wide it revealed a flash of uvula.

Octavia was considered to be of pale skin, but not compared to this man. His skin seemed drained of pigment, so clear that the veins in his neck were visible to the eye. His hair was almost equal in tone, a stark, silvery white, but not because of age. Acne flecked the broadness of his cheeks and his flattened, crooked nose—not a feature he was born with, she was quite sure of that. His smile revealed dark gaps in his teeth.

"Eh, Alonzo," said the bearish man, yawning again. His chest seemed to swell as he craned back, biceps tight through the poor fit of his crimson uniform jacket. A jacket that was completely unbuttoned in the front. The union suit beneath was as brown-stained as a nappy passed down to the third consecutive babe in a family.

Mr. Garret cleared his throat and tilted his head toward Octavia. The man eyed her up and down, his jaw still agape, then grabbed at his chest. His eyes widened and both hands reached beneath his waist and below the bar. He turned and showed the expanse of his back, his fingernails clumsily scratching at buttons. She pressed a fist against her mouth to keep from laughing.

"Well then, er." The man turned, still working the buttons on his coat. Crookedly, she noted, but at least he tried. "Sorry then, er, miss, but see, I don't fit in any of the bunks aboard ship, so I sleep back 'ere during the day. Not supposed to get patrons in the morning, not normally."

Mr. Garret was a man of strong build with broad shoulders and a narrow waist, but this man seemed twice as big at the same height. *He doesn't need a bed. He needs a stall suited for draft horses.*

"'Tis not a normal morning, Vincan," said Mr. Garret. "We have sickness aboard and everyone is a smoker."

"Now, Mr. Vincan—" she began.

To her surprise, he burst out laughing. "By Allendia's ghost! Listen to that, eh? Mr. Vincan. I sound all fancy 'n something when put like that. The surname's Page, but not a soul ever calls me that. We're not so formal down here, miss."

"I see. Mr.—er, Vincan, did anyone act sickly or strange last night?"

He grinned again. "My goodness now. She makes it sound like she's a proper medician or somethin'." He chuckled at his joke.

Mr. Garret's expression pleaded for tolerance. She shook her head, smiling. "Mr. Garret, you said you had a list of the ill?"

"Certainly, m'lady." He passed her a pad of paper. She skimmed the names. Only Captain Hue's was familiar.

"Well, Mr.—um, Vincan, I need to know where these men were sitting or if they shared the same drink or snack. Do you know where a Mr. . . . Wexler sat?"

Vincan stared at her, blinking.

Mr. Garret clucked his tongue. "He will not know them by their surnames. Mr. Wexler. A tall, reedy fellow with a mustache about the width of a toothpick—"

"Oh, 'im." Vincan nodded. "Yes, I know 'im. 'E sat there." He pointed a beefy arm toward the far corner of the room, in direct view of the bar. "Drank whiskey. When his drunk was up, he had a wheezy laugh, like some sneezing dog."

"I believe the next on the list was Mr. Grinn," said Mr. Garret. Octavia passed the list back to him. "Mr. Grinn is a big fellow. He has a gut like a bag of grain." He mimed the curve of a pregnant belly. "The fellow speaks only a few words in Caskentian."

"Yes, 'im. Fluent in grunt. Favored malt beers. Hiddly Hops, mostly, though he may have had a shot 'r two of harder stuff. He was just on t'other side." Vincan leaned to tap on the wall between the bar and the sitting area.

"Hmm. They had different drinks, then." Octavia drummed her fingers on the counter. A bowl of flatbread crisps sat about a foot away. Her stomach groaned. "Did they eat any of this?"

"Well, yes, miss, jus' 'bout everyone does."

"Did you?" she asked.

"No, not me. If I did, that bowl'd be empty, wouldn't it?"

For now, at least, she could eliminate alcohol as being

suspect. That was a relief, as there had to be a hundred bottles along the wall. Testing each would present a tedious chore. She knew better than to ask if the patrons had ingested water; at a place like this, it was unlikely. Unless . . . "Do you serve ice in your drinks?"

Vincan looked at her as if she was daft. "Most assuredly I do, miss. Keep a cooler under the bar an' fetch more ice from the kitchen if needin' more."

She turned to Mr. Garret. "I'm afraid I have a rather grotesque favor to ask of you."

"For you to preface it like that does not bode well." He braced himself. "Ask away, m'lady."

"I need a sample of . . . expulsions from an ill man."

"Oh, is that all?" An eyebrow arched high, his lips already contorting in disgust. "Miss Leander, as I said before, you do bring new life to a dull job. I will be right back." The air-lock door whooshed shut behind him.

"He's fetching . . . er, what?" asked Vincan.

"Vomit, most likely," Octavia said in an upbeat tone. "It'd be the pleasanter choice."

"You are a strange one, aren't you, miss?"

"So I've been told." *And I'm about to prove my oddness once again.*

Mr. Garret returned with a chamber pot in hand. The foul, fermenting stew of stomach acids and alcohol caused her to crinkle her nose.

"I intercepted a steward just out in the hall. Everyone is on cleanup duty." His expression turned grim. "And you should know, the copilot is now ill as well."

No. Don't picture the flames. Don't imagine the screams. She took a steadying breath, and immediately regretted it. "How soon until we're forced to land?"

"Less than thirty minutes. If anyone else in the cabin shows symptoms, sooner." He set down the pot.

"Kethan's bastards. I dunno if I should be around for this," muttered Vincan. "Miss is the real deal, in't she? Magic 'n all? I just . . . I don't know . . ."

"Go back to sleep, big lug. 'Tis far past your bedtime," said Mr. Garret.

"Yes. Yes. Believe I shall." Vincan lowered himself behind the bar.

"I confess, Miss Leander, I am not sure what you are doing either," muttered Mr. Garret.

"Are you afraid of me?" she asked softly. *I'm so sick of being feared.*

"Afraid of the chaos in your wake? Perhaps. But of you, m'lady? Certainly not." His smile created cozy warmth in her chest—quite an accomplishment, considering the task at hand.

She looked down at the chamber pot, steeling herself. "I've only done this once before. It's only been done once, period."

"Surely medician texts—"

Octavia shook her head, loose hair whipping her cheek. "There's nothing similar chronicled. I may be the only one who's done this, ever." The words emerged as a whisper.

He arched a black brow. "Most interesting."

"In this regard, perhaps, though I fear I'm rather dull

at parties." She tucked the strand of hair behind her ear and set her satchel on the floor. "Can you lock the door, please?"

Octavia pulled out the bag of honeyflower and crouched close to the chamber pot as she created a tight circle. "You're aware of the science of zymes? It comes out of Tamarania."

Mr. Garret shook his head. "I am Caskentian, born and raised. I have never been to Tamarania, though my mother maintains Father's old household there."

Octavia stood, dusting her fingers against her parasol. "Zymes are living creatures so small they cannot be seen with the eye, though they show up in a magnifying scope. Some zymes make a person ill, while others do nothing at all."

"I note you are not using your blanket this time," said Mr. Garret.

She studied him before answering. His eyes were keen as he absorbed every detail of her operation. Mr. Garret did a decent job of playing an amiable lackey, but a man of his class didn't belong in a servile role on an airship. Compared to that bragging buck on the promenade, Mr. Garret would make an excellent Clockwork Dagger—he had the agility and intelligence—but he was far too . . . nice to take on such a callous role. Of course, with the economy as it was, even displaced earls begged on street corners. A man had to earn his bread somehow.

"For this, I prefer to use the smaller circle. It focuses the magic." She looked toward the bar. "Vincan, is it possible to pull out that cooler?"

There was a feral grunt. "'M pretending not to be here,

miss. Magic and me, we's not friends, even if it's the pleasant sort."

"He was branded." Mr. Garret's voice was barely audible.

In that instant, Octavia understood. Branding was a peculiar act committed by Waster infernals—a perverse show of respect for soldiers who managed to get within range of physical touch. Such marks were small, painful, and always left scars as they were far too minor for doctoring.

Magic terrified many people. For a person's sole exposure to be the violence of an infernal—Vincan was certainly not the first she had encountered with such an aversion to magi.

"Vincan, I'm a medician, as you surmised, and I need your help. This does involve magic, yes, but I suspect that Wasters may be at fault for these illnesses."

The floor shuddered as Vincan emerged, his pale skin strangely ruddy. "Wasters, on *my* ship?"

She nodded. "Not long before armistice, they used zymes to poison the water at the northern pass—"

"Oh, damn the day, miss, my brother was there and lived and has a wee baby girl to bounce on his knee now. Whatever you need, s'yours, specially if it's Wasters causing the fuss."

He ducked down again and groaned, staggering out with a cooler that looked to be of lead. Condensation and ice coated the lower half of the cube. He set it down at her feet and tossed the lid aside.

Octavia made another circle in honeyflower and lowered herself to the floor. The wood was hard and cold through the cloth at her knees.

"Lady, hear my plea," she murmured. "There is illness aboard this ship. Your Tree is the encourager of all life, roots mooring the world. I fear that zymes are being wielded as swords. Please, Lady, reveal the rhythm of this illness, so that I may find the cause and treat the suffering."

When she closed her eyes, images loomed in her mind: the Tree, the branches, the bobbing leaf she yearned to catch. She breathed in the mustiness of a world freshened by rain and extended her hands beneath the leaf, waiting. Praying. The drop fell slowly, like a single coursing tear. It trailed along the membranes and to the very tip of the five-pointed leaf, hesitating, and then fell. She shivered at the warmth of the drop as it met her skin and lapped the length of her forefinger to her palm, as though she had submerged her full hand in water.

She bent in basic Al Cala pose, arms extended to reach the chamber pot's circle. Powdery honeyflower dug beneath her nails.

Awareness flared through her body, adrenaline surging through her nerves as if reacting to an exploding incendiary. Her ears seared and throbbed, but not with pain. It was heat and sensitivity and a pressure beyond all comprehension. She opened her eyes. The world outside the circles looked the same as before. She leaned forward, knees grinding into the hard floor, and tapped the circle around the icebox.

"Grace me, Lady," she whispered. The sound began,

like the gnawing of a hundred mice beneath the floorboards. *Being surrounded by humanity is bad enough. If I could hear microscopic beings everywhere, I'd go mad, that's for certain.*

This was what Miss Percival had termed a new eccentricity—something no medician had ever asked before of the Lady. When Octavia had performed this at the front, with a thousand men dying around her, her fellow medicians could not replicate the act. Nor could Miss Percival.

That horrible, ugly envy on Miss Percival's face. That's when things changed between us.

And yet—Miss Percival asked Mrs. Stout to be here with me, and that action says a great deal. She still loves me, even if she cannot show it.

The music wavered, and she focused. Octavia bowed over the chamber pot. The fetid stink no longer assaulted her nostrils. The noise increased, the clacking rhythm of the zymes. They sounded like a marching band featuring tinny drums and a high whistle, looping in a brief and singsong manner. Octavia let her eyes half close as she hummed the tune beneath her breath.

She shifted to the icebox and listened, still humming. The rhythms matched. They met together, note to note, and she could swear the song was the same one she had heard months before.

This sickness wasn't an issue of some filthy hand glancing the ice in passing. The entire block is rife with contamination. The Wasters chose water as their medium again—appropriate, since the last war started with irrigation rights as the excuse.

She touched the circle around the icebox. "Lady, thank

you for extending your branches." The heat in her ears and beneath her fingers vanished within a breath. She looked up at the men.

"Vincan, can you pick up the box again? The entire thing needs to be purged, and the rest of the ice supply must be checked as well." He didn't move. "I'll use my wand on your hands and most everything else in here soon. I won't let you get ill, I promise."

That was good enough for him. Vincan grunted as he moved the icebox several feet away.

"Is it that bad, m'lady?" asked Mr. Garret.

For my herb supply, yes. Still, she didn't hesitate. "Please assemble the afflicted. I'll treat the captain and copilot first, and any other crewmen. When you have the chance, I'd also appreciate it if you could fetch breakfast for Mrs. Stout." She lowered her voice. "There's also a hungry gremlin."

"Consider it done, Miss Leander. If there is anything else I can do, please let me know."

Yes. Can you restock my herbs, even with supplies so low across the kingdom since the last war? Or explain to the people of Delford that I'm still worthy of a home there, though my doctoring is probably as good as what any local midwife or physician can already offer?

She squeezed her hands into fists, allowing herself brief seconds of selfish fear and frustration, and then she stood. Lives needed saving.

At this rate, by the time the *Argus* landed in Mercia, Octavia's charity would leave her begging on the streets for charity as well.

Chapter 7

After Captain Hue and the copilot, she healed each man in turn, starting with the most severe cases. Her supply of bellywood bark dwindled pinch by pinch. Mrs. Wexler succumbed to bedside theatrics due to her husband's condition, and had to be treated as well.

Her last patient was Mr. Grinn. As Mr. Garret had described him, he was a hefty man with a gravid swell to his gut. He stood in the disengaged circle of the blanket, teetering slightly, and reached for his stained suit jacket.

"Dank," he mumbled as he thrust an object at Octavia.

It took her a moment to realize he wasn't commenting on the moisture in the room but was trying to express gratitude. She accepted the item from his hand—a watch, the glass cracked and the once-ornate case worn smooth by use.

More useless payment. The other men had also offered what they could, poor as they all were—another broken watch, a scattering of copper coins, and a voucher to visit the Museum of Amazing Mechanicals in Mercia. The fine print on the latter stated that it had expired six months ago.

"It's appreciated, Mr. Grinn," she murmured. "Please rest so your body can continue its recovery."

He stared at her, froglike face vacant of expression, and then he shuffled onward.

"No other illnesses have manifested. Are you well?"

She turned to see Mr. Garret in the entrance of her makeshift clinic. The crew had set up stanchions to block off a quarter section of the promenade, even going so far as to lay down oilskin tarps to protect the carpet.

She packed up her supplies. "Tired, but that's to be expected. How is Mrs. Stout?"

"Much improved," he said. "People have inquired, and with regret I told them she also had a mild touch of sickness, but as her roommate, you treated her privately during the night."

"Well put, Mr. Garret, thank you. And . . . ?"

He stepped closer. "The beastie has been sleeping each time I checked on him, and the food I left vanished. Tonight we pass over the Saint's Road. It may be difficult to release him, with the smoking room and promenade busy until late."

"Oh! I've always wished to see the road, especially by air. Do you really think people will frequent the smoking room, even after the events of the day?"

Mr. Garret snorted. "You have been to the front, m'lady. Threats of poison or death do not make men relinquish a favored vice."

"True. I've seen soldiers shot because they simply had to stand outside for a smoke, even though it made them an easy target against the snow. Some of them still had the cigarette between their lips as they were hauled in for a healing." She shook her head. "By the time Miss Percival was done scolding them, the bullet seemed minor in comparison!"

Mr. Garret grinned. "Miss Percival sounds fierce as a threem."

"Oh, she could be at times, but she always meant well. She just couldn't abide it when people brought injury upon themselves. 'Sometimes, they deserve a little pain,' she'd say." Octavia stared into the distance and smiled. It felt good to speak openly of Miss Percival. It felt better to even think of her, knowing Mrs. Stout had been sent along.

"On the contrary, I believe you deserve some pleasantness. If you want to see the road, I could awaken you late tonight. And Mrs. Stout, of course," he added hastily.

A peculiar heat warmed her belly and, despite her weariness, brought a wide smile to her face.

"Oh, goodness. Yes, I'm interested. I can ask Mrs. Stout if she'd like to come." She studied his face, trying to gauge the intentions behind his offer. Viewing the Saint's Road was considered . . . well, intimate. It was a holy landmark in existence for fifty years, a cobblestone road whose principal builder was blessed with the peculiar gift to set the stones aglow. Octavia had heard more than one person say they had been there, but beyond that, they'd say very little. It was the sort of memory that made people smile and stare into the distance as though an old friend waved at them from far away.

When will a chance like this come again? It's not like anything will happen. He's a steward. He's being polite.

She cleared her throat. "How has Mrs. Stout been . . . treating you?" She kept her voice low, in case someone stood on the other side of the partition. She couldn't help but wonder how Mr. Garret would regard Mrs. Stout if he knew the full truth—tattoo, vault, and all.

Trusting him with the secret of my occupation was one thing—risking the lives of Mrs. Stout and her family is something else entirely.

"If that woman were an infernal, a solitary glare would down this entire ship. I wish she would permit me some small show of faith—a simple chance—so that it would relieve some tension between us."

"Why show that faith? What've you done to earn it?"

Mr. Garret leaned closer, his expression sober. "Then why do you seem so trusting of me?"

"I just am," she said, keenly aware of how lame the words sounded. She looked away, her cheeks warming. "I should check on Mrs. Stout."

"Oh, of course. I will check on the beastie for you, and after that I will slumber for the next while. Try to stay in the public areas of the ship as much as possible, Miss Leander." His face softened to a smile. "I will see you tonight, show you the road?"

She hesitated for all of a second before nodding.

"I will knock on your door when 'tis time. The hour will be late, likely after midnight." With a final nod, he briskly walked away.

Several people sat in the promenade and gazed out the windows. Octavia barely registered their presence as she walked through. Mr. Garret's warm smile dominated her thoughts instead. *I'm daft. I shouldn't encourage the man. When this journey's done, I'll never see him again.*

A day away from the academy, and Octavia already displayed the moral flippancy of the heroines of those pulpy copper novels Mrs. Stout read.

Not that Octavia would ever read such a book, of course. And never in *public*.

She pushed through the door to berthing and ran directly into Mr. Drury.

She had a brief glimpse of his eyes going wide and then he spun backward. Literally. His arms whirled in a pinwheel as he pivoted on one foot, bounding back toward the stairwell like a dancer. He caught himself there in a crouch. His arms curved out in boneless grace, reminiscent of a standing Al Cala pose. No ordinary suit allowed such flexibility; it had been tailored for use in fighting. Octavia pinned herself against the doorframe. The presence of warm metal in her hand surprised her—by instinct she had pulled forth her capsicum flute.

"You." Mr. Drury jerked upright and his trim suit jacket shrugged into place again. His salesman's smile resumed a comfortable position between the soft lines of his face, that sausage of a mustache curving along his upper lip. "You gave me quite a start, Miss Leander."

Beside her, the caged mechanical birds tweeted, their little metal feet and wings clattering.

"The feeling is mutual." Her heartbeat fluttered against her breastbone. His fluidity was that of a supreme martial artist, a Clockwork Dagger. The thought of him in such a position of power turned her blood cold. "Were you a soldier, Mr. Drury?"

Wariness crept into his gaze for the first time. It wasn't the haunted look that had drifted over Vincan earlier; no, this was pure shrewdness. "Why do you ask?"

"Some soldiers practice acrobatic arts as a means of fitness and entertainment." *Or to slit throats.* She nodded toward him. "Moves such as that, for instance."

"I used to dabble a bit." He brushed off his suit, though it had no dust now. "Old instincts and all."

"Quite."

"The *Argus* was quite fortunate to have you aboard today. Your miraculous work is the talk of the ship."

"It's unlikely anyone would've died before we moored in Leffen," she said stiffly. *Barring a crash landing, of course.*

"Ah, but they may have wished they had." That salesman's smile returned to his lips as his eyes twinkled at her in obvious pleasure. Her stomach soured. How long until he circled the conversation around to that blasted tea again? "You are very gifted. Most medicians would still be at work. I heard you are unusually efficient in your herbal applications as well. Mrs. Wexler in particular noted how not a single excess piece of bellywood bark littered her husband's skin, quite the contrary to her previous experience with your kind."

"And what of you, Mr. Drury? Are you experienced with . . . as you put it, my kind?"

His lips thinned in a smile almost obscured by the furry width of his mustache. "As you noted, I have endured action at the front. It's a rare man who escapes unscathed by bullet, climate, or zyme. It makes the comforts of my current occupation all the more enjoyable, and for such a joyous product as well."

Ah yes, there was the overdue reference to his precious Royal-Tea. "It's been nice to see you again, Mr. Drury. I really must rest."

She made to go around him and he neatly sidestepped to block her. Octavia's eyes narrowed and she squeezed the small pipe within the sweaty well of her palm.

"Would you, perhaps, like to join me for dinner later?" he asked. "Lunch is quite soon, of course, but I understand you're tired. Perhaps I could even persuade you to try some Royal-Tea? It revives the spirit like nothing else."

"No, I would not like to join you for dinner, Mr. Drury. I'll dine with Mrs. Stout, as she's recovering from her bout of illness and may need assistance." Her eyes scanned side to side. Using her flute in such proximity wouldn't be wise, but she had no desire to retreat or show submission in any way. This called for drastic action and anatomical knowledge.

Mr. Drury opened his lips to speak again. She drew back her fist. The blow landed several inches beneath his sternum. Clearly caught off guard, Mr. Drury dropped like a swatted fly, his eyes appropriately bugging out as the wind was knocked out of him.

Octavia didn't mind that a strike to the celiac plexus

was likely to cause a good bit of pain. *Miss Percival is right. Sometimes people deserve a bit of suffering.*

"When I say no, Mr. Drury, I mean no." She circled around his crumpled form, scurrying lest he try to grab her ankles. A mechanical bird hooted as if in approval.

Adrenaline seemed to drain from her as she reached the door to room 3. Her knuckles rapped on the wood. Lady be thanked, Mrs. Stout promptly opened it. Octavia jumped within and slammed the door with her backside. Her fingers fumbled as she did the lock again.

"Well!" Mrs. Stout stood there, arm still raised from where she had held the door. "What was that fuss about?"

"An unwelcome suitor who can't comprehend answers in the negative." Her fingers trembled too much to put away the flute so she let it stay in her fist.

"Not that steward? You can't trust that sort, Miss Leander! Give them an inch, and they'll want a yard. Need I remind you what's at stake?" Mrs. Stout was looking like herself again, her hair coiffed in its massive bun and shimmery blue eye shadow in place. Her rouge, however, seemed too stark and red against her pallor.

"No, not him. A passenger." She didn't wish to reveal that Mr. Garret's advances weren't truly unwelcome. Or were they? The man muddled everything.

"I see. Come and sit down. You must be run off your feet, you poor thing. There. I'll get you some water."

The room had been remade for daytime use, their bedding packed away and the top cot flush against the wall. Octavia collapsed against the bench seat. A different pulp book sat beside her, this one featuring a woman in a trendy, loose-waisted frock fleeing from a sinister flock of mecha ravens. She murmured thanks when Mrs. Stout pushed a cup into her hand.

The woman remained over her, fists planted on her broad hips. "I'm sorry that you're garnering such attention, child. I know you didn't want anyone to know what you are, and I understand perfectly well why. I feel like that's my fault—"

"Oh, Mrs. Stout. You didn't stab yourself, nor did you poison the ice in the larder."

"You know very well what I mean. Once someone knows a secret, it . . ." Her voice trailed away. Octavia looked away, already detecting where the conversation would lead. "You must be careful about who you trust."

If Mrs. Stout knew about Mr. Garret's invitation to view the Saint's Road, she'd turn it into some sordid affair, and likely alert the captain and anyone else in range about Mr. Garret's impropriety.

Octavia understood there were fights she could win, like the one against Mr. Drury, and others where she might as well attempt to fill a dirigible by mouth. So she nodded and smiled as if she agreed with everything Mrs. Stout said, even as she mentally ticked down the hours until midnight.

Octavia waited in the top bunk, filled with equal measures of dread and eagerness. Her hand on the smooth panels of the wall felt the faint quiver of the engines, akin to the distant pulse of a heart. A slight tap came from the door.

He's here! I shouldn't move too quickly or he'll think I've been waiting at the door. But I don't want to be too slow either. She pushed aside her blanket and scooted to the ladder.

The chill of the ladder rungs bit through her thin socks. She paused before stepping onto the floor. Mrs. Stout wheezed in her sleep, grunting on occasion as she tossed to and fro. Octavia eased onto the carpet, as light as a bee upon a flower, and pulled on her boots. Octavia had worn a sailor-collared dress in light blue since the afternoon, and told Mrs. Stout the day's activities had simply left her mind too active for sleep. Not a total lie, at least.

A glance out the peephole confirmed the fact that Mr. Garret stood on the other side. Octavia grabbed her satchel and slipped through the door. Locking it, she murmured over her shoulder, "I do worry about leaving her alone."

"She will not be joining us?" He sounded politely disappointed.

"No," said Octavia, and left the matter at that.

"The flight over the road will not take that long," he said, then frowned. "I should have told you to wear a coat. The best view is with the windows open, and 'tis quite chilly."

Indeed, he wore a pea coat over his usual crimson jacket. The double rows of buttons and thick cotton weave gave him an even more imposing form. His thick ponytail was tucked within his collar, and she resisted the urge to flip it to lie free on his back.

"Oh, I'm no nesh. At the northern pass, our chamber pots would freeze during a winter's night. I can handle the cold here. Besides, Mrs. Stout is asleep, and digging around in the closet would be sure to wake her."

"The lady certainly deserves her rest." He led the way toward the promenade. "I checked on the beastie a short while ago. A few crumbs of food remained in his cage. I assume you fed him?"

"Yes. I visited during supper when everyone was in the promenade. He was well."

More than well. When Octavia had opened the cage, Leaf had flung himself at her with both wings around her neck. Judging by the tone of his chatter, she was being scolded most brutally. Quite understandable, considering he'd been locked up with a dour portrait of the Queen. A few of his gruffer clicks and clacks would no doubt have translated as profane.

He quickly calmed down when she pulled out a cloth napkin mounded with pecans and little cheeses on toothpicks. She demonstrated how to eat a piece of mozzarella so he wouldn't eat the stick as well, and he mimicked with his delicate three-fingered hand. A single cube of cheese made his cheeks swell like that of a hoarding squirrel. The line between hideous and adorable had blurred substantially.

"I could probably let the beastie out late tonight, after the smoking room calms down."

"Oh. That's . . . very kind of you, Mr. Garret."

Leaf should be free. He's not intended to be a pet. But he is so small, likely a baby—were all of his kin slain? Where will he go? Vorana is a day away.

She gnawed on her lip. *Oh Lady. I should never have gotten attached to him in the first place. Just as I shouldn't be with Mr. Garret now.* And yet her legs seemed to move of their own volition to follow the man.

Most of the lights in the promenade had been shut off. A few lamps swayed in the center of the room, casting soft and subtle illumination; dim glowstones embedded in the tiles added to the effect.

"I thought you said it'd be busy in here?" Her heart beat a little faster.

"On some trips, most every passenger comes to view the road. Other times, none at all. Here. The library will offer the best view."

I'm alone with him, but I've been alone with him several times already, even in my own berthing. He's a gentleman.

Mr. Garret worked the latches and slid a window open. A gust of cold air caused her to gasp, her skirt lapping against her thighs. She smoothed her wayward dress and stepped closer to the window. The forty-five-degree angle of the opening caused her to gaze into almost complete blackness below. She noted a faint string of road and a distant glimmering light.

"Is that it?" She pointed as she set down her satchel.

He bent down to look. "No, 'tis likely a house amidst the marshes. You will know the road. The ship will turn to follow its brief length."

"I see. Well, I understand. I don't actually see it yet, of course." *I'm yammering like a ninny. I should stop talking.*

So close, his sleeve brushed hers and his radiant masculine warmth was bold against the chill of the night. "Tell me, Miss Leander, about the destination of your journey."

She blinked, surprised by the question. "Oh. Uh. I've been employed by the village of Delford. It's a two-day wagon ride from Mercia, to the south of the Giant. There are no medicians in the vicinity. The Wasters staged an attack there, you see, some new kind of poison. It didn't kill people immediately, but has created slow and terrible suffering."

"I have not heard of any such attack."

"Oh, there's a reason for that. Their representatives told me that Caskentia has kept their suffering quiet, lest it create a panic amongst the greater population."

He grunted. "That I can believe. Secrets would keep well there. 'Tis quite remote."

"You've been to Delford?"

"I have been all around the Giant. If you think it appears huge looking south on a clear day, wait until you stand within the foothills and gaze up." He shook his head, hair whipping at his shoulders.

"I read up on it as much as possible, of course. They sent three men to the academy's hiring fair. There's a house for me there, barely more than a shed, but I can build onto it in time. The winters are a tad milder in the south with a mere touch of snow, but they said bellywood trees grow and pampria and heskool are native and . . . oh dear, I am going on, aren't I?"

"Quite all right." His grin seemed to glow in the faint light. "Your enthusiasm is a delight. You are blessed to have such a bounty awaiting you."

Anxiety twisted in her gut. *I will scavenge the underbrush to find herbs, take on most any farm labor needed to earn food. I'll prove to them that I belong, even if I cannot tend to the worst of their maladies straightaway.*

She forced her dry throat to swallow. "I do look forward to settling in. I want to plant my own roots, like the Lady's Tree."

"'Tis the hope of most." Something sad seemed hidden in his words.

"Not pleased with a steward's life?" Octavia cocked her head to one side.

He remained quiet for a time, staring into the darkness as if he could see something of interest. "I had hoped to make a career as a soldier."

"Ah." Mechanical limbs greatly improved quality of life, but they weren't allowed in the enlisted ranks. Conditions in the field were too adverse, and even the best of mechanicals could fail.

A glimmer of light caught her eye and she pointed out the window. "Look! Is that . . . ?"

"Indeed. Feel the airship turning?" The rumbling of the ship shifted, deepening. The little stub wing of the craft gleamed silver in the darkness, its rotor a constant blur as the airship turned. The thatched lines of a city emerged, tucked between the hills, and beyond that lay the Saint's Road.

Stones glowed in white, green, and gold, the colors braided. The airship was low enough that she could see people on the ground below, but none on the path itself. The mob shifted in a peculiar way. A faint melody rang in Octavia's ears.

"They're dancing," she whispered. Tears smarted her eyes, and not from the gushing air.

In the colorful illumination of the road, skirts twirled and black coats gleamed, but not all to the same beat. Some moved slowly, as if to a waltz, while others twirled like Mendalian dagger fighters.

"The road sings, but no one hears the same song," Mr. Garret whispered, reverence in his tone.

Blood screamed in Octavia's ears, but the road purred its melody. A memory flashed in her mind, one long lost to time. *I awakened in my bed. I was so little—maybe five, with that sheet of alphabet letters glued by my bed. Mother hummed a melody in the kitchen. There was no denying that Mother sang like a hungry cat, but her humming—off-key as it was—conveyed pure joy at the start of a new day. The sound made me smile and wriggle deeper in my nest. The scent of fresh-baked bread sifted into the room. The world outside my blankets was fiercely cold, but I was warm, so perfectly warm.*

A strong beat carried through the rhythm of the song, matching time with her mother's hummed melody.

A sob choked out. She pressed a fist to her lips. "I . . . I always heard people traveled here, even from the southern nations, and everyone always said it was beautiful, that there was nothing like it, but . . ."

"No one can do it justice with mere words." Tears left glistening trails down his cheeks.

How is his song different? Does he hear his father? But she knew she could never ask, never pry in that way.

She held an arm out of the window, the wind a weight

against her spread fingers, almost as if she could feel power like an aether magus.

"Careful. Do not lean far." Mr. Garret laid a heavy hand on her forearm as if to bind it to the sill.

"The road has such a presence. To think, one woman laid that, stone by stone." *This is probably as close as I'll ever get to the Lady's Tree: a place sanctified and alive.*

"'A constellation bound to soil, by sweat and loss and toil,'" Mr. Garret sang, his baritone husky and surprisingly soft. "'Stone by stone and tear by tear, fear ye not for God is near.'"

"You show yourself to be a poet again, Mr. Garret. My father . . . he loved that verse." A tear dried on her cheek and stiffened the skin.

He shrugged, suddenly shy. "'Tis a pleasant tune, especially with strings in accompaniment." His hand remained on her arm, his fingers thick and dark against the pale blue. The road's song was already fading as the airship sailed on, but the strong beat lingered. Octavia looked from her arm to his face.

It's Mr. Garret. His body's song. It was one with the road's melody, with Mother's humming. The three braided together like the colors of the Saint's Road itself.

What does that mean?

The world beneath them darkened. The motors revved again. She sensed the subtle shift as they redirected due south.

It was cold. She knew, logically, that the window was open and she should be feeling quite numb by now, but the sensations from her childhood memory had returned to her like a real thing, like her visions of the Lady's Tree. Octavia was warm, cocooned in the strange awareness that this was one of the most perfect moments she would encounter in her life.

So she kissed him.

She leaned forward, her lips swooping onto his. The tiniest gasp escaped his mouth. His lips were soft, broad, strong. He kissed back with a gentle intensity, his fingers crawling up her arm to cradle her cheek. She almost jerked back—his fingers were like ice cubes. Instead, she opened her eyes. His were shut in bliss, but as if feeling her scrutiny, they opened. His blue eyes regarded her with wonderment.

They pulled apart, staring at each other, blinking.

"Miss Leander." He croaked out her name.

"Mr. Garret, I . . ." *I'm sorry? No, I'm not sorry, but why did I do that? What if he thinks I'm some floozy?*

A bell rang from the stewards' station on the far side of the promenade. They jolted farther apart as if scalded.

" 'Tis a summon to the berths."

"Yes." She stared down at her arms against the sill.

"I am the one on duty upstairs. I will be back as soon as I am able."

She couldn't even look at him. "Do your duty, Mr. Garret."

He lingered there a moment, as if he would speak, and then trotted away.

She buried her head in both hands. *What am I doing? I've known him for scarcely a day. A few spins of the world, and I'll never see him again. Just like Leaf, and Mrs. Stout. I'm only creating more grief for myself. Stupid, stupid, stupid.*

Octavia briskly ran her hands over her face. She knew the cold now—the tip of her nose numb, her eyes as dry as the Waste. The light of the road was utterly gone, the landscape rendered even blacker in its absence.

Her feet nudged against her satchel as she leaned on the sill and stared out. "Oh Lady, what am I going to do?" she whispered.

Then two hands pressed against her lower back and shoved.

CHAPTER 8

Octavia's scream sounded shrill and impossible to her own ears as she tipped forward, floundering in space. The sleek, silver roundness of the hull came into view as her legs kicked out, seeking hold on the window, on something, anything. Her skirt slipped forward, and of all of the ridiculous things, she realized she would die, splatting into the ground with her skirt upended. *Knickers exposed for all the world to see.*

Then she saw the swag fluttering beneath the window.

It had been a minor detail when she boarded, but now that triangle-adorned ornamentation was her lifeline. She grabbed hold of the swag's cord with both hands just as her full body weight tipped out the window. The coldness of the metal sliced into her palms. Blood rushed to her head as another scream tore from her throat, her legs swinging downward. She dangled on the string like an acrobat, the sudden pain in her fingers so overwhelming she almost let go. Almost. The entire world became a vision of darkness as she swayed. She forced herself to twist in place, switching her hands around so she faced the silver lines of the hull.

Agony burned through her palms as blood wept rivulets down her arms.

Don't look down. Don't look down. Terror and bile rose in her throat as she continued to rock on the swag. Her boots kicked the underbelly of the airship, seeking purchase, instead pushing her away.

"Help!" she screamed. She bobbed and managed to look up.

A massive bulk of flesh filled the angled window overhead, froglike jowls looming. Mr. Grinn. The last passenger she healed, the one who didn't speak Caskentian.

"Help me!" she cried. He stared at her, jaw agape, as though frozen in shock. *Oh, sweet Lady. He shoved me out the window.*

"Octavia!"

There was a blur of motion. Mr. Grinn rumbled something in a foreign tongue and vanished from sight. Thunks resounded through the wall at her head level, and Octavia forced her gaze forward as sudden dizziness overwhelmed her. She adjusted her grip, screeching again as the cord sliced into her fingers. Thank the Lady, the swag was made strong to withstand wind along the hull. Agony quivered down her arms and burned through her strained muscles. Her swaying decreased and the toes of her boots found the tiniest bit of a ledge along the hull. Probably no more than an inch in width, but it was something. She pressed her body against the iciness of the curved base of the airship, trying to take as much weight off her hands as possible. Little triangular flags rippled along the rope.

An especially heavy thud caused her head to jerk up. A blob filled the window and blocked light like an eclipse. Then the blob fell. Toward her. Toes edging over on her slight ledge, she forced her bloodied hands to move, and just in time. The hulk of Mr. Grinn dropped from the window. She didn't see him grab the swag, but she felt it. The cord went taut in her fingers and dipped in a most precarious way. Mr. Grinn had to be three hundred pounds of solid weight. Soft yet wild music drifted from his hands and face; without seeing him clearly in the dark, she surmised that his nose had been bloodied.

A soft pinging sound pulled her gaze to the left. It sounded like a button popping from a coat. The swag dipped again. *Oh Lady. It's ripping away from the hull.*

"Octavia!" She looked up. A pair of black boots dangled about six inches above her head.

"Mr. Garret!" she cried.

"Grab hold of my leg! I have a grip on the sill!"

It was a brilliant idea, making his body into a human ladder. Unfortunately, Mr. Grinn agreed.

More fortunately, Octavia knew which leg to grab.

They each grasped Mr. Garret's legs at the same time. The swag's bolts continued to ping and loosen around them. Octavia wrapped one hand around the curve of Mr. Garret's ankle, and then gripped with her left. Her boots worked up the hull and found another small ledge. Blood and pain challenged her grasp, and she relied on the extra buckles on his boot to enhance her hold.

Beside her, Mr. Grinn grappled for purchase. She

caught a glimpse of his face in a pained grimace and then came the sound of wrenching metal. Mr. Garret screamed, raw and deep. Mr. Grinn dropped away.

Don't look down. She tried to press against the hull and was nearly kicked in the face by Mr. Garret's heel.

"Haul 'im in!" bellowed a deep voice. *Vincan.* She jerked upward. Adrenaline flooded her senses as her feet lost their hold, sending her legs flailing. Time seemed to slow, her maimed fingers slipping on the slick leather. Her weight was too much.

"Oh Lady," she whimpered, clenching her eyes shut.

Lightness wrapped around her being. She was reminded of how it felt when she was a child, swung in her father's arms. Legs outstretched, toes pulled straight by centrifugal force. No gravity, no cares—but in this case, no joyful laughter either.

Is this death? Was the fall that fast?

She opened her eyes. Gray hazed her vision. She pulled her hands close, staring into them. Her body was weightless in space. Darkness shifted around her and then the air itself seemed to change. There were faces, blurred. Octavia squinted through the mist as she ached to recognize her parents.

Then the blurriness was gone. The tingle of dissipating magic shocked her chilled skin. Arms reached for her, chattering voices melding into cacophony.

"Octavia. Octavia. Miss Leander." Mr. Garret's face filled her vision, his eyes wide in concern.

"Mr. Garret." Her voice was a croak. "How did we . . ."

"They brought in the aether magus from the cockpit and he seized you in time. You . . . you fell."

"Yes. Thank you for stating the obvious."

"Ah, miss. What're you doin', falling outta windows like that?" Vincan hovered close by, shaking his head. This time, she noted, his jacket was properly buttoned.

The burden of life struck her chest like a physical blow. Her breath rattled as she gasped. She had never felt such a thing before, but knew from the tales. Knew what one of the other Percival girls had said after a soldier grabbed her from the path of a stampeding wagon. The Lady prized life, and prized those who saved the ones who labored in her name. As the girl had said, "It's a pressure, on your heart. A reminder. No matter what I did, I had to find that soldier again and bless him."

Two. The number sang in her head, just as the bodies around her sang their own melodies. She owed a life debt to two people within this room.

"Here." Mr. Garret wrapped his coat around her. The instant warmth came as a shock, creating a violent shiver. She hunkered down and pulled the jacket closer, crying out as her palms touched the cloth. The jacket carried the coziness of Mr. Garret's body heat and his lingering scent. She breathed it in, soothed in spite of everything. Mr. Garret adjusted the coat on her shoulders, the backs of his fingers stroking her neck, ever so gently.

Her head jerked to the side and their eyes met. Sadness—relief—shone potent in his gaze.

If he continues to look at me like that, I'll thaw in no time.

Little Daveo flung a wad of cloth napkins into her lap. She murmured thanks and pressed the clean cloths to her hands, gasping at the pain. Mr. Garret's hand braced her shoulder, steady as a mooring tower.

"I want to know what happened!" An authoritative voice boomed over them. Captain Hue stood there in a thick crimson jacket. The straight, tailored lines couldn't quite hide the late-life roundedness of his gut.

Mr. Garret stepped back as Captain Hue leaned over Octavia. A whiff of onions filled her nostrils. The captain's face was craggy and wrinkled, yet in a noble, handsome way. A slight tilt to his brimmed hat completed the look. Octavia blinked, suddenly realizing all the lights were on in the promenade, and half of the passengers and crew seemed present as well.

"Oh my goodness! Oh my goodness!" Mrs. Wexler wore a voluminous white nightgown, her voice high and hysterical—nothing unusual, from Octavia's brief acquaintance with the woman. Everyone jabbered, words overlapping, body songs forming a low murmur of background noise.

"Miss Leander." Mr. Garret held a glass of water directly in front of her face. She reached for it, then stopped.

"Um, Mr. Garret, could you . . . ?" How embarrassing, to ask him to help her drink. He smiled in understanding and tipped the glass to her lips. She sagged in relief at the coolness of the water in her dry throat, and motioned him back. Water trailed from the corner of her mouth and she wiped it away with the back of her hand.

"Captain, sir," she said. "Mr. Garret, your steward, was kind enough to inform me when the Saint's Road would be viewable and stayed with me a time." She certainly hoped saying that wouldn't get Mr. Garret in trouble; he nodded to her in encouragement, while Captain Hue was as readable as marble. "Then . . . uh, Mr. Garret was summoned away and I stayed at the window and then . . . there were hands at my back, and next thing I knew, I was out the window.

"I looked up and saw Mr. Grinn looking down at me. Then Mr. Garret . . . I daresay, events at that point are blurred. I was just trying to hold on."

"Mr. Grinn, our passenger." The captain's eyes narrowed, vanished beneath thick lines of wrinkles. "You tended him earlier, did you not?"

"I did, yes. He was my last patient."

"Did he take offense to this? Did he come across as disturbed? Were any words spoken?"

Octavia forced her spine straight. "Sir, *I* take offense at the idea that I somehow invited or caused my defenestration. Mr. Grinn spoke mostly in grunts, but he seemed grateful enough."

"Mr. Grinn doesn't speak our tongue, sir," added Mr. Garret.

"I'm well aware of that, Mr. Garret. I take the time to welcome each of my passengers." Captain Hue's tone was icy. His gaze didn't shift from Octavia. "And he said nothing when you dangled together below?"

Octavia shook her head. "No, sir, not that I can recall. I don't . . . I don't even remember if he screamed."

The captain reared back, breath released in a huff. "You can take care of yourself?" He nodded toward her.

"Oh. Yes. Speaking of which, I need to inspect the damage." The napkin tugged at the gluey blood as she pulled the cloth from her right hand, sending another fierce stab of pain down her arm. The flesh at the base of her fingers was cut almost to the bone; if she had struck with any greater velocity, the cord may have sliced through her hands entirely. It's a wonder she had managed to hold on as long as she had.

No, not a wonder. Strong as I am, I couldn't have held on to that cord for more than a few seconds on my own. It's as though the Lady endowed me with extra strength for a time.

"I need to place myself in a circle right away, before infection sets in." She sucked in a sharp breath. "My satchel?"

"Still by the window," said Mr. Garret. He carefully sat down a few feet away, tucking his shredded and vacant pant leg against his thigh.

Octavia bit her lip. "Oh, dear. Your leg—"

He waved a hand in dismissal. "It contains a tracking device. I will seek it out."

"We're over the marshes, aren't we? Oh Lady. All that water . . ."

"In any case, it can be recovered and save a mechanist the trouble of measuring me again." Mr. Garret was far too flippant. The way that the leg had been wrenched away, it could have created major damage to the connectors. Then the water, and the fall . . . Even a quality prosthetic such as his had limits.

"I'll make a peg leg, Alonzo," said Vincan.

"I appreciate the offer, my friend, but I cannot fasten a peg on. It would grind the connectors into my skin. A crutch will have to suffice." Alonzo heaved himself onto his single foot. The crowd around them had begun to disperse. "Where has Mrs. Stout gone?"

"Mrs. Stout was here?" Octavia asked. *At least Mrs. Stout is safe now. Mr. Grinn must have stabbed her before, in my stead.*

"She was the one who rang me," he said.

"Oh." *Mrs. Stout must have been brimming with suspicions—some of them valid.*

Mr. Garret continued, "We were entering the promenade together when we noted your absence and saw Mr. Grinn at the window. Thank you." Little Daveo offered his stubby body for Mr. Garret to use for balance. "Mrs. Stout ran to the stewards' panel to summon more aid."

"I suppose all my screaming didn't do much good, did it?" Octavia asked.

"Over the wind? No, m'lady." A hard glint flashed through Mr. Garret's eyes. "I am grateful I was gone but for a minute, but if I had not left . . ."

"Don't torment yourself in such a way, Mr. Garret. Please." Octavia stood. The coat slid from her shoulders to create a puddle of black at her feet. The extra warmth slipped from her skin, yet she noted the absence of the cinnamon scent most of all. "Captain Hue. Pardon." The captain turned from the crewman he was speaking with. "I would appreciate some privacy to conduct mediations for Mr. Garret and myself."

"Certainly. You can heal in here. No point in making the man hobble all about. Garret, you're off duty until your leg is fixed."

"Understood, sir. I will remedy that as soon as possible."

The pressure on Octavia's chest intensified, as though squeezed in a giant's fist. She looked at the crewman alongside Captain Hue. He was younger than she was and wore his gawkiness like a garish coat. A knob protruded his throat, like a turkey's gullet. His body exuded heat along with a song, his mild magic a palpable presence.

"You're the aether magus who saved me."

The youth blushed. "I'm not a magus, m'lady. Not yet. I have a few years in training to go, and work as an elevator man aboard airships between sessions. I just lifted you, that's all."

"It was no mere thing to me. Fully trained or not, thank you, and may the Lady bless you." She reached out, a napkin clutched in her fist, and tapped the side of his jaw with her knuckle. His stubble prickled her skin. He jerked back, eyes going wider.

Blessings required no circle: simply gratitude from the heart for the preservation of life, channeled from the Lady. The boy would find that he slept soundly and healed quickly for the next while. The pressure against her heart eased, but it still took effort to breathe.

She owed that same debt to Mr. Garret, but had a sense that he'd know to dodge her if she reached for him like that. However, dodging would do him little good in his current condition. She eyed Mr. Garret, suppressing a smile.

"Out, out!" barked the captain, shooing people away. He looked at Octavia. "If you need anything else, m'lady, ring for assistance." He motioned to the far wall with its pull cords.

"Thank you," she said. The other people cleared out.

"I suppose I should sit down again," said Mr. Garret. He grimaced as he leaned against the wall to lower himself.

"Well, there was no call for you to rise in the first place."

"You stood as well."

"I'm not the one missing half my leg!"

"True." He sat with a grunt and propped himself up on his good knee. "So what now? Shall I pass your satchel?"

"No. You'll remain still while I bless you."

Mr. Garret's eyes went wide as she dove at him. He yelped and tried to scoot to one side, but Octavia was more agile yet. She stepped over his good leg and pinned it between her calves. His head was indecently placed, trapped between her skirt and the wall. She tapped her knuckle against his cheek. His skin was soft but for the pinprick beginnings of a beard. And goodness, he was warm against the lingering iciness of her skin.

"For saving my life and risking yourself for me, the Lady blesses you," she murmured. He shivered. *From the coldness of my touch? The blessing? Or something more?*

"You did not need to do that," he mumbled.

"Actually, I did." Octavia took in a full breath, expecting the onerous pressure to be gone. It wasn't. She almost cursed aloud. *His leg is still missing. That must be why. Surely the Lady knows I will help Mr. Garret of my own free will? This doesn't make any sense.*

Confused, she backed away, reaching for her satchel. She worked it open with slow, fumbling moves.

"I can help," he said quietly.

"No. I can do this." She pulled out the blanket by pinning it between her thumb and knuckles. Agony from her sliced hand muscles sent a jolt straight to her skull. She half closed her eyes, breathing through the pain to stay conscious.

"Miss Leander, please."

Unable to speak, she nodded. Mr. Garret moved quickly to fluff out the medician blanket. It filled the floor space between the wall and several tables. She crawled on her knees and centered herself in the oval.

"The jars. In red and blue." Her voice was hoarse from pain, but the agony was more bearable with her hands still.

I'm letting a man handle my jars. This is far more intimate than that kiss, yet I'm not that perturbed about it. Pain puts things in perspective.

"Anything else?" he asked.

She jerked her head in the negative. "Are you in much discomfort right now, Mr. Garret?"

"If you are trying to place me first in the queue, it will not work. I will not acquiesce."

Curse the man. He knew she couldn't heal him against his will. "Then answer me truly, knowing you must wait your turn."

"I am not in any pain. My leg feels . . . strange. Ghostly, if that makes sense. I feel as though 'tis there right now."

"Hmm. How quickly was the leg attached after initial amputation?"

"Six weeks."

"A brief wait, compared to most."

"I am friends with Kellar Dryn, of Leffen."

Octavia perked up. "Oh! That explains the high quality of your leg! Dryn's creations are sheer artwork. No wonder it has a built-in transmitter. His works are known to be stolen for their parts."

"Indeed. Though I fear Kellar has not tested his products for durability if dropped from six hundred feet into a marsh."

"Not forgetting, of course, that it was wrenched free by three hundred pounds of weight."

His smile twitched in amusement. "No, I would never forget that."

She looked toward her parasol. He followed her line of sight and set it in front of her. "Thank you. Can you grab one of the clean napkins, Mr. Garret?"

"Certainly."

"Okay. Wait for a moment." Tears filled her eyes as she tugged the napkins from her crusting wounds. The world wobbled before her eyes. Her throat clenched tight and breaths ragged, she continued, "Now, stuff the cloth in my mouth."

His eyes widened but he forced the cloth between her lips. The dryness of cotton invaded her tongue. Before she lost all nerve, she passed her hands over the wand.

Lightning bolts of agony raced down both arms. Black spots swarmed her eyes as she heard her own scream, muffled and hot, against the gag. Hands steadied her waist, her forehead bowing forward to meet Mr. Garret's shoulder. He didn't offer any ridiculous words of encouragement, no shushing, no telling her that it would pass. He simply moored her upright as the violent pain began to fade. Her breath caught in an aborted sob.

Her hands were decontaminated. That was the important thing, especially considering the malevolent zymes aboard ship. However, the wand had also dissolved the clots. The wounds bled anew. She sat up and bobbed her head. Catching the hint, he pulled the gag free.

"Thank you, Mr. Garret." Octavia's voice was raspy.

"Good God. You are welcome, though I pray we do not have to do this again." He actually appeared shaken, his eyes wide.

"Oh. I thought it was my duty to keep your life aboard ship exciting and unpredictable." Tears streamed down her cheeks.

"In that, you have succeeded most brilliantly." Without waiting to be asked, he moved the two jars to the perimeter of the circle. She nodded her gratitude.

Octavia bowed forward, hands extended with the palms facing up. The softness of the blanket pressed against her nose. Closing her eyes, she could see the copper and honeyflower band that surrounded her, the dormant magic like a smoldering flame. At her intensified focus, heat flashed against her skin and came as a welcome relief.

"Pray, let the Lady mend her healer's ills," she whispered, her words hot against the silky cloth. She dipped her fingers into the pampria and pressed both palms together.

In the openness of her mind, the wind howled through the branches of the mountainous Tree. Cold seeped into her hands as if she had dipped them into a bucket of ice water. The sensation crawled up her fingers and wrists, inching along her arms. It found her brachial artery and flared out in an instant, her breath seizing for several seconds as the sudden chill clenched her heart and lungs. Then she sagged. The pain was gone. *Lady be praised.*

She sat upright and applied a gelatinous Linsom berry to each hand. In an instant, they were absorbed.

"Thank you, Lady." She pressed her hands together again, bringing her thumbs to her lips as she opened her eyes. With a resounding zap, the seal around her dispersed.

More pampria gone. Not that I'll quibble about this use.

Mr. Garret sat just off of the blanket. His arms were wrapped around his good knee, his expression scrutinizing as always.

"Would it help if you took notes?" she asked.

His sternness collapsed in a relieved grin. "Pardon. I cannot help but find it fascinating. I am accustomed to modern machinery, not magical arts, and certainly nothing of your caliber."

"I do believe you're next in the queue, Mr. Garret."

He glanced over his shoulder as if to see if anyone was behind him. "I suppose so, but I am not sure 'tis even necessary. My leg is simply . . . gone. As for the fight, truth be told, it was not honest. Mr. Grinn faced the window and I had the jump on him."

"Is that a confession of sin, Mr. Garret? I'm a medician, not a sister."

"Well, yes. 'Tis a confession of . . . something, I suppose."

"Honor has a time and place. Now is neither."

They exchanged places. Octavia tapped the circle and began the ritual. His body's tune flared even louder than before—a military marching band, the brasses bold and triumphant. It suited him all too well, and proved his health to be sound.

Maybe his strong rhythm blended with the song of the road and Mother's hum simply because it is such a basic rhythm. There may be nothing more to it.

Maybe it provided a good excuse for what I wanted to do, anyway. Oh Lady, that kiss.

She smiled to herself as she bunched the cloth of his trousers above the knee. His thigh felt taut beneath her glancing touch—not that she was taking any liberties, of course. She frowned as she bent to take a closer look at the amputation.

As she suspected, the artificial leg attached just below the kneecap. A conical cap of silver marked the site, dozens of miniature connectors exposed to the air. She touched a few that she knew were most inclined to loosen, but they seemed sound. One small mercy.

She straightened and tapped the circle to break the bond. "This side of the socket seems to be in good care. I suggest placing some padding over the site, just in case you fall or put pressure on it."

"Miss Leander." His body's song quickened. Surprised, she glanced up at him. Mr. Garret stared down at the blanket, frowning. "You speak of honor, and I confess, I have not been honorable in how I have presented myself to you."

"Whatever do you mean, Mr. Garret?"

"You realize that twice now someone has tried to kill you aboard this vessel?"

"Yes, and now Mr. Grinn is dead."

Mr. Garret looked around, confirming the emptiness of the promenade. "No one . . . here should be trying to kill you, least of all a Dallowman like Mr. Grinn."

She froze. "Mr. Grinn is a Waster? How do you know—"

"I am on this ship because an agent from the Dallows was sent to kidnap you, Miss Leander. They need a medician for their cause, and your actions on the front caught their eye. But they have no reason to kill you. They want you alive."

For a moment, she felt as though she were dangling beyond the hull again, her legs kicking in vain against the air. "I don't . . . I don't understand, Mr. Garret. If you're not a steward, then what are you? Who are you?" *Who did I kiss?*

He gazed into his palms as if expecting an answer there. "A secret agent of the Caskentian government, m'lady. I am a Clockwork Dagger."

Chapter 9

"*A Clockwork Dagger. You.*" Octavia gawked at him.

He met her eyes, his brows pained. "'Tis so hard to believe I could make those elite ranks?"

"That's not what I meant." Or it was, partially. She always pictured a Dagger as something . . . more. A spry figure in black, slitting throats in the night, like the romantic lead—or villain—in one of Mrs. Stout's pulp novels.

Mrs. Stout. An agent of the Caskentian government knew Mrs. Stout could be the princess? *Oh, thank the Lady I didn't tell him the full truth about that tattoo.*

"What of Mrs. Stout?" she asked, voice trembling.

"I have no intention of divulging who she may be. 'Tis not relevant to my mission."

Yet both times he had stepped away to perform duties, something terrible had happened. Mrs. Stout was stabbed, and Octavia pushed out the window. He could have pushed her. She never saw the person standing behind her. But then why dangle himself from the craft to try to save her? To throw her off his trail, to earn her loyalty? If so, then why tell her any of this?

"I doubt your employers would agree," she said.

"No, they would not. We tend to disagree on many subjects." Exhaustion weighed on his features. "But she is obviously no threat to the established order. I have no wish to see or her family assassinated." As if that was the worst of it. Perhaps he didn't know of the ward or the contents of the vault.

She met his eye. "Why is someone pursuing me?"

"The Dallowmen want you alive. 'Tis all I know. I have been undercover for three months, waiting for you to board. The *Argus* is the cheapest flight south to Mercia."

"Undercover? You gave me your true name when we met."

"Now, Miss Leander. How many Tamarans do you see in a year? Could I truly work in full secrecy? No, I was never secret in that regard. I am who I am the son of a disgraced general, sent to make sure that one of the government's top medicians does not fall into enemy hands."

Top medician? Me? She knew it was true, but it was odd to hear it. "They sent you here, specifically, yet they never told you of my parents?"

"Your parents?"

"I lost my family in the crash of the *Alexandria*. We . . . resided in the village."

Shock dawned on his face, followed by horror. "No wonder you acted ill when I said my name. Your family—I thought no one survived in that village at all."

"I was the only one." She lifted her chin, as if to still defy death.

"How did you survive the conflagration?"

At that, her gaze lowered. "I don't speak of that night."

Me, a rebellious twelve, stubborn and obsessed, slipping out of my bedroom. I read of a flower that only bloomed under the light of a full moon, and though I resided in the wrong region entirely, I was determined to find it. I was crawling on moss when the first explosion shuddered through my bones. A fireball fell to earth. The screams flared; the crackles broke apart so many songs. Mud mired my feet. The taste of ash, blood, death.

Never again would she feel such powerlessness. That was her vow. If she could help someone, she would.

"I am sorry," he murmured.

"The grief is old." She shrugged the sorrow away, trying to cover the trembling in her voice. "And now the Wasters are trying to kill me. Is it vengeance for healing so many Caskentians?"

"I do not think they would hold it against a medician. You have healed their prisoners as well, have you not?"

"Oh. A few, yes. Higher-ranking officers. None died under my care."

"Mr. Grinn's death will not dissuade them. The next leg of our trip is the most dangerous. Leffen is a major port, and from there the southern pass is easily accessible. My orders"—his voice faltered, his gaze slipping to the floor—"are to stop you from falling into the Wasters' hands, at any cost. The best way I can secure your safety is to take you into my charge in Mercia—"

Her spine stiffened. "No one is taking charge of me, Mr. Garret. Delford needs me—"

"And what is to keep the Wasters from kidnapping you within Delford? How many men can you hold off with a single flute of capsicum?"

"I'm not without resources."

"I have full admiration for your abilities, Miss Leander, but I have no desire to see you as a tool in their hands. Or dead." He met her eyes then, expression pained.

"But what is the point of taking me into your charge now, so soon after armistice?"

"Must you even ask? Is the peace ever kept for long?"

"No," she muttered.

Certainly, it was poppycock that the Waste was under a curse—Caskentia had no such powers—but those plains were a place to die miserably, not live. Women were considered old if they lived past thirty. Hardscrabble farms vanished overnight, consumed whole by wyrms that resided within the dirt. *To be a prisoner there . . . oh, sweet Lady, no.*

Yet the alternative was Mercia. Smokestacks, industry, streets thickened with refugees. *People everywhere, drenched in soot and poverty. Living, dying, dead. The dead, at least, are silent. I've been told a person can wander the city for a full day and never see a living tree, only steel, bricks, and a sky of fetid gray.*

Not that I should fret too much over that. I doubt I'd be free to walk the streets at all.

The only other choice was to spurn all other choices. To land in Leffen, flee from Mr. Garret, and find her own way in the world. Somewhere, somehow. North to Frengia? No, the Frengians had allied with the Waste when it suited them. Tamarania would be an interesting choice with its emphasis on logic and education. Besides, they were also a source of cocoa and chocolate. Octavia could become a plump academic medician and leave Caskentia to rot amidst its political intrigues and chronic debt.

Tiredness soaked her to the bone. She didn't want to think about this—about which death to choose. "It's been a long night, Mr. Garret. We can discuss this tomorrow."

"Do you still wish for me to take care of the beastie? The hold will be unloaded in port tomorrow. He must be gone." His mouth was a hard line of concern.

She looked away, unwilling to look at the lips she so foolishly kissed.

I'll repay the Lady's life debt to him and mend his leg. I will do that much. It's only right.

"No. You'll have a hard enough time managing the stairs by yourself, Mr. Garret. I'll take care of it. You can't be expected to carry a cage, even if you expect to put me in one in Mercia."

With that, she stiffly stood and left.

As she approached her berthing, she couldn't help but listen closely to ensure that all was well. Blood didn't scream or beckon; that much was a relief. She did, however, note a light shining beneath the door. She softly knocked as a warning and then proceeded inside.

"Well, it's about time! Good gracious me, child." Mrs. Stout swung her legs over the side of her bed as she tucked a book beneath her sheets. The tenting was up but the overhead lights were still on.

"Were you waiting up for me?"

"Of course!" Mrs. Stout released a heavy huff. Her face looked pale without any cosmetics, her eyelids strangely plain. "You . . . goodness. Praise God you're still with us, child! I couldn't . . . I couldn't stay and watch. My heart couldn't take it. One of the men told me that you'd been retrieved, thanks to that steward." Her tone turned brittle.

I won't tell her that Mr. Garret is a Clockwork Dagger. I can't. She's too anxious as it is. And odd as it may be, I believe him when he says he'll keep his word about her identity. He didn't have to tell me anything, but he did.

"I must go and free our little gremlin, Mrs. Stout."

"Oh my." Mrs. Stout pressed a hand to her cheek. "I am a terrible person to forget our dear little creature. Here I was, sleeping away half the day while he stewed in captivity!"

"You needed that rest, and please, go ahead and sleep now. I don't know how long I'll take."

"I was sleeping earlier, and quite well at that. What possessed you to sneak off like that, child?" Mrs. Stout sounded truly wounded by the deception.

"I wanted to see the Saint's Road, that's all."

"With him? Surely I don't need to—"

"No, you don't," Octavia snapped. "I know very well how you feel about Mr. Garret, and I can assure you, nothing inappropriate is going on between us." *And certainly nothing will now.*

"I swore to Miss Percival that I'd watch over you, but now this is a task arising from the fondness of my heart.

My dear Miss Leander, you're old enough to make mistakes, ones that will linger for some time." She arched one silver eyebrow, leaving the rest unsaid.

"Oh, Mrs. Stout, really." Octavia couldn't hide her exasperation.

"Now, now, you meet a certain someone and things can happen very quickly. Buttons can be undone, stays can be loosened—"

"Mrs. Stout!"

"You get my meaning."

"Far too well." If Mrs. Stout knew how far things had already gone, the woman would go into conniptions. "Now please, get your rest. I must take care of our gremlin before I sleep on my feet. Should I turn off the light?"

"Yes, I suppose so. I can always read again tomorrow. But, child, don't take long, and if that steward—"

Octavia flipped the switch and practically dove out the door. She locked it, tested the handle once, and then skedaddled down the hallway to the stairs.

She was past the smoking room when she heard a muffled voice behind her. She ducked into the nearest doorway, satchel banging against her hip. Someone laughed. She eased her heels backward and then thought to take in her surroundings.

It was the ship's galley. She approved of the sharp odor of lemons and noted a small wand, like hers, hanging on the wall. A gleam of silver caught her eye. She reached into the little basket of the shelf and pulled out a circle. Someone of great strength had bent a fork fully around, like a bracelet.

The tines touched the base of the utensil. Gremlins liked silver things. Perhaps this could do, as a gift. She brushed some dust from the object and clutched it in her hand.

Going back to the doorway, she peered out. No one stood in the hall. She proceeded through the next door, past the crew areas, and into the hold. Something scurried in the darkness. She paused there for a moment, the knob digging into her spine as she let her eyes adjust to the dim light.

She found Leaf's little cage in the shadows. A sharp squeak welcomed her, and despite everything that had happened, she couldn't help but smile.

"Hello, Leaf." The lock released with a slight pop. The door burst open and Leaf scurried up her arm and around her shoulder like a crazed squirrel. She giggled as his stubby fingers tickled through cloth. "It seems you missed me."

He emitted a most perturbed squawk. His head butted against her jaw and she leaned into his affections. Tears brimmed in her eyes. *Oh Lady, I'm lonely. I miss Miss Percival, how she used to be. The other girls—well. No wonder I've been so stupid and vulnerable.*

Octavia opened her hand to reveal the bent fork. "Leaf, I brought you—"

Those beady black eyes opened wider as Leaf gasped. He scampered down her arm and grabbed the fork, holding it up in the meager light. The silver band gleamed. His fingers worked over the surface, taking in the curved lines.

"It's a fork. An eating utensil. Someone very strong, likely very bored, bent it in a circle like that." She laughed as Leaf tugged at the tines. His smile was all toothy and vicious. "I don't think you'll be able to . . . oh."

Despite being the size of an adolescent kitten, Leaf had pried up one of the tines. Then another, then the last. Her jaw gaped. How could the creature be that strong? Leaf lifted up his left arm and slipped the band over his flesh, right between the juncture of wing and shoulder. He reached across at that awkward angle and pressed the tines down again.

No wonder gremlins had such fondness for silver, if it was so pliable to their touch. Octavia laughed. Leaf could have opened his cage at any time. He hopped to her lap and tested his wings.

"Leaf, I need to set you free," she murmured. "You need to find more of your kind, and be safe." He only chirped and rubbed a triangular ear against her hand. She swallowed down a sob as she unzipped the middle section of her satchel.

"Here." She patted the open compartment. "Just like we did before. I need you to stay quiet and hidden while we go upstairs."

He leaped to her satchel and tucked his batlike arms against his body. She nudged him down a little more and drew the flap over the gap.

As she backed up, her heels kicked the Queen's portrait, the wooden frame clattering. She glanced down at Evandia's shadowed face. "One of your Daggers is looking after me. Me!" Octavia whispered, her brow furrowing. "I thought they looked after Your Majesty to the exclusion of everyone else. The Queen is Caskentia, they say. The rest of us . . . well, scrap metal possesses more value."

Wait. If a Dagger is involved, that means if I fall into the Wasters' hands, it's paramount to a direct threat against the Queen. How could I possibly hurt Queen Evandia? It's not like those artifacts of the Tree in the vault could be that dangerous either.

The royals—Mrs. Stout included—are just plain full of footle when it comes to the Lady and medicians.

Octavia crept out of the hold. She was halfway down the hall when the knob of the door ahead began to turn. Panicked, she looked to either side. This was the crew berthing, packed with men. She was as good as trapped.

The door opened to reveal Captain Hue, his face expressionless.

"Pardon me, Captain, sir," she said. Her fingers clutched her satchel's strap as her mind raced. "Oh, um, you see, I thought I would check on Mr. Garret to see if he needed any soporifics for the pain, but now that I'm down here, I can find no one awake, and I'm not about to go blundering into these chambers." She ended her babbling with an embarrassed smile. Never mind that Mr. Garret was in no pain, and that she didn't carry any soporifics.

He eyed her up and down and grunted. "No one's awake because the shift change is done. It's their place to be asleep."

"Oh. Of course. Silly me. I would appreciate your help, sir, and then I'll retire for the night as well."

Captain Hue's broad form occupied the aisle as he approached. "I'll check on him," he said in a growl, and opened the door to one of the rooms.

She released a long breath and placed a reassuring hand atop her satchel. *Please, let this not take long.*

Captain Hue emerged. He gave her a pert nod and edged past and to another door. With his hand on the knob, he turned to look back at her. "Next time, ring for a steward from your room or the promenade. This is no place for a lady."

"Yes, Captain, oh, I completely agree," she said, well aware she sounded like some empty-headed hoyden. A husky throat cleared behind her and she turned around.

Mr. Garret stood there in naught but a pair of gray underpants. His exposed arms were cords of muscle, his chest defined. Dark nipples stared at her like eyes.

Oh my. No wonder he moves with such grace, even with half his leg gone. The man could qualify for Clockwork Dagger on the basis of his physique alone.

"The captain said you were looking for me," he said, his voice a low, lilting rumble. His eyes went to her satchel and back to her face. She gave him a tiny nod.

"Oh, yes. I wanted to see if you needed any soporifics. To help you sleep. Because of the pain." She didn't hear the door behind her close, and had a strong hunch that the captain was listening from his berth.

"I should be able to rest on my own. I would rather not medicate and risk sleeping late, as the search for my leg will occupy much of the day."

She stared at him a moment. "Your leg. You intend to

search for your leg on your own? We're flying over endless miles of swamp now, aren't we?"

"Yes, m'lady, but I have a tracking device. I will find it." The determined set of his jaw said he'd find it, or die trying.

Octavia's eyes half fluttered shut. "I should have been more careful in my examination. I must have missed a head wound."

"Miss Leander?"

"You have one leg. What do you intend to do, swim?" The life debt nagged at the back of her brain—as if she needed the reminder. She ground her teeth together. "I can handle a wagon. Maybe, if the Lady's with us, I can even reattach the leg while we're still in the swamp."

I will help him and be done.

He gawked at her, clearly not expecting this development. "But . . . m'lady, I am overwhelmed."

"So am I." No point in mincing words, even if the captain listened. "You saved my life. Who knows? With the way this journey has progressed, you may need to save it again. Won't it be better for all involved if your legs are intact?"

He slowly nodded. "I am grateful to you, Miss Leander. We will speak more as you debark in the morning, then."

Her satchel swayed without her swinging it. Her smile stiff with renewed anxiety, she scurried past and made a dash for the stairs.

Upstairs, the promenade was empty, the only illumination from the glowstones within the floor. Her slow steps echoed against the white panels and windows.

She walked to the far side of the dining room, away

from where she fell. She had no desire for that particular view again. Cold wind gusted inward as she lowered a window on its hinge. The smell of moisture was ripe in the air, though she could see no rain falling yet. She snorted. *Yes, fine weather for traipsing through the marshes with Mr. Garret.*

A small arm pushed open the flap of her satchel. The green head followed, scrunched nose sniffing at the air.

"Smell that?" Octavia said, holding out her arm to Leaf. "That's—"

Instead of scurrying up her arm, he sprang from the satchel, wings stretched out. He paused on the sill, head tilted up, eyes wide. His wings flashed out with a slight snap and then he was gone. She leaned toward a shut window, throat raw with emotion as the deep gray clouds swallowed him up.

"Live well, Leaf," she whispered.

No long drawn-out farewell. No final chin rubs. *It's for the best.* More lingering, more likelihood they would've been caught. She pulled the window handle, wincing at the iciness of the metal, and latched it shut again. She hoisted up her satchel.

A loud clatter at the window made her jump. She turned. Leaf was sprawled against the window.

"Leaf!" She let her satchel slide to the floor as she fumbled the window open again. Cold wind slapped her face. Leaf's little hands inched along the glass as he pivoted his head toward the opening.

He came back! Joy and terror brought tears to her eyes.

"Leaf, no. You have to go. It's not safe on board."

His mouth moved but she couldn't hear his trill against the wind.

"They'll kill you! Go!"

A little green hand worked into the gap. She pried his fingers up one by one to shove him back outside, but his grip perfectly capped the tip of her thumb. The rest of his body stayed plastered against the glass.

"You can't come in, Leaf. Go! Fly away! Shoo!" She wiggled her hand free and jerked the window shut. The cold air lingered like a burn in her nose and lungs.

Leaf's mouth opened and closed. The fork rattled against the glass as his arm moved in an arc, as if waving.

"Go!" She waved him away. Those black eyes stared at her, unblinking.

Octavia did the only thing she could. She picked up her satchel and walked away. Tears thawed trails down her cheeks, and she didn't look back.

Chapter 10

"You cannot be serious about going out with that man. Child, really. You must reconsider." Mrs. Stout huffed as she pushed open the curtains. Sunlight flooded their room at the Hotel Nennia, the intensity burning Octavia's eyes. She had only gotten half her usual amount of sleep, and on top of the drama and a self-healing, she was feeling the effects of her exertions. Another lecture from Mrs. Stout was about as welcome as a ward of virulent pox patients.

"Don't start this again, please. The man saved my life. And assisted in saving yours, I might add." Plus, the Lady's burden pulsed like a headache, the word "debt" repeating itself in her brain like a relentless, breathy chant.

Octavia could only have afforded a doss house along the docks where certain beds sold by the hour, so it was something of a relief that Mrs. Stout had insisted that she accept her generosity and room with her. Their chambers were easily the size of the entire promenade aboard ship and glimmered with a sort of opulence that made Octavia feel profoundly out of place. A wide window showcased the bay and a sky speckled with airships and puffy contrails.

The sight of the sky made her flinch. She hadn't even gone to the promenade that morning. She didn't want to hear gossip of a pesky gremlin lurking at the windows or how he was tended to.

Please, Lady, let Leaf have given up and flown away.

"Well! Not to be ungracious, but Mr. Garret's arrival was rather peculiar in its timing. Some men might use such gratitude as leverage for other favors. And now you intend to gallop across the swamp together! Alone!" Mrs. Stout gestured toward the ceiling with both hands, as if expecting God to chime in with agreement.

"I'm not about to leave the man one-legged on my account." *Though I'd have an easier time escaping him that way.* She shook away the awful thought. She could never live with herself for abandoning a patient in such condition, even if the man in question was an overly pleasant government agent who intended to imprison her for her own well-being.

"I don't like it! Not one bit. You're inviting trouble, if you ask me."

No one asked you. Octavia took a deep breath to calm her tongue. "If you look at everything that's occurred over the past two days, there's little to like. You were stabbed. Someone poisoned the ice using a distinctly Waster method. I was shoved from a window."

"It is a curious cluster of events! If these things are indeed connected, we'll figure it out," said Mrs. Stout, a devious gleam in her eyes. The woman seemed to regard their recent history as if it was a chapter in one of those pulp novels she kept close at hand. "I'll be staying here today to do a spot of reading, taking things easy as I recover. But! Perhaps tomorrow we can walk around. Leffen is a lovely little town, truly."

The view from the ritzy window made it seem so, but the perspective from the mooring mast had shown Octavia a skyline cramped with narrow buildings, with tall smoke-stacks belching soot.

Another blighted city of refugees and day laborers. Nothing on the scale of Mercia, but bad enough.

"I would like that," she said in a small voice. "I must visit the bank to withdraw money from Miss Percival's account." Five silvers—not even enough to cover two nights in a room like this, but it'd get her to Delford.

If she was still alive then, or Delford even an option. *Stop thinking like that.*

"If you're going to wear that into town"—Mrs. Stout nodded toward her outfit—"be prepared to get some attention!"

Octavia looked down at herself. "It's only for today. We'll be headed straight to the swamp. At least these clothes won't be ruined out there."

The white cloth of her Percival uniform glimmered from its underlying enchantments as it covered her from neck to wrist to ankle, yet not in the stodgy fashion sported by Mrs. Stout. A medician needed to move and breathe freely. A high slit in the skirt extended past each knee to reveal a flash of trousers beneath. The dress showed curves but not too much, the femininity blunted by a deep-pocketed apron that obscured the breasts and widened the hips. Beneath the basic gown, she didn't wear a corset—those things disrupted a body's song in a terrible way—but a modern brassiere for basic support. Knee-high boots completed the garb. Like the layers of cloth, the leather had been blessed with endurance and resistance to harmful zymes.

Then there was the headband. Octavia had no great love for hats, not like some girls, but she did love how the three inches of crisp white lace adorned her coiled-up hair. It fit from just past her bangs to tie at her nape. She had embroidered the front of the headband with the image of a small tree in brown and green threads.

She checked herself in the mirror. Crazed ringlets of brown dangled in front of her ears. No matter how she wet and coaxed her hair, the strands stayed unruly.

"Now, now, that won't do much good. It's the moisture," Mrs. Stout said, noting her labors. "It's even worse in the thick of summer! Just let it be, child. Weren't you supposed to be downstairs about now?"

Octavia looked at Mrs. Stout in the mirror. "You're practically pushing me out the door!"

"Yes, well, you may as well fulfill your obligation to the man." She waggled a thick finger. "But only that! And if he tries anything . . . !" *Mrs. Stout can nag him to death.*

"Yes, Mother," Octavia muttered.

She reached the lobby as a massive grandfather clock boomed out the hour. The notes reverberated through her feet, reminding her of the airship rumbles to which she had become so accustomed. The lobby was even more ornate than her room. A white marble floor, scuffed by constant use, still gleamed in an austere manner. Wooden wall panels held polished whorls and waves. A candelabra featured rows of lights, alternating between dull yellow glowstones and gleaming electric bulbs.

Mr. Garret motioned her toward the door. He wore common workman's garb and leaned on a crutch. The sight of him caused Octavia to feel a small twinge of regret. Her anger at his revelation had faded—after all, he only meant to keep her alive—but she still had no desire to linger in his company longer than necessary.

"I did not expect you to be in the full Percival attire," he said.

"It'll clean well, that's why. At the rate this week has gone, I would soon be out of dresses." She realized the improper implication of her words and added a little shrug.

Mr. Garret chuckled. "Yes. Until your arrival on ship, I never realized how handy it was that the *Argus* has crimson jackets. They hide blood all too well."

Whereas my uniform drinks it in, just as the Lady accepts my bloodletting from the ground.

"I should tell you, there was some consternation on the ship this morning," he continued. "Someone rifled through Mr. Grinn's luggage last night before any stewards could secure his belongings."

The street smelled of fresh, salty air. Just down the way, rows of masts tottered with the waves. A buzzer rumbled somewhere overhead.

"Was anything stolen?"

Alonzo stared into the distance, a tweed cap shading

his eyes. "Not that we could ascertain, things ransacked as they were."

Something green fluttered over the street and vanished over a facade on the far side.

She gasped. "Is that . . . ?"

"M'lady?"

"I thought I saw something." *It can't be Leaf, not here.*

A gaggle of women passed by, brilliant plumes in their hats and their parasols aloft. Their bodies rang with the burble of indigestion. Their eyes widened at the sight of Octavia, and they whispered among themselves.

Just past the view offered by their window above, part of the street had been torn apart. Large construction equipment, darkened by grease and abuse, idled there.

Mr. Garret motioned that way. "They are pulling out old tramway rails. The trolleys were smelted during the war. I suppose the city gets along well without them."

"I see." Across the way, the broad side of a brick building wore a painted advertisement for Royal-Tea. That horrid drink was everywhere.

"Miss Leander! Oh, Miss Leander!"

Octavia stiffened as she turned. It was that unbearable Mrs. Wexler from the ship, the one who grandly swooned during her husband's illness.

"Oh, I did hope I would see you again." Mrs. Wexler panted slightly. A heavy cloud of jasmine perfume assaulted Octavia's nostrils. "Thank you so much for tending to my husband on the ship. He's resting now, the poor man. I am out on errands. Can you believe this city? So backward! No rails! Glowstone lights and all." She tsked beneath her breath. "It's almost as bad as Vorana, and Vorana was dreadful. Dirt streets, like some Waster village. Not at all like Mercia, mind. There I can take a trolley wherever necessary."

Octavia opened her lips to speak.

"I wanted to invite you to a symposium tonight," Mrs. Wexler continued. She plucked a sheet from the velvet satchel she was holding. "My husband was going to argue on how science can eradicate the Wasters quite tidily from afar. I mean, they claim we already did that centuries ago, so why not make the myth into reality? But! We were both inspired by our encounter with you, and he will instead speak on the science of medicians."

The sheet of paper was shoved into Octavia's hand. She looked to Mr. Garret for aid, but his eyes were on the passing carriages. His hunched shoulders told her that he didn't wish to be recognized by Mrs. Wexler.

"The science of medicians?" Octavia echoed.

"Well, yes. How your work is really a manipulation of cellular matter within both the body and plants."

"What of the Lady?"

Mrs. Wexler tittered behind her hand. "Oh, really. We're in a modern age. Please, don't tell me you really believe in the quaint notion that some giant Tree keeps the world alive."

A hot flush traveled up Octavia's neck to her cheeks.

"Well, I must be getting along. Such a busy day! I will see you at eight o'clock, Miss Leander! Perhaps we can speak afterward." The woman flitted off.

Octavia barely resisted the urge to ball up the paper and toss it at the back of Mrs. Wexler's head.

"You are going to find a lot of people who think like that, especially in Mercia," said Mr. Garret.

"You mean converse with themselves and order others about like servants?"

He smiled, shaking his head. "You will have that sort everywhere. I meant her beliefs on the Lady and the Tree. 'Tis considered a rather . . . antiquated notion."

That wasn't a surprise, really; Octavia hadn't known much about the Tree until she was taken in by Miss Percival. "Then how do you explain what I do, Mr. Garret?"

He turned up both palms in supplication. "I know you can work miracles, Miss Leander. You will get no argument from me. On that subject, anyway." His motioned with his head. "Our wagon is just up the way."

"Something Mrs. Wexler said . . ." Octavia paused to think as they walked. "Could Caskentia destroy the Waste from afar? I would think that if it were possible, it would have been done back when all this started, after the princess's kidnapping."

He frowned down at the sidewalk. "I confess, I have not had dealings with that area of research, but it seems like something Caskentia would consider in order to end the conflict in one fell swoop."

"One fell swoop indeed," she said darkly. "War. I'm so sick of it. I'm so sick of needless death. Ours, theirs."

She felt the pressure of gazes around her, heard the whispers. She walked faster.

"We save the ones we can," Mr. Garret said, his voice husky and soft. Octavia nodded, thinking of Leaf. She spared a glance at the sky and didn't even see birds—just smoke, exhaust, and glistening dirigibles on high. *Live, little one. Please.*

They walked a block off the main thoroughfare, to a buggy parked in front of a Frengian baker. The sweetness of hot sugar lingered in the air. Mr. Garret untied the reins from the hitching post. A slim bay horse was in the shafts.

"As we are venturing beyond civilization today, would it be forward of me to call you Octavia?" He didn't look at her, focusing the harness instead.

The cultured lilt of his words seemed to meld with the sugariness in the air, and she shivered at the sound of her first name on his lips. From him, it sounded like music. Music that tasted like confectionary delights. Strange heat filled her chest, and for a moment she couldn't speak.

"I . . . I suppose you could. Wouldn't be too forward, I mean. Should I call you Alonzo as well?" *This all would be easier if I hated him outright the way Mrs. Stout does.*

" 'Tis up to you," he said, holding out a hand. His gaze was shy, as it had been after the kiss.

Don't think on that.

"Chivalry's all well and good, but you possess one leg. I'm helping you up first."

"That might be easiest, true." He grimaced as he set the crutch against the wagon. She stepped close, angling her shoulder. He placed his good foot on the single step and used her shoulder to pull himself up the rest of the way. His jacket flared out. His belt held a gun within a holster.

"Oh. That's a Gadsden .45," she said.

"Indeed 'tis. You are quite astute to recognize it that fast."

"I'm most familiar with the consequences of the weaponry, though my mother did teach me to hunt when I was young. Don't look so surprised. I'm not averse to eating meat." *Though I used to be, for different reasons.*

"My pardon. 'Tis good that you can shoot, just in case."

"Just in case," she echoed.

She slipped off her satchel and passed it up to Mr. Garret and then climbed into the seat. She edged around his legs, noting his gaze politely turned away from her skirts, and then sat down next to him. Her left arm ached, just slightly, and she frowned. The need for bloodletting was upon her already. She'd need to tend to that later, before it became bothersome.

"I assume you have your tracking device?" she asked.

"Yes. And lunch is packed in the back."

The paper from Mrs. Wexler rustled in her hand. "Well, whenever we need to make a privy stop, at least this paper will come in handy," she said pleasantly as she tucked it into a pocket of her satchel. Mr. Garret chuckled softly.

OUTSIDE THE CONFINES OF the city, Octavia encouraged the bay steed to proceed at a steady clip. Despite the gloom of the sky some hours before, the clouds fled as the morning progressed, revealing bright blue heavens. The landscape was as flat as the palm of a hand, composed of marshes, tall grasses, and waving reeds. Infrequent trees offered variety to the eye. The smell could best be described as a middle ground between carrion and ripe mud. Still, to Octavia, the terrain was far pleasanter than that in the city.

Alonzo pulled a small, silver cube from the pocket of his jacket and cradled it in his palm.

"That's the tracking device?" she asked. "How does it work?"

"The crystal within is aligned with the one inside my mechanical leg. I turn it on, like so." He pushed a small grate on the top open to reveal cross-hatching and darkness. "This will emit a noise when we are within a few miles, the volume increasing with proximity. Even if the mechanism of the leg is destroyed, the crystal should be well nigh invincible."

She gave him a baleful look. "My concern is finding it at all in such a wide area." *Debt, debt, debt* nagged in the back of her head.

"'Tis not as dire as that. We are on the northern road between Leffen and the monastery at the Saint's Road. This is the route airships trace. Had I the funds, I would have rented a buzzer for us and we could have flown this way."

"Pardon me if I'm prying, but your father invented the buzzer. Doesn't that grant you certain . . . prerogatives?"

Alonzo's smile thinned. "He invented it for the Caskentian military. They own it, not him. Besides, my father's name does not earn me any favors."

"I see." Octavia pursed her lips. "At times you seem rather bitter toward Caskentia, yet you work for them as a Clockwork Dagger. Why?"

The grind of the wagon's wheels filled the silence as Alonzo stared into the marshes. "You do not mince around, do you?"

"You needn't—"

"I can answer, once I find the words. I have battled and embraced my father's legacy my entire life. He was a brilliant man, and brilliance does not often fit with a military that wishes one to conform. I always assumed I would follow in his footsteps and rise through the ranks. Then I found myself without a foot at all." He stared at the folded pant leg over his stump. "I am little more than an apprentice as a Dagger. My Tamaran heritage makes my appearance too memorable to work undercover. If not for the sway of my mother, I likely would not have this job at all."

"And what is this job exactly?"

Something shifted in the song of his body. The tempo of his heartbeat increased. His posture stiffened. "Clockwork Daggers are the defenders of the realm, the guardians of the royal family. By preserving the Queen—"

"Oh, I wasn't trying to say that I was . . . like her. That would be ridiculous. I'm just not sure why I'm important enough to warrant this attention at all." She clicked her tongue and the horse began to trot.

Silence stretched out between them. "Octavia. You have no idea how dangerous you are, do you?"

"Dangerous?"

"You're the most powerful medician in recorded history. You use a minimal amount of herbs. You ask the Lady for aid, and she answers with swiftness. Your fatality rate at the front was three percent, compared to a forty-four percent average for the other Percivals—"

"Wait, there are statistics on us? I never . . ."

"The only other person we know of with such gifts, such blessedness, was the Lady herself—and in Mercia, she is largely regarded as a mythological figure. There is no one like you in Frengia, the southern nations, or across the sea. Caskentia has Daggers abroad. They have searched. They know. There is no one who can do what you do, Octavia. *No one.*"

"Oh." She folded her arms against her stomach. Was she supposed to be proud, pleased? Instead, she blinked back tears.

"Yes, you are dangerous. What is Caskentia supposed to do with someone of your skill? You are a conduit to God, Octavia. How can the government control that?"

Control. With Caskentia, things always came back to control. Rage flickered in her chest. "Then it'll certainly be to your benefit when you bring in a rogue like myself, alive and well," she said, and immediately regretted the words. She took a few long breaths. "Pardon my tone. It's the lack of sleep."

And Mrs. Stout's nagging, and the itchiness of the life debt, and the fact that people are trying to kill me, and that Caskentia regards me with the same fear as the other Percival girls. "But I've no desire to stay in Mercia. That kind of life . . . isn't living."

That line between his brows persisted. "If you think the people of Delford have suffered already, how much more will they endure because of your presence and the danger it brings? I am sorry, I know these words pain you. If anything, Wasters are stubborn. In Mercia there are safe houses and guards aplenty. It may not be ideal, but you will live. *You will live.*"

Locked in a city of endless cobblestones and smokestacks and crushing humanity and disease in every song. "And how long will I be expected to live like that? How many years? I . . ."

A red-leafed bush caught her eye and she abruptly pulled up. Her fears of Mercia slipped from her mind in an instant. "Is that . . . ?" she asked breathily. She slid off the seat, reins still in hand, and her feet impacted on the ground with a cloud of dust.

"What?" asked Alonzo as she looped the reins over a gnarled, cutoff trunk.

"Pampria." *Pampria!* She wanted to whirl and dance as she had as a child. "Do you mind if . . ."

"Not at all, though it goes without saying we should not tarry."

Octavia nodded and half slid down the embankment. The bush stood as high as her shoulder, its red brilliant as blood. She leaned over to breathe in the faint odor of cinnamon. Her arm throbbed again, as if the proximity to pampria intensified the need to bloodlet.

She passed a hand over the wand. Keeping her satchel on her shoulder, she opened it to dig out a treated leather bag. With her clean hand, she plucked the waxy leaves from the bush. It would take them days to dry, but a full bag would be enough, once it was ground down, to replenish her jar.

"Can I help?" Alonzo asked. The wagon creaked as he eased off, and as she turned to advise caution, he came down the embankment. Down, hard. He all but tumbled head over heels and practically decapitated Octavia with a swipe of his crutch.

"Sorry about that," he said, gasping. He somehow managed to land on his working leg.

"Please be careful, Alonzo!" She frowned at him. He looked suitably chagrined. "When you look at the leaves, get ones that are fully red. The slightest tinge of green to the tip, they're not ripe."

"Understood." He began to pick leaves. His fingers were fast, and the bag quickly filled as they both worked. Alonzo shifted slightly, reaching over her, and the crutch found a soft spot. She sensed his loss of balance before it happened. The bag fell from her hand as she leaned to catch him. He had moved to catch himself as well, relying on the most stable object within reach: Octavia. One hand landed on her shoulder and the other on the narrowness of her waist. Her hands slammed against the solid warmth of his chest, the crutch hitting the earth with a soft thud.

"Oh." She gasped. That particular cinnamon smell wafted across her nostrils again, stronger due to the proximity of the pampria, and she breathed in deeper.

Alonzo's face hovered inches above hers. "Balance is an art form I have taken for granted. My apologies."

Her fingers pressed into him through the cloth. His chest was as firm as it had looked when she had seen him shirtless aboard the *Argus.* She was keenly aware of how his hand curved against her waist as well, like interlocking puzzle pieces. Heat crept up her neck and to her cheeks.

"Oh. Uh. There's no need to apologize, but you should certainly be more careful. If I wasn't here to catch you, you could've broken your hand or arm when you struck the ground."

He grinned. "Perhaps 'tis a way to earn your continued attention." His lilt was soft, dangerous.

Instead of fading, the warmth in her face worked downward into her chest and belly. She swallowed drily. "Surely there are ways to attract my eye that don't involve maiming oneself."

He arched an eyebrow. "Truly? Do tell. It may come as a surprise, but I am not keen on self-injury."

He's a Clockwork Dagger. He wants to take charge of me in Mercia for my own safety. Being this close, wanting to be this close, is absolutely idiotic.

"You could always do this." She eased a hand from his chest, slow to make sure he had regained his balance, and did a tentative wave in front of his face.

"Yet that seems so . . . common." His breath was hot against her cheek as he leaned closer. She placed her hand against his chest again, her fingers curling.

"Sometimes . . . sometimes common approaches are surprisingly effective."

"I must keep that in mind. I suppose it would not always be convenient to fly laps over the Saint's Road at night."

"Oh. No. The road—that was extraordinary, but afterward . . ."

Alonzo's lips quirked. "I promise, if ever we fly over the Saint's Road again, it will only be pleasantness."

"You mean, I won't be thrown out of the window?"

"I promise." His hand found hers and their fingers twined together. Octavia's heart threatened to lift off like a dirigible.

It was at that moment that a sharp beep emanated from his pocket. She jerked back with a yelp.

"Oh! It beeped," she said, stating the obvious. She was surprised at the huskiness of her own voice.

"Indeed." His blue eyes searched hers for a long moment and then he stepped back. His breathing, his heartbeat were rapid, his song quickened. "We must move along. Do you have enough?"

"Enough what?" She blinked. "Oh, yes. The pampria. Of course." The bag had snagged on the lower branches of the shrub. She checked the amount, nodded, then stuffed the bag inside her satchel.

Alonzo stooped to pick up his crutch. "Here," Octavia said, holding out her right hand. Leaning her left arm against the embankment, she practically dragged him upward. His crutch was useless against the loamy soil.

They sat on the seat, maybe a little closer than before, though not quite meeting each other's eyes.

They rode on. The beeps grew louder and closer together mile by mile, and the silence between them deepened. Finally, with the sound from the device almost continuous, she drew the wagon just off the road and secured the reins to a tree branch. Alonzo worked his way down from the seat and grabbed hold of his crutch. The instant he placed weight on it, a solid six inches of the crutch sank into the earth. He tipped forward. Octavia leaped to throw out an arm and catch him by the sleeve.

"Damn it." He tried to stand erect and the crutch only sank more.

"Hold on to me," she said, her tone quiet. Alonzo pivoted to grab her. Her face was at the level of his shoulder, his hand a warm weight.

Octavia stepped back so that he could lean on the wagon. The crutch stood straight up like a sapling. She uprooted it, the mud gushing in an obscene way, and threw it into the bed of the wagon. The detector continued to squeal. She motioned for him to pass it over, and she tucked the device into her apron.

"Pardon my language, but if I feel infantile without my leg, and in a swamp . . ."

"I understand it's quite frustrating, but you'll work yourself into a fury if you try to manage on your own." *To think, that was his original plan. He'd have died out here.* That awareness sent a terrible chill through her. "You have two choices: you either wait at the wagon, or you lean on me."

He grumbled beneath his breath. "You do not mind? We will have to be in rather close proximity."

"I'll try not to grope you without a legitimate medical excuse."

Alonzo barked out a laugh. "Perhaps I should fall down more often, then."

Mud squished beneath Octavia's boots as she stepped

into the water. She cringed at the repulsive sound. Alonzo's hand was steady on her left shoulder as he hopped alongside her. The foulness of the place increased.

"Let's be honest, Alonzo. This isn't an ideal place for wooing." She kept her steps slow as she tested the ground. The tree behind them faded behind tall stands of tule reeds.

He grunted a reply as he fought for balance. Their breaths huffed as they slogged onward.

The detector beeped from her pocket, but soon the sounds waned, so they turned to walk north again. The beeps increased in volume and frequency. Water lapped just above her knees and stank of things dead and dying. Alonzo's hand draped to grip at her elbow, his weight often heavy against her side. The mud sucked on his boot, causing them to take slow, wobbly steps together.

"Tell me, Octavia, what would be a good locale for wooing you?" He spoke between heavy breaths. Sweat and swamp water had soaked him through.

The words stopped her in her tracks. "What?"

Alonzo's expression was as mild as if he had inquired about the weather. "You said a swamp was not ideal. What would you prefer?"

"Goodness." She staggered onward. "Someplace green, with trees. I love to work in a field, or forage in a forest. I need space to breathe, to feel the Lady breathe. I suppose that I'm happiest when I'm busy and no one is hurting."

"You despise cities." He spoke loudly to be heard over the device.

She glanced at him in surprise. "Is it that obvious?"

"I have watched you in Vorana and now Leffen, how you react at the mention of Mercia. You seem far more at ease here, even with me as a burden."

"You're not a burden. Not much of one."

He looked at her in a way that sent a jolt of heat straight to her belly. Something in the water snared her foot and she jerked her gaze away as she caught herself on reeds. The detector beeped without ceasing.

She forced her dry throat to swallow. "It's rather cruel to ask questions about wooing me considering the temporary status of our relationship." *Medician and patient; passenger and steward; prisoner and jailer.* Her gaze went to a cluster of cattails ahead and she sucked in a sharp breath. "Also, rather inappropriate with dead bodies about."

The arm dangled over the reeds at about her shoulder level. They hobbled closer, and dread filled her stomach. Not that she was perturbed to face a dead body; no, it was the manner of his death. The corpse sprawled facedown on its prickly bed. Several reeds impaled him completely, their soft brown heads drenched in blood that did not scream.

"He was likely killed the instant he landed," she said. *Good. He didn't suffer.*

"'Tis a shame. He could have wallowed in his misery for a little while," Alonzo growled. She stared at him, speechless. He let go of her arm and clutched the thick reeds as he hopped around.

"Do you think the leg's under him?"

"No. More likely, they drifted apart as they fell."

Octavia stepped away from Alonzo, all the while keeping an eye on him in case he stumbled. She studied the surface of the water and wondered how likely a leg was to float. The detector paused in midbeep and she turned back toward Mr. Grinn.

"I found it!" Alonzo held on to the reeds with the leg in his other hand.

She hurried over, water sloshing against her thighs. "Wonderful! How does it look?"

"Wet through, but the boot looks good. I would hate to lose one of my favorite boots."

She opened her pocket and shut off the blaring noise. The sudden quiet was a surprise. She wiggled her head as if to adjust her ears. The sound of buzzing lingered, along with the persistent nagging of her life debt. Perhaps she had sustained temporary hearing damage from that obnoxious device.

"Well, let's get back to the road and I can take a thorough look at your leg," she said.

Alonzo frowned and gazed up. The skies were pale blue with infrequent clouds. "Do you hear that?"

"Hear what?"

"It sounds like a buzzer."

"Oh." Octavia looked up again. "I thought it was an echo from that device."

"No. 'Tis definitely a buzzer." He hopped forward and away from the tules, and Octavia caught him against her side.

"Probably someone following the road?"

Alonzo pointed. She could see the craft now. The lower

part of the buzzer resembled a bicycle, though broader and flatter with a three-wheeled design for landing. On a high shaft, the propeller whirled about five feet above the sitting pilot.

Alonzo's hand stilled on her arm. "The sun, the way it glints on the front passenger seat. 'Tis wrong. It looks like the military version of the rig."

Yellow lights flashed at the front of the buzzer. "Get down!" yelled Alonzo, throwing himself over her as bullets pinged around them.

Chapter 11

Octavia stumbled backward and they both went down, water splashing to her shoulders. Stones and debris stabbed into her derriere. Bullets zipped past and sliced into the nearest stand of reeds. Alonzo sputtered in the water and managed to regain his footing. His hat had vanished but his grip on the leg seemed quite secure.

"Are you well?" he asked, panting. Water dripped from his face.

"No, I'm not well! Someone's shooting at us!" Cold dread trembled through her veins as they both scrambled for the shelter of the thicket of reeds. The buzzer whirled overhead again.

"Hold me steady." He set the leg in the water and unholstered his gun. Octavia placed her hands on his waist, gripping at his flesh beneath sopping layers of cloth. The buzzer passed overhead and began to turn. Alonzo brought up the gun, squinting, and fired. Her eyes caught the glint of the bullet bouncing off the chassis of the craft hundreds of yards away.

"You're a crack shot!"

"Or I would be, if I had my damned balance." He glared at the sky, holstering the Gadsden and picking up his leg again.

Octavia took in a deep breath to calm her fluttering heart. "How much diesel do buzzers hold?"

"Probably six hours' worth. If it took off from Leffen, they probably have four hours' worth left."

The sound of the buzzer faded as it made another loop. Octavia sidled forward, half dragging Alonzo by one arm as she shoved through the reeds. The sour smell of the water caused her stomach to roil. She hooked her arm to hold back the tules as she checked the area ahead, revealing a patch of clear water. Dozens of elegant white egrets glided across the pool. She glanced up. The buzzer was making another direct approach.

"Lady, forgive me," she said, touching a wet finger to her lips as she shrugged off Alonzo's hold. He grasped hold of the reeds. "Hold this, please." She shoved her satchel's strap into his hand. In a snap, she had unfastened the parasol.

"Octavia, what scheme are you hatching?" The buzzing grew louder.

"One that works, I pray. Wait here."

Leaving him clutching the reeds, she sloshed out into the exposed pool, all too keenly aware that the shimmering white of her uniform would lure the craft in like a beacon. A few egrets fluttered their wings. She marched forward and then the ground was gone. Octavia went under, the world turning black and fetid. Gasping, she kicked out her legs and found solid ground again, the parasol still clutched in her hand. She spat out water, gagging at the taste, and flared out the dripping parasol. She dug her boot soles into the mud to propel herself forward and screamed as she stampeded the egrets.

The birds squawked and rustled as they rose in a mass. The sharp whine of bullets pierced the air. Octavia threw herself into the water and opened her eyes. Everything was black and she couldn't see far, but she did spy several perfect trails of bubbles. The wakes of bullets. She yanked down on the parasol handle but the cursed thing was too buoyant, marking her location with all the clarity of skyward beacons and glittery dancing girls. She emerged, gasping, flung the parasol away, and hurled herself into the nearest thicket. Reeds sliced at her arms but she barreled her way inside the shelter. The ground was higher here, and she sank to her knees to rest. Gasping for breath, she needed several seconds to realize how quiet it was. The buzzing had gone away.

She thrashed her way out of the thicket again and into thigh-deep water. Her parasol was upside down in the pool, lazily circling. She searched the sky.

"The birds took him down," called Alonzo. She looked toward him, and then past. A black plume of smoke rose into the air.

"Excellent!" she said, wading to her parasol. She dumped out the water and held it overhead as she made her way back to him. The guilt hit her then, followed by the backlash of adrenaline. She had, after all, forced innocent and beautiful birds to die in her stead. Closing her eyes, she paused in the middle of the water.

"Lady, I'm sorry," she whispered. "Please, take them to your branches. I pray they didn't suffer."

She reached Alonzo and found herself quivering without control. Saying nothing, he wrapped an arm around her shoulders. Her lips pressed against the soggy cloth of his jacket and she took in the reassurance of his embrace.

Even without a leg, he's solid as an oak. She pressed closer against him, trembling as if boneless. After a long minute, she pulled back.

"Thank you," she said softly. His arm rested on her shoulder to keep him upright.

"You were very lucky," he said. He pointed up at her parasol. Two neat holes had pierced the fabric.

"Oh." She took in a rattling breath. *I'm well. He's well. Thank the Lady.*

Octavia accepted her satchel and draped it over her shoulder again. With Alonzo holding tight to his leg, they worked their way toward the plume of smoke in the west. Toward the road.

"Here," he said as they got closer. She accepted the leg and had her first good look at it. Most of the mechanical limb was covered by a black leather boot. At the top was a shred of cloth—from a union suit, perhaps—and an inverted cone of metal. Divots and gears showed where it would lock in place with the rest of his leg. It all looked quite intact. Whether the internal mechanisms worked was something else entirely.

Alonzo unholstered the Gadsden .45 and hefted it in his hand.

"Are you shooting to kill?" she asked.

"The pilot may well be dead already, but I would much rather bring him in alive. I have a few questions to ask."

"True. The dead aren't quite so forthcoming." She paused. "If we're under fire, don't hesitate on my account. The Lady understands matters of self-defense. So do I."

He nodded. His queue of hair was a dark lump on his back, several curling strands dangling free to frame his face. They trudged forward, taking cover behind rushes as they approached. The raised bank of the road was visible not far ahead—thank goodness—and the buzzer had crashed beneath a small cluster of big-leaf maples. It smoldered in a heap of metal.

"No movement," Alonzo muttered. "Proceed with care." They worked their way up an embankment and onto dry land for the first time in hours. Octavia yearned to flop down and rest, but not yet. Not now. She could feel the tension carry through Alonzo's hand, as though he were a cat ready to spring.

Upon their arrival at the buzzer, it was clear why there had been no movement. No one was there. Blood and charred tissue smeared the cockpit where the legs would rest. The burns were serious, but evidentally the pilot could still walk.

Nausea struck her like a hoof to the gut. *The stillness of a purple dawn. The house a crisp shell. Mother and Father's bodies blackened, embracing. My bare feet lodged in mud as though I'm a tree. The air: smoke, ash, and the faint scent of cooked meat.*

"Lady, spare me," Octavia whispered, forcing her mind

to the image of the Tree. The branches swayed, stroked by light rain. She breathed through her Al Cala exercise and straightened, casting a glance back at Alonzo. His focus was on the wreckage. Calmer, she considered the smoldering heap as well.

Our attacker was seriously injured in the crash, the legs in particular. Burned flesh radiates a particularly loud song. If this person tries to strike at close range, I might have some warning.

"Damn." Alonzo glowered. He clenched his jaw and he holstered the gun again, staring at the empty craft as if he could make a body magically appear.

Octavia's arm ached, the pain sudden and penetrating to the marrow. She bit her lip to hold back a yelp. She circled the grove. The pressure in her arm intensified step-by-step, pain drowning out sensations in her fingertips. Peculiar, how sudden it was.

"I need a moment of privacy," she called over her shoulder.

"Oh." He paused. "Do be careful."

She edged around a thick bush, but instead of lifting her skirt for privy business, she rolled back her sleeve. Pain prickled like hot nettles, causing her fingers to fumble. She worked the bandage loose. The seal of wax practically popped into her right hand, followed by a gush of blood that pattered on the ground. Octavia gasped.

"Octavia?" Alonzo's pitch rose in alarm.

"I'm fine! I almost slipped. Mud." She stared at the blood still flowing from her arm, at the ground where little green leaves were sprouting. The tiny incision was vertical so that it would release a mere trickle of blood, but this . . . Why was the Lady demanding this much of her? The flow resembled a tipped teakettle. For most medicians, a few drops would suffice.

Finally, the blood slowed to a dribble. With trembling fingers, she replaced the wax, then rewound the bandage. Her wand eradicated any spatter on her hand and clothes. The loss of blood left her cold, shivering. Scared. A waft of cinnamon caused her to turn, afraid Alonzo was spying on her, and then she realized the scent came from her feet.

Where her blood fell, pampria grew.

Octavia choked back a hysterical giggle. Were her herbal woes that easy to remedy? No. These sprouts would need months or years until they were large enough to be harvested. She had never heard of a bloodletting causing the Lady's own blessed plants to grow.

At least now I'm away from Miss Percival and the others. This . . . this would give them another reason to hate me.

Alonzo wouldn't hate me, if he knew. He'd perk up like a cat spying a mouse, want to know more details. That coaxed a slight smile. *I almost wish to tell him, just to point out how dangerous I am—look, plants grow from my blood. Caskentia should be terribly frightened.*

I'm peculiar, not powerful.

She headed around the bush again, skirting the road, and glanced down. Footprints in the mud led back toward the road.

Alonzo was half sitting on the backside of the wreck as

he dug through the remnants. "I found the placard," he said, not looking up. "The craft is from a rental company out of Leffen. 'Tis a normal two-seater, as I suspected. The automatic gun was hastily installed on the front seat. The bolts are clean and new, likely done today."

"Ah. Someone was hunting for us."

"Yes." When he did look at her, his face was grim. "Either there is another assassin on the *Argus,* or Mr. Grinn failed to meet with someone this morning and they tailed us."

"Or perhaps both."

Alonzo's caramel skin seemed to darken. "Yes. Though I do not like to think of that possibility. The Dallowmen want you alive. No one in his right mind would want you dead." His expression was fierce.

"Well, someone's obviously not in his right mind." She motioned behind her. "I found footprints in the mud leading toward Leffen."

He stared south. "Might it be possible to reattach my leg?"

"I'll do my best."

She found a dry patch of dirt and grass and spread out the medician blanket. After drying the socket and mechanical leg, she tapped the edge of the copper circle. The Lady's scrutiny tingled across her skin as the conduit opened.

Usually in such operations, the medician would apply pampria to enhance the connection between nerves and wire while the mechanist verified that the mechanism worked. The task required synchrony between the two professionals as they melded magic and machine.

She pushed the leg into place. The sockets fit, but there was no change in the song of Alonzo's body—a song already strained by the stress of the day. She closed her eyes, then sprinkled the tiniest amount of pampria over his leg as she focused on both the intense muscle strain in his good leg and the connections in the amputation.

"Try to move your mechanical foot now." She placed a hand on his quadriceps just above the knee. The muscles hardened in quite an appealing way as he tried to move. The toes didn't bend.

"Can you feel anything?" she asked, frowning.

"I can feel the connection, but 'tis as though the leg is asleep. Dead." The stoicism in his words couldn't mask his concern.

"Drat. Perhaps the mechanism is shut off. I dare not open the compartment; I'd likely cause more harm than good. Can you try standing up within the circle?"

"Certainly." Alonzo pushed up from his hands, placing all his weight on the good leg as he stood erect. She eyed the mechanical leg. It didn't fall off, which was a good sign. The connectors had locked as soundly as the royal vault. He placed the sole against the blanket. The ankle flexed, barely, making the leg appear quite wooden.

"I think that's as good as we'll get," she said, shaking her head. At least the application of pampria would make him feel better. A curl of hair brushed her cheek and she tucked it beneath her headband again. She murmured thanks to the Lady as her fingers touched the copper threads of the blanket.

"At least 'tis connected, which is more than I had before," he said, stepping from the blanket. "Thank you."

"I wish it fully functioned. Do be careful. You can't move fast. You won't feel your toes if you trip on something, and you'll be more conscious of the weight of it as well."

"We do need to move, as fast as possible," he said, his jaw set grimly. "Or we have an even longer walk ahead of us."

Her head jerked up as she caught his meaning. "Oh. The wagon."

She quickly packed her satchel. Alonzo didn't need constant support but they still remained close, just in case.

It didn't come as a great surprise that their horse and wagon were gone. Fresh wheel tracks showed that the vehicle had gone south toward Leffen. Alonzo stood there for a moment, his jacket stained dark, his fists balled at his sides. If he still had a hat, she suspected he would have thrown it to the ground.

"I think I'm most upset that the assassin stole our lunch," said Octavia, sighing. She pressed a hand to her hollow, growling stomach. After that heavy bloodletting, she needed food, meat. She clenched her fists to hide the trembling.

Alonzo said nothing as his shoulders heaved up and down. She stared at him in alarm, and then his laughter boomed out so loudly it scared the birds from the tree above.

"You . . . after all that . . ." He faced her, wiping tears from his eyes. "Ah, Octavia. You do keep things in perspective." He looked toward the sky, where the sun had already descended forty-five degrees toward the horizon.

"Someone will drive along this road," she said.

Alonzo sighed. The poor man's good leg probably throbbed like fire, and Octavia had her own share of stiffness and strain.

"Eventually."

They both stared to the tapered point of the horizon, no horses or cabriolets in sight, and they began to walk.

Chapter 12

"*Now, really! Are you* going to sleep until that Lady's Tree of yours dies and turns the world to ice?"

Mrs. Stout's voice rang, clear and obnoxious, directly into Octavia's ear. Octavia moaned and turned her head away, her arm flailing to find a pillow. A beam of sunlight sliced through her shut lids and she couldn't help but wince.

"Tired," she said, the words hot and muffled against the pillow.

"Of course you're tired, child. You didn't get here until an obscene hour of the night." The words sounded harsh, but Mrs. Stout spoke with the same scolding fondness she had used for Leaf.

"Timeszit?"

"Past eight."

"Eight? Balderdash." She propped herself up. A mat of crazed brown hair blinded her. She shoved the hair from her eyes to see Mrs. Stout sitting on a chair beside the bed. She appeared especially prim in a powder-blue gown far superior in quality to anything she had worn on the airship. The shimmery blue complemented the bold streak in her hair. An antiquated corset uplifted her bosom in a spectacularly gravity-defying way, creating planets of flesh that hovered above an unblemished satin sky.

Octavia pushed her feet out onto the floor. Fierce cramps jolted through both legs and sent her sprawling backward onto the bed. They had walked for hours until a farmer with a wagon had come along.

Mrs. Stout's expression softened. "Oh, child. You should see about healing yourself."

"There's no time." *And definitely not the supplies.* She gritted her teeth and made herself stand, sparing a moment to massage both calves. Her stomach rumbled, clearly still in need despite the four stale scones she'd inhaled when they arrived at the hotel. The blood loss and the day of exercise had drained her. "This is the only full day in Leffen I have. You said it could take hours at the bank, and I must reattach Mr. Garret's leg this afternoon."

"You'll be the death of me, child." At that, Octavia arched an eyebrow, and Mrs. Stout burst out laughing. "Sorry."

"It would be funnier if it didn't nearly come to pass." Octavia stepped behind a dressing partition and found her burgundy and sailor dresses already laid out. Goodness, she had been sleeping soundly. She sniffed at the red dress, approving of the lingering lavender scent from the hotel laundry.

"I do need to talk to you, Octavia." Mrs. Stout stood on the other side of the screen. Octavia flinched in full expectation of more nagging about Alonzo, and at the same time was surprised to hear the woman use her first name. "I understand your circumstances yesterday were quite . . . extraordinary."

Octavia snorted softly as she slipped off her clothes. She had relayed some story about the stolen wagon, conveniently omitting the whole strafing assassin episode.

"I had a brief chat with Mr. Garret last night." Mrs. Stout spoke with the enthusiasm of one discussing a loved one's terminal illness. "He was quite apologetic, for all that means. But my concern is not with his behavior, but with appearances."

Octavia paused as she pulled on the burgundy dress. "Appearances?"

"You're young. He's young. You spent the entire day together in the countryside and return covered in muck—"

"Now, really, Mrs. Stout. You make it sound as though we took a rest day's carriage ride through the country and rutted like pigs. It was a *swamp*."

Not at all a proper locale for wooing. The memory of that conversation made her smile, even as it vexed her. What did Alonzo Garret really intend? His interest in her was clear, but it seemed unlikely they'd stay together long enough for anything to come to fruition. Whether she traveled to Delford or—Lady help her—stayed in Mercia, Alonzo would soon be out of her life.

Like Leaf. Please, let him have flown away somewhere safe, somewhere away from people.

"I just worry about you, that's all." Mrs. Stout sounded as if she would cry.

"I'm more concerned with staying alive," Octavia muttered.

"What was that?"

"Nothing." Octavia stood in front of the full-length mirror. She ran a hand through her thicket of hair. It was free of tangles due to a thorough brushing last night, yet still the slightest bit damp because she had fallen asleep so soon afterward. She worked her hair into three segments and formed a quick braid, then used some pins to bind it in a bun at her neck.

A quick check of her satchel found the signed letter from Miss Percival to present to the bank. Lifting the satchel strap into place, she discovered her shoulder sore as well.

"Come," Octavia said. "This will be a busy day."

LEFFEN WAS BUSTLING, BUT it was a different sort of bustle than that of Vorana. Certainly, there were draymen and steam cabriolets and horses, all competing for the same spot of road at the same time, but the buildings here were taller and more austere. The gray bricks wore a patina of soot. Wide cobbled sidewalks allowed people to flow like a river in spring thaw. In the press of humanity, Octavia found it hard to know which way was which. There were too many clashing hums of music, too many conflicting smells. She detected the hollow echo of amputated limbs, the weak notes of hunger, the distorted wails of severe infection. Alone in the crowd, Octavia would have hunkered against a wall and fought the urge to scream to block out the disorienting burble.

Mercia will be a thousand times worse.

Thank goodness, Mrs. Stout showed no hesitation,

advancing through the crowd like a barge on a river and forcing lesser boats aside. Octavia's fingers clutched at her satchel strap as if it were a lifeline in a tempest, and she followed. As if the cacophony of ill health wasn't enough, there was also the fact that her would-be assassin was somewhere out there, biding time until he struck again.

Alonzo had been grieved that he couldn't guard her as he had to work this morning, and last night Octavia had been dismissive of the risk. Now she acutely felt her vulnerability.

"News! Get your news from Mercia!" a man shouted over the din. "Waster kidnappings! Faltering banks! Auxiliary League Protests Eradication of Death Village! Read it all for a copper!"

"Waster kidnappings?" Octavia looked at Mrs. Stout, whose face had paled. "Have you heard anything about this?"

"No, child. I stayed in my room all day yesterday. I wonder . . . !"

Octavia wondered as well. If other medicians were being kidnapped, her recent ordeals might make more sense. No way was she paying a copper for the news, though. Trailing in Mrs. Stout's wake, she edged closer to the street and studied the ground as they walked several blocks. Finally, in the gutter she spied a discarded newspaper. With a quick eye to traffic, she stepped out and scooped up the sheet.

The signs for the Golden Harvest Bank jutted from the building. Glowstones lined the top and bottom, creating a mild glimmer even in broad daylight. Sheaves of wheat in shimmering bronze accompanied the words.

Octavia gasped as they entered the building, and the sound echoed. The Hotel Nennia had nothing on the opulence of this place. The floor was black marble so shiny she could see her own image at her feet. Crimson velvet panels adorned the walls accompanied by wainscoting of alabaster and gold leaf. Any metal surfaces gleamed in gold as well. Probably some forty people stood ahead of them, mostly men in suits, clutching hats. Ahead of the snaking line, attendants sat behind a gilt cage and a marble counter.

They shuffled into the queue. Octavia's feet throbbed, but she did her utmost to ignore it. She glanced at the newspaper in her hand. A bold headline read CASKENTIA FIREBOMBS DEATH VILLAGE; LADIES' AUXILIARY PROTESTS. "What is a death village?" she asked.

"That's a newfangled term for a village overwhelmed by pox. Caskentia has taken to eliminating everyone to prevent the spread of disease. Now, child, calm yourself—"

"Everyone?" Octavia did her best to keep her voice low, but several men turned to frown at her. "Pox is survivable, especially by healthy adults if they have proper hydration and care. Caskentia can't, they . . ."

She closed her eyes for a moment, swaying. She shouldn't be surprised. This was the country she loved, the country she labored for, and she knew well how they treated their own. The war was over. The killing needed to be over.

"Tut, tut. Of course they can. If killing a hundred means stopping the spread of illness that could kill five thousand. It's all about control."

"You can't believe that this . . . firebreak strategy is

right, Mrs. Stout. Or just. Pox is terrible, that's true, but it can be survived with some care."

"Oh, child." Mrs. Stout's expression was of pity. "Who do you expect to care? The Queen?" She kept her voice at a discreet level. "Her Daggers—which likely include some infernals who set that village ablaze—would raze the majority of the kingdom if it meant preserving the royal family. The crown *is* the kingdom. They won't risk this new bout of pox working its way into Mercia or the palace."

"Ah yes. It's easier to burn the illiterate nothings. No one will miss them." Octavia barely managed to utter the words. Just as no one spared a memory for her village, no one but her—and Alonzo.

Fire. Caskentia using fire, just like the Waste.

"I wish this were a different world, child." Pain flashed through Mrs. Stout's colorfully shaded eyes. "Now, to change the subject! Where's that story about the kidnappings?"

Yes. The kidnappings. As if that were a pleasanter topic. Octavia blinked the heat of memory away and read on. YOUNG SOCIALITE KIDNAPPED; THIRD GIRL IN MERCIA THIS WEEK: "IT'S THE WASTERS!" CRIES FATHER. A small picture of the man showed his face as distraught and ruddy in shaded gray.

A quick scan revealed no mention of medicians. The kidnapping incidents involved teenage girls of solid moral repute and upper-tier families.

"I had hoped the news would be more relevant," Octavia muttered, shoving the newspaper onto a credenza as they shuffled forward. She certainly didn't fit with the pattern. She was too old and too poor.

"Kethan's bastards!" a customer at the counter yelled, grabbing her attention. Two bank clerks in white grabbed the man by the arm and dragged him toward the door. "One payment late, and you take my farm? Where'm I supposed to live, what do I tell my—" He sobbed as he was shoved out the door.

Mrs. Stout flinched. "I do hate when people say that. King Kethan . . . was a man of discretion. He should be remembered for the Gilded Age, not in tavern footle!" She lowered her voice to a murmur. "I suspect my cousin was behind the popularity of the saying."

"Did you know your . . . cousin well?" Octavia thought of the haughty-looking portrait stashed aboard ship.

"A bit, yes, but we were never close. She was a nesh of a girl. Would sob at the slightest thing, quite insecure. Certainly not the one anyone expected to be Queen."

At long last, they stood at the head of the line. Octavia pulled out the sealed paperwork from Miss Percival. Her thumb stroked the circle of hardened wax. A light flashed at a teller station far down the row, and she headed that way.

"Greetings!" Octavia said, smiling at the woman on the other side of the golden cage. Mrs. Stout's footsteps stopped just behind her.

A dour face stared through bars. The woman's cheeks were elongated, the nose flat. Dull eyes gave a cursory glance that betrayed no actual interest. Octavia was reminded of a horse—a very plain, sell-for-meat kind of horse.

"Do you have an account?" the teller asked.

"No, but I have a withdrawal slip for an account here. Five silvers, please." She slid the paper through a designated slot in the bars.

The woman took it up with fumbling fingers. "Percival, of the Medician Academy, to Miss Octavia Leander. Wait here."

She turned and walked through rows of desks to the back of the room. The entire wall consisted of wooden drawers, a thousand at least. The teller opened several and pulled nothing out. She walked through a doorway and returned minutes later with a decidedly round fellow. A few strands of hair made a bold attempt to lessen the intense glare from his shiny pate.

"You are Miss Leander," he said, greeting her with a clipped Mercian accent. A monocle made one eye appear monstrous and magnified.

"I am." She frowned, suddenly ill at ease.

"There appears to be a bit of a problem here, m'lady. The paperwork you brought is in order and matches the account holder's signature and seal in our records, but her account here was closed six months ago."

Octavia's mouth went dry. "What?"

"Perhaps she forgot about that fact while drafting her letter for you," the man continued. The teller stood beside him, her head tilted as if she were listening, but her eyes were as vacant as those of a mechanical.

"No. Miss Percival wouldn't forget something like that." Panic clenched at her chest. This couldn't be happening. "This is the money I'm owed for my last year of work. Miss Percival knows I need the funds."

"I am sorry, Miss Leander." The man's voice cooled. He waved an arm, and Octavia heard heavy footsteps behind her. He was calling a guard—on her?

"Pardon me." Mrs. Stout stepped forward and leaned on the ledge of the counter. "I'm a friend of both Miss Percival and Miss Leander, and I have difficulty believing that such an old, dear friend of mine would error in such a way."

"Perhaps it was no error." His gaze made no effort to surmount the magnificent summit of her cleavage. "We hear this throughout the day, Mrs. . . . ?

"Stout. Viola Stout."

"Yes. Mrs. Stout, these things happen. Perhaps she forgot about the closure of the account, or addressed the wrong bank, or it was no error at all. But the plain fact is, we have no money under her name and we cannot help Miss Leander."

Mrs. Stout seemed to poof up like a riled cat. "Now listen here—" The guard placed a hand on her shoulder and she flushed.

"Mrs. Stout, it'll all be fine," Octavia said. Dizzied by this development, she looked to the manager again. "I will contact Miss Percival and get to the truth of this matter. Thank you for your time."

Lies, all lies. It'd cost Octavia a silver for an urgent courier to travel north by buzzer to connect with Miss Percival, but she knew very well the academy had no money. She wouldn't have the other girls starve on her account.

She tucked the paperwork back in her bag and all but fled. Behind her, Mrs. Stout's footsteps stomped like a shod draft horse.

"The audacity of that man! This is most assuredly a scheme. No wonder they were forcing out so many people. This bank is holding money hostage, no doubt. Insinuating that Miss Percival is in such poor control of her funds—"

"But she is in poor control of her funds," said Octavia. Mrs. Stout gaped at her. "Caskentia has not paid her for our work at the front."

"None of it?" Mrs. Stout was aghast.

"Not a copper, last I heard. The academy survives by farming. We haven't been able to buy any of the Lady's herbs, prices being as they are. Everything must be grown on site. Most patients pay through barter."

Octavia pushed open the door. A chill wind blasted her in the face, but seemed mild compared to the new coldness against her heart. Her supplies of herbs were low, her supply of coins even lower. The two-day wagon ride from Mercia to Delford would probably cost a silver for cramped quarters in a livery transport, without accounting for bedding or food.

"I will write her a letter later in the day, and also address a note to my solicitor! The correspondence may reach him in Mercia the day before we arrive. Oh, that bank manager!" Mrs. Stout shuddered, bosom quivering. "I know they are holding something back, child, I know it."

Someone was holding back, yes. But Octavia was no longer confident that the bank was the guilty party.

Chapter 13

Mr. Garret awaited them outside the hotel. “Miss Leander.” He frowned. “Is something wrong?”

She managed a tepid smile. “Minor things compared to attempted murder and mayhem.”

He didn’t seem quite sure how to take that. “I see. Mrs. Stout, good afternoon to you.”

“Mr. Garret.” Mrs. Stout’s greeting was a growl. “Miss Leander, I’ll write and—”

“Thank you, Mrs. Stout. We really must be going,” said Octavia, cutting her off with a wave of her hand. “I’ll see you later.”

Alonzo tipped his hat and murmured farewell. Octavia matched his stiff stride as they walked down the street. The crowds around them were too thick for the sort of conversation they needed to have, and so she welcomed the companionable silence.

Rows of smokestacks lined the horizon. Black clouds were belched into the clear afternoon sky. The smell of the place carried in the air; it stank of heated metal and coal and the grime of industry. Workers, men and women both, were smudged by coal from head to toe. Automated work carts rumbled by, treads clacking loudly on the cobbles.

Disgust twisted a knot in her gut. No trees in sight; no birds. Her lungs felt constrained as if squeezed by a corset.

The crowds around them thinned. She turned to Alonzo and murmured, "Have you found out anything in your investigation?"

He glanced around, casual yet wary. "Yes, in fact. Our stolen wagon was returned to the livery stable yesterday evening, everything in good care. No one saw the thief. My crutch was left in the back, though the assailant did help himself to our lunch."

"Well, it would have spoiled by evening, anyway."

"Quite. I also went to the Leffen Buzzer Company. They rented out a buzzer yesterday morning. The entire exchange was done through a courier, the payment in hard coin, and no names were exchanged due to the generous funds involved. They were most cross when I told them their vehicle's whereabouts."

Octavia arched an eyebrow. "Interesting." *Now he sounds like a Dagger out of a novel.*

"I believe you will find this place interesting as well." He pointed to a tall shop ahead, its facade blackened by soot. Brass pipes snaked the outer walls, and on closer look, they were not merely for function. Whirligigs in metal shades from gold to nickel spun from fittings atop the pipes. The lower blades were wrapped in steel cages, but the highest adornments on the wall spun free, the blades clinking with the stiff breeze.

A man stood in the doorway, bulky forearms crossed at his chest. He was thin yet solid, a shock of black hair draping over his forehead. Silver streaks in his hair caught the light. Beneath smudges, his skin had the texture of gently worn leather. The hum of his body denoted the loss of both hands, which were covered by black gloves.

"That's a pretty rigid walk you got there," said the man, jerking his head toward Alonzo.

"'Tis this or hop." Alonzo grimaced as he stepped up onto the doorsill.

"Walking is your best choice, unless you wish to pantomime a spring rabbit," said the man. "I could rig up some long ears for you, maybe find some cotton fluff for a tail. If you're going to hop, you may as well have some style."

Alonzo glowered.

The man's face creased in a wide grin. "I take that as a no. And you are, m'lady . . . ?"

"I'm Octavia Leander, sir," she said with a curtsy. Her satchel swayed against her thigh. She stood to find his dark gaze had narrowed.

"Alonzo. You said you were bringing a medician, not that you were bringing *her*. She's the one who . . . ?"

Alonzo mutely nodded.

"Damn." The man ran a hand through his hair. "Caskentia, Caskentia."

Octavia felt her hackles rise. "Is that a problem, sir . . . ?"

"Dryn, Kellar Dryn." He openly appraised her. "I know your work. Had more than one boy come here from the front with a nice, clean amputation, perfectly prepped for attachment. No issues with straight cuts or gangrene. I had to nose about to find out that a single Percival was behind all of that handiwork. Then there was that water contamination at the pass."

"I—I had no idea I had a reputation. It's not really me who heals, of course. It's the Lady."

"You might be the conduit but your hand still has a signature. Please, come in, we can go straight to the workshop."

His handiwork carried a signature as well. She certainly never would have expected a master mechanist to possess two mechanical hands. It made his work all the more extraordinary.

The atmosphere within the shop struck her as bright, a contrast to the makeshift sheds of mechanists at the front. The heavier stink of a forge wafted through the first doorway, but Dryn continued to walk through an archway at the end of the hall.

A stained glass window as tall as Octavia herself depicted the Saint's Road in all its glory and cast dappled color onto the floor. The floor tiles contained an inlaid copper oval easily seven feet in length. A wooden platform with adjustable panels had been wheeled into the middle, the brakes in place. Alonzo leaned against the platform, grunting as he pried his boots off.

Dryn stood back, hands at his hips, lips clicking in reproval. "What exactly happened again?"

Alonzo related the tale of his leg as Octavia set up her supplies.

"Well, you two had quite the day, didn't you? So we have the possibility of water damage or an unaligned crystal or disengaged wires."

Alonzo settled himself in the seat within the circle, his trousers rolled up past the knee. Dryn hummed as he palpated the surface of the mechanical limb. With a small screwdriver, he unfastened an inner panel along the calf. He peered inside.

"It's dry," he said. "And there are loose connectors."

Alonzo's sigh of relief was audible. "Is that the worst of it?"

"We'll see," said Dryn. He glanced back at Octavia. "Are you ready?"

"Yes." With the oval so large, it required fully working within its confines. She crossed the copper lines to stand near her pampria, and then stooped with her fingers hovering over the circle.

"Pray, by the Lady let me mend thy ills," she said.

The circle crackled into life. She felt how readily Alonzo acquiesced in the sureness of his body's song. He had absolute trust in her. That warmed her even more than the Lady's presence. She stood and rested her hand on his bare knee. Hairs felt prickly yet soft against her palm, the skin warm.

Dryn leaned over Alonzo's good leg as he tweaked the wires within the case. The mechanical leg jolted, and he cursed, shaking his head. "There's a single gear out of alignment and it won't budge. Perhaps it needs the Lady's persuasive touch?"

"Let me see." He and Octavia switched positions.

A glowstone within the leg illuminated the minute mechanical construction within. The confines were tight, every inch occupied by gears and flexing bands and the solid central supports of the metal tibia and fibula.

"This," said Dryn, motioning with tiny forceps.

She could see the gear in question, on the far side. It was so small it would be easy to dismiss, and yet it connected to the belt system that played the role of tendon. She closed her eyes and breathed as in her Al Cala.

"Lady," she whispered, "gaze through your poor servant's eyes and lend your aid, so that this man's leg may work again."

A vision of the Tree brightened her mind. Despite the clear heavens above Leffen, this sky stewed with clouds. Thunder rumbled as wind whipped the high branches and sent debris falling to the canopy of normal-size trees far below. Keen awareness of the Lady trickled through her veins as warmth whirled in her eyeballs.

Octavia opened her eyes. The errant gear, in reality the size of a thumbnail, now looked as large as a belt buckle. She had expected greater awareness, but nothing of this magnitude. Stunned, she almost closed her eyes, but remembered herself and forced them open. The heat reminded her of a kettle billowing steam in her face, and yet there was no pain.

She took in deep breaths. *The Lady is using me. No reason to fear. This is like lifting Mrs. Stout.* She focused on that single errant gear. It shifted. It was a movement of millimeters that loomed in her vision. In that instant, the magical magnification vanished. The world swam slightly as she shuffled aside. Dryn resumed his work inside the cavity.

"Impressive." Dryn spared her a glance. "My usual medician requires thirty minutes of meditation to get the sort of results you achieved in seconds."

She shrugged off the praise and scooped up some pampria. The fragments of leaves vanished upon contact with Alonzo's knee.

Alonzo propped himself up on his elbows. "Kellar, has your wife heard interesting news from the Waste of late?"

"Why not ask her?" Dryn offered, his tone casual. He grabbed pliers from the tray. His arm swung out and banged against the invisible barricade of the circle, the impact soundless but for his gasp of surprise. "Good God." He stared at Octavia.

"Sorry. When I make a circle, it has a certain . . . potency."

"That's no joke. A circle usually feels like a wall of spiderwebs. This is akin to brick." Dryn shook his head, clearly awed.

"Kellar." Alonzo cleared his throat. "I thought it best to ask you first. We have little time remaining in Leffen. Also, your wife can be more intimidating than my mother."

Dryn snorted. "I'll have to tell Adana that. She'll take it as a compliment." He reached over and tweaked the row of metal toes, testing the joints.

Octavia recognized her cue and focused. Heat surged beneath Alonzo's skin. She imagined the connections between the leg and brain like the Lady's roots and branches, the unique duties of roots and leaves. She drew her finger down the hard knob of his knee to the smooth metal extension, dragging the heat with her all the way to his big toe.

Alonzo's leg jerked, his toes flinching. She smiled.

"Thank you, Lady," she whispered. The faint buzz in the back of her mind dissipated, the sudden silence strange and almost disturbing. The burden of her life debt had been removed, but more than that she was grateful for Alonzo's sake. She stooped down to touch the copper bands, and that pressure released as well. "You're able to leave the circle now," she said to Dryn.

"Thank you, Lady, indeed," said Alonzo. "And thanks to you, Kellar, Octavia."

"It's the least I can do." She inclined her head. "Now I'm curious. What do you expect Mr. Dryn or his wife to know of the Waste?"

Kellar Dryn nodded. "Exactly. I'm just a mild-mannered mechanist."

"You, mild-mannered?" Alonzo snorted. "You have all the domesticity of a wild boar. This is where I stop pretending that you are ignorant of my mission. Octavia needs to have you available as a resource. You both know things about Caskentia and the Waste, things you are not meant to know."

"Alonzo, shut up." Dryn's voice held an edge.

"Damn it, Kellar. The Waste has changed tactics. They are trying to kill Octavia, and have made more than one attempt. I could very well be caught in the cross fire. Octavia must have someone to turn to if I am gone."

Alonzo's words caused a vicious twist to her gut as she turned to stare at Dryn. "You're spies? Daggers, like Alonzo?"

"Now really, Alonzo. You tell your mark what you are? Softhearted fools like you aren't meant to be Clockwork Daggers." Dryn's eyes fluttered half shut as he sighed. "But she is favored by the Lady, more than any other medician I've ever encountered. That's both a blessing and a curse. God knows what Adana endured.

"To clarify, we are not Daggers. Caskentia uses my wife as a resource for translation, but only that. We work to preserve knowledge, the sort of knowledge that'd get us arrested and declared collaborators of the Waste."

"If not shot outright," Alonzo murmured.

"True. Why waste any expense or effort on imprisonment?" Dryn grimaced.

"I love Caskentia, but I'm not blind to the government's machinations," said Octavia, frowning. "If Alonzo is a Dagger and allied with you, does that make him a sort of double agent?"

Dryn barked out a laugh. "No. Not in Alonzo's case. Oh, he walks a fine line, that's for sure, and Caskentia wouldn't be pleased, but he's something worse—an idealist."

"'Tis a sad day when optimism is mocked."

"Every day is a sad day here." Dryn sobered. "Queen Evandia is at the head of a body beset with gangrene. How long until the heart fails?"

She thought of the soldier rotting in the alley in Vorana, of the clock with its burden of bodies, of Miss Percival and the academy left utterly destitute.

"The heart already fails," she whispered.

"Maybe that's why the Lady has brought you here," said Dryn, expression contemplative.

Octavia frowned. As if she could heal a government. She could scarcely heal anyone at all.

Dryn looked to Alonzo. "When does your airship leave?"

"Late morning tomorrow."

"Adana will be in her office then. Both of you, go to her."

Alonzo sat upright. "My thanks to you, Kellar." He tottered and Octavia grabbed his forearm to steady him.

"Take it slowly. Put the pressure on your good leg and then bear down on the mechanical toes first."

"I have done this before, you know." He stared at where her fingers clutched his arm. The muscles were tight in her grip, his skin delightfully warm, but she shivered as if she were cold. She relinquished her hold and looked away, making sure her supplies were packed.

"Knowing this fool, he'll be back again," Dryn muttered.

Alonzo gingerly stepped across the floor, with Octavia lingering behind as a precaution. By the time he reached the hallway, his stride was back to normal. The song of his body rang as strongly as when they'd first met. The blessing had allowed him to mend from yesterday's travails abnormally fast.

Relieved as she was, she felt a tinge of regret, selfish as it was. She'd lost her excuse to touch him.

Kellar Dryn stood by the door to the atelier. "It was an honor to meet you, Miss Leander." He bowed and extended a hand. Octavia recognized the gesture and reached outward. His kiss to her knuckles was quick and professional.

"Thank you," she said. "I'm glad to know you're here, in case."

But Alonzo will not die. I won't let him.

Factory exhaust blotted out the sky. Octavia gagged at a foulness like ammonia. Bells chimed from the nearest building, and not two seconds later, workers exited in a flood. They scarcely talked. They were an exhausted mob, blackened by coke. Even the children looked old beyond their time—backs stooped, faces sagging with exhaustion.

She took it all in as she struggled to breathe against the stench. "Mercia is like this, isn't it?"

"'Tis. With a thousand more factories and far more people, besides."

"The beautiful places you spoke of before. I would never see them, would I? What about blue sky? Here, there's a strong wind, but in Mercia . . ."

"Octavia . . ."

"Yes, yes. I know you mean well. But this . . . everything . . . I want a cottage and a garden. A home, a family." She flinched, not intending to say the last out loud. It wasn't something she even wanted to think about.

"Trees," she continued, looking around. "I cannot imagine living without the sight of trees."

"I am sorry."

"Will sorry keep me alive? Will sorry grant me freedom and peace? Oh Lady. I'm the one who's sorry, Alonzo. This isn't your fault, not at the heart."

He stopped. "Do not apologize, Octavia. You asked for none of this. But I want you to look around us, right now."

She did. They had entered the commercial district, and the crowd had thickened around them like a stew set to simmer for hours. Cabriolet horns blared their crude symphony as a buzzer whined somewhere above.

Alonzo stepped closer, dangerously close, his shoulder at face level. She breathed in, detecting the clarity of his scent even through foul exhaust from the smelters.

"I do not want you to die." His voice was soft, tender. His eyes searched hers. "Anyone around us could be your assassin. They could trail us, even now. I am one man, Octavia. One inadequate man." Bitterness seeped into his tone. "I have . . . my orders, but I think that once we are in Mercia, you will be in good care. Medicians are few. This arrangement will be temporary. Caskentia should be blessed to have you."

"Oh. Keeping me alive is for the benefit of Caskentia. I see." For some silly reason, she was disappointed.

He brought his hand to her face, and with one callused finger he followed the line of her cheek. The pressure was as glancing as a feather's stroke, and yet it sent shivers through her. "Perhaps I have my own selfish reasons," he said, then turned toward the hotel again.

"Oh," Octavia said, and followed.

Chapter 14

"I need to speak with Mrs. Stout," Alonzo said. The high brick spire of the Hotel Nennia was visible ahead. He had said nothing for blocks, and now his voice had lost that huskiness that caused Octavia's heart to race a little faster. Instead, he sounded confident, assured.

"Do you, now? If you're truly in need of more prickling wit and lectures on morality, I would be happy to oblige."

A half smile softened his face. "I will endure her sharp commentary. This is necessary."

She eyed him with suspicion. "Very well."

The hotel lobby was bustling with the evening's flow of guests. She recognized several people from the airship and nodded greeting. A mechanical dog scampered underfoot and emitted tinny barks. At the far side of the lobby was the other steward, Little Daveo. He wore similar clothes to Alonzo, a brown suit tailored to his small body.

"Look! There's Little Daveo," she said, nodding toward him.

"Indeed." Alonzo and Daveo waved to each other across the room.

The lift doors opened. "Oh! Miss Leander!" Mrs. Wexler stood there, her pale-faced husband at her side.

"Mr. Wexler, Mrs. Wexler," said Octavia. Beside her, Alonzo bowed low and repeated the names as well.

Mrs. Wexler focused her steely gaze on Octavia. "You did not come to our symposium."

Octavia didn't reply immediately, taking several long seconds to grind her teeth. "I never said I would, Mrs. Wexler. I had other engagements. Mr. Wexler, how are you recovering?"

"Well." The Wexlers stepped from the lift, and she followed Alonzo's lead and slipped inside.

"Miss Leander—" Mrs. Wexler began.

Octavia granted her a pleasant smile and pressed the button to close the doors. "Have a good evening." The wrought-iron doors shut with a whoosh of air, as tight as the royal vault. Octavia sagged against the wall as the lift began to rumble upward. "Goodness. That woman is like a barnacle."

"That barnacle is on the passenger list for the final leg to Mercia."

She sighed. "And here I am, unable to afford laudanum."

"As pesky as Mrs. Wexler may be, 'tis worth keeping an eye on her and her husband, even from afar. As you noted, they have stayed close to you."

"Oh, no. You . . . you think they could be behind these attacks?" She couldn't repress a chill.

"We must consider everyone." A bell dinged and the cage doors opened.

Octavia unlocked the room door without a sound. She heard mumbling and the rustling of papers as she entered the parlor of the suite. Mrs. Stout sat hunched over an ornate desk, leaning on one elbow and scribbling with her free hand. A stack of books sat beside her—thin composition books, their bindings worn and in shades of yellow and blue.

"Mrs. Stout?" Octavia said.

Mrs. Stout screeched and leaped up. The chair toppled backward and papers danced through the air. She whirled around, pen in hand like a dagger. "You!" She sagged forward, gasping. "Don't startle me like that, child! Oh goodness, you gave me a start! I thought someone . . ."

The dread expression said it all. "I'm sorry, Mrs. Stout. That wasn't my intent at all. I brought up Mr. Garret as well. He wished to speak with you."

Alonzo plucked one of the papers from the floor and examined it as he stood. "I do believe that Mrs. Stout may wish to speak with us as well." His face turned stony as he held the page toward Octavia.

She squinted to read it. "That's sheer footle." Line after line consisted of absolute gibberish, dashes and lines and shapes that bore no resemblance to letters of the alphabet.

"No, 'tis not." His grim gaze focused on Mrs. Stout. "This is a cipher. And who are you working for in this regard?"

Octavia looked between them. "Are you suggesting Mrs. Stout is . . . ? That's as likely as Caskentia creating the Waste, Al . . . Mr. Garret."

Mrs. Stout raised her chin, eyes defiant. "I work for no

one but myself, Mr. Garret. I do not have to explain myself to an *airship's steward*."

"Then explain it to me, please," said Octavia, matching Mrs. Stout's imperious tone.

Mrs. Stout pursed her lips. "Well, yes. I should explain this matter to you, but must *he* be present?"

"I believe Mr. Garret to be much more knowledgeable than I in the way of ciphers, and I trust him with my life. Whatever you're doing, please, kindly explain it to the both of us."

"A steward, knowledgeable in ciphers? That does not comfort me any. Quite the contrary."

"Please, Mrs. Stout," said Octavia. Mrs. Stout sighed heavily and nodded as she motioned to the vacant chairs of the parlor.

Octavia set down her satchel and claimed one of the plush armchairs. Alonzo's body seemed strung so tight he could have been played like a harp. He sat straight in a chair, one hand near his waist where his gun was holstered. *Surely he wouldn't shoot Mrs. Stout?* Octavia felt the urge to get between them, to soften this terrible tension, but forced herself to sit and wait. To listen. Mrs. Stout gathered that stack of books and carried them to Alonzo. He accepted them, surprise on his face.

"If you must know, I've been deciphering this code for the past day and a half. I have made some progress, I think." She sat down, primly, ankles crossed. Her white-gloved hands rested on her lap. At that moment, she was the very picture of a dowager queen.

"And where have you seen such codes before?" Alonzo flipped a book open and scanned through its pages, all while keeping a chary eye on Mrs. Stout.

"Well! You know, or suspect. I may as well not pretend otherwise. I encountered it as a girl, of course. Father often used such codes in communicating with his Daggers throughout the realm. I wasn't supposed to pay attention to such things, but being of a stubborn nature and an only child, I did as I would. These books came from the luggage of Mr. Grinn."

"Mr. Grinn!" Octavia gasped.

Mrs. Stout granted her a small nod and smug smile. "When we walked into the promenade and I saw him at the window, I knew he was suspect. I knew it! While Mr. Garret ran to the window, I struck the service bells. With everyone clustered at the windows, I dashed to Mr. Grinn's berth. I picked the lock—yes, gape as you will, but I do have some tricks up my sleeve! My immediate assumption was that Mr. Grinn was behind my . . . incident and the poisoning as well. I wanted proof. I found it."

"This is a highly sophisticated code from the Dallows," Alonzo said, frowning as he skimmed. "These are your pencil notations?"

"Yes. You do know your ciphers. By my count, there are over four hundred different symbols used in those pages. It's a work in progress, of course. I first tried applying mathematical formulas or letter codes, but with that number it was clear that the method was more complex. I believe that each symbol represents a syllable of speech."

Alonzo rubbed at his bristled chin. "I do believe in one day you have progressed further than some of the best minds in Mercia have in months."

"And where have *you* seen such codes before, Mr. Garret?" Mrs. Stout's tone was ice.

"You did not tell her?" Alonzo said, looking at Octavia.

"Of course I didn't! What do you take me for? It was enough that we both knew who she . . . might be. I had no desire to compound things unnecessarily." *Mr. Grinn, Mrs. Stout, Alonzo, the Dryns—is anyone who they appear to be?*

Alonzo leaned back. "Majolico."

"What?" Octavia stared at him. The word was nonsense, same as that code on the page.

"Oh my." Mrs. Stout raised a hand to her lips. "You're a Dagger."

"'Tis an old code word," he said to Octavia. "Still used with the royal family. Pretend you didn't hear it."

She nodded as she committed it to memory, picturing the spelling in her mind.

"You're a Clockwork Dagger. And you know who I am. Oh God." Mrs. Stout leaned forward, both hands against her face. "You've sworn an oath to Evandia, haven't you? Then you must . . . I . . ."

"I have sworn no oath to your cousin the Queen, not yet." His tone was gentle. "I am, in truth, little more than an apprentice. My taking the oath has been delayed by my superiors. I am not breaking my word to Queen Evandia by keeping your secret. It will not be forced from me."

Mrs. Stout nodded. She worked her jaw as if she would

speak, jowls jiggling, and was quiet several long moments. "The word of a Dagger is everything, or so my father said. Trust above all."

"Trust above all," Alonzo repeated.

"But I have no reason to trust you. Clockwork Daggers—Caskentia itself—are not what they used to be. Evandia, she . . . sits in her palace as everything rots around her. Even if you say you're not part of that lot, the corrosion is on you. If you keep my promise, it means you violate your oath as a Dagger once you have taken it. What will your word mean then, steward?"

Mrs. Stout and Alonzo stared at each other from across the room. The tension between them was thick, suffocating.

"I trust him." Octavia broke the silence.

Weary gratitude softened Alonzo's face. "That means much to me, Octavia. As for what my word becomes, Mrs. Stout, I see what Mercia is. I do not plan to stand by idly and accept corruption as the status quo. Things have changed for the worse. They can change for the better."

"He's an idealist," Octavia said, echoing Dryn.

Mrs. Stout arched an eyebrow, revealing the broad purple of her eye shadow. "You intend to take a stand against Evandia? Truly?" A smile quirked the corners of her lips. "Well, you're a fool then, albeit a noble one." Like one of Mrs. Stout's book heroes, no doubt. She scrutinized Alonzo, nodding as if he suddenly met some standard of approval.

"Yet I am left wondering how you were able to break

such an advanced code on your own, Mrs. Stout," said Alonzo. "Surely as a child this was not your hobby?"

"It was all a game to me, back then. But I have developed the skill in recent years. My husband was Donovan Stout, you see, of Cloak and Cowl Publishing."

Octavia burst out laughing. "You mean, all of those copper novels you read . . . ?"

Mrs. Stout beamed. "Are from my husband's company, yes. Well, my company now. I have penned some fifty novels myself. Dreadful, delightful little things, under a dozen different names. I often incorporate ciphers based on the ones I recall as a child. Simplified, of course, but it adds to the aura of mystery. We've even published a few books composed entirely of codes and they sold quite well. Most of the books are murder mysteries, of course."

"Speaking of murder mysteries." Alonzo met Octavia's eyes, and she had a sudden sense of dread. "The reason why I wished to palaver with you, Mrs. Stout, is to help me to convince Miss Leander here that voluntarily coming with me to Mercia is in her best interest. You see, in the past day there has been another attempt on her life—"

At that, Mrs. Stout exploded in indignation. "What?" She stood, face flushed, bosom heaving. "Are you all right, child?"

"I'm quite all right," Octavia said, giving Alonzo a pointed glare.

"As you see, she is intact and well." He said this the way a person soothes a spooked horse. Immediately, Mrs. Stout's agitations decreased. "The latest attempt—"

"The second," interjected Octavia. "Saying 'latest' makes it sound as if there've been a dozen."

Annoyance drove his brows together. "Second, yes. It took place in the swamp yesterday. A buzzer with an automated gun attacked us. It crashed, and the assailant then stole our wagon."

"A thief and a would-be murderer," muttered Mrs. Stout. Her flush darkened and she sat down again as if deflated. "My goodness."

"I have the jurisdiction, of course, to take Miss Leander into my custody and force her into a ward in Mercia." Or do the same to Mrs. Stout. The intensity of his gaze made Octavia turn away and study the paisley pattern on the parlor walls. "She is opposed to this for various reasons. But damn it all, whoever is behind these attempts will not give up."

"Oh dear. This is quite serious," Mrs. Stout said in a most droll tone. "Child, you have driven this man—a Clockwork Dagger—to swear in the presence of ladies."

"I haven't driven him to do anything!"

Alonzo cleared his throat. "You know what I am up against, Mrs. Stout."

"Yes, quite. A stubborn girl is a particular sort of creature. I know from experience." She gave Octavia a gimlet eye. "I've had to be in such a position before, of course, leaving behind my expectations and loved ones." Mrs. Stout took in a deep, quivering breath. "To survive, I sacrificed part of myself. My name, my heritage, the very essence of who I was. You may very well need to do the same."

Octavia stood, fists balled. "I know that guarded custody in Mercia will likely preserve my life, but . . ."

Gray skies. Gray buildings. People gray with soot and sickness. No Delford or garden or greenery or birds.

But if that's what it takes to stay alive . . .

"How long would I need to stay in Mercia?" Octavia asked, forcing the words through her clenched throat. She knew he didn't know the answer, but she had to ask nevertheless.

Deep inside, it was as though part of her started to atrophy and turn gray as well.

Alonzo remained quiet for several long seconds. "I must speak with my superiors, make them understand . . . the situation has changed."

"Wasters." Mrs. Stout's voice was sharp. "I still cannot see why they would want Octavia dead. Her worth is greater than gold. Even during combat, Wasters have never targeted medicians."

" 'Tis why the situation is so perplexing. No one should desire her death." Alonzo sank into his chair, haggard and weary.

"I'll go with you to Mercia, Mr. Garret," said Octavia, the words a hoarse whisper. "With the hope that it's temporary, that you and your Daggers can figure out why this is happening and that I can carry on soon."

The people of Delford will continue to die. I may not have been able to do much for them now, with my supplies as they are, but I could have doctored them. Done something.

"Oh, child, I know this is hard for you." Mrs. Stout

walked over and embraced her, the scent of rose water like a cloud around her. Octavia allowed herself to be squeezed. "But it will keep you alive. Focus on that!"

Octavia could only nod.

Mr. Garret stood as well, hat in his hands. "I must get to work now that my leg is fully functioning again. Oct— Miss Leander, I will see you at nine in the morning for our appointment? And these books . . . I know this is your dedicated project, Mrs. Stout, but tomorrow we meet with an authority of the Waste and its literature. She would find this work most intriguing."

"A woman, is it? A Caskentian agent?" asked Mrs. Stout. Her eyes narrowed.

"Not directly. An academic with a full department at her disposal. She is a resource for the government, but is her own person, without question."

"Mercia is less than two days away with a good wind. There's no way I can translate it all on my own." Mrs. Stout released a huff of breath. "The words in those books may save Miss Leander's life. That's the only reason I will hand them over, you understand?" She aimed a pudgy finger at Alonzo's face. "It's not because I trust you, or that woman academic. It's not even because I like you. I don't. But if you can help keep this girl alive, then so be it. Give me tonight to draft my own copies of my work. I can hand you the books tomorrow."

"Understood. Miss Leander, I wish you a good night." Mr. Garret bowed, his gaze on her heavy.

"Mr. Garret." She bobbed her head stiffly.

He left with a quiet click of the door. Mrs. Stout immediately turned to her. "Oh, child. I know this is so difficult for you—" She stepped forward as if to hug her again and Octavia retreated, a hand raised.

"Please, Mrs. Stout. I know you mean well. I just . . . I need to be alone for now."

"I see. Of course. Whatever you need. Let me know when you are ready for dinner. Oh goodness, I have a lot to do. I'd best get started again . . ."

Octavia retreated to her room. *Mercia. I'm going to Mercia. Just for a while. Just to survive.* The pressure of withheld sobs tightened her chest. She looked out the window. The winds had shifted, bringing billows of filthy gray to suffocate downtown and blot out the blue heavens. Below, people walked with veils and scarves draped across their faces, most all of them accustomed to the foulness.

Could I adapt like that? Will I?

She curled up on the carpet, her face pressed to her knees. The vision of the Lady's Tree came to mind, as brilliant and green as ever beneath a gray sky—a cozy one, the scent of rain thick on the air.

To think, I'll be locked in that landscape of steel and brick, so very close to true artifacts of the Lady, and I will never know them myself.

Tears flowed, and in her mind, even the Tree was deluged by the torrents.

Chapter 15

Mr. Garret awaited her outside the lobby the next morning. "Miss Leander, I hope sleep was kind to you." He accepted the extra parcel from her arm. Mrs. Stout had gathered the stolen materials and packaged them in burlap and twine.

"It wasn't, but I appreciate the thought." The brisk morning air did little to improve her mood.

His expression was guarded as he nodded, taking her arm snugly against his, as if he could keep her safe by sheer force of will.

She studied their fellow pedestrians with suspicion. Everyone looked absolutely normal. Many men openly carried a sidearm. Any cabriolet or wagon could become a weapon. She glanced up, as if expecting a buzzer to come barreling from the heavens. Death could come in so many forms. She might not even see its approach.

She smelled trees before she saw them, and deeply inhaled, a smile already easing the hard lines of her face. They rounded a corner to find a sentinel row of oaks, their trunks scarred by scrapes with cabriolets and buggies. Even so, the trees stood resolute and strong, leading them toward the university just down the drive.

Leaves crunched underfoot. A bluebird chirped on a branch and hopped to the sidewalk, beak jabbing at detritus, then fluttered away as it realized their proximity. More bicycles than cabriolets rolled by, most everyone quiet. Reverential.

A piece of paradise tucked away here, just when I needed it most.

"'Sing, sweet bird, of crowns and kings, of armies and castles and various things,'" said Alonzo, his deep voice finding the singsong rhythm. "'But the bird said nay, of these I sing not: of men who died, and battles fought. I sing of flowers and bees and trees and sun; I sing of spring to everyone. I sing of cool dew and the crunch of seeds, I sing of what the heart truly needs. Lo, I sing of spring.'"

Octavia looked at him in surprise, not sure whether to be delighted or annoyed.

Alonzo shrugged, suddenly bashful. "I contrived the verse as a mere boy and the words stuck in my memory, wretched as 'tis."

"Oh, it's not that bad. Really. You would have liked my father. He adored verse. He was a teacher, as was my mother before she married and began to doctor instead. But Father loved his poems. He would work on the farm in the wee hours of the morning, and I always knew where he was because he composed poetry out loud. He then would come inside and scribble like a madman before walking down to the schoolhouse."

"I have been known to have my own madman moments." He continued his surveillance as they walked. "Less frequently in recent years, I fear. But the thoughts are always there, even if I lack a pen in my hand."

"You could carry a little notebook, like Mrs. Stout. Do you work on verses out loud?"

"Sometimes, if I am alone. Not often these days. Aboard ship, someone is always sleeping in the berths. 'Tis always unpleasant to be awakened by a voice, but for it to be the musings of a poet . . . ! I may as well stand in place and accept my beating."

Despite the fact that death could await her in any shadow, Octavia laughed.

Student tenements huddled together as if trying to keep warm. A tall wall skirted the walkway and wore a thick layer of posters for various events. Her eyes skimmed the mishmash of colors and words, and she was pleased that she couldn't find mention of the Wexlers' lecture on medicians.

Mr. Garret squeezed her arm against his. "You know I will do my utmost to keep you safe on the remaining journey, and to have you in the best of care in Mercia."

She forced her gaze ahead. He had admitted himself that he was barely more than an apprentice and that only his mother's influence had gotten him the job.

She couldn't completely rely on him, or Mrs. Stout.

The university literature building consisted of gray stones almost obscured by thick honeysuckle. With winter near, the vines had shriveled, the dead growth still tenuously clinging to the facade. They passed through the entrance and into an echoing atrium. Octavia gazed up at the high point of the ceiling, her hands clutched together at her waist. Alonzo told a clerk of their appointment, and her footsteps faded down the hall.

After a brief wait, they were guided into a room. Octavia took in high bookshelves and the delightfully musty smell of leather before noticing the figure at the desk. Adana Dryn's silver hair was cropped short in a most unconventional yet flattering way, her eyes almond-shaped and as intense as knife blades. She seemed to assess Octavia in a piercing glance, nodding.

"Welcome. Please, take a seat. I understand we have little time."

"Yes," said Alonzo, clearing his throat as he sat.

Octavia claimed a chair as well, doing her utmost not to gawk at the rainbow of soiled leather bindings around her. It was rare to see so many old books; Caskentia lost its greatest libraries in the fire-bombing of Mercia. In Tamarania, sights like this were likely commonplace. Octavia looked past Adana Dryn and noted a familiar window of stained glass that was almost obscured by heavy curtains. A beam of sunlight framed Adana in white.

"That's the same window as in your husband's atelier, depicting the Saint's Road," Octavia said.

Adana glanced over her shoulder. "Oh. Yes. They were gifts. I forget it's there most of the time. Not as though I need a reminder." Octavia blinked, not understanding, and Adana cocked her head to one side. "You didn't tell her, Alonzo?"

"I saw no need to."

"Well, Octavia, perhaps you'd know me better by my maiden name, Adana Murg."

Octavia straightened. "Adana Murg, the Sainted Fool? The one who finished the Saint's Road?" She gaped in awe.

"With the aid of my husband forty years ago, yes, though his role is often forgotten. That suits him quite well." By the way Adana shifted, it was clear that she would rather the matter were forgotten, too.

Adana Murg, the one chosen by God to finish the road. Her touch alone had been able to set stones aglow. The man who aided her had only been able to help because his frost-damaged hands had been amputated. His mechanical replacements didn't cause the stones to dim. Kellar Dryn had indeed lacked both hands.

Goodness. The tale of the Sainted Fool was my favorite as a child. To be in her very presence . . . !

Adana averted her gaze and Octavia flushed, realizing that she had been staring. "Alonzo," said Adana, her voice rusty with age, "Kellar has already told me about your discussion, and I'm not sure what insights I can offer."

"We have discovered something more since speaking with your husband. Allow me to show you these books."

Alonzo handed over the burlap bundle. He explained that Mrs. Stout was a pulp book publisher with a keen interest in ciphers, and pointed out her marginalia.

"Your friend is brilliant," said Adana. Octavia imagined Mrs. Stout preening at the praise. "I have seen many Dallowmen codes before, but to possess such a trove! Usually the most Caskentia intercepts is a note or two within a year, nothing like this. Whoever this man was, he was high up in their organization or a scholar himself. You say he had no traveling companions?"

Alonzo shook his head. "None registered. He was the only non-Caskentian-speaking passenger."

"The Dallows encourage settlers from all nations. Most of them are multilingual by necessity. I would guess that he could understand Caskentian, even if he couldn't speak it." Pages crinkled as she flipped through. "I believe at least one of these volumes consists of bound correspondence. I recognize the formality in the formatting. This seems to be quite recent."

"Perhaps it will explain these attempts on my life?" asked Octavia.

"We can certainly hope. I will have my assistants begin work on this immediately." Adana rose from her desk and walked toward the door. Octavia blinked.

The glow of the window stayed on Adana.

Her entire body was illuminated by a thin white nimbus. It clung to each strand of hair and traced the tailored lines of her high-waisted pants. Octavia looked to Alonzo. He showed no reaction, but he had said that something was intimidating about this woman.

"Alonzo," she murmured. "Do you see anything . . . strange about her?"

"Ah, her trousers and cropped hair? She is quite bold, is she not?" His nod was of admiration.

"I . . . never mind."

Octavia gnawed on her lip as she studied the glow. *This is some new insight from the Lady. Adana once bestowed light on stones; maybe some of that blessing lingers on her still.*

"How soon will the deciphering be done?" asked Alonzo as Adana returned to her desk.

"The booklets are slender and your Mrs. Stout already did the hard work of unraveling the cipher. I have thirty eager students ready to translate, and I'll join them once we're concluded here. Please inform your captain that a buzzer will arrive this evening, by supper if all goes well."

"Goodness. By supper!" Octavia couldn't help but be impressed. To her, the pages still made as much sense as trying to read raindrops.

Alonzo stood, and Octavia followed suit. "I am relieved and grateful for your aid, Adana. We must return to our hotel if we are to make our departure on time."

Adana nodded briskly and walked them to the door. "It has been a pleasure to meet you, Octavia. Perhaps we can meet again and speak at greater length. I'll keep you in my devotions as you continue your journey."

This close, the light of Adana's presence caused her eyes to ache. "Mrs. Dryn—Adana—thank you. It's been a special honor to meet you."

"Alonzo?" Adana's voice was soft as she faced him.

"Yes?"

"Be careful."

Alonzo nodded as he hooked Octavia's elbow. They walked out together, murmuring their thanks to the clerk as they passed. Alonzo seemed lost in thought as they headed away from the university. Their footsteps crackled on drying leaves. Octavia breathed in the musty scent as if she could carry it with her.

Along the street, the construction equipment wasn't idle now. Instead, it clattered and boomed, mighty wheels turning as a refitted tank mounted with a shovel blade worked at the pavement. Another large machine followed close behind, its large scoop mounded with steel pipes. Octavia covered her nose and mouth with her hand and pressed through a cloud of foul exhaust, the joyous scent of the trees utterly gone. Alonzo's lips moved but she heard nothing. The black cloud cleared, and she could see people and wagons before the hotel entrance.

A man near the doors turned, twiddling with his mustache. Octavia stopped cold. Mr. Drury. She hadn't seen him since jabbing him aboard the airship, and had no desire to see him now. Especially as the timing of his departure meant he was likely boarding the *Argus* again.

"Octavia?" Alonzo's lips were beside her ear, his breath hot and tickling.

She shook her head. Walking past Mr. Drury was unavoidable, but she refused to show any fear to that man. Mr. Drury faced them, his thick eyebrows rising. Octavia glared. He smiled as if nothing were amiss.

"Miss Leander." Mr. Drury's voice was almost obscured by the noise of construction. Behind him, a small child in homespun clothes bounced and pointed toward the machinery, his face rapturous with delight.

Leaves rustled and brushed against her face, almost

ticklish, and she raised a hand to force them away. There were no plants nearby, only the street. As she lowered her hand the sensation came again, a twig scratching against the high bones of her cheek. She turned to look that way and caught the glint of light off flying metal.

Yelping, she dropped to the ground, dragging Alonzo with her. The steel beam flew past. Her gaze on the cracked pavement, she didn't see the metal impact with the child, but she heard it. She felt it. The violent smack, the rush and scream of blood, the mother's wail. Behind it all was the roar of the machine. Octavia looked across the street. The smaller of the refitted tanks spun in a tight circle, the scoop's burden of metal rendered into missiles with each rotation.

Something heavy struck her, knocking her flat onto the sidewalk. Grit cut into the tender flesh of her hands. Glass shattered. Screams resounded. Screams of voices, screams of blood—more blood. She remained still, dizzied by the sudden barrage of traumas around her. Chaos rang out around her, horses neighing and wagons rattling, but all she could see was the pool of blood expanding around the child's limp and upturned hand.

Chapter 16

"*My boy! Someone help* my boy!" Out of all the surrounding noise, that voice rang out the loudest.

The cacophony of screams and hooves kicking at buckboards was muted by the sudden flare of music from the boy's blood. It wailed, stomping a frantic jig for attention. Not two seconds had passed since the child fell, and the very life was seeping from his body. Octavia pressed herself onto her forearms, struggling to rise, move, edge over a foot more to see the injury for herself.

"Stay down, woman." The voice was cool at her ear, a hand pressed at her waist. The scent of cloves wafted over her. Mr. Drury. Revulsion shuddered through her body.

"I must get to him," she gasped, struggling to rise again. More yells, more breaking glass. A horse emitted a sharp scream, only to suddenly go silent.

"Get her out of here." Alonzo's voice was sharp. "I will get the boy."

Another attempt on my life, and this time others are dying in my stead. Horror paralyzed her against the sidewalk as another metal beam whirred overhead.

Mr. Drury wasted no time. She had witnessed his agility on the ship but was stunned at his speed now. In one deft move, he scooped her up, arms around her waist, and hauled her toward the spinning lobby doors. She thought to screech or fight, suddenly more afraid of Mr. Drury despite the fact that he had used his own body to shield her from an assassin, but she wouldn't run from him. That meant running from that child, dying there on the pavement.

Dying because of me.

The ornate lobby held its usual crowd of stewards and idlers. Trained by years of war, they all remained prostrate on the glimmering marble and handwoven rugs, hands over their heads. Two children peered from behind a heavy chair, their eyes wide even as a maternal arm yanked them back again. Mr. Drury whirled her to the side and away from the windows and doors. With a wall at her side, her feet alighted on the floor. She flinched from him, already dropping her satchel. Two seconds later and the medician blanket fluffed out.

"You shouldn't do this here. It's still too vulnerable," said Mr. Drury.

She spared the split second to shoot him a venomous glare and then Alonzo backed through the doors. The child was a bloodied doll in his arms, the mother as their shadow.

"Oh Lady," Octavia choked. *Pampria. Heskool root, to ward against infection brought into the wound. A pinch of bellywood.* Her shaking fingers twisted open the lids as Alonzo set the boy down in the midst of the woven oval.

"My boy!" The mother was like a shawl draped from Alonzo's arm, limp and ragged.

A sharp whistle of the wind had joined the dismayed symphony of the boy's body. *Brain fluid.* Louder than the screams of blood, the whistle pierced the chatter of faceless others in the lobby and the whistles coming from somewhere beyond.

Oh Lady, Lady. A brain injury, the most dire.

"M'lady. Come with me. Let her work." Alonzo pulled at the mother, dragging her back.

The browned skin of her face had blanched. "My son, he's all I have left, I—" Alonzo yanked her away.

Octavia touched the circle and heat surged. "Pray, by the Lady let me mend thy ills." She waited, breath held, watching. *Is his soul still present to acquiesce?*

"Don't die because of me," she whispered. Her gaze darted to the street. There were others in need. Not even the horses should suffer, not because of her.

Horses had screamed the night her parents died, too. She heard them in the fiery barns. Trapped. Octavia's fingers trembled.

The conduit opened. The music of the boy's body was like the susurrus of an airship high above, more distant by the second. She scooped up the pampria without looking and let the dried leaves sift over his face. The pallor of death had already claimed him, his jaw slack and lips devoid of color.

This boy was all his mother had left. Octavia knew what it was like to lose everyone. She couldn't let that happen.

The fresh scents of pampria and heskool root replaced

the coppery scent of blood and the chemical odor of brain, but only for a matter of seconds. His colors hadn't shifted. *Bartholomew's tincture. Shards of the skull may be lodged in the flesh, preventing healing.* She unscrewed the lid and used a small spoon to scoop out the blessed white powder.

She hunched over, her prayer wordless in its agony. A loosened curl tickled her cheek but she didn't brush it away. With both hands, fingers colored with herbs, she clutched the boy's limp and pliable fingers. They were so small, so delicate. He couldn't be older than six.

The boy's chest arched upward as he took in a sudden gasp of air. His eyes shot open.

"What happened?" His voice was soft with wonder.

Octavia sagged forward. "You were injured, but the Lady intervened."

She expected blankness, confusion. So few children knew of the Lady. To her surprise, his face brightened.

"The Lady. I saw her. The Tree, I mean. I sat on a branch and swayed my legs and swung from a vine. She talked to me. She told me to tell you something."

Octavia stilled as ice crept through her veins. "The Lady told . . . told you something? For me?"

"Yes. She said, 'Listen to the branch and look to the leaves.'" A smile lit his face.

And then he died.

The music snuffed out in a single instant. His head fell slack against the reflective marble, eyes closing gently. A wisp of a smile lingered on his lips.

"Child?" Octavia stared, sitting up on her knees. She

squeezed the hand in her grip. It was limp, already cooling. Certainly, she had seen death before. There were always ones who were too far gone, whose pain the Lady could only relieve as she soothed their passing. But this? *He came back. He spoke, and then he . . . he . . .*

"Octavia." Alonzo's voice was hot and husky against her ear. "He is gone."

She glanced back. Alonzo had penetrated the circle. Octavia had never even disengaged it. The Lady had withdrawn entirely on her own.

Listen to the branch and look to the leaves. What did that even mean? It's as if the Lady had revived the child just long enough for him to speak, to make him the conduit, and then withdrew her breath of life.

"That doesn't happen," she whispered out loud. "The Lady doesn't . . . doesn't do that."

"Octavia." Alonzo's hand rested heavily on her shoulder. "We cannot stay here. The police are questioning witnesses. If we are held, the *Argus* departs without us."

She began to sway but Alonzo grip's anchored her as strongly as a steel girder. "There are others who were injured. I need to—"

"No."

"I can't leave them. This is . . . someone . . . how?"

"The rig driver was bludgeoned and someone set the machinery to drive in a tight circle, just as we passed. 'Tis shut off now." He took in a shuddering breath. "Do you have money?"

That took her off guard. "Wh-what?"

"We must bribe the investigator. All my money paid for the wagon and Kellar's services. I . . . I have not been paid by Caskentia in three months. I live on my steward's salary and that alone."

They were equals in their poverty. Part of her wished to laugh, but she knew it'd only trigger hysterics. "I have coppers . . ."

"Coppers are not enough." He pulled back so she could see the chagrin on his face. No, outright embarrassment.

"A silver, then." It's not as if she had any use for the money where she was going. "Can you pass me my wand?"

"Of course."

The smooth staff of wood and copper was a comforting weight. She tended to her hands, clothes, and jars. She packed everything, then looked to the boy.

"Where's the mother?"

"She swooned. Hotel stewards are tending to her."

Why, Lady? Why use this child in such a way? Octavia pressed a fist to her chest and fought a tide of tears. She was meant to be the conduit, not him. Why bring him back—with such sweet hope—only to take him again seconds later?

"I can lift him up," Alonzo said, his voice gentle.

"I'll take his feet." Mr. Drury had been standing some distance away, near the door, but now he approached and stepped onto the blanket. Octavia was so numb she registered his return without any fear or revulsion. The two men hoisted up the lad and set him to one side. Her hands folded the blanket, knowing the creases without aid of sight.

"I don't even know his name."

Alonzo stood over her and she knew what he wanted. She nestled the blanket into its place and then went to the coin pouch to pull out a silver.

"I am sorry," he said. Whether he spoke of the child and the others, the shameful matter of the money, his failure to provide protection . . . she knew not. Some nebulous emotion wavered in his eyes and he approached a nearby officer. There were many, she realized as she looked around the lobby. The real world returned to her ears as though a fog lifted. The chamber echoed with dozens of conversations.

"They'll blame the Waste," said Mr. Drury, his tone one of disgust. "They always do, even with no evidence. As though only men from there are capable of crime and vice."

"Men and women in Caskentia are quite capable of vice." She watched Alonzo shake the hand of an officer in a gray suit, the silver coin slipped from hand to hand.

"You are well? Unhurt?" Mr. Drury asked.

"I'm unhurt. I'm not well."

"What is this? What has happened?" The regal voice of Mrs. Stout carried across the room.

Octavia sucked in a breath as she stood. "Spare her this scene. Please."

"There's another exit," said Mr. Drury. "On the far side of the counter."

She scooped up her satchel as Alonzo rejoined them. "There are others who are still alive, even horses, I—"

"Miss Leander, no." Alonzo shook his head. "We must

get you aboard before that investigator decides to gouge us for more money."

Rage and frustration flushed her cheeks as she glared past Alonzo to the officer, but the vivid red on Alonzo's clothes caught her eye. "Wait. Mrs. Stout hasn't noticed us yet. Let me clean you up." Octavia pulled out the parasol and made quick passes over his attire. A hand clenched her upper arm and she cringed.

"My dear lady, I'm so very glad you're unhurt. I must say farewell to a companion." Mr. Drury tipped his hat as he released his hold on her. "I will see you on board." He stepped aside just as Mrs. Stout advanced on them, almost shoving her way through the crowd in the process.

"What has happened? So many screams! Are you—"

"I'm fine," said Octavia, surprised at the evenness in her voice. She tucked the parasol away.

One of the hotel bellboys lingered behind Mrs. Stout. He pulled a small cart of luggage. Octavia recognized her suitcase on the bottom.

"This . . . does it continue the same matter as before?" Mrs. Stout asked. Her lower lip tucked in against her teeth.

"It does. And we must board now and pray we leave the assailant behind." Alonzo put a guiding hand at Mrs. Stout's elbow to direct her toward the far exit.

"Oh dear. Oh dear," muttered the woman.

"And what if we don't leave them behind?" asked Octavia.

Alonzo paused. "The next stretch will be the most perilous. The route skirts close to the southern pass and various other winding trails through the mountains." His voice was soft. "But Mercia is a day and a half away. We are almost there."

A day and a half fraught with danger, before her relative safety in imprisonment. Octavia nodded as she wavered in place, her hand clutching the strap to her shoulder, and forced her suddenly wooden legs to walk onward.

THIS TIME AS SHE boarded the *Argus,* the prevailing scent was of chicken and rosemary. It was normally one of Octavia's favorite dishes, one that evoked fond memories of Mother's cooking, but now the redolent scent did little to relax her.

A child was dead because of her, and countless other people as well. The airship did not feel like a refuge. The corridors seemed to press in on her shoulders, the warm wood of the walls dark and confining. She kept one hand near her torso and the capsicum flute, though she knew it might be in vain. Thus far, her assassin—or assassins—had only gotten close enough to push her from behind. And if more than one attacked at once, she only had a singular shot of pepper from her pipe.

She kept seeing that young boy, the brilliant smile on his lips when he returned to life just for an instant. *Why, Lady? Why?* This was a time when she knew she should absorb herself in her Al Cala and take comfort in the cycle of life and all it entailed, but instead she ached to scream and cry and hit and pummel at the faceless figures who kept committing such atrocities in their pursuit of her.

I'm a medician. Why kill me? What have I done?

Alonzo escorted her and Mrs. Stout to the same quarters as before. It was a tight fit with the three of them together, but he closed the door to address them.

"I must dress and attend to our embarking procedures." Alonzo's hard gaze focused on Mrs. Stout. "Stay together at all times. Watch for anyone suspicious."

"I'll do my utmost to take care of her." Mrs. Stout raised her chin. "And she will tend to me, as she already has. Now go about your duties, young man. It will help neither of us if you get the chuck."

That coaxed a weary smile onto his face. "Yes, m'lady. Octavia . . ." His voice faltered, emotion swimming in his eyes.

"You have done all you can, Alonzo," she said softly. "Go."

His gaze lingered on her and then he nodded. The door shut behind him with a soft click. Octavia sank into the bench seat as if her bones had turned to porridge.

"Oh, child." Mrs. Stout sat down beside her, plush hip pressed close, and wrapped an arm around. "It's a terrible burden, I know it is. I'm just glad you're all right."

"The Lady . . . I don't understand . . ."

"Well! Some things aren't meant to be understood. I mean, look at me. I've seen parts of the Tree, but the nature of the Lady . . . well, she wasn't for me, but I fully accept she exists." Mrs. Stout's hand squeezed her upper arm. "Do remember, the Lady suffered as well. She was the mourning mother, beseeching God for those she had lost. Whatever burdens your heart, she understands, even if you don't."

Octavia nodded. Hot, slow tears coursed down her cheeks. "Yes. You're quite right, Mrs. Stout. Thank you for putting things in perspective for me."

Not that her grief had been assuaged so quickly. Her anger and frustration at the Lady stewed in her chest, but Mrs. Stout was right that the Lady would understand those very emotions. The Lady would accept the turmoil, mighty branches waving as if in a typhoon, and eventually the storm would pass and the sun would shine through again.

Just not today. For now, the storm will continue.

A bell dinged in the hallway. Octavia braced both hands against the edge of the seat. Despite her readiness, when the lurch came, her stomach heaved at the abrupt motion.

"Well," said Mrs. Stout. "It may be tempting to hide away in here, but considering the threat against you, I think it would be best for you to be seen by as many people as possible. They must know you are present and alive, and therefore if you are absent, you'll be missed."

"Under such guidelines, it sounds as if I should be installed in the smoking room for the rest of the trip."

Mrs. Stout snorted. "That might not be a bad idea. There are several men on board who are already indebted to you for your kindness after that zyme poisoning! They would likely watch your back under unpleasant circumstances."

Mr. Grinn should have also been indebted to me for my kindness, and we know how that turned out. The image of him flashed in her mind: his bed of blood-drenched cattails, the limp thickness of his arm.

As Octavia entered the promenade, the first person she spied was Mr. Drury. He stood by a table chatting with another man. A wood-slatted box of canned drinks sat in front of him. Mr. Drury met her gaze across the room and granted her a gracious nod, as if nothing had been amiss in town.

In the library was a mother with two young girls whose hair was done up in sagging bows. *More children. Will they die because of me as well?* Octavia shuddered. The very figure of a husband stood behind them, a newspaper in his hands. The headlines of the previous day returned to her mind, the death villages and kidnappings.

So many questions, no answers. Only the echoing screams of blood and a mother's cries. The mechanized band played a jolly tune, and she wished to tear apart the metal constructs with her bare hands.

Several other passengers idled with drinks by the windows. She had no desire to go that way. *The last thing I need right now is to see Leaf, waiting against the glass.*

"Oh, Miss Leander!"

Octavia's spine went rigid. *Not Mrs. Wexler. Not now.*

The woman was alone and her smile focused on Octavia. "I did hope to chat with you again. Our symposium in Leffen was such a grand success that we'll continue the series in Mercia and I had hopes—"

"No."

Mrs. Wexler blinked rapidly. "I beg your pardon?"

"Now, Miss Leander." That was Mrs. Stout, a note of warning in her voice.

"No, Mrs. Wexler. I believe in the Lady." Even with deaths weighing on her, Octavia could say that without a doubt. She didn't need to see inside the royal vault for physical proof. "I believe in a Tree whose roots anchor the world, whose branches stir the wind. Science is a glorious thing, but it's not my faith. Please, do not approach me again."

"Well." Mrs. Wexler stiffened. "If I had known you were a pagan, I would not have invited you at all. You are young, and you have time yet to change your quaint ways. When you do—"

"I will say this bluntly, Mrs. Wexler. Shut your pie hole."

The woman blinked rapidly as she backed up, then turned, her skirts flouncing as she hurried away.

"That was uncalled for," snapped Mrs. Stout.

Octavia stared at her hands against the table. Somehow she thought that putting Mrs. Wexler in her place would vent some of the awfulness that weighed on her spirit. Instead, she felt neither guilt nor catharsis, only emptiness.

"Miss Leander, Mrs. Stout."

She wasn't surprised to turn and find Mr. Drury there, smiling, his box in his hands. "Mr. Drury." Octavia kept her voice cool.

"You are recovered from the incident at the hotel?" he queried as if she had stepped in a puddle and soaked a stocking.

"Well enough."

"Ah, the resiliency of a master medician." His broad,

toothless smile stretched his mustache. Her distrust in him flared again. *Though he did just save my life. I cannot dismiss that fact.*

"Ah. You are the vendor of Royal-Tea. On our last trip, I heard that one of our fellow passengers peddled the drink." Mrs. Stout stared into the box.

"I am indeed, good madam." He bowed with grace, showing no strain from the weight of his burden. "I have an excessive inventory after my stop in Leffen and am offering tins to everyone aboard. Please, take one at no cost."

Octavia did not like this man, but some small measure of gratitude was warranted. She reached into the box, probing lower for a cooler can. Mr. Drury's smile softened into something more genuine.

"Do let me know what you think, Miss Leander. We only use the best ingredients. Mrs. Stout . . . ?"

"Oh, no thank you."

"Do you need assistance in opening your tin, Miss Leander? I have—"

"No, thank you. I have my own opener."

"Very well. I will speak to you ladies again later, I'm sure." With another graceful bob of his head, he continued to the next table.

Octavia examined the can in her hands. It was slender and fit perfectly within the cup of her palm. The container bore the crown logo of the company and fine calligraphy touting the health benefits of the drink, including boosted energy, salved spirits, ease of digestion, and steady hands for fine motor work.

"This is nothing more than a paroxysm pill," she said in disgust. "No medicine can do all of that."

"It's a sales pitch, no more." Mrs. Stout tried to wave down Little Daveo across the room, but he didn't seem to see her. "I'll be right back. I believe I need a glass of aerated water."

"Very well. Don't go far." Octavia kept an eye on her surroundings as she reached into her satchel for her tin opener. Using the triangular tip, she pressed down on the lid. The tin emitted a slight spurt. She raised it to her nose. Bubbles fizzled through the small hole. Mr. Drury was watching her from ten feet away, his face impassive. His bland observation set her on edge, as if he expected something to happen.

Goodness, I am being paranoid. It's just canned tea. Everyone else is drinking it. She took a sip.

The flavor of tea lapped against her tongue, mild and fragrant. She detected a subtle note of cinnamon. To her surprise, it was quite good. Not as good as chocolate, but then nothing could equal that. She shot Mr. Drury a brief nod and he returned to his conversation with the others. She had another long drink, the fluid bubbling in her throat.

It struck her then. Her head jerked toward Mr. Drury and then her gaze flew to the window, where the roofs of Leffen were fading to the size of miniatures. *Mr. Drury saved my life and yet I feel no obligation from the Lady, no debt. When I was pulled from the side of the airship, awareness of the debt was almost instantaneous. The Lady knew the aether magus had assisted in saving me, though I had never seen the man before.*

And then there was the obvious debt to Alonzo, which lingered on her until his leg had been restored.

Mr. Drury had shielded her and she felt nothing. *What does that mean? What does the Lady know that I do not?* Octavia set down the can and opener, unwilling to finish the drink despite the pleasantly warm fizz it left on her tongue.

"Well!" Mrs. Stout plopped down in her seat again with a slight huff. She set a glass of effervescent water on the table. "I do believe that little steward injured himself when we were in port. The poor man!"

"Oh?" Octavia forced her attention to her companion.

"He has quite a limp. Said he had a close call with a drayman's cart! The driver didn't see him due to his size. Drivers these days, all fuss and hurry." She tsked under her breath. "I asked if he wanted healing from you, but he quite adamantly refused, said he could never afford a medician."

"That hasn't stopped anyone else." *Or taught me how to say no when their bodies call to me with such great need.*

"Watch the attitude, child. I was going to point him out so you could judge his injury yourself, but it seems he's gone about his business. These stewards never stay still, do they?"

Octavia touched the can, gliding her fingers along the cylindrical curve. She had no desire to drink any more; she had little desire to do anything at all. Simply sit there, staring into space as Mrs. Stout's voice droned on. *Empty.* She felt empty. A day from now, Octavia would either be dead or, if she was lucky, imprisoned.

So this was how it felt to lose hope.

Chapter 17

The sun had dwindled to a pink sliver in the western sky when Octavia heard the telltale buzzing of the arriving craft. She set down her fork in her half-eaten dinner. Silently, she headed to the far side of the ship, Mrs. Stout following close behind.

In the increasing darkness, the silhouettes of the mountains loomed just beyond the window. Octavia sucked in a breath. The Pinnacles, the only wall that stood between her and the Waste.

Small-engine cars protruded from the sides of the *Argus.* She had scarcely paid them heed before, other than noticing that a bundled-up crewman seemed to be out there at all times. Now another person crossed the gap to the port car, hands on the railings, his back hunched against a buffeting wind. Without seeing his face, she knew it had to be Alonzo. He would trust no one else to handle the delivery from Adana Dryn.

The buzzer loomed close like an oversize wasp, the propeller a dark blur.

"Goodness! If it gets any closer, it could hit us!" shrieked a woman beside her. Octavia recoiled in surprise. Most of the dining room had gathered to watch the show.

"Calm yourself," said an older man. "This is a common occurrence. Buzzers are trained to make such deliveries." Still, the man watched with curiosity that dulled the impact of his words.

Octavia's gut lurched as the buzzer came alongside, almost directly above the engine. A long shaft extended downward and joined with the car. Using that pole, a black object slid down and directly into Alonzo's hands. He disengaged the staff and it telescoped up again. The buzzer pilot pulled away, sparing one brief wave for the audience at the window. Alonzo clutched the parcel against his chest as he marched back inside.

"Come," Octavia said to Mrs. Stout. They headed down to deck B to intercept Alonzo.

Octavia had her hand on the door to the crew compartments when she spied Alonzo's face through the circular window. He was still attired in a thick leather jacket. A woolen collar fluffed out like a mane. Thick goggles rested atop his forehead, the glass fogged from the sudden temperature shift. He smiled briefly in greeting and opened the door from his side to allow them through.

"Follow me. I explained to the captain that you expected urgent news from Leffen and he has granted us the privacy of the officers' mess."

Alonzo motioned to a door farther down the passage. The heavy scent of aether and ozone hovered around him like a cloud.

The mess was a small, cramped space, barely larger than their berthing. The walls were patchy and ugly with bared bolts, and she surmised that some metal entertainment apparatus had been removed and sold for scrap. Two tables, one rectangular and one round, were each surrounded by scuffed brown leather seats much like the ones in the smoking room. Octavia immediately went to the circular table at the back. Mrs. Stout wedged in beside her, the medician satchel between them. The staff of the parasol gouged Octavia's thigh. She clutched her hands together and stared up at Alonzo.

He locked the door and then worked at the latches on the leather satchel. It was slender, not much different from a shoulder book bag used by university students. He pulled out papers and let the bag fall to the table. Octavia glanced inside and saw nothing else.

He was silent for a long moment as he skimmed, and she felt as if she would burst. "Can't you just hand out sheets to everyone?" Octavia snapped.

"There are only two. Adana summarized everything as best she could and inscribed it in one of her codes. I fear handing it to you would be of little help."

Octavia slumped over, most unladylike.

"Oh gracious! I would like to see," said Mrs. Stout, perking up far too much.

"Maybe later, Mrs. Stout." Alonzo took in a deep breath and met Octavia's gaze. The pale blue of his eyes seemed to stare into her soul. "We were correct in surmising that Mr. Grinn was an agent of the Dallows. He, along with the rest of his crew, were tasked with crossing the mountains to retrieve Miss Octavia Leander, a recent graduate of Miss Percival's Academy, and rendezvous with the rest of their team at a place that has some vernacular name. They dubbed it Black Heaps."

"A team? You said they have a team?" Octavia shivered as if chilled, even as sweat rolled a long course down her spine.

"Yes." His jaw was set in a grim line. "No numbers set. It may not be as daunting as you fear."

"Still too many," muttered Mrs. Stout. Her red nails drummed on the tabletop. "What of the attempts on Octavia's life?"

Alonzo shook his head. "There is nothing. On the contrary, it states that they are to do everything possible to protect her. They used the phrase 'guard her as you would a daughter,' which is a high-level vow amongst the Dallowmen. Their daughters live hard, short lives and are prized more than oil."

"Oh Lady. I don't understand. Why did Mr. Grinn push me? Was he a double agent?" Octavia pressed a hand against her brow.

"Nothing in the booklets suggested such. Instead, it seemed as if they had selected the best of the best for this mission, regarding it as a primary operation for the Dallows."

"Primary operation." Mrs. Stout's voice was dull. "That's what I was."

Me, a prime target for an entire rogue territory? Octavia's scant supper threatened to make a return visit. *Maybe I truly am a threat to Queen Evandia and Caskentia. But how?* Alonzo's eyes skimmed the paper, one hand at his mouth.

"This is not good," he said.

"You mean it gets worse?" asked Octavia. "How can it get worse?" She regretted the words the instant they escaped her lips.

Alonzo's eyes shifted from her to Mrs. Stout. "When they bring in Octavia, they are also to retrieve her roommate, a Mrs. Viola Stout, wife of the late publishing magnate Donovan Stout. There is no exact reason given, though the matter is presumed—"

"No." Mrs. Stout stood. "You did this. You're the only one here who knew. Octavia wouldn't tell! I know she wouldn't, but you. Oh God." Her lips opened and closed for a moment, no speech emerging. Her jowls jiggled.

"Mrs. Stout. Viola." Octavia stood and grasped the older woman by the shoulder. "That is completely absurd. You can't possibly believe—"

"No, she is right to suspect me, even if she is wrong," Alonzo said, his voice quiet. "She has survived by keeping her identity under strict confidence. How many people know the truth, Mrs. Stout?"

"My husband. You. Octavia. Nelly." She sank into the cushioned seat and stared into space. "Nelly." The name was a gasp.

"No," said Octavia. "Absolutely not. You're trying to suggest that Miss Percival . . . no." *She wouldn't. She couldn't.*

"She begged me to escort you on this trip," Mrs. Stout

murmured, her eyes wide with horror. "Said it would be good for me to get out, that I could take you under my wing, we could be roommates. Just like she and I used to be roommates. Oh God." She shrank and shielded her face behind her hands.

Alonzo paced in short, abrupt strides. "These letters go back for weeks. This was not a spontaneous operation. Now, Octavia—"

"Don't even look at me. Don't consider this. Miss Percival raised me from the time I was twelve. She was a second mother to me." *Not only a mother. My only friend. The only one who understood how it felt to be different, blessed . . . until I proved to be the more blessed.* "Why would she . . . ?"

"Money." Alonzo said it with a shrug. "Caskentia has not paid her. How much does it cost to run that institution?"

That's why I wasn't paid what I was owed. It's because I was the one who had been sold. No. No, it can't be. Miss Percival wouldn't do that. Not to me.

But she's been so cold these past few months. Was it all leading up to this?

"Nelly would do anything for that school of hers," murmured Mrs. Stout. "Anything. But even then, I never thought . . . she has kept my identity a secret for fifty years. Why now?"

"Desperation," said Alonzo. "No one has coin these days. How close is the school to failing completely?"

Octavia struggled to piece together enough logic to prove his argument invalid. "But the letters never identified who Mrs. Stout used to be, correct? Wasters are kidnapping young women for ransom. The Stout family has money. Maybe this has nothing to do with her past after all. Maybe it's all for ransom."

Alonzo shook his head. The fluff of his collar scuffed against his prickly jaw. "Even if someone high up in the organization knew, they would not inform a lackey of the truth. There would be too much prestige in being the one to finally kidnap or kill the princess. That attempt on Mercia was the Dallows' first great offensive toward independence, and their greatest failure."

"Back then, they thought to wed me to Archibald Taney, the one who became grand potentate ages ago. He had a dozen titles, probably as many wives. In my brief time in their hands, I was told I would be a princess of the Dallows, my children raised in the wild Promised Land. And now . . . I am too old for children, but my own children . . . the babe . . . if someone knows the truth about me . . ." Mrs. Stout's words were muffled behind her hand. She stared at Octavia. "Remember what I told you?"

The royal vault. Mrs. Stout's blood was the key. Caskentia could certainly misuse the contents of the vault, but the Waste . . . *Oh Lady.*

"Your family needs to go into hiding," said Alonzo. "Leave Caskentia. Head to the southern nations."

"All my children know of my history is that I'm an orphan and a failure as a Percival girl," Mrs. Stout said. "To force them into that sort of life, I . . ."

"Caskentia would want them dead just as much as the

Waste." Alonzo's voice carried a grim tone that made Octavia shiver. "The Queen will not abide with living rivals for the throne, not during this time of unrest. Too many people are desperate for a bowl of food and a ruler to save them. Your father and grandfather are still idolized, and some would believe you are the very person to create a new Gilded Age."

Mrs. Stout emitted a wordless moan against her hands.

"There's no hard proof that Miss Percival is behind this," Octavia said. "She's not named, is she?"

"No. The Dallowmen would not be that foolish. As 'tis, I am sure these letters were meant to be burned as soon as Mr. Grinn reached Leffen. Adana noted that some pages were missing. Those likely contained the most sensitive data."

Oh Lady, why is this happening? "Will Adana be handing this information over to the government?"

"Yes. Too many people know of the books for them to be secret. But the interpretation would be that Mrs. Stout is intended for ransom. Not even Adana suggests any other truth."

Octavia had known the news wouldn't be good, but she had never expected such a turn. She stood, leaning on the table with both hands. "I would like to retire to my room and commune with the Lady." There was much to dwell on. The dead boy. Miss Percival. The peculiar nature of Mr. Drury. Mrs. Stout. Her throat burned, and she had the sudden longing to scream, as if that would vent her worries and make everything well. Instead, she forced herself to swallow, a taste as bitter as bile on her tongue.

Alonzo nodded, empathy clouding his eyes. "I understand. I suggest you sleep in shifts tonight as well. I will watch over you as best I can, but I cannot always be at your door. In an emergency, go to Vincan."

"Vincan? Who is this Vincan?" asked Mrs. Stout.

"The bartender in the smoking room," Alonzo said. "Big fellow, very pale."

"Oh. I do believe I saw him once. Can he be trusted?" Her voice quivered.

"I know 'tis not in you to trust him, and I well understand, but I served with Vincan at the front. I trust him with my life. If anything can be said for him, he hates the Waste."

Mrs. Stout sucked in a breath. "In our desperation, that must suffice, though I fear those loyal to my cousin just as much. And you think that these Wasters will make their move soon?"

"Within the next day, while we are still in the countryside."

Mrs. Stout nodded, eyes closed, the gesture automatic like a mechanical bird. "Very well. Sleep in shifts. I can do that. We'll be over the sprawl of Mercia soon. It's not that far, truly."

Octavia had no faith in sleeping at all this night, shifts or otherwise. Too many things stirred in her head, roiled in her gut.

They walked down the hall and Alonzo motioned them to wait. He entered the open kitchen door and exchanged quick words with one of the cooks. The man opened the hatch beneath the stove. Alonzo stuffed the papers into the flames. The sheets curled and blackened as he shut the door again, giving a quick nod of thanks to the workers.

They headed upstairs, Alonzo guarding their flank. Octavia rounded the stairwell and stopped, a familiar sound assaulting her ears.

"Blood," she said. Alonzo bounded ahead of her.

Fresh blood cried out along with a drumbeat of fists on flesh. The wall ahead shuddered and an idyllic print of an airship and clouds tilted off-kilter. She rushed forward right behind Alonzo, one hand at her waist, the other on her satchel. The door to their room was open, and in the narrow hallway tussled Mr. Drury and Little Daveo, both men battered and bruised and showing no indication of ending their fight.

Even Alonzo was rendered still for several seconds. One nearby berth door cracked open to reveal wide, frightened eyes.

Mr. Drury flew back against the wall, arms up, and in an instant sprang forth again, just missing a low-aimed kick from the little steward. The wooden boards on the wall clacked and rattled against the metal frames beneath. Watching the two men in action was like witnessing a fight between two tomcats. Mr. Drury moved with delicacy and finesse, sinuous as a snake. Little Daveo may not have grown above five feet in height, but the man had brute strength and agility. His stubby legs dodged a kick and he practically bounced off the wall. Daveo caught himself on his hands and spun around.

"What is the meaning of this?" barked Alonzo.

Mr. Drury's eyes raked over them and settled on Octavia. He seemed to nod to himself, not responding to a solid jab to the chest. "This steward intended to poison Miss Leander!" He faced Daveo again to block another assault.

"Daveo? What is this?" asked Alonzo. Nearby, an alarm bell dinged four times.

The steward offered no reply. He wiped a line of blood from his cheek and had eyes only for his opponent. Several gold buttons had been ripped from his jacket, leaving the flap dangling open to show the worn silk beneath. Strains of blood sang stronger and Octavia wavered, catching herself against the wall. Both men's noses were bloodied, their faces cut, but she couldn't see any knives or evidence of stab wounds.

"What manner of poison?" she called.

"Tampering within your faucet." Mr. Drury panted heavily as he dodged another punch. "I suspect he added a filter laden with zymes, in the very method of the Dallows."

Is Little Daveo my assailant? She narrowed her eyes as she laid a hand on Alonzo's arm and he tilted an ear toward her. "He offers no defense or explanation."

"He does not."

Mr. Drury smacked into the wall again, this time with adequate force to break a wall panel in half with a resounding crack. Even so, his next kick landed in Little Daveo's gut, causing the shorter man to double over. The two men crashed into the floor in a mad knot of legs and arms.

Octavia stepped past Alonzo, following the call of

blood. It reached a crescendo over the men. There was something else, too—the quivering note of extended agony.

"Lady, lend me your aid," she whispered, and breathed in, willing her olfactory sense to extend. It was subtle, that note of charred flesh, the lingering stink of diesel, but she knew it all too well. Her gut clenched in response as screams—human, equine, blood—boomed in her memory.

She pried out the capsicum flute. Raising the weapon to her lips, she leaned forward and exhaled through the short pipe.

A red plume of mist flowed over the fighting men. Octavia's nose burned at the harsh pepper, but their reactions were more blatant. The tussling ceased. Screaming and writhing, they pulled apart, hands covering their eyes.

"Oh God! Oh God!" cried Little Daveo.

Octavia was in no mood for sympathy. "The steward's injuries indicate he was the pilot in the buzzer that pursued us. He's our man. Or one of them."

Alonzo stared at her, agape. "How . . . ?"

"I just know."

That was enough for him. Alonzo motioned to some stewards who had gathered behind them. They grabbed the two men. Mr. Drury sobbed, tears streaking a path in the red powder on his face.

"Where are you taking them?" asked Octavia.

Alonzo spared her a glance, his eyes blinking rapidly. "The promenade is where we assemble in most emergencies."

The stewards had already corralled the dining passengers at the far side of the promenade, where they jabbered amongst themselves. The windows showed absolute darkness. The captain had already arrived. Octavia stalked forward with Mrs. Stout in her wake.

"Captain," Octavia said.

He grunted in greeting, his breathing heavy. He must have run from the control room. "It seems you are the focal point of more disturbances aboard my ship."

"Much to my regret, yes."

"This have anything to do with that buzzer drop earlier?"

She hesitated. "Perhaps."

Alonzo bound Daveo's wrists together and poured a pitcher of water over the man's face. Another steward was doing the same with Mr. Drury, though he was not bound. Excess water coursed along their faces and puddled on the dark carpet.

"Thank you, thank you," murmured Mr. Drury with a smile for his steward. He stood and staggered away. Octavia opened her mouth, wanting to shout for them to stop him, to do something, but had no reason. As if reading her mind, Mr. Drury looked at her with a patient smile as he walked by, as if saying all was forgiven.

Octavia forced her attention back to the more immediate matter. "Al—Mr. Garret, I think it'll ease matters if someone—I'll put it bluntly—undoes Daveo's pants to show the extent of his injuries."

"Undo his pants? Here?" The captain waved an arm. "Clear the promenade. There are ladies present."

"Could take them to the mess, sir," muttered one of the stewards.

"I'm not having capsicum in a smaller enclosed space. Get someone cleaning that hallway, too," he growled.

Octavia turned to Mrs. Stout. "You don't have to stay."

"I will. I'm not leaving you, child! Besides, I've seen wounds before. And if this man . . . if he has done what you think . . ."

Octavia doubted Mrs. Stout had seen the ugliness of poorly treated diesel burns, but she nodded. She would have felt ill at ease had they separated, anyway.

"And what, pray tell, is it you think my steward has done?" asked Captain Hue.

She met Alonzo's eyes, wondering how much to tell the man.

"Captain," said Alonzo. He set the pitcher down. "When we ventured to retrieve my leg in the swamp, we were attacked by an assailant in a modified buzzer. It crashed and the pilot escaped, but not without injury."

"What makes you suspect Daveo?" Captain Hue asked, arms crossed over his chest.

"I . . . I am close to the Lady. I have a way of . . . sensing these things," said Octavia.

Daveo blinked rapidly, his eyes still red. His jaw was set in a defiant grimace.

"Like how you managed to find the source of that poison in the smoke room? Magic!" An expression somewhere between disgust and fear twisted Captain Hue's lips. He did a quick turn to look around the room, then faced Daveo. "Nothing to say for yourself, eh? Drop his trou."

Two of the other stewards tugged down Daveo's pants.

Mrs. Stout made a slight clucking sound and cleared her throat, but Octavia was unmoved. The dark trousers wadded around his ankles. Both legs were swathed in bandages, filthy in rusty red. His skin—what was left of it—warbled in its agony without need of a circle to enhance the sound, and she detected frantic notes indicative of infection.

"Blimey," muttered one of the men.

Captain Hue grunted beneath his breath. "This is a matter of increasing sensitivity. Men, strip him of his coat and sleeves and check for armaments, and secure him to the post. Then go and guard the door."

The crewmen did as asked. Little Daveo's chin continued its defiant tilt as they stripped him to his undershirt. When his pants were lifted up again, they found two knives strapped to his boots. Another small blade was sheathed close to his forearm. Had Mr. Drury been less of a fighter, he likely would have been stabbed. They hauled Daveo back and used decorative cord to fix him to the pillar. Daveo sat on the carpet half undressed, his mauled wounds weeping through the bandages. The men backed away, offering bows to the captain, and headed toward the entry.

For Daveo to tolerate his injuries in such a way suggested heavy doses of tinctures or training in matters of extreme pain, or both.

Octavia met Daveo's gaze evenly. "Why?"

"As a citizen of Caskentia, you are subject to the rules and laws of Caskentia," Daveo said, his voice husky with pain. "Therefore, as an agent of the Queen—"

"You, an agent to the Queen? You are naught but a brigand. You have no power to arrest Octavia," said Alonzo. "She has committed no crime. And as a Clockwork Dagger and agent of the crown, 'tis I who shall arrest you for repeated attempts at homicide." He straightened and stood, as if he wore regalia and not a common steward's garb.

Daveo laughed. It began with a low wheeze and grew to a wild cackle. "Oh, listen to the general's son, talking as if he still owns the world. I do indeed have the power to arrest her, general's son, and to kill her as I will, just as you were supposed to."

"What?" squeaked Octavia. Alonzo's face was of stone. "Kill me?"

Daveo continued, "I am a true Clockwork Dagger, tasked to eliminate Octavia Leander lest she fall into the hands of the Dallows and turn traitor to Queen Evandia. The key Dallowmen agent here is Mr. Drury, whom you just let walk away."

Alonzo, kill me? All along, it could have been him. Was supposed to be him. And I trusted him. I was that stupid.

The captain sucked in a sharp breath. "Two Daggers aboard my ship, playing rivals?"

"You, a Dagger . . ." Alonzo's expression stiffened in disbelief. "All along, it was you?"

"What does he mean, you were supposed to kill me?" demanded Octavia. The words were raw in her throat.

Alonzo shook his head. "Octavia, believe me, I never would have. By orders, your death was to be a last resort. That is why I wanted you to return to Miss Percival—to scare you away with that note in your quarters—or for you to be escorted to Mercia, where I could convince—"

Believe him? Why should I believe anything this man says? From the very moment we met in the streets of Vorana, his close proximity was intended to realize one purpose: my death.

"And what if you hadn't been able to convince them?" she asked, a quiver in her voice. To Caskentia, she had been nothing more than another pox-ridden village. It didn't matter how many lives she had saved, or would save.

If I cannot be controlled, I will be killed.

"Oh, he wouldn't have. But he would have tried, I grant him that. We would have provided a cleaner death within Mercia, in any case." Daveo paused as he spat out a tooth and then looked to Alonzo. "Do you really think they would send someone as inexperienced as you on a mission this vital? We wanted you out of the way for months, to silence your mother's trap. We doubted you had the nerve to carry through. You're too much like your father, a diplomat. Soft." His face contorted in disgust. "Not even I thought you'd become besotted with the quarry."

"'Trust above all' is the Daggers' motto. This deceit . . . I do not believe you," Alonzo said stiffly. But she could see he did believe, and how gravely the words wounded him. The words were intended to wound him.

Little Daveo sneered. "Come closer, then, if you doubt."

"Are any of my damned stewards who they claim to be?" asked the captain. No one paid him heed. Alonzo edged forward.

"Is it wise to get so close to him?" Octavia asked. What

if they had not found all of the man's weapons? What if this was all some terrible ploy? And should she care what happened to Alonzo? His allegiance to the Daggers would have led to her death, despite his best intentions.

His best intentions. He was supposed to kill me. He didn't. That means something—everything.

"I must," said Alonzo. He leaned closer to Daveo as the short steward whispered something.

Alonzo straightened. The lean skin of his face had gone haggard, taking on a yellow tint in the lamp and glowstone light. "He is telling the truth."

"That's it?" Octavia stared.

"'Tis proof enough for me." Alonzo sounded as though he was the one who had been beaten and peppered in the face. She recalled the code word he had uttered to Mrs. Stout in Leffen. Daveo must have offered something similar.

"You have a job to do, general's son," said Little Daveo. "Can you do it? Can you act in the name of Queen Evandia?"

The Queen who would burn thousands of her own people to keep her precious palace safe, who did nothing as her people starved and corruption ruled. What was one more body on the pyre?

"Oh God," Mrs. Stout murmured behind her.

Octavia's blood ran cold. *Kill me. Alonzo can kill me and prove himself as a Clockwork Dagger.* She clutched a hand to her waist, where her capsicum flute used to be. *First Miss Percival, now Alonzo.*

His gaze met hers, eyebrows drawn and expression

agonized. Her heartbeat seemed to slow. Alonzo lowered himself as if to speak with Daveo again and then his arm blurred in motion. There was a magnificent crunch and spew of blood as Daveo's head flew back, chin skyward. The back of his head smacked the pillar. The man's head lolled on his neck and drooped downward. Octavia flinched at the hue and cry of the gore, but couldn't help but smile as Alonzo stood and shook out his fist.

"Kellar was right. I make a lousy Dagger." Alonzo looked to the captain. "If what Daveo said about Mr. Drury is true, he must be apprehended, and quickly."

Captain Hue nodded and turned toward the door. "Rogers! Mayhew!" He looked back to Alonzo, his voice lowering. "I know well what a Clockwork Dagger is, boy, and if you two are at odds and he is the superior, you just created a fine mess of trouble for yourself. You'll be the quarry next."

"Indeed." Alonzo's face was grim. "But if Mr. Drury is a Waster, we need to—" He froze in place. "Do you feel that?"

Captain Hue extended a hand, as if feeling for a breeze. "God." His leathered face clenched.

"What? What?" Octavia looked between them.

"We're turning." Cold anger sparked in Captain Hue's eyes. "Someone is piloting the *Argus* off course."

Chapter 18

Octavia thought Alonzo had an imposing figure, but no one could match Captain Hue in presence. He stalked through corridors, not running and yet urgent in his stride. A gaggle of gossiping passengers had stayed around the top of the staircase on deck A. At Captain Hue's approach, they parted, wide-eyed and wordless, allowing him clear passage to the stairs.

Alonzo dropped back to join Octavia. "I want both of you to go to Vincan in the smoking room. Tell him to shut down. He will know what that means."

"Is he a Dagger as well?" she said in a whisper, panting as she hopped down the stairs. She could scarcely hear herself against the thudding of so many feet on metal.

"No, nor does he know I am one, just that I am an agent of some sort."

Octavia flinched at the tautness in his voice. He had defied orders to keep her alive, believing he could persuade his superiors of their error. In truth, he had been regarded as a child at a Solstice dinner. Meddlesome, unwanted, and best exiled to a far distant table.

"I want to stay with you," she said. "I need to. This is about me—"

"And why is it about you?" Captain Hue stopped cold, whirling on his heel to confront her. He stood a few steps below but seemed to tower over her.

"I . . . I am close with the Lady, and the Waste desires my skills," she stammered, the words sounding lame and boastful.

Captain Hue snorted. "Religion be damned." He continued down the steps, his breaths an enraged huff.

"I need to stay with Octavia," said Mrs. Stout.

Alonzo released a heavy exhalation. "You all will be the death of me."

"Then it's a good thing I'm a medician."

Captain Hue rounded a corner on deck B, going in the opposite direction from the smoking room and through another door. A few crewmen stood in the hallway. "Both of you, follow me."

"Yessir," they chimed in melody.

Captain Hue reached into his jacket and pulled out an ivory-handled knife. With the flick of his wrist, he extended the blade. He then shoved his way through the next door and into the control car.

It was a narrow space some ten feet in length. At the far end, rounded windows stared into the bleak night. Men in trim crimson uniforms stood in various positions throughout the room, utterly silent. Mr. Drury stood at the far end beside the rudder wheel. He faced them, his expression cool, eyes bloodshot from the capsicum. He held a young crewman, one hand gripping his hair and the other holding a knife to his throat.

"Miss Leander," he said pleasantly, as if they had just encountered each other on the street.

"What are you doing to my ship?" snarled Captain Hue.

"A slight detour, that's all. I do hope you kept that little steward in custody. I would like to talk with him some more." Mr. Drury leaned to one side as if to nudge the rudder wheel.

"You don't know what you're doing," said the captain, his chest puffing like a roused prairie grouse.

"Actually, I do. I have piloted airships for over twenty years. Don't worry, I'll return your ship and your son to you soon enough." He gave the boy's blond hair a hard tug, jerking his head back more.

Octavia had no intention of squandering any more time. "Mr. Drury, are you a Waster?"

"'Waster' is such a crude term, my lady. We prefer the term 'Dallowmen,' don't we, boys?"

At Mr. Drury's motion, the two crewmen they had met in the hall stepped forward. One pounded Captain Hue in the back of the head while the other kicked the backs of the captain's knees, sending him crumpling to the floor. The hostage whimpered and struggled against the knife. Octavia heard the cry of the blood before she saw the red drip down the pale line of his neck. Alonzo backstepped, herding Octavia and Mrs. Stout toward the hall.

"Get to Vincan," he muttered over his shoulder. "See if he can get you out through the aft keel. I will hold the hallway as long as I can. If they get you off the ship, I will follow."

"Alonzo—"

"Where are you taking my medician?" asked Mr. Drury. The captain groaned on the floor.

"Don't you *dare* get yourself killed," Octavia whispered.

"Go!" yelled Alonzo.

Octavia gripped Mrs. Stout by the arm and half dragged the woman down the hall. She hated fleeing, but she was no use in a fight, not in there. Her satchel bounced between her hip and the wall. Deep yells echoed behind her. The women burst through the door to the public quarters of deck B. A few passengers were on the stairs coming down.

"Mutiny!" Octavia cried. "Wasters have taken control of the ship!"

Their expressions shifted from curiosity to outright panic. Yelps from above indicated her voice had carried up the stair tower. Octavia pushed through to the hallway.

Mrs. Stout panted and whimpered at her arm. "Wasters, Wasters," she repeated in a dark mantra.

Past the lavatories, through the double-doored air lock. She entered the smoking room, pausing there for a moment, heaving for breath. The freshness of cloves and tobacco assailed her nostrils. Vincan stood behind the bar, a glass in hand. He resembled a pale wall against a dark backdrop.

"Wasters!" Octavia managed. "Have taken over the control car. The captain. Alonzo's trying to hold them off."

"Wasters." Vincan bristled. The word echoed in the room as a few other men stepped forward.

"Wasters, here?" growled one, guzzling down the rest of a beer. He wiped his mustache clean with a swipe of his wrist. "Where?" In front of him, two mechanical warriors continued to skirmish for dominion atop the pyramid board. Metal ground on metal, and a mecha snake tumbled to the floor with a pathetic cry.

"They are piloting the ship. Mr. Drury is a Waster, and at least two of the crewmen are as well." Octavia dropped her satchel to the ground, even as Mrs. Stout collapsed into the nearest seat.

The men slammed their glasses on the counter, heading out into the corridor. Octavia looked to Vincan. "Alonzo said to tell you to 'shut down,' whatever that means."

"Eh. Means all the bloody hell's 'bout to break loose. B'why?" he asked, his gaze direct.

"Me. They are after me." Part of her wanted to sink into the floor and sob. *I don't want anyone to fight, to die. Not over me.* "Alonzo said you could get us out the aft keel hatch?"

"Aye, if we're fifteen feet off the ground," growled Vincan. "Hardly gonna toss y'out at five hundred feet, am I?"

Alonzo's intention became clear as the ship tilted to one side. Octavia gripped the sill of the door with one hand and her satchel in the other. Mrs. Stout's thick calves flew up in the air as she grasped the table for dear life. Glass tinkled behind the counter and there were a few resounding crashes from the seating area. Something cold slid against Octavia's leg—it was the mechanical snake, its fangs still bared.

"Oh Lady, he's trying to get control of the ship. That blessed, stupid man." The ship righted and Octavia bumped back against the doorframe. She kicked the little snake, vaulting it into the far wall with a metallic ping.

"Come'n," Vincan said. He reached beneath the counter and pulled out a knife as thick as his forearm. He wedged past Octavia and into the hallway. Before Octavia even had a glimpse of the corridor, he shoved her back again. "Fighting at the stairwell, and somethin' going on down by the crew area as well." A gunshot cracked through the ship and Octavia hit the ground flat.

"Thank God this isn't a hydrogen vessel," said Mrs. Stout in a quivering voice.

"Oh, it can still crash and burn, maybe not so pretty like," Vincan said, quite matter-of-factly.

"That's enough of that talk." Octavia scampered to her feet again, picking up her satchel.

"Eh. So who all is playin' traitor on the crew?"

"Two men that I saw," said Octavia. "One maybe in his twenties, pock-faced, no mustache. The other is bald with a red face and—"

"I know 'em. They like their whiskey."

Something clattered against the outer door. It flew open, revealing a man in steward's garb with a shiny bald pate and ruddy skin.

Vincan's grin was gap-toothed and wide. "Why 'ello."

Octavia retreated behind the inner door, but could still hear the faint mew of blood and the thuds and grunts of combat.

"We can't get out? We're trapped?" asked Mrs. Stout. Her skin was impossibly pale.

Octavia's mind raced. She had a strong feeling that Drury had more than two men on his side aboard. He had planned this operation far too well. If that traitor crewman had already gotten past Alonzo, she had to assume that Alonzo had fallen. *Lady, let him be alive, please.*

"Mrs. Stout, come around here. There's more shelter behind the bar." She motioned Mrs. Stout behind her and toward the corner, near what appeared to be Vincan's pillow and assorted toiletries.

The airship wobbled again as Octavia dropped to both knees and opened up her satchel. Upon her capture, they would undoubtedly take her satchel away. It was the most assured way of keeping her in line. That, and using Mrs. Stout or Alonzo as leverage to keep her cooperative. *I'll need my supplies more than ever. How can I smuggle them on my person?*

"Mrs. Stout, are you quick with a needle?" Octavia began unbuttoning the front of her dress.

"I cannot fall into their clutches." A terrible quiver in Mrs. Stout's voice caused Octavia to glance up. Mrs. Stout held a knife against her own throat, her hand shaking. *Oh, blessed Lady.*

"Mrs. Stout, lower the blade, please."

"You don't understand, child. I can't—I can't be used against Caskentia. I love this land too much! I love it so much, I gave up everything, everything, so that the fighting would stop! So that it wouldn't be over me. I know things didn't happen that way because of Evandia and the Waste, but God, I wanted peace." The loose skin at her neck shivered. "I don't want to be used against Caskentia. I don't want to be a figurehead, or a key." To the vault, and whatever darkness lay within.

Oh Lady. Can I kill Mrs. Stout if necessary, if it will truly avert some sort of cataclysm? Like Caskentia, obliterating hundreds or thousands of people to contain pox?

"Mrs. Stout, I'm begging you, don't do this. Have some faith. If you die, what of your children?"

That caused the older woman to flinch. "I should have told them, warned them. I can't . . . oh, child, I don't know."

"You need to be the one to tell them, Mrs. Stout. Who else will they believe? I wouldn't even believe you were Princess Allendia had I not touched your tattoo and seen the scar. Please."

Mrs. Stout lowered the knife, then dropped it to the floor.

Her eyes on Mrs. Stout, Octavia grabbed the blade and tucked it behind her, on the shelf again.

"You must promise me, Miss Leander. If things seem hopeless, if they seek to somehow get me into Mercia . . ."

"I will do what I can for you, but please, don't ask me to kill you."

Mrs. Stout nodded. "I know. I understand. I'm sorry. The burden that would place on you, violating the Lady's way . . . I'm sorry."

More yells echoed from the hallway. Octavia put a hand to the buttons at her chest again. "We don't have time for apologies now. Can you work a needle, Mrs. Stout?"

"Yes. I think so. What of it?" Mrs. Stout tore off her

gloves while taking in a deep breath. Terror glistened in her eyes, but her hands seemed steadier.

"I have a plan. This pouch has my doctoring supplies. Pull out the needle kit, and pardon my lack of modesty." She let her dress open wide to reveal the padded buttresses of her brassiere. The design was simple, like a wide band of ribbon to restrict the breasts and elasticized cloth extending to the navel. With a twist of her wrist, Octavia undid the eye hooks in front. The air chilled her breasts and made her break out in goose bumps. Taking care not to meet Mrs. Stout's eye, she grabbed a scalpel and tore out sections of thread and tugged out the cotton padding with her fingers.

"You're going to stuff the brassiere," said Mrs. Stout, awe in her voice. "We could do the same with mine—"

"If we have the time." With the fabric hanging loose from her chest, she caused the holes in the seams to gape as she began to pour in her herbs. Honeyflower first, for forming circles. Then pampria, and bellywood bark. Mrs. Stout reached over and began to mend the gaps as Octavia moved across her chest from left to right. Their knuckles bumped and herbs spilled, but they worked in swift concert. Octavia didn't dare pour in all of her supply; she had to take care that the band of the camisole was not too lumpy, and the Wasters would be suspicious if all her jars but wet Linsom had been emptied.

Mrs. Stout put the needle and thread away as Octavia quickly palpated the cloth to even out the herbs on both sides of the eye-hook closures. As long as she kept on her underclothes, she was not powerless.

And if I'm without my underclothes, I have a whole new set of worries all together.

Male yells reverberated through the thin walls. She heard Vincan's deep voice and heavy smacks. The wall shuddered. The fight was getting closer. The Wasters must know where they were. Her eyes raced over her satchel. What else could she take? A hand went to her hair, already a wild mess of curls.

"Mrs. Stout, I'm redoing your hair."

"Think you can fit a bag of honeyflower in there?" Mrs. Stout asked with a nervous giggle.

"No. Sharper objects, as long as you don't intend anything foolish . . . ?"

"No. No. Do what you will, child."

Octavia plucked out pins and released Mrs. Stout's silver mane, silky and slightly oily to the touch. She hid her smallest pair of scissors within and rolled it up again, then secured the bun with two of her scalpels, their blades obscured in the mass of hair. As much as she disliked doctoring, Octavia felt better with some basic implements at hand.

"Turn around, child. I'll do the same."

Octavia did, facing the inner shelves of the bar. She could see part of the entry just beyond. Heavy steps thudded down the hallway accompanied by more yells. She finished the buttons on her dress and patted her chest to see if any lumps were visible to the eye. It looked as smooth as before, even as she felt the uneven pressure against her sensitive skin. *Lady, grant the fabric some extra strength so the herbs don't poke through and drive me mad with itching.*

Mrs. Stout's fingers combed through her hair, swift and strong without being painful. "Your hair has such life and body. Unlike my daughter's. Hers is thick but straight. It can go as limp as corn silk."

Octavia closed her eyes for a moment, as if she could pretend this was a moment of casual gossip, not that they were hiding behind a bar with Wasters in pursuit.

"What should I put in your hair?" Mrs. Stout asked.

Octavia craned back and fumbled in her foldout kit. "These," she said, and passed over two bullet probes in dull gray. A heavy clattering near the door reverberated through the floorboards. She barely swallowed a whimper. *This is how the gremlins felt.*

"Done," said Mrs. Stout. Octavia touched the tight bun at the back of her head. Through the thickness of hair, she could barely detect the two small nubs of the probes. She reared up on her knees and reassembled her satchel with trembling fingers. The top flap had just closed when the door to the smoking room burst open.

"There!" Mr. Drury.

Octavia whirled around, elbow angled out. A pock-faced boy dodged with a slight yelp. Blood warbled from their bodies, the notes varied. Some of the blood was their own, but not all.

"What have you done with the others?" Octavia asked. She pushed Mrs. Stout against the wall, shielding her with both arms. She wanted to ask after Alonzo but she dared not draw more attention to him.

"That's none of your concern." The door behind Mr.

Drury opened again and admitted one of the academic fops, his nose bloodied and a wound in his arm hastily bound and dripping red. Each plunk of blood to the floor welled as if in crescendo. The man carried Octavia's suitcase with both arms.

"I should have struck you harder with that tray," she said, tone icy.

The man seemed reluctant to meet her eye as he set down the case.

"Now," said Mr. Drury. "You must change into your Percival garb, as it will survive travel best. Anything you wish to keep, put in your satchel."

She glared. "I'm not going anywhere. I bought passage on this ship and—"

"Oh, don't pretend to be such a silly ninny. I know better. My men are in control of the ship and are now mooring it. We'll disembark in a matter of minutes. You will be dressed and ready, or I will begin to execute your fellow passengers, one by one. Starting with this one." He waved his hand at his back.

The man behind him opened the outer door. One of the little girls from the promenade was shoved through the gap. Tears streaked her face and she gripped a filthy doll with one hand. Mr. Drury tugged a .45 Gadsden from his waistband and lowered the muzzle to the child's head.

"Well?" he asked.

Octavia forced herself to take in a deep breath and fill her lungs, as she did in her Al Cala exercises. She held it for a moment, focusing on the Lady and her Tree, envisioning a branch as thick as a horse crushing this man flat. No guilt twinged in her chest at the blasphemous thought. She stood with effort, as if weighed down. Mrs. Stout scrambled up behind her.

"I'm not changing in here," Octavia said.

"No. Go in there." He motioned to the sitting area. "Your friend can block the doorway to grant you privacy. Leave your satchel on the floor."

She had expected as much. Octavia reached behind her and found Mrs. Stout's hand. Her flesh was cold, like chicken flesh from an icebox. Octavia gave her fingers a squeeze and pulled Mrs. Stout forward.

Mr. Drury opened the suitcase. Her medician gown lay on top, carefully folded and glimmering. She grabbed the gown, trousers, and apron in one hand and retreated toward the sitting room. Mrs. Stout stayed in the doorway, her back to the little room. She made for a good and broad barrier, her legs braced wide and arms out, even as she violently trembled. If not for the doorframe, she likely would not have been able to stand on her own.

Mr. Drury hasn't shown interest in Mrs. Stout yet. Maybe he doesn't know of the extra instructions provided to Mr. Grinn. Or maybe he's simply biding his time.

Octavia pushed herself into a corner and began to change into her uniform. Each movement was brusque and determined. Now that Mr. Drury had them cornered, a determined peace had settled on her. *Alonzo will be okay. Surely he's holed up somewhere in the ship. I must stay calm. I must keep Mrs. Stout calm. The ship will be safer without me aboard. And once we are in the mountains . . .*

Her heart fluttered as if it could fly away. She took in another deep breath as she pulled up her trousers. The vivid scent of honeyflower overwhelmed her for a moment, as if she held the laden brassiere right next to her face. The scent was of coziness and comfort, everything embodied by the Lady. With it came strength and resolution. *The Lady is with me.*

And then the image of the boy returned to her mind. Bloodied. His fingers curled, his hand limp. The scent of honeyflower faded as terror flared in her chest again. *Why me? Why him? What did the Lady mean by such an act?*

Octavia pressed her gown to her lips and struggled against the bile in her throat.

THE MOORING TOWER WAS a black obelisk in the darkness of night. Lights circled the top of the structure and created a blinding glare as Octavia disembarked. Her shoulder and hip felt naked without the comforting weight of the satchel, which was now in Mr. Drury's hands. The metal deck clattered underfoot, the echo more pronounced compared to the more solid construction of the ship.

An enemy mooring tower, concealed here within the very borders of Caskentia. Such a thing wasn't supposed to exist.

Mrs. Stout was a shadow, emitting occasional whimpers like a hungry pup. Two crewmen followed close behind them. Blood cried from their bodies but neither had serious wounds. There had been blood in the hallways as well, though no corpses. No stink of death. She tried to take that as a positive sign, though the absence of any news made her lungs tight with frustration. Mr. Drury made no mention of any casualties aboard. Despite seeing her with Alonzo on multiple occasions, he dismissed the man as a mere steward.

Octavia prayed with every breath that Mr. Drury's arrogance had kept Alonzo alive.

The mooring tower had been fitted with stairs, not a lift. As she rounded the docking station, she could see more figures on the ground below, and a large cluster of horses. A dozen perhaps, though it was hard to judge amidst the play of light and shadows. She reached the ground and breathed in the dankness of the wet grass. Mrs. Stout made a strangled sound. Octavia turned. The woman had sunk to her knees, shivering.

"Be strong," Octavia whispered, eyeing their guards as she dragged Mrs. Stout to her feet. The woman's eyes were wide with terror.

"Drury!" called one of the men.

"Lanskay! I hoped it would be you." The two men walked up to each other, greeting with claps on the back and chuckles. Drury wore his trim suit and cap, a stark contrast to his countryman in his workman's scruff. "Here, my friend. You must meet our talented recruit."

Recruit. Anger curdled in Octavia's stomach. The two men approached and a beam of light from the tower illuminated the newcomer. He was tall, like a weed bursting to growth after a rain. His thick blond hair had been pulled back into a tight queue, showing the severe angles in his cheeks and jaw. The warmth of his presence flowed ahead of him like an invisible fog and she felt herself standing straighter as she scrutinized him.

"An infernal?" she asked. *Oh Lady. The Wasters have a fire-wielder, here? For what ill purpose?*

"She is good!" said Lanskay. His thick accent reminded her of Mr. Grinn. A wad of tobacco bulged against his cheek.

Drury's wide grin appeared to be genuine for once. "You should see her in action. The Lady has bestowed her with a particular touch. She diagnosed and treated our zyme contamination entirely on her own. There were no extended illnesses or fatalities aboard ship."

"You . . ." Octavia said, almost speechless with rage.

Mr. Drury bowed with a flourish. "Indeed. All designed as a test of your talents. Zymes are my specialty, in truth. I was most dismayed when you resolved the matter on the front so quickly." *Quickly!* Thousands of men died and hundreds more spent weeks in intestinal agony, too many to be treated by medicians who had exhausted their supplies of bellywood bark for Drury's "test." "But upon hearing that one young woman was behind the brilliance, my thoughts took a different turn."

"Aye. He was smitten." Lanskay elbowed his comrade. "The man delights in being outfoxed. Makes his brain begin to truly work."

Drury's smile sickened her. *No wonder he didn't take my hints—or my jab to his stomach—in their proper context.*

Loud scrambling on metal caused her to turn. A mustached crewman walked Daveo down the stairs. The steward had been stripped to the waist, revealing a torso darkened with blood and contusions. His hands were secured behind his back and a gag muzzled him. Even so, his chin was tilted up and defiant. Octavia looked up the tower. A man at the top was disengaging the airship. The *Argus* was going to leave.

"Who is the little man?" asked Lanskay.

"One of the stewards on the ship. I do believe he is the Dagger sent to kill our medician." Drury stepped forward to wrest Daveo from the other guard, half dragging him to his companions.

"Kill the medician!" Lanskay drew in his breath with a hiss. "With so few born with the gift . . . !"

Drury loomed over Daveo and then bent to look him in the eye. "Even more, he let our friend Mr. Grinn be blamed for one of his attempts on Miss Leander. Did you not, little man?" He grabbed him by the scruff of his hair and shook him.

"You mean, Mr. Grinn was . . ." Octavia began.

"Likely trying to save you when the others found him there and assumed the worst. Not that I can blame them, as the appearance was quite deceiving. And I bet you were hiding under one of those tables in that dark room, like a little cockroach, now, weren't you?" He shook Daveo again. "Do you know what we do with cockroaches in the Dallows, steward? We eat them."

"Sometimes you can feed a whole family on cockroaches alone," added Lanskay. The other men laughed.

"Where are Mr. Grinn's books, little man? Did you send

them along to your friends in Mercia?" Drury lowered his voice to a deadly hiss. Behind Octavia, Mrs. Stout gasped. Octavia gave her a sharp look to silence her.

"Take off his gag, Drury. I can make him talk. I might even make him sing," said Lanskay.

Oh Lady, let them keep him gagged so he cannot utter a word about Alonzo. From twenty feet away, Daveo's eyes met hers, dark and cold. The airship's motors thrummed above as the craft began to pull away.

"His actions have condemned him more than any words. We can't waste any more time on this filth." Drury let Daveo drop to the ground with a solid thud. He made a quick gesture and a group of men advanced. They hauled Daveo away, his heels dragging through the grass. "Secure him. We'll grant him prairie justice."

A muffled yell escaped from Daveo's gag as he began to wrestle and kick. The other men subdued him in a knot of fists.

"Prairie justice. Oh God," moaned Mrs. Stout.

"Who is this other woman?" asked Lanskay. "Surely not another medician? Did you find a sale price on Percivals?"

Octavia stepped to shield Mrs. Stout. "She's someone who should have been left on the ship."

"Such nobility in guarding her friend," said Mr. Drury, quite pleased. "This is one Viola Stout, the publisher's wife. Taney advised us to bring her in."

A Taney used to be grand potentate. Is this a relation?

"Surely she isn't a virgin!" said Lanskay. The others laughed. Some fifty feet away, the sound of pounding metal rang out. A stake was being driven into the ground, and Daveo secured to it.

"No, no. She has two grown children, from what I gather. But Taney has something in mind," said Mr. Drury. Octavia reached behind her and found Mrs. Stout's cold and trembling hand. "Tell me, Miss Leander, do you ride?"

"I can give her something to ride!" called one of the men.

Drury whirled on his heel. "Who said that? Come forward, please."

The man left his horse ground-tied and approached. He stopped before Mr. Drury, head up and hands clasped at his back, and without a word he accepted Mr. Drury's knife to the gut. The man sank to his knees, groaning. Blood and bowel fluid screamed, high and anxious.

"Mr. Drury!" Octavia couldn't help but step forward. *Oh Lady. Not another death, not because of me.* "He's going to—"

"See, men? Look at her benevolence. Insulted in such a crude way, yet still willing to save him. My dear lady, he's not worth the herbs. Unlike in your corrupt land, we do not tolerate such behavior. We live by a higher code." Mr. Drury waved to the other men, who waited close by, motionless, and pointed toward Octavia. "That woman is one of God's chosen. Regard her as a High Daughter. The next man to commit such an affront will not have such a merciful death. Is that understood?" They murmured assent. The screams of blood dulled to a whimper.

"That means you're regarded with the esteem of a daughter of their potentate," Mrs. Stout murmured, her voice trembling.

"I'm quite content as the daughter of a village doctor and teacher," Octavia whispered back. The Dallowman's blood quieted, his soul departing. *So fast. Mr. Drury kills with chilling efficacy.*

"Now." Mr. Drury turned to Octavia. "Do you ride?"

"Yes."

"And you, good woman?" He looked to Mrs. Stout.

"I do not." Her voice was scarcely audible.

"Bring forward their mounts, please."

A chestnut bay and an all-white mare were led forward. In that instant, Octavia knew that the mare was intended for her. Despite the remoteness of their location and the burs in the grass, the mare's mane and tail had obviously been brushed through recently, her legs free of filth. This wasn't a mere horse. It was a symbol, and here she was in her shimmering white medician's garb, groomed to match.

Mrs. Stout's chilled and sweaty fingers dug into her hand. "We have to do something. We can't go with them. We can't."

"We can't run here. If I try to fight, they'll kill you or others," Octavia murmured.

"Run away. We have to run away." Mrs. Stout shrieked and tried to pull away, out of Octavia's grip.

"Listen to me." Octavia bent her head close. "We will live. We will get out of this. But for now, we must play along. Don't draw attention to yourself. Please. I can't bear to lose anyone else." She focused on keeping her voice level. Despite her terror, despite the shakiness of her faith, she refused to show weakness before these men.

Hooves crunched in the grass and Octavia faced the two men. A beam from the tower highlighted them for mere seconds. They wore the rough dungarees of workmen, their faces creased by sun and toil.

"M'lady," said the one leading the white mare. "I can help you up—"

"No. But let me assist my friend first. She is very scared, and with reason. I expect you to show her the same regard as you do me, do you understand?" The fierceness of her tone caused his eyes to widen.

"I—of course, m'lady."

"Her skirt isn't suited for riding. May I have a knife to cut a slit?"

To her shock, he instantly handed over his knife. The blade was warm from its proximity to his thigh, the handle worn. She hesitated for a moment, wondering if she could strike. *No. That's not my way, not the Lady's way. Besides, we couldn't escape this number of men, not here.* Octavia crouched down before Mrs. Stout's skirt. The blade sliced through the cloth with ease, and she returned it to its owner.

"I'll stay with you right here," said Octavia, soothing Mrs. Stout as she would a patient. As the other man held the bay still, Octavia helped Mrs. Stout to clamber into the saddle. The older woman sat awkwardly, thick thighs jutted out on either side, her hands clutching the saddle horn for dear life. Under Octavia's glare, the man secured Mrs. Stout's wrists to the horn. Octavia noted that the rope was slack enough to not immediately chafe.

Octavia mounted up on her own. The mare shifted

beneath her, light on her hooves, and calmed with a quick stroke to the withers. This was not the thick-furred pony or heavy draft horse one associated with the Waste, but a creature of fine breeding, probably from the southern nations. The sick knot clenched in her stomach again. *How many months have they planned this escapade, to fetch such a horse?*

Mr. Drury trotted up beside her. His stallion was chestnut like so many of the others. "Miss Leander, I want you to note that your hands are free. I have your satchel here." He motioned to where it was secured behind his saddle. "And we have your friend. I believe you're familiar with the expert marksmanship of the men of the Dallows. Should you make any move to escape, Mrs. Stout will be shot in the head. Is everything clear?"

She ground her teeth together. "Perhaps you should go ahead and secure my wrists, then."

"That would hardly build a relationship of trust between us, now, would it?" His smile was pleasant and toothless. The symphony of his body was calm despite his injuries, the blood crusted and quelled.

The lights from the tower flicked off, casting them into complete darkness. Octavia blinked rapidly to encourage her eyes to adjust.

"A small crew will stay behind and dismantle the tower and then catch up with us," he said. "We will be riding for some hours before we set up camp. Do let me know if you are hungry. Lanskay?"

The blond man pointed toward where Daveo sat, tethered to the ground. Prickles of magic whirled in the air, stinging Octavia's nostrils and whirling across her scalp, and then the heat came. It was a flash from this distance, a beam of flame from Lanskay's fingertip to Daveo. The little steward screamed, arching his back, and then the flames consumed him whole. His agony smacked into her senses, dizzying her for a moment, and then it stopped. Another quick blast, and the dead Dallowman was incinerated as well. The image of flames burned in her retinas for a second more and then there was only the blackness of the night. She sucked in a breath and almost retched at the odor of cooked meat. *Oh Lady, Lady.* She could only stare at where Daveo once knelt. *He's dead. Burned alive, like Mother and Father.*

"Could I hit the airship from here, you think?" Lanskay called.

Octavia sucked in a breath. The *Argus* was a gray cylinder above, well beyond accurate gun range, but that meant nothing to an infernal. "No!" she yelled, digging her heels into the mare's sides. The horse took off with a snort. Some of the others yelled, but she rode directly into the mob of men, not away from them.

"Those are innocent civilians," she snapped as she reined up in front of Lanskay, as if she could shield the ship from him. "Don't you dare."

He cocked his head, his lazy smile growing colder. He worked the tobacco against his jaw and then spat into the grass. "No one in Caskentia is innocent."

She wouldn't win any argument on that subject, not with a Waster. "Then I beg you, spare my friends aboard. Please."

He hummed a lively tune beneath his breath, casting idle eyes to the starry heavens. It disturbed her to think he must have a lovely singing voice. "Oh, very well. I should save my energy, anyway."

And energy he had. It rolled from him like heat from a house fire. Powerful as he was, he might feel the same from her.

Lanskay burns people. He burns them with a flick of his fingers. An infernal like him stood on the deck of the Alexandria, *ready to destroy my village, only that time the magus burned with everyone else.*

How many times has Lanskay fire-bombed Caskentia? How many thousands burned as he lit a load of oil that was dropped upon a city below?

Octavia hated him from the depths of her soul.

"Come," said Mr. Drury. His tack jingled as he rode alongside them. "Let the ship be. They can carry word to Mercia, work the government into a tizzy, make them pretend they can actually rally their troops to try and stop us." The other men raised a cheer, and she was filled with dread at the dark intentions left unsaid.

Octavia cast a glance to Mrs. Stout, hunkered over the saddle horn and sobbing, and then to the airship dwindling in size above. "Lady, be with us," she whispered, and encouraged her mare to join the rest in a canter toward the looming mountains.

Chapter 19

Unseen birds cawed, wings flapping somewhere in the ebony night. The group accelerated from a lope to a gallop. Octavia and Mrs. Stout were kept penned in the middle of the pack. They entered the hills and found a trail that quickly narrowed so that only two could ride abreast. Branches slapped at Octavia's legs, gouging them. The moon played peekaboo with the clouds.

The men were quiet. Far ahead she could see the silhouette of Mr. Drury's hat and the pale sheen of Lanskay's ponytail. Their armaments gleamed in the scant light. Every man had at least a pistol, while others had rifles holstered to their saddles. As Wasters and soldiers both, they no doubt were excellent shots. Then there was the matter of Lanskay.

If—when—Alonzo comes in pursuit, he'll be slaughtered.

No. There must be a way for us to escape. Somehow.

Al Cala meditations would have soothed her spirit, but right now Octavia wanted to be angry. And though she knew the Lady was there with her, the fragrance of blessed herbs drifting from her chest, she didn't wish to fixate on the Tree. That would only make her think of that boy, of the life that flared so briefly in his eyes.

If I'm supposed to be so extraordinarily blessed, why did the Lady betray me at that moment, toying with a child as one would a puppet on strings? I've had patients die, but none like that. None claiming to see the Lady and bearing a message to me, only to expire once the enigmatic words were uttered.

Her chest ached deep within, tears smarting her eyes.

"Father said . . . Father always said be strong. Be strong. Like a little soldier, hair done up in curls," Mrs. Stout mumbled beneath her breath. She was hunched over like an old man hauling full water jugs on a yoke.

"Mrs. Stout?" Octavia whispered.

"I can get back home. Guards will be looking for me. The whole kingdom will be looking." A strange keening sound escaped her throat. "I just want to get home."

Oh Lady. Octavia had seen this sort of behavior before in soldiers who had endured some terrible trauma. Even if they emerged with sound bodies, it was as though mental shrapnel had lodged in their brains, sending them back to the past. Once a soldier had witnessed his brother immolated by a Waster infernal's blast. The man lay in his cot, reliving some childhood moment when that brother had burned his leg on a stove and his mother had doctored him with an aloe salve. "Mama will make it all better, Mama will make it all better," he had chanted all night long.

"Mrs. Stout." Octavia reined her horse closer to the other woman, causing their legs to scrape together. "Viola. Viola."

Mrs. Stout showed no response, her mumbles continuing as her gaze focused on her horse's withers.

Octavia had to ground Mrs. Stout in the present, as unpleasant as it might be. It would be safer than focusing on the past and everything that came with it. "Mrs. Stout. Viola? Viola?" She sucked in a breath, lowering her voice even more. "Allendia? Princess?"

Mrs. Stout's head slowly turned, her shoulders not moving from their stiffened state.

"Look here. Remember me? Octavia Leander? We are roommates aboard the *Argus*. You are Viola Stout. Your husband was Donovan Stout. Your children . . ." Her voice trailed away. She was certain Mrs. Stout had mentioned their names, but she couldn't recall.

"My children." Mrs. Stout's voice cracked. Tears flooded her eyes. Octavia reached over and squeezed her hand.

"Hey now," called one of the men behind them. Octavia shot him a venomous glare.

"We are going to get through this," Octavia whispered. "I know you're scared, but you must maintain control. You must remember who you are. You must have hope."

"But they are taking me . . . us . . . to Mercia or the Waste . . . the Waste."

"They are trying, yes, but we're not there yet. That'll take days or weeks, depending on the route and the passes." She paused. Snow could fall this early in the season. She and Mrs. Stout weren't attired for extreme weather, though she was sure the men would tend to them should the need arise. Snow would make them far too easy to track if they did try to escape, though. Wasters were master huntsmen and horsemen, crude technologically yet capable of making do with little at their disposal. They had to be to survive in that desiccated land. "Look at me, Mrs. Stout. Focus."

Soft sobs shuddered through the older woman's body. "They are going to use my babies to kill people, then kill them. It's my fault. I should have warned them. I shouldn't have stayed here. Nelly . . . how could Nelly do this?"

Those words sent a nauseating chill through Octavia. "Look at me, Viola. Don't focus on the past or what might happen. Say to yourself, 'I am Viola Stout and I am brave.'"

Mrs. Stout's tongue darted out to lick the dry crevices of her lips. "I am Viola Stout and I am brave?"

"Yes. But say it like you believe it." The trail widened and hoofbeats approached them from behind.

"What's wrong with her?" asked one of the guards. He wore a black beard thick enough to shield him from frostbite.

"She's terrified witless," Octavia said, hoping for sympathy.

He snorted. "The women of Caskentia are too soft."

Octavia stiffened. "I'm a woman of Caskentia, and I assure you, I am *not* soft."

"You are of the Tree." He raised a fist to the center of his chest and nodded.

This esteem for me might be the best way for me to keep Mrs. Stout safe and alive.

"I am, and this woman is both my patient and my dear

friend, and I'm worried for her. She's not of an age to handle such strain."

"We won't ride all night. It'll help her to get some sleep." His voice was softer, almost kind. Octavia afforded him a polite smile in thanks, and he pulled back to join his comrades as the brush squeezed in on them again.

"I am Viola Stout and I am brave, I am Viola Stout . . ." The crackling whisper kept time with the thud of hoofbeats. Viola took in a deep breath and sat straighter. Octavia recognized the regal carriage that had become so familiar in recent days.

"Thank you, Octavia," said Viola, her whisper hoarse. "The fear, the memories, it all came back to me. It felt so real. More real than this." She shuddered. "I'm sorry."

"There's no need to apologize. You're a strong woman, Viola, and this is a terrible test to endure again. But you will endure."

Viola nodded, tears glistening in her eyes. "Yes. Yes. We will endure. I am Viola Stout and I am brave." She lifted her chin, her chest puffing outward.

Octavia shifted in her saddle and looked to the moon where it sat between the hills. Somewhere far away, that same moon hovered in the branches of the Lady's Tree.

"I am Octavia Leander and I am brave," she whispered. Her chilled hands clenched the reins as she repeated the mantra.

TIME LOST MEANING AS they rode on. Adrenaline was replaced by weariness that seeped into Octavia's bones. Mrs.

Stout's whispers faded and she slumped forward, this time dozing. On occasion she awakened with a start and Octavia calmed her again, reminding her of where she was and why. But Octavia shook off the urge to nap, alert for any useful scrap of information on their whereabouts or plans. To her frustration, the men remained silent, or murmured too low for her ears to catch.

Then the trail opened up to reveal a clearing. Mr. Drury raised an arm and the column shuffled to a halt.

"Set up," Mr. Drury said. "Get the ladies' tent established first."

"Yes sir," answered one of the men. He and the others dismounted and scurried into action.

Octavia groaned as she dismounted. It had been a few months since she had ridden—the academy had sold everything but the Frengian draft horses for the plow and wagon—and she felt the strain. She took Mrs. Stout's horse by the bit and led both it and her own to one side. Mrs. Stout dozed in the saddle, and Octavia was unwilling to wake her until the tent was ready. She noted that several men stayed quite close to her. Another guarded the trailhead whence they had come. Beyond the clearing and the shadows of trees, it was difficult to ascertain their surroundings.

Something chittered in the branches above, sounding rather like a gremlin. She glanced up but it was far too dark to see anything. A guard looked up at the tree, frowning.

How quickly would Alonzo follow? *Could* he follow? The airship didn't dare linger close to those Wasters disassembling the mooring tower. As it was, the *Argus* would have to hover close to the ground for Alonzo to make a jump, which held plenty of dangers for both man and ship. The Wasters hadn't taken pains to hide their trail—these men were an arrogant lot—but with Alonzo on foot, he would never catch up.

Or he was already dead or dying on the Argus. *Oh Lady.*

She wasn't going to wait for rescue. They needed horses. Octavia needed her satchel. She could set simple snares so they wouldn't starve once they escaped. But how to prevent pursuit?

"Tent's ready," said one of the men gruffly. He cut through the ropes at Mrs. Stout's wrists. The woman awoke with a start.

"What? Where are we? Octavia?"

"I'm here, Viola." Using Mrs. Stout's first name seemed prudent, and showed the closeness of their friendship. "Lean on me and I'll help you down." Gravity did the rest. Mrs. Stout landed in a heap and stood again, bowlegged.

A faint sound came from above, and not the jabber of a gremlin. Octavia tilted her head toward the night sky. Around her, the men stilled as well. The man who held the horses' reins placed one hand to his gun and looked up.

"A buzzer?" one man asked, his voice low.

"Yeah. High up." Another man spat on the ground. "Could be following the pass."

The man with the horses grunted. "Maybe, maybe not." The buzzing sound was gone.

Mr. Drury made a crude motion to the men. "If a buzzer

comes low, shoot it down. We can't afford to be seen. You, get these women prepared for their respite."

Octavia and Viola were permitted a few minutes of privacy in the bushes and then led inside the tent. The space was small but adequate. Two bag-blankets had been laid out along with a single glowstone to grant them some light.

"I don't suppose I should take off my dress," said Viola, brushing some dirt from her skirt as she sat on a blanket. Her voice trembled, but that defiant gleam had returned to her eyes. She was doing her utmost to be strong.

"No. Keep on your shoes as well." Octavia claimed the blankets nearest the door and touched the fabric of the flap, testing it. The weave was coarse, with the outer layer soaked in oil to render it waterproof. The scissors concealed in Viola's hair would probably pierce it, but go dull all too soon. Perhaps one of the scalpels could slash through.

"Miss Leander." Mr. Drury's silky voice caused her hand to immediately go where the capsicum flute once lay against her ribs.

"I'm here."

"I would speak to you alone."

"I'm not leaving Viola. We're both awake."

"Very well." Mr. Drury entered, doffing his tweed cap as he did. "You ladies are well?"

"As well as prisoners can be," she said.

"It's my hope you will not see yourself as a prisoner much longer. We are blessed to have you among us."

"The feeling is not mutual, Mr. Drury. I want to know your intentions."

"The good of the Dallows, most assuredly. But it is not my place to speak more on that matter. We'll be joined by more comrades in the morning."

Her stomach clenched as in a fist. "More comrades?"

"Are you hungry? Thirsty?"

"I am surprised you haven't offered some of that Royal-Tea of yours."

Mr. Drury laughed, the sound so light and casual it made her wince. "I do have some with me. Its properties are quite useful at times, but you will learn more of that in the morning as well. Do you need food?"

Octavia didn't trust these poisoners, but she and Viola needed their strength if they were to escape. "Yes, please. Viola?" The older woman nodded, her lips compressed tight as if she didn't trust herself to speak.

Mr. Drury turned and hollered, "Bring the ladies some food." Octavia heard heavy footsteps outside. Mr. Drury looked toward her again and held out a small parcel. She accepted it and looked inside, angling the bag toward the weak glowstone light. There were several cakes of corn pone, the disks as wide as her hand, and a few broad pieces of dried meat.

"If you have need of anything, ask one of the guards." Mr. Drury turned toward the flap again. The compulsion overcame her and she had to ask.

"Mr. Drury." Oh, how she hated how his eyes lit up when she spoke. "Tell me, did you kill anyone aboard the *Argus*?"

"A few fools put up a fight. One man was shot and a few

were stabbed. We didn't go out of our way to kill anyone, but . . ." He shrugged and his eyes narrowed. "Be sensible, Miss Leander. Don't expect anyone from the airship to come to your rescue. They will limp toward Mercia to spread their tales of woe, but they'll all be silenced soon enough."

"Silenced? How?"

"Why, they'll be dead." Mr. Drury's smile was dazzling. "Sleep well, Miss Leander."

Octavia did sleep, but only due to sheer exhaustion. Her restless slumber was plagued by the sensation that she was still swaying back and forth on a saddle.

And then there was the matter of Mr. Drury's threat. *How can these Wasters slaughter a city of Mercia's size and scope? Are they plotting some attack with zymes, infiltrating the water supply? Are they going to access the vault—and can they somehow use the elements of the Tree against Caskentia?*

She wasn't sure how the Tree could be dangerous, but she couldn't completely ignore the words of King Kethan. The city itself was strongly warded so that infernals such as Lanskay couldn't enter. The Wasters would have to choose some other means of attack.

A streak of daylight and the ruckus of horses finally caused her to fully awaken. She lay there for a moment, breathing through sudden panic at her whereabouts. Mrs. Stout was curled up in her blankets, her face a mask of peace. Octavia pushed herself upright and went to the tent flap.

The massive peak of the Giant dominated the southern sky. She had never seen the volcanic mountain so close before, its broad cap white with snow all year long. Though it had to be several days distant, it looked close enough to reach out and touch. Closer, there were large black mounds as big as the surrounding hills. The surface looked strangely rough in texture, though not like a hillside charred in a wildfire. It took her a moment to recall a similar sight in the north. The blackened mounds were copper slag; this was, or used to be, a copper-mining facility. *This is the Black Heaps mentioned in the correspondence of Adana Dryn.*

Noise drew her attention to the camp itself. A large cluster of men were on horseback, milling at the far side. Was the camp packing up so soon? She eyed her surroundings. No. Many men were still lying on the ground near their fires, though one large tent had been erected in the center of the camp. The rattle and creak of wagon wheels was new as well. That meant a passable road was nearby.

It also meant reinforcements had arrived.

"Do you need anything?" asked a gruff voice. The guard stood only a few feet away.

"I am hungry."

"Food will be brought." With his fingers to his mouth, he blew a piercing whistle. Behind her, Mrs. Stout stirred with a loud gasp. Near one of the fires, a man shuffled forward and ladled something steaming from a pot.

"What's going on?" Octavia asked.

"Taney's here." The guard accepted the dish and passed it on. The bowl was cozily warm between her palms, almost too hot to hold. The beans smelled fragrant and wonderful, and her parched mouth watered in response. She had no great fondness for camp beans, but appetite overruled taste.

Octavia retreated into the tent, the bowl cradled near her chest. Mrs. Stout sat up, her hair a wild bird's nest. "Did he say Taney?"

"Yes." She extended the bowl to Viola, who shook her head with such violence that one of the scalpels fell out.

"I know I should eat, but I've barely kept down that corn pone. Taney is here?" Viola shuddered. "He was one of the men, back when . . ."

Octavia put a finger to her lips. The tent cloth was too thin for any illusion of privacy. "You know the name from your youth."

"He was the one . . . who started the first war." And they both knew how that war had started. Viola looked deathly pale.

"Surely this can't be the same man fifty years later."

"Probably not." Viola's whisper was hoarse. "He's the one I escaped from."

Taney. The man who had wanted to make Princess Allendia a princess of the Waste, create a new royal lineage, and carry the Gilded Age to the Dallows. The leader of the settlers. This Taney is likely still a leader high up within the Dallows' military.

And if someone of that caliber is here, that says even more about their intent with this mission.

Viola crawled on her hands and knees to the side of the tent and retched. Octavia immediately set down the bowl and went to aid, bracing the older woman's shoulders as she emptied her gut. Then Octavia kept her steady as Viola's shoulders heaved in sobs.

"Keep faith," Octavia murmured. She said it to herself as much as to Viola.

Viola leaned forward, weeping. Octavia could do little else, so she unpinned Viola's hair and combed out the snarls with her fingers. She pulled out the scissors and tucked them into her apron pocket. They were the length of her palm and wouldn't be visible to the eye, nor was she likely to be searched. She hoped. She coiled Viola's hair up again and secured it with the pins and scalpels, then returned to her beans. They were cool enough to eat. Octavia restrained herself from eating more than half and set down the bowl near Viola. The older woman had stopped sobbing and sat there, very still, her eyes closed. Her lips moved mutely, and Octavia recognized the mantra from their midnight ride.

"Miss Leander?" The voice came from the other side of the tent flap.

Her stomach immediately soured again. "Mr. Drury."

"Your presence is required in the main tent. Mrs. Stout's as well."

Viola emitted a long, low moan.

"Come." Octavia gripped her by the shoulders and helped her to rise.

"I can do this." Viola patted her arm, her walk stiff as they stepped out into the brightness of day.

"What is that smell?" Mr. Drury asked, wrinkling his nose.

"Viola was ill."

"Hrm. She has a rather delicate constitution, doesn't she?"

"Nothing about me is delicate, Mr. Drury," snapped Viola.

Anger flared, Octavia's cheeks heating. "Mr. Drury, you think she should be docile and handle this like an afternoon picnic? Your people grab us by force, ride us through the night, and you expect what, gratitude?"

Mr. Drury remained cool in the face of her outburst. "A lady of the Dallows would think nothing of it."

"A lady of the Dallows can catch and cook a wyrm for breakfast, I'm sure. She'd also likely be dead by thirty after birthing a dozen children."

"I thank God each day that I am not a woman of the Dallows." Viola practically spat the words.

He shrugged and motioned Octavia to the large tent. "It's a blessing to be of the Dallows, Mrs. Stout. An honor. Even at your age, there is time to correct your thinking." Mrs. Stout snorted in reply.

"You kidnap the lady and insult her age and constitution," Octavia said. "For shame."

Mr. Drury bowed his head to Mrs. Stout, his fingers on the brim of his cap. "My pardon, Mrs. Stout." He looked to Octavia as if for approval. She shuddered.

A man held open the tent flap for them. Mrs. Stout's eyes narrowed and she said nothing to Mr. Drury as she stalked past.

Upon entry, the first thing Octavia noticed was her satchel sitting atop a small table. The second was that the infernal, Lanskay, spoke with a man whose back faced the entry. Third, there was a girl secured to a stake driven into the dirt floor, almost invisible in the dim light. Her eyes widened above a gag as she stared at Octavia.

Octavia immediately closed her eyes, focusing on the music drifting from their fellow captive. The song was steady yet strained, not unlike Viola's, with no indication of injury.

"This is the medician!" a baritone voice boomed. The strange man approached them with commanding strides. Thick black muttonchops extended from his ears to his clean-shaven chin. Blue eyes sparkled against deeply tanned skin. Most of all, Octavia was stunned by his youth. By the glow of his skin and the slenderness of his build, he couldn't have been more than sixteen. Certainly a common age for soldiers, but not for a commander, as she presumed this man to be.

He tilted his head to one side, scrutinizing her as a man would in buying a horse. "She's young."

"Twenty-two this year," said Mr. Drury.

"Quite nice." He circled her. Octavia clutched Viola close against her hip.

"I'm not a piece of meat one buys at a market," Octavia said, her tone icy. Out of nowhere, intense pressure increased in her left forearm, as if the flesh were about to balloon. Considering what happened the last time she bloodlet, that might be true. *Lady, this is not a good time to bleed. Not at all.*

"No. You would be far too expensive."

In the background, Lanskay chortled. Octavia shot him a glare.

"Who is the girl?" asked Octavia. "Why's she bound in that manner?"

"Ah, the true spirit of a medician, thinking of others instead of herself. Or asking who I am." The man's pompous smile reminded her of Mr. Drury, but his voice was the most peculiar thing of all. Despite her situation, she was awed by his words. His pronunciation lured her in, pleased her ears. Mr. Drury may have had the slick voice of a salesman, but this stranger utilized sheer charisma. When he spoke, all would listen.

He continued, "The girl is of no consequence to you. She's about to leave, actually." At his motion another man entered the tent. The girl made some mumbled objection, digging her bare feet against the floor. Octavia took a step forward, her fists balling. Her gaze met the terrified eyes of the girl as she was hauled past. Her face and body were smudged with dirt, her hair a yellow whirlwind.

"Don't hurt her!" said Octavia, suddenly overwhelmed by helplessness.

"I assure you, we will not. We need her alive."

For what purpose? Octavia was afraid to ask, so she turned to a more immediate question. "Who are you?"

"I am Reginald Taney, grand potentate of the United Dallows." Alas, the bold voice did not yet match the body. He braced his shoulders, a gesture that might have been more menacing if he did not have a child's face framed by a beard.

The grand potentate, here within the borders of Caskentia. Oh Lady help us.

Viola emitted a soft whimper. Her body dipped as if she might fall, but Octavia hooked out an arm to keep her upright.

"Viola," she hissed.

"Viola. Such an interesting name." Taney smirked. "Lanskay, Drury. Secure the room."

"Yes sir," the two men said in unison. They both approached the entrance, indicating something to the guard beyond, and then lowered the heavy flap. The only illumination came from lights draping from ceiling hooks and a single lamp on the table near her satchel.

"Viola is quite a fine name," said Octavia, her voice trembling. "Not that uncommon."

"No, it's not. It blends in quite well, doesn't it?" Taney continued to stare at Viola. "Unfasten her dress, Percival."

"Absolutely not!" Octavia said. The loudness of her heartbeat pumped in her ears, her arm throbbing as the need to bloodlet increased. *Oh Lady. He knows.* "I will not disrobe a lady for your sordid purposes—"

"Interesting. Perhaps the medician doesn't know." Taney squatted down, his scruffy dungarees shedding a cloud of dust at the movement. "Did you tell her, eh? Does anyone else know?"

Viola rocked slightly, closing her eyes. Her chin lifted in defiance.

"Know what, sir?" asked Drury. "I thought we took her for ransom."

Octavia sucked in a breath. Ransom. That girl. She might have been one of the kidnapped girls from Mercia

Octavia had read about in the paper. She felt the urge to run after the girl, to save her, do something, but knew there was nothing she could do in this camp of armed men. Frustration tightened her throat and squelched her ability to speak.

"That's how it was meant to appear until this very moment, and why I only have my two most loyal men present."

Octavia couldn't help but notice how Lanskay preened at the praise.

Taney reached out and tapped Viola on the chin, forcing her head up. Her red-eyed gaze was sullen and fearful as she shrank back from his touch. Taney burst out laughing. "To think, you could have been my grandmother."

"Sir?" asked Mr. Drury, his mustache curling in a frown.

Taney stood. "I present to you two gentlemen a solution to the greatest failure to plague our efforts for independence. It's my honor to introduce to you . . . the long-lost Princess Allendia."

Chapter 20

"Princess Allendia?" Drury's jaw gaped.

Taney looked to Octavia. "Medician, unfasten her dress to the waist or I'll do it."

"You will not." Viola's voice was raspy, her eyes narrowing. Taking a deep breath, she nudged Octavia away so she could stand on her own. "I am Princess Allendia of the Fair Valley of Caskentia, crowned true heir to the throne of Mercia, daughter of King Kethan and Queen Varya, granddaughter of the good King Rathe, cousin to the ruling Queen Evandia."

In that moment, Viola Stout was in every way a princess. From the tilt of her head to the stance of her wide hips, she was royalty, even with her skirts slit to the thighs and stained with dirt.

"Well, well." Taney's eyes sparkled. "The old gal has some life in her yet."

Viola crossed her arms against her broad chest. "Your grandfather was the Grand Taney."

"Yes. And I would like to see the scar given to you by your own soldiers, evidence of their poor aim."

Without hesitation or shame, Viola unfastened the buttons lining the satin bodice, then pried down the cup of the full corset beneath. The prominent scar shone against the pallor of her skin. Taney leaned forward, nose almost in her bosom, and nodded his satisfaction.

"Yes. Exactly as described," he said as he straightened.

"And who described it to you?" asked Viola coolly.

Octavia braced herself, already certain of what he would say and dreading the confirmation.

"The esteemed Miss Percival. You should both take pride in the fact that you were quite expensive. That woman drives a hard bargain."

The world swam for a moment. *Miss Percival did this. Sold me. The only mother I've known for ten years sold me.*

Alonzo was right. It was all about the money, saving the academy.

"How much?" Octavia heard herself ask, her voice so husky she almost didn't recognize it.

"Now, now, we don't need to discuss the particulars. It's vulgar to speak of finances with a lady." Taney stalked back toward the other men.

"That's the lost princess," muttered Lanskay. "A publisher's wife. Alive all this time, right there in Caskentia. I'll be damned."

"What are we going to do with her?" Mr. Drury asked, his expression thoughtful.

"My children do not know of my past," said Viola, her voice cracking. "I haven't left any written record, no proof. I have no desire to seek the throne. I beg of you, leave them out of this. Let them live. Do whatever you want with me. Please."

"This has nothing to do with whether or not you *wish* for the throne." Taney cocked his head to the side. "Others will. Caskentia is in ruins. Your people are sick and starving, and what does your queen do? She hides. Your people are weary of war, as are mine. We want autonomy. We want a cure for the curse on our land. If you sat on the throne, you would grant us that, now, wouldn't you?"

Viola fastened her dress again and smoothed it with a dainty flick of her wrist. "If your land is cursed, good. You can all starve to death and the world will be the better for it."

"Such an unfortunate response." Taney turned to Octavia with those pale, scrutinizing eyes. "Which leads us back to you, Percival girl."

"Don't call me that," said Octavia. The very name of Percival made her clench her fists.

"Very well. Medician. I know your kind needs to work willingly, and your patients must be equally willing. I can understand if you're not positively disposed to us at this time."

"No. Near-constant assassination attempts and our kidnapping did not improve my opinion of your cause."

"Now Miss Leander, those murder attempts were not directed by us. We tried to save you," said Mr. Drury. He gave her a frown of great consternation.

"No one would have tried to kill me at all if not for you!" Octavia's voice rose, and Taney waved a hand.

"Enough. Medician, you are aware of the enchanted seals of Mercia and of their nature."

She couldn't help but look at Lanskay. "Yes. They will cause extreme illness and death if an infernal lingers too long within the city."

Taney continued, "There are similar wards placed around the Giant, that fine hulk of rock just to our south." That took her aback. He smiled at her reaction, his thick muttonchops curving with his lips. "Caskentia's infernals have focused on securing Mercia. The dormant volcano has been a lesser priority. I need you to keep my infernals alive as they venture to the Giant."

"I'll do no such thing, and if you think the Lady would bless such a mission, that's ridiculous!"

"Spare me the moralizing. That Tree of yours takes no sides, as you well know. Otherwise, you would never be able to tend an ill soldier, lest he go back on the field and take more lives. Besides, we have a very special relationship with the Lady. Mr. Drury, did the medician try some of our Royal-Tea?"

Mr. Drury bobbed his head. "Indeed, sir."

Taney looked to her. "And tell me, what did you think of it?"

The tea? Their tea? Oh Lady, what did I ingest?

"She seemed to like it," volunteered Mr. Drury.

"As well she should," said Taney. "Congratulations, medician. You drank of your precious Lady."

"What?" Octavia asked with a squeak. The pressure in her arm spiked, as if to remind her of its presence.

"We have found the Lady's Tree. Royal-Tea is made by brewing the dried bark."

The Tree. They found the Tree. Not simply pieces of the Tree, but the entire thing. This time, it was Viola who caught Octavia and held her upright with an arm.

"You cannot expect us to believe that you're using the Tree as an ingredient in a commercially sold tea," said Viola, the trembling in her voice gone. "That's preposterous. You would never even be able to get close to the Tree. It defends itself, has creatures to defend it. Or so the stories say."

"And the stories are true, which is why we require a supply of virgins who are able to get past the threems and other defenses that prevent the tainted likes of soldiers from approaching."

The realization struck Octavia like a blow. "Oh Lady. That girl." She straightened. "That's why you're kidnapping girls from Caskentia. It's not merely for ransom. You're using them as ferries to get the bark. The Lady would never attack the innocent." Virginity and innocence were two very separate entities, not that she expected Wasters to grasp such a distinction.

"Now you begin to understand." Taney nodded. "Lanskay, bring out the branch."

Sudden pain seared in her arm, dazzling her vision with black spots, and faded to a dull ache.

Lanskay lifted cloth from an object on the ground and carried the item over. The branch in his hands was as long as a forearm, the bark green and mottled by lichen. The twigs were bare of leaves. As he neared, she heard the thrum and swell of an orchestra, the beat of a chlorophyll-filtering heart.

The branch was as alive as any person, and screamed its music as if bleeding and near death.

Even more, it sang in accompaniment with the instruments, the voice wispy-light like that of a teenage girl. *"Growmegrowmegrowmegrowme."* The chant was as steady as the one uttered by Viola the night before. Octavia stared, awed, and sank to her knees. Viola's hand rested on her shoulder.

"It's just like . . ." Viola whispered, and stopped.

Just like the branch of the Tree that Viola saw as a girl. "Can I touch it?" Octavia whispered.

"Certainly. You can hold it," said Taney.

Lanskay's radiant heat seemed dimmed by the presence of the branch. She ignored him, her fingers clutching for the piece of wood. A shock nipped at her fingers and whirled up her arms. The sensation zinged through her scalp, her hair prickling in response. The pain in her arm dwindled to a tingle. She stroked the bark, taking in the scaly texture, breathing in the lingering musty scent. *The Tree. I'm touching part of the Tree.*

"That branch was retrieved three years ago. As you can see, the bark and the lichen on it are still alive. The legends are not true in all respects, though. There are many things we have learned about the true properties of the Tree." He paused, but Octavia had no words for him. He continued, frowning, "For example, the leaves are said to bring back those recently killed. It's a lie. Chewing, brewing, doing anything with the leaves induces a grotesque death. As far as we have found, the leaves contain a juice that acts as a potent poison, too potent for us to handle with safety. The green bark is equally fatal. We only use absolutely dried bark that is found on the ground beneath the Tree."

"The cans of Royal-Tea," said Octavia. "All those things the product claimed to do. It's all true." *I actually ingested part of the Lady.* The thought made her giddy and horrified all at once. How many cans of tea were sold each day? The advertisements for Royal-Tea papered the walls and buildings of every city. No wonder the Dallows had no issues with money, even as Caskentia starved. Caskentia's people funded the Waste with every purchase.

The Lady certainly wouldn't object to helping people improve their health, but to treat them in absolute ignorance and use the profits to fund a war—that went against her every belief.

"Growmegrowmegrowmegrowme," sang the branch in its constant yearning to rejoin itself. She stroked the wood like a cat, as if she could quell its need.

"Yes. The tea is something of a miracle product. Mr. Drury here was behind the development of that." Taney acknowledged him with a nod.

"Yes, as I understand it, Mr. Drury has a talent for brewing many things," Octavia said.

"We have yet to find the fabled seeds of the Tree," said Taney. "But perhaps that is just as well."

Those were the first sensible words from his lips. The seeds were said to resurrect anyone, regardless of decomposition. Viola had said a seed existed in the royal vault . . . so Caskentia had that capability, and not the Waste?

No one should hold that power.

The branch shifted in her arms, almost like an awakening baby. Octavia stroked the bark again as tears beaded on her eyelashes. She was holding the Tree. Truly holding part of it. *How many times have I imagined such a thing in my meditations? The feel of the bark is just as I envisioned. Strange, really.* Her fingers explored the ragged crevices and lines.

"If you have seen the Tree, how can you still pursue war? It's against everything that the Lady represents," she said, her voice hoarse.

Taney cocked his head to one side. "The Tree is a thing, medician. Like a field of wheat, ready to be harvested. Certainly, there is a God out there, but if the Tree is proof of anything, it's that we of the Dallows are blessed with a resource that will enable us to be independent at last."

She stared at the branch cradled within her arms. *How can he not see this as proof of the Lady's divinity? How can this be a mere thing to him? Would he look at the Saint's Road and see no lights, hear no song?*

"If you willingly keep my men alive as they journey to the Giant, they will guide you to the Tree."

"What?" she said, dragging her gaze to him.

"You keep my infernals alive as they climb the Giant to release its flow, and in turn, they'll guide you across the plains so that you may see the Lady's Tree with your own eyes."

A pilgrimage to the Lady's Tree. But the cost . . .

"You want to activate the volcano." She stared at him. "The lava and mud flows would go directly into the city. The ash alone—"

"The ash would mostly impact the southern stretch of the Dallows, which is not settled. Our aether magi have already studied the wind patterns. A potent eruption would eliminate most of Mercia and have little impact on those of us beyond the Pinnacles." He said this in a matter-of-fact tone.

Blessed Lady. Half a million people live in the industrial sprawl of the capital. The majority of the entire population of Caskentia. Burn. They would burn or be smothered.

"I can't," Octavia said hoarsely. "To participate in the death of that many . . . the Lady . . ."

"By killing that many, the Dallows will have its independence. If Caskentia will not undo the curse, then we will succeed in spite of it. The destitute of the southern nations will migrate north without concern for Caskentia's endless war. We will have freedom to traverse the mountains and irrigate our lands. Within years, we will form our own cities and grow our population by thousands. Those deaths would create many, many new lives."

Viola's nails dug into Octavia's shoulder. "My daughter lives in the outskirts of Mercia, in the valley beneath the Giant." Her voice was raw, as if the words could bleed.

The branch quivered in Octavia's grasp.

"Keeping infernals alive past the wards is one thing," Octavia said, "but not even I can keep men alive during a volcanic eruption."

Lanskay cleared his throat. "You are a miracle worker, yes, but not even we would expect such a thing of you. The eruption wouldn't be an immediate event. We manipulate fire. It would be a matter of drawing the lava upward and creating a bubble, giving us time to evacuate to the north. Think of it as akin to chipping away at a dam. The earth would eventually break under the strain. Likely within days or a week."

"And after that, you would take me to the Lady's Tree?" she asked. Viola's nails bit into her shoulder even as the branch squirmed at the mention of its whole.

"As soon as it would be safe after the eruption," said Mr. Drury.

"And after that? After I saw the Tree? What would happen then? I couldn't . . . I couldn't come home to Caskentia."

"Octavia! You can't actually consider this!"

Taney's fingers combed at his beard. "You would be embraced by the Dallows. A heroine, a queen. You would have your freedom. Some of the Lady's herbs are not native to our land, but we would provide what you needed. Or you could stay near the Tree and serve our settlement there."

Stay near the Tree. Live there, in its shadow.

It's not as if Caskentia holds any fondness for me. The Queen has signed a warrant for my death. The city of Mercia is a blight on the land.

But to visit the Lady's Tree after committing such a deed . . . would the Lady even accept me, being party to such a sin? How can I even weigh such a thing?

All those lives I saved in the war—could I undo them? It would mean everyone I ever healed . . . it was all in vain.

Taney continued, "If you do not choose to assist in this mission, you'll be brought back to the Dallows and wed to one of my men. Mr. Drury has expressed great interest."

"What?" She recoiled, reality grounding her like an anvil. Mr. Drury smiled in his toothless way. "I won't marry any man against my will. That's barbaric, a travesty."

"In our land, fathers arrange the marriage of their blessed daughters. Your father is dead. Therefore, I would assume that role," said Taney.

Her anger returned, and she was grateful for the emotion. "My father is dead because of an attack committed by your people." *He burned, because of them. And they would burn thousands more.* Octavia stood, the branch clutched to her chest like a babe.

"That is no matter." Taney's eyes were cool. "As of this moment, you are no longer a citizen of Caskentia. You are ours. You can either embrace that willingly or the promise of our land will come upon you regardless. And you'll come to love the Dallows, as all do. But if you choose to resist us, you will never see the Tree. I can promise you that, medician."

She clenched her eyes shut, blocking out the disgusting hope on Mr. Drury's face and the pompous tilt of Taney's hairless chin.

"The Lady cannot be that hard to find," said Viola in a haughty tone. Octavia opened her eyes. "Everyone knows the Tree exists beyond the Waste. Surely a tree taller than the mountains cannot hide that well."

"You would be surprised," said Lanskay. "Our hunters have roamed the far stretches of the Dallows for near a hundred years, and yet this discovery is recent. It is a long, hard trek for our caravans. We still lose men on the journey."

Taney held up a hand to silence his subordinate. "This is your choice, medician. And you must make it today. This is the fork in your path. Choose wisely."

"Growmegrowmegrowme," sang the branch.

"I have to think," Octavia said. "Give me time. Please."

"Keepmekeepmekeepme."

She was so stunned at the sudden shift in the song that she nearly dropped the branch. "Can I . . . hold on to the branch in the meantime?"

Taney cocked his head to one side, smirking. It was clear that he saw the branch as her greatest temptation, what would seal the deal in his favor.

"I can give you an hour, no more. You will be returned to your tent."

Mr. Drury walked behind them to open the flap and motioned them to walk outside.

Sunlight pierced Octavia's eyes and made her cringe. The Giant loomed to the south. Before, it had been a landmark of comfort, but now the dark possibilities made her stomach clench in a knot.

"I am a man of means," said Mr. Drury. "I could provide well for you."

"I am a woman of means. I need no man to provide for me."

"After you travel to the Tree, I hope you will keep me

in mind." The brightness in his eyes wasn't simply from reflected sunlight. "I understand that in Caskentia, women have some ideas of independence. It's a necessity, I suppose, when men are away to war so often."

"As if women are not alone so often in the Wastes," she retorted. The camp was quieter than before. The men on horseback were gone, as was the wagon and the girl. However, there were new men present, as if they had rotated crews. Sudden, prickling heat across her skin made her draw in a hiss of breath. *Infernals.* They noted her presence, too. Four men turned in unison, their gazes curious and somewhat awed. *Oh Lady. Five infernals present, each abnormally attuned.*

"We have large families who share a household, and many sons. Women are not expected to face the strain of life alone."

No, they were meant to die amidst the labor of childbirth. "I must have time to consider my options, Mr. Drury."

"Of course," he murmured, and opened the women's tent for them. The smell of vomit was gone, the cold bowl of beans removed. As soon as the heavy flap dragged shut behind them, Viola whirled around, grabbing Octavia by the shoulders.

"You can't actually consider what they offered." Her eyes searched Octavia's face. "There are half a million people in Mercia. My daughter, my son-in-law, my grandbabe-to-come. They would all die, Octavia, and it would be on your soul. You can't expect that after such a thing, the Lady—"

"They presented you an offer, too."

"Yes! One I promptly refused, even at the risk of my life." Viola's voice softened. "You asked questions as if you are considering this. You can't, child. This isn't you. Even with the possibility of the Lady's Tree, if you can believe they would truly take you there."

"I told them I needed to think," Octavia said. "That didn't mean I needed to consider their offer."

Viola's expression was quizzical, but when she parted her lips to speak, a deep voice came from the flap instead.

"Ladies." One of the guards came through, a hand to his chest as a gesture of respect. His eyes stayed on Octavia. "The potentate has requested that I secure you as a matter of precaution." He held up a chain in his hand.

Octavia bit her lip. Perhaps Taney hadn't been left certain of her choice after all. Another man entered and drove a tall spike into the ground. She heard the metallic rustle of other guards hovering just outside. *Trapped.* Fighting back would be futile. Despair clogged her throat as Viola was motioned to sit and her wrists were chained to the spike, a key clicking in the lock. Then it was Octavia's turn. She sat, her back against Viola's back, and glared at the guard. His expression was apologetic, his touch on her skin brief.

"Can you set the branch on my lap?" she asked.

"Certainly, m'lady." He obliged and backed out of the tent.

Octavia jostled the chain. "Viola, I don't suppose your literary research has taught you how to pick locks while your hands are behind your back?"

"I write about characters who do such, but that hardly means I'm capable of such brilliant escapes."

Octavia stared at the leafless branch resting against her thighs. Even through layers of cloth, she could sense its thrum and warmth, hear the relentless song of its ache to grow again."Our escape would need to be especially brilliant, considering the number of armed men and the five infernals."

"Five?" She felt Viola wrest away as she tried to turn and look at her. "Five infernals together? My God. That must be all the living infernals in their army. I think Caskentia only numbers a dozen since the last war."

"Ten, last I heard." Octavia took a deep breath. "Escape seems impossible, but we have to try. Death is a kinder choice than what these Wasters are offering even if . . . even if it means I never see the Tree with my own eyes."

"Then you are not truly considering . . . ?"

"You know me, Viola."

"I thought I knew Nelly." Her voice was small. "You notice, they didn't even mention the vault? All these years, I've been so dreadfully afraid . . ."

"They have the Tree."

"Yes. Yes. Such things should not be trusted to any man's hands."

Octavia agreed with the sentiment, but at the same time she basked in the weight of the branch upon her lap. She closed her eyes and took in a long, slow breath. She yearned for the Lady, for the sight familiar in her mind. Likely all she would ever have.

The massive form of the Tree filled her thoughts. The canopy of ordinary trees lay a mile below the topmost branches, like a carpet of grass beneath an oak. She breathed in, tasting the mustiness of the true branch on her lap. A tear traced a meandering path down her cheek.

"Lady," she whispered. "Be with us. We need you. These men . . . they commit acts against you and believe they are justified by their cause. All seems so hopeless. Alonzo . . ." Her throat tightened. "Please let him be alive. Please let him help us and not suffer in his efforts. Be with the rest of the airship's crew and aid them, even without me physically present as your agent. As your roots delve through the earth for a drink of water, guide us to an outlet of escape, to a life free of the terrible choices they have presented us today. Show us a way that means life for both the Waste—the Dallows—and Caskentia. Peace. Please, let there be a way of peace."

Octavia bowed her head, chin almost resting on her chest. The Tree in her mind swayed as if considering and she felt the chill of a breeze against her cheeks. She lifted her head, basking. The trail of her tear dried on her skin. A strange chirping sound caused her eyes to open.

At the back of the tent, just feet away, a gremlin had crawled between the fabric and the ground. It wriggled to stand erect and shook out its wings. Something metallic rattled and drew her eye to a bent fork that adorned the base of its wing.

"Leaf," Octavia whispered.

Chapter 21

This was impossible. Absolutely impossible. But as the gremlin leaped into the air and flapped over to her feet, the grin on the creature's strange little face left no doubt that what she saw was quite real.

"What was that?" asked Viola, trying to crane around again.

"Leaf. Our gremlin. Oh, little one, you're in so much danger here!" At her scolding tone, Leaf's ears wobbled.

Viola forced her body to pivot to one side, her hands still firmly restrained against Octavia's. "Is it . . . ? Oh, goodness! Can it possibly be our gremlin? What's on his arm?"

"Keep your voice low, Viola. Please. It's a gift I gave him before freeing him. This is our Leaf, no doubt."

"You named him." Viola's chuckle was dry. "I shouldn't be surprised! But however did he get here? You released him before we reached Leffen, did you not?"

"Yes." Leaf gracefully sprang into her lap and landed on her thighs, right before the branch. His black eyes widened and his head tilted to each side, a mechanical movement like that of a curious owl, but he did not reach forward to touch the artifact. Instead, his attitude seemed . . . reverential. His small hands clasped at his chest, wings extending past his little hips as he looked between the branch and Octavia.

His timing cannot be an accident.

"Leaf, look at our chains. Can you set us free?"

Leaf's ears swiveled to attention as she rattled the chain, and he hopped from her lap. His touch was feathery soft against Octavia's bared wrist, and then he grabbed the chain. With him so close, she flinched at the split-second flash of magic as he touched the metal. There was the distinct clink of a lock and the weight on her arms lightened.

Oh, bless him. She caught the chain with her fingers before it struck the dirt with any noise. Upon setting down the chain, her hands immediately went to the branch. Its song had been incessant but now it seemed to flare.

"Growmegrowmegrowme."

Gunshots punctured the air along with yells and the roar of surging fire. For a half second Octavia stood there, paralyzed in horror.

"Alonzo." Octavia said his name as a breath. *Here. Now. This is our chance.* She turned, branch gripped in her hand, her arm throbbing with the intense need to bloodlet. Leaf pried apart Viola's lock. Octavia grabbed the scissors from her pocket. Small as they were, they were the best weapon at hand.

"Grab the woman!" yelled one of the Wasters.

No. Lady, no. She forced her legs to work, heading to the front of the tent as if to fend off their attackers as Viola was freed. Fear lay against her chest like a leaden vest. *If we're trapped by the men with their guns and fire, Alonzo will not give up. He'll suffer the same fate as the boy. Limp. Bleeding. Dead.*

The branch screamed and writhed in her grip. *"Growme!Growme!Growme! Waterme!Waterme!Waterme!"*

The dead child and his message from the Lady. The pampria Octavia grew in the swamp. Pieces slipped together in her mind.

"I can water you," she whispered to the branch. Sparing no time to unwrap the bandage on her forearm, she slashed the open scissor blade across her thumb and pressed flesh to the branch.

It screamed in a tone that could only be described as ecstasy.

Octavia stabbed the branch into the ground before the tent flap. "Now grow."

The bare twigs quivered, and then buds began to form. Tight green ovals emerged along the limb. It grew, shooting five feet upward in a single breath. Cracks in the earth radiated outward as the ground trembled. Viola's chains clattered to the ground.

The roof of the tent was ripped open. Octavia staggered backward, catching Viola's arm and dragging her away. The branch expanded in height, zooming past Octavia's head, out of the roof and ever upward. Thick branches sprouted all around and grew as they traveled toward the heavens.

This isn't the tranquillity of the Lady I know. This is . . . something more. Something incomprehensible.

Mrs. Stout had mentioned the powerful miasma that

surrounded the artifacts in the vault, and now Octavia could taste that heady, electric power against her tongue.

She hopped back as another branch nearly snared her. The twigs at its end extended like a hand and waved as it passed her face. The tent shuddered and fell apart, revealing the chaos of battle beyond. Several men stood on the other side of the tree, guns in hand as they stared upward with slack jaws.

"Growgrowgrowgrow," The tree hummed, its rhythm content.

"Oh my God," said Viola with a gasp.

Despite Octavia's terror, she understood that this was the Lady. She could . . . trust the Lady. She had to trust her.

"Viola, sit on a branch and rise with it. The tree will protect you."

Viola's jaw dropped. "Go *up*? I can't! The tree, this power. This is even more than—"

"Don't question me, just go!" Octavia grabbed Viola's hand and thrust her forward. The sight of the women seemed to encourage the men to approach, even with the massive tree in their way. Something welled and pulsed beneath the lichen on the bark, and a vine emerged. It whipped out, past the flattened front of the tent, and slapped the two nearest men across the face. They flew backward, toppling the others like ninepins. Octavia shoved Viola to sit astride on a branch. Her thick knees jutted out, wiggling for a secure hold. Leaf leaped onto the visible bloomer ruffles at Viola's thigh and chirped encouragement to Octavia. As Viola rose past Octavia, more vines emerged, but these slinked like snakes to wrap around Viola and hold her in place. Octavia had one final glance of Viola's face, pale and wide-eyed, and then the woman vanished into the thickness of the canopy above.

And it was indeed a thickness.

The tree must have extended at least several hundred feet in the air, far surpassing the nearby heaps of black slag. The air was ripe with the smell of spring growth and freshly turned earth. The shadow of its canopy was deep and black, and Octavia shivered at the sudden drop in temperature. The trunk itself grew in roundness, its circumference well over twenty feet. More of the approaching men were whipped back by vines, while others inched toward Octavia. One of the vines drifted to her eye level and beckoned like a hand.

Nervous terror filled her stomach again. *This is the Lady. There is nothing to fear.* "I know it'll be safe up there," Octavia said to the vine, her voice quivering. "But I can't retreat. I must find Alonzo."

The vine gripped her by a wrist and tugged her forward, almost jerking her off her feet.

"No!" She slapped the vine away. It shuddered and lashed at her again, coiling around her arm to the elbow. She jerked back. The vine whined like a spoiled child. Branches emerged from the still-expanding trunk, twigs stroking her as if to grab hold as well.

"I can't go up there, I can't! Alonzo needs me! I've had to walk away from too many people. I will not retreat now!"

Octavia switched the scissors to her left and slashed at

the vine. The open blades parted the green tendril from a growing twig. Free, Octavia flailed backward, striking the ground. The breath gushed from her lungs. Leaves fluttered around her. The vine around her arm shriveled and fell to dust.

Horror froze her for a second. She looked at the tree, terrified that the entire thing would disintegrate in the same way, but still it grew.

"Lady, I'm sorry, I'm sorry." She scrambled to her feet. Leaves scattered across the ground—full, green leaves. Taney had described them as profound poison, but everything she had ever read described them as possessing a power to bring back those on the boundary between life and death. Octavia didn't have gloves, or possess the time to dawdle. She grabbed a handful of leaves just as another vine began to wave her way.

"Lady, no. No." She motioned it back. "I'll keep fighting if I must, but I will not hide."

The vine stopped, as if considering, and slinked back toward the trunk, dejected.

The nearby crack of a gunshot forced Octavia to the ground. More men attempted to approach; more vines unfurled. Leery of the violent greenery, she took advantage of the deep shade and crawled on her belly away from the camp, going toward the shelter of other—more normal—trees.

Once there, she scrambled behind a trunk and crouched down to get her bearings. The growing tree dominated the camp, the hills, even dwarfing the haze-enshrouded Giant in the background. Most of the fighting seemed to be clustered around the main tent, where the men had formed a protective ring. Several Wasters sprawled on the ground. Those who were shooting aimed north, toward the path Octavia and Viola had taken the night before.

How did Alonzo catch up so quickly? She rubbed her arm where the vine had grabbed her, terrified at her active defiance of the Lady, yet resolute. *Where is he?*

Her eyes searched the tree line and the ridge of a black hill. Several of the Wasters' horses were tethered there; one thrashed on the ground. Sympathy welled in her chest and she uttered a prayer to the Lady to ease its pain. Thinking of the Lady, she remembered the leaves in her hand.

She counted five of them, each the length of her palm and an inch in width. The color was the vibrant green of spring grass. A deep depression extended upward from the stem. The line and the size reminded her of a human tongue. *"Look to the leaves."* She sucked in a breath. She had no idea that the Lady's attributes included precognition.

Octavia glanced at the massive tree. *I could be up there, harvesting enough leaves to revive an army.*

Instead, she shoved what she had into an apron pocket and looked to where Alonzo must be sheltering.

The space between trees was fully exposed to the Wasters. The glistening white of her garment, already shedding its layer of dust, would leave no doubt as to who she was.

She lay flat on the ground and crawled forward, her focus on another cluster of trees not far from the horses. A shot whistled overhead, another thudding into the dirt not far from her legs. *Aiming to disable me, not kill. Their heartfelt apologies would follow, I'm sure.*

She tried to press herself impossibly lower into the hardness of the ground. Dust stung her nostrils and she swallowed down the urge to cough. A dark figure was behind the trees ahead. Octavia crawled faster, the wail of blood beckoning. A cold sensation crept down her spine. Alonzo was hurt—no, not Alonzo. The song wasn't his, but—

"Eh, the medician! Good to see you, miss."

She proceeded into the shelter of the trees. Vincan sat, massive legs sprawled out, a rifle across his lap, a Gadsden holstered at the waist. In an instant she took in his two bullet wounds, one to the shoulder and one to the thigh. The thigh wound was close to the femoral artery and wept blood into a screaming puddle.

"Vincan! Lie down so I can form a circle."

He glowered. His pale skin showed deep bruises on his face, complete with a purple halo around an eye. "Bandage it 'n I'll be fine. Gots to keep up fire. Alonzo was circling round, trying to get into that tent. Not sure if he saw you and the Stout woman. By Allendia's ghost, how'd you make a tree like that?"

"You're losing too much blood. Lie down!"

"Medicians. Always bossy," he muttered. The Wasters opened fire again, some shots aimed toward them, others pinging elsewhere. A man screamed. Vincan turned and raised the rifle to his shoulder.

"There are five infernals," she said.

"Three. Took out t' first two who showed flame. Infernals." He spat a viscous wad of spittle into the dirt, then fired. One bullet struck, a man groaning in the distance. Vincan turned and set the gun on the ground. "Getting cold, miss."

"It's the blood loss. Stretch out here, behind the bushes. Is there anyone else here on our side?"

"Just us. We's all that could squeeze into that courier buzzer. Some woman in Leffen, Alonzo said, she paid the buzzer to play guard all the way to Mercia. Came round, and we asked to borrow it."

"Asked to borrow it. I can imagine how that went. Pardon me." She reached into her dress and used her grimy fingernails to rip the hastily done threads of her brassiere. The scent of the mingled herbs welled in her nostrils and renewed her resolve. She pulled out a conservative scoop of honeyflower, wincing at the contamination of pampria leaves and unsure how it would impact the circle.

Well, the Lady has provided thus far, so she must certainly understand.

Unless I have upset her plans by defying that vine.

Vincan was a massive man, and Octavia did her best to encompass him with the thinnest possible of lines, keenly aware that the Wasters would approach if it took too long for him to return fire. "What happened on the ship?"

Vincan's face was pale even by his standards, his clothing drenched by sweat and blood. "They drove us back into the crew berths 'n blockaded the door with tables and chairs. Two of the crew shot, the captain banged about a bit, 'nother man stabbed, boy slit 'cross the neck but well's can be expected."

She completed the circle. Heat immediately flared below her hand; the circle had been activated, even without her touching the honeyflower on the ground. *The Lady is here.* Tears of relief warmed her eyes. Vincan's readiness to be healed lapped against her skin like warm water.

Another song burbled close by, the notes erratic with injury, but more than that, there was heat.

"Vincan, is the Gadsden loaded?" she whispered, already reaching for his waist.

"Aye. Five bullets."

She brought up the pistol and pivoted on her heel just in time to see a shadow just on the other side of the bushes.

Octavia fired.

The jolt almost caused her to commit the ultimate beginner's error and drop the gun, but she was no beginner—though it had been years since she'd practiced. *I shot someone. Oh Lady, I shot someone.*

Close as she was, she hadn't missed. The infernal had been knocked far enough away that she could scarcely tell he was there.

"Percival!" The voice was bold and commanding. *Taney.* "We have your servant."

Octavia dove forward and peered through the bushes, anxiety driving her heart. Mr. Drury had Alonzo on the ground, a gun to his head. He still wore the leather jacket, but now the woolly collar was stained with red.

"Vincan, get her out of here!" yelled Alonzo, his words slurred. The shade of his skin almost hid the puffiness of his cheek at this distance.

"Miss Leander! I require your help," called Mr. Drury. "Lanskay is injured, just feet away from your location. He's my blood brother. Save him."

She looked between Vincan, still bleeding out and bound in a circle, to the supine body five feet away. *I just shot Lanskay. It'd be more prudent to land another bullet in his skull, Lady forgive me.*

She scooted back to within arm's length of Vincan and set down the gun. "I don't have my satchel!" she yelled, delving a hand into her bosom. Her fingers knew the flakes of pampria by touch.

"We are hardly going to hand over your satchel in the midst of this poorly executed escape attempt, Miss Leander. You are an accomplished doctor when the situation requires." Drury lowered his voice, and exchanged indistinguishable words with Taney.

She flung pampria over Vincan. His body sucked in the herbs like oxygen. His eyes shot wide open. She dug into the other brassiere cup, seeking out a chunk of heskool.

"I do not desire to lose one of my most valuable men either." Taney's voice rang out, luscious as cream. "Check on him. Try to save him. We'll provide you some additional motivation."

She found the heskool and dropped it over Vincan's thigh.

Alonzo screamed, the sound of a throat ripping itself raw. Octavia lurched away from Vincan, her fingers dragging to break the circle.

The other young infernal had hold of Alonzo's arm.

Even at this distance, she saw the glow of the man's fingers, how they traced Alonzo's forearm to drag out another horrible scream.

Burning. He's burning.

"Stop!" she screamed. She started forward, but a heavy weight on her skirt pulled her back.

"Miss, they's Wasters, y' know it's a trap."

"I can't leave him with them." She tugged her skirt free, speaking fast. "If I don't make it back, Mrs. Stout and a gremlin are up in that tree. Please find a way to get them down. The tree . . . should know who you are, that you mean well." *Or may be too helpful.*

Alonzo was no longer screaming, but she could hear his heavy panting, the ragged sobs. The fire may have stopped, but the burning continued. *That's always the way of it.*

Octavia stood up, revealing herself above the bushes. She straightened the collar of her dress, making sure everything was covered. Her fingers went to the headband and the embroidered emblem of the tree, and her eyes to the true embodiment of the Lady only a few hundred feet away.

Then she stalked forward to save Lanskay.

Chapter 22

Lanskay was dead.

The terribleness of that fact lodged in her gut like a bag of coal. *Save him. How am I going to save him without my satchel? What will they do to Alonzo when they know Lanskay is gone?*

The blood of his shoulder wound sang with freshness, though the music dimmed with each passing second. She stooped over Lanskay's body. A graze to his back was older, quieter. So little blood overall, the exits wounds clear, the locations nonfatal. Both of his hands clutched his throat, his eyes wide.

She didn't need a circle.

Octavia flung herself onto Lanskay, hands pressed together to land on his chest. His body curved at her impact as a wad of tobacco shot from his mouth with an audible smack. He wheezed as his lungs took in air. The Wasters broke out in cheers. Lanskay rolled to one side, gasping.

"Well done!" cried Mr. Drury. "Lanskay, how do you fair?"

"Don't hurt Alonzo any more!" Octavia yelled.

"We won't. Not if you cooperate," said Taney.

A campfire breathed smoke feet away. A keg of Royal-Tea sat to one side, the top punctured. Nearby, several Wasters lay utterly still and silent.

"Alonzo?" she called.

"It's not . . . that bad," he managed to croak out. *He'd say that if half his other leg were lopped off.*

Lanskay groaned and rolled onto his back, swiping his mouth with the back of his hand. "My thanks," he said, guttural accent and spittle thickening his words. As his body returned to normal, that extra heat rolled and radiated from him, flickering with every breath. Her lips contorted in disgust.

"Take it as a sign that chew is bad for your health," she said.

"Another thing bad for your health. Getting too close to infernals." He grabbed her wrist.

Octavia felt the fire then. Tiny as it was, it evoked a scream of surprise. Her wrist searing with agony, she jerked back, swinging her arm. Her palm caught the side of his face and sent him into the dirt. The Wasters erupted in hoots and cheers as she scooted away from him.

"That's how you people show thanks?" she screamed, half sobbing. She looked to her wrist. The mark was small—the oval of the very tip of his thumb and the indentation of the nail like a crescent.

Vincan bellowed like a bull about to charge. The bushes shivered. "Miss! He branded you, miss. S'what they do. S'what they did to me. Counting coup." He took in a terrible, rattling breath. "I shoot him, Alonzo dies, but I wants to shoot." The quaking of his body carried through every syllable.

"Don't," she said, then lowered her voice. "Not yet." Iron tainted her tongue; she had bitten her lip.

"It's an honor, medician!" called Taney. "To be so close to an infernal and allowed to live. Only the best of soldiers are granted such a brand."

Vincan growled.

Ten feet away, Lanskay grinned as he shakily stood.

"I don't understand you people," she said. "You incinerated one of your own men because he made a single lewd comment, and you hurt me, like that, and everyone cheers."

"Pain is different from honor," said Lanskay, "Though honor can come from pain." He sobered, regarding her. "I am truly thankful to you. That would have been a sorry way to die, tobacco in my throat."

Her wrist pulsed with heat and she pressed it to her chest. *He needs to die, but his death needs to be painful. He needs to feel what he has caused to so many others.*

"Miss Leander," called Mr. Drury. "I still have a gun to this steward's head. Do come over here, please. The sooner this is resolved, the sooner we can put salve on your wrist."

"Miss . . ." began Vincan.

"Remember Mrs. Stout," Octavia said, then pushed herself upright. She counted the men ahead of her. Two infernals and a third man, and then Lanskay, Mr. Drury, and Taney. Three infernals, three men with guns.

Herself, Vincan, and the Lady.

She looked to the massive tree. *Lady, I know I chose*

the hard path, but you're still with me. What do I do? I used the branch. I have some leaves. What else is there?

Her gaze lowered to the keg of tea. A drink powered by the Lady. She felt the burn on her wrist, the cut on her thumb, and a myriad of other aches and agonies acquired over the past few days.

My blood fed that tree. That tea is steeped in the Lady's own bark.

She kicked the large Royal-Tea tin. It tipped with a slosh. The brown liquid poured out and flowed across the dirt.

Nothing happened.

"I would expect you to be more kindly disposed to that tea, medician," said Taney with a guttural drawl.

"My preference is for the source, not the product." The tea soaked into the ground as would any normal liquid. Octavia gnawed on her lip as she walked forward. *Nothing is happening.* The wind was still, as if nature itself held its breath in anticipation.

Most of the men had been bloodied in the fracas, but of them, Lanskay's flesh wounds and Alonzo's burns screamed the loudest. Alonzo stared straight at her, his expression calm now. Accepting. *He expects to die.*

"You are rather fond of this Tamaran, aren't you?" asked Mr. Drury. "You were frequently in his company in the city."

"Mrs. Stout enlisted him so we wouldn't be women traveling alone, not after that incident with Mr. Grinn." The lie came easily.

A wave of grief passed over Mr. Drury's face. "Mr. Grinn was my dearest childhood friend, Miss Leander. He would have done anything to save you."

"Yes, so he could enslave me to your cause." Her bitten lip continued to ooze. Every word tasted of blood.

"Our cause is about freedom. Your powers can save many lives."

Octavia had almost reached them. So close, she could smell Alonzo's burned flesh. *Like supper meat.* That old revulsion roiled in her stomach again, worse than it had in years. Sweat beaded Alonzo's skin, the swelling around his eye like a ripe plum. She stopped, facing the men, willing something to happen.

Maybe the tea had no power unless it was ingested. *What am I missing?* The foul taste of blood covered her tongue.

Me.

I am the missing ingredient.

She spat blood into the spilled tea.

Hot prickles began in the soles of her feet and whirled upward, causing the hair to rise on the back of her neck. The same sensation as when she activated a circle, only stronger. Power, raw power.

Vines burst from the ground, a countless number in a flailing sheet of green, and whipped toward the men. Octavia hit the ground as the expected gunshots rang out, her hands shielding her head. None of the vines lashed toward her this time—no, they had a different focus.

Shrill screams quivered in the air and were cut short.

More shots, Taney yelling, more screams, the roar of fire. Heat rippled overhead, a shock against the autumn cool. She raised her eyes. The vines were everywhere, making it nigh impossible to see who was who in the thrashing mess of flora and men. The harsh scent of cut grass assaulted her nose. A new cry arose, different from blood, a terrible and pathetic whine—the same sound she heard when she sliced the vine, only multiplied. These vines lived and bled.

"Alonzo!" she shouted, sitting up on her knees. A vine as thick as her forearm glided past, dragging a man's leg in its wake. She forced her gaze away.

The Lady did that.

The Lady maims. She kills.

The Lady manifests through blood. My blood.

"Alonzo!" she screamed.

Fire billowed and the vines bowed and crested like an ocean wave. A flash of blond hair above revealed Lanskay. Vines clenched his waist like a fist and hauled him upward. Flames trickled from his hands and singed several vines, causing them to curl back, but others took their place. Her eyes met with Lanskay's, his face determined yet fearful, and then he plummeted to the ground.

Taney was there beside Lanskay, a sword in his hand. *A sword? Where did an antiquated weapon like that come from?* Severed vines draped from Lanskay like a child's play costume gone wrong and disintegrated as he leaped up. Taney and Lanskay retreated together, Taney driving back vines with the blade.

"Alonzo!" Octavia half turned. "Vincan! The potentate

is getting away!" She stepped forward. She held a breath for a moment, frozen in fear, but the vines shrank back to create a path. A few seconds later and they all began to withdraw into the cracked, dry earth.

The walls of the tent had collapsed. Several men, or bits of them, adorned the ground like the aftermath of a canon blast. Something squished underfoot. She didn't look down.

A lump of man lay on the flattened canvas of the tent. His leather-adorned arms hugged his body limply, his mouth agape. The exit wound of the bullet was a black hole in his temple. It wept blood and matter.

Octavia stopped. Her breath burned in her throat. "Alonzo?"

"I wasn't trying to shoot him." Mr. Drury sat just behind him, leaning on his knees. "The vines reached for me and I fired and he tried to lurch up, get away."

"No," she breathed.

"Come with me, Miss Leander." Mr. Drury stood and brushed off his suit. It still fit him with tailored excellence, even stained by the trail and spatter. "We can meet with Mr. Taney and Mr. Lanskay. I'm sure we can work out a compromise, and that they won't force you to do anything you do not wish to do."

It took effort to breathe, as if her lungs had turned solid. "That will never happen. You're lying to yourself if you believe that, Mr. Drury."

Something in his eyes hardened. "I want you to come with me, Miss Leander."

"I will not."

His gun remained on the ground beside Alonzo. As Mr. Drury stepped forward, she was keenly aware of his proven strength and agility and how well she would fare against him in a melee. She retreated several steps.

Lady, help me. The vines were gone, the earth shattered and uneven underfoot. Mr. Drury loomed in her sight a mere step away. He grabbed her upper arm, the clench of his fingers firm. She reached behind her head. Her fingers found the metal shaft of the bullet probe used to secure her bun. She grabbed hold and jerked her arm forward. The world blurred.

His eye screamed—a juicy squirt—followed by a crunch and that distinctive whistle and whiff of brain matter. Mr. Drury groaned as he toppled backward. The medical instrument protruded from his eye. The music of him bleated and wailed.

She stared at him for several long heartbeats. *A bullet probe. I . . . what did I . . . Mr. Drury. His eye . . . his brain.*

Other music called to her, the brilliant brasses going dull. She turned and staggered forward. *Alonzo.*

Octavia fell hard to her knees and bent over him, her hands resting on the smoothness of his cheeks. He was still warm to the touch. Life lingered in him yet. She fumbled her hand inside her dress and to her brassiere, even knowing that her supply had been exhausted by tending Vincan. *My satchel. It's somewhere beneath the tent. Where's an opening? Can I cut my way inside? Oh Lady. There's no time.*

His heat was fading, his skin stiffening. The brass band of his soul had quieted to the soft rat-tat-tat of a lone drum.

His glazed eyes stared toward the sun, the blue more pale than it had ever been in life.

"Lady," she gasped, "Lady. Please." She curled her back and shut her eyes, willing herself into Al Cala, drawing herself to the image of the true Tree. An icy wind numbed her face. *This isn't my imagination.* A child's laugh caused her to recoil in surprise. Her vision swooped like a bird in flight and found a figure in the thick of the branches. A young boy, on a swing of weathered rope and driftwood.

"Listen to the branch and look to the leaves." His words returned to her with the lash of the wind. *Look to the leaves.*

She opened her eyes to the desolation of the camp and shoved a hand into her apron pouch. The leaf fit in her hand, her thumb tracing the midrib. *Taney said the juice is poison. Chewing it is poison.* She tugged Alonzo's jaw fully open and with her filthy fingers lifted the limp weight of his tongue. The leaf, so tonguelike itself, fit in the depression behind his lower teeth; his tongue lay on top as a lid. She withdrew her fingers and nudged his mouth shut again. Her warm tears plinked like rain as she brushed the softened leather of his shoulder.

"Lady, please bring him back. Please bring him back." She opened his jacket, and the crimson steward's coat still underneath, peeling back the layers of fabric until she found flesh. Her skin, even tanned by labor, was so pale against his nutmeg tone. Her fingers curled against the muscled knoll of his chest.

"Live," she whispered, and brought her face over his. Without the probe in place, her hair shifted and unfurled behind her headband. A crazed ringlet drifted to rest on his cheek.

Alonzo twitched. Beneath her fingers, his heartbeat surged. Music flared in her ears, the triumphant fanfare of trumpets. His lips opened with a gasp. His eyes blinked wildly and then focused on her. The bruised knob on his cheek wavered like the ocean surface and sank in, revealing unblemished skin and the perfect angle of his cheekbone. The thick sludge of blood along his cheek and ear evaporated, the screams quelled. The wounds sealed and the music withdrew as well, resuming its quiet background hum.

The cooked stench of his burn wound dissipated. She breathed in, fully.

"Octavia." He said her name with his first exhalation. He frowned, his tongue finding the leaf obstructing his mouth.

"Don't bite it! Here, open up." He did, his expression puzzled. She pinched the leaf out again, and even as she lifted it away it faded into dust.

"I saw the Tree," he whispered, and she knew he wasn't speaking of the one nearby. He wiggled his lips for a moment, as if shaking off the rigor of death. "It spoke to me, it told me . . ."

A harsh chill quaked her body. *No. No. This can't be as it was with the child. Not again. Not to be taunted with life, with him, to lose him anew.*

" . . . 'Go.' "

Octavia blinked rapidly. " 'Go?' That's it?"

"Isn't that enough?" A grin creased gentle lines into

his face. She felt the warm heaviness of his hand on her shoulder, and she lowered her lips to his. The texture was chapped yet soft, his heat sending a giddy whirl through her stomach. A slight whimper escaped her throat. His hand glided to her neck, his thumb brushing her skin. With his lips moving against hers, his breath surprisingly minty, everything felt right.

Her eyelids fluttered shut for a few seconds, and then she realized she wanted to see this. See him. His pale blue eyes were open as well, studying her in that intense way he studied everything. A smile turned her lips even as she kissed him again, fiercer. A moan escaped his throat as he pulled her closer.

His song grew stronger, her awareness more keen than ever before. She felt the very reverberation of his life force against her lips, the way a tree's leaves take in the heat of the sun.

As if—as if I can feel his heart, wield power over his life right now, without a circle, without any herbs in hand. It wasn't like this just a few days ago at the Saint's Road—but my blood didn't cause pampria to sprout before the swamp either.

His body, his song, quivered through her awareness as if she were a composer. She had read the musical notes of bodies for so many years, but now it was as though she could pry apart the wind instruments and drums and brass by her very will. Control them. Rewrite the song.

She jerked back, frightened.

The ground shuddered. She glanced up. The giant tree was shrinking. The motion was slow, nowhere near as fast as it had been in growth, as it withdrew toward the ground. Alonzo propped himself up on his elbows, his gaze still on her. One hand went to his chest as if to check his own heartbeat.

"That . . . that was nice," she said with a shaky smile. *I wanted it to be nicer. Lady, what's happening to me?*

"Helloooooooo down there!" Mrs. Stout's voice was high and far away.

"Octavia . . ."

"Viola will be down in a few minutes." The words were raspy.

"That infernal burned you."

She looked at the welts on her wrist. "It was nothing compared to the way they tortured you."

His sleeve was still clumsily rolled to the elbow, cloth stained by gore. Faint pink lines showed where they had scorched him. "'Tis not fair, really. I am healed, yet you, the healer, are still hurt. When we find your satchel . . ." Alonzo's body brushed against the canvas tent as he worked to stand. His breath caught sharply. "Drury. Did you do that?"

"Oh Lady. I did." She crawled over to Mr. Drury, already bracing herself for the sight of him. Shrapnel to the eye was never pretty. "I can save him." Her fingers fumbled out another leaf.

"Are you sure you want to do this?" Alonzo asked.

"I'm a medician. I can't . . . I can't just let someone die. Not even him."

Still, she cringed as she touched his lips. She tucked the leaf beneath his tongue and shut his jaw.

"Was that truly the potentate here?"

"Yes." Keeping her gaze away from Alonzo, she rested a hand against Mr. Drury's forehead. She spoke of what she had learned of their plot against Mercia, that Miss Percival had indeed sold out both Octavia herself and Viola Stout, that they were using young girls to harvest the gleanings of the Lady's Tree. The words flowed fast, and as the minutes passed Mr. Drury's skin only grew colder.

"Did I do something wrong?" she said aloud. Through her, the Lady had mended thousands of strangers over the years. She knew the Lady was currently present, even without a circle to draw her eye.

I could press my lips to his, see if I feel any thrum of life as with Alonzo. Personal revulsion was an adequate excuse to avoid that, but even more, she knew there was nothing there to feel.

Octavia opened Mr. Drury's mouth and withdrew the leaf. It looked the same as before, only glossy with saliva. It remained whole in her hand.

"The Lady didn't want him healed." She stared at Mr. Drury in awe. "I have never . . . never seen her deny someone so utterly. But after he saved me from that machine at the hotel, I never felt the burden of a blessing on me. She . . . she . . ."

"Considering his sins, that is her choice to make."

Octavia nodded mutely and traced the crusted slash across her thumb.

The Lady killed. She killed Mr. Drury by denying him life anew, and she killed the other Wasters whose body parts still lie scattered across the ground. Who is the Lady, really?

Who am I? A medician—and something more?

She shivered, discomfited by the very blood running through her veins.

VIOLA RETURNED TO EARTH shaky but well. Leaf had made a comfortable nest for himself on the shelf of her bosom, one wing draped over her shoulder to hook himself in place. He chirped in greeting but seemed content.

"My goodness," said Viola, plopping down on an overturned bucket beside a smoldering fire. "My goodness. I saw everything from up there. Every awful thing."

"Everything?" Octavia asked sharply, half expecting a lecture on impropriety.

"Well, I may have averted my eyes a time or two." Mrs. Stout offered Octavia a not-so-subtle wink.

Alonzo greeted Mrs. Stout and then stared at the gremlin, shaking his head and grinning. "This day is full of surprises."

Octavia dug out her satchel from beneath the tent and almost wept to feel that familiar weight in her hands. She immediately ran the wand over the leaf she had retrieved from Mr. Drury. Four leaves left. As for the mighty tree, it had not shed a single leaf. All that remained was the bare branch upon the ground, alive and humming some wordless song. Octavia looped the artifact into the top straps of her satchel.

Vincan returned soon after Alonzo and Octavia had gathered most of the dead to burn. His pale skin was ruddy and drenched with sweat.

"Wasters got away," he said simply as he heaved himself

to the ground. "Some more o' their horses got free. They snared 'em and rode off. I was on foot, but I tried t' follow. Got off one shot but had only two bullets left, didn't want to be without."

Exhausted, they all gathered around the fire to eat beans.

"The big question is what we do now," said Alonzo. He rubbed his face with both hands.

"Well! It would be better to say you're dead," said Viola.

Alonzo looked at her in puzzlement. "What?"

"I was there in the promenade! I heard what that little steward said, that other Clockwork Dagger. You were intended to fail, to appear as a fool."

"I was a fool, naive. I thought I would prove myself by keeping Octavia alive, even as I defied my orders. That . . . I worked for a greater good."

"You did, and I'm grateful for it," said Octavia, her voice soft. Gazing at him evoked a cozy warmth in her chest, even as the sensation was tempered by fear of what she had felt in their last kiss. *Not just what I felt in him but in myself—my own potential.* "But the truth is that you were treated like a child underfoot in the kitchen, and you deserved better."

Alonzo stared into the fire as he ate.

"Caskentia will still want me dead." Octavia knew that with certainty. "Taney and Lanskay know what I can do with the blessing of the Lady."

Viola nodded. "Yes. The people of the Waste are nothing if not stubborn, and you caused a full tree to grow before them, child. Your worth was confirmed."

Whatever that means. She gazed into the bowl as if she

could scry in legumes. "There is much I don't understand about the Lady. Alonzo?" He looked up. "We can't stay in Caskentia, that much is clear. The southern nations are known for their libraries, their academies."

He swallowed and set the bowl to one side. "The southern nations." He nodded slowly. "Yes. There are said to be libraries there so large a person can get lost for days. This enigma of the Lady's Tree—perhaps we can find some answers there. Maybe we can find a way to her."

That rekindled desire brought tears to her eyes. She laid a hand on the branch. It was quiet now, satiated, even as it still hummed with life.

"The ride south will be hard, Octavia. Wilderness, on the brink of winter." Alonzo's expression was equally hard. "Once we cross the ravine to the city-states, there is no guarantee of our safety. Both Daggers and Dallowmen will be in pursuit. The southern nations take no sides."

"What other choice do we have?" asked Octavia.

"Death."

She shrugged. "Well, I've made clear my thoughts on that."

A small smile rounded Alonzo's cheeks. "Mrs. Stout, Vincan can fly you to Mercia in the buzzer. Vincan, about me . . ."

The big man nodded. "Eh. You're dead. The Wasters strung you up like a Solstice ham. Not sure what t' say about the miss. Are you s'pposed to be alive or dead?" he asked, looking to Octavia.

"Say you do not know," said Alonzo. "Soon enough, the

Waste's continued interest in Octavia will alert Caskentia to the fact that she lives. Perhaps some ambiguity will buy us time."

"I won't be safe either, nor will my children be." Viola straightened, causing the slumbering gremlin to shift and yawn on her shoulder. "We will also head south. Besides, that region boasts more readers than Caskentia. It may be a prudent business move in the end."

Dawdling wasn't wise. With the meal concluded, Vincan and Alonzo clapped hands. Viola embraced Octavia, the slightest hint of rosewater still lingering on her skin.

Leaf stirred with a wide, fang-tipped yawn. The gremlin flexed one wing and then the other, then hopped toward Octavia. She caught him on her forearm.

"I didn't get to thank you properly earlier." Octavia scratched at the wrinkled flesh between his ears. She felt the faint line of what could be a seam. "I wish I had some of those little cheeses you loved on the ship. You earned handfuls of them, little one."

Leaf trilled. He cocked his head to one side, round black eyes staring as if he could see through her. He leaned forward and she brought her arm closer. His wing brushed her cheek as his stubby fingers pressed against her headband and the embroidered emblem of the Lady's Tree.

"That's the Lady," she whispered. "Like the tree you were in a short while ago, though more permanent."

He chirped. His fingers rubbed as if to take in the texture of the threads.

"In the south, they say, men can speak with gremlins,"

said Viola, her voice far softer than usual. "What would our creature say? I wonder."

Leaf's grip on Octavia's arm shifted, and with a twist he took off. She touched the emblem on her headband as she watched him fly away. His fork armband glistened in the light as his wings flapped east—toward the mountains, the Waste, the Tree.

The Lady is somewhere out there. The Wasters found her. Maybe Alonzo is right, and we can find our own path.

"I'm not sure if Leaf truly needs words or a translator. It's clear he was sent to aid us." She lowered her gaze to Alonzo. He was passing several items over to Vincan.

"Considering the day, I don't doubt that a bit. I am sure you haven't seen the last of him, child!" Viola followed Octavia's line of sight and clucked her tongue. "As for Mr. Garret, that so-called steward of yours! A few days ago, I had far different opinions, but I daresay he has surprised me."

"Does that mean I'm spared the lecture on the impropriety of my gallivanting about in the woods with a man?"

"Well! He's not just a man, is he? He's a Clockwork Dagger. He's the sort a woman wants to gallivant about with." Mischief sparkled in Viola's eye. "Oh! And I mustn't forget." She reached into her cleavage, and after some fumbling, pulled out a small satin purse. "You'll need this." She pressed the purse into Octavia's hands. It was warm and moist with sweat.

Octavia opened the bag to find jingling golden coins. She sucked in a breath. "Oh, no, Viola. I've never held this much money in my life. These are gilly coins. I can't—"

"You can and you will." Viola's tone was imperious. "You need the money to travel and survive, and at some point you'll need new medician attire that is not the pure white of a Percival disciple." Sorrow sagged her face.

"About Miss Percival . . ."

"I will not correspond with her further. I will not let her know I live." Viola's jaw hardened as much as it could. "If there's anything of the old Nelly still there, the guilt is eating her alive. And it should. It should." She looked past Octavia. "You take good care of this girl, you understand?"

"If things continue as they have, she will likely be the one taking care of me," Alonzo said.

Viola and Octavia hugged a final time. "Octavia," she whispered, "I know you love your Lady, but don't do so blindly. Remember my father's warning. Remember what you saw here today."

As if I could forget. "I'll remember." Octavia couldn't help the tears that fell as she watched Viola and Vincan trudge along the trail together. Alonzo stood behind her, giving her time to compose herself before she turned around.

"Well, that's that, then. I suppose we should head out?"

The two of them, alone together in the wilderness. *Well, Miss Percival was right in her advice about shunning the presence of men. Nothing proper has happened, that's a certainty.*

Alonzo had cobbled together supplies to load a horse for each and a gray packhorse besides. Octavia mounted her white mare. Alonzo had claimed a chestnut stallion with a long blaze. Downwind, the pyre of the dead had been lit. It crackled in the distance like a body's song.

They took a path going south, silence dwelling between them for a time. Octavia's mind was a weary jumble. A gentle breeze rattled through the branches above. No bodies cried out in need. No one spoke but birds, and they sang of all the glories of autumn. Squirrels scampered from tree to tree like little gray ghosts. The smell was of mustiness and dirt and everything she loved about life.

Octavia laughed, the sound causing Alonzo to swivel in his saddle.

"What . . . ?"

"Here. Where we are. It's beautiful. A piece of paradise. Delford isn't far away, is it? Just to the south of the Giant?"

"'Tis a few days' ride away."

"Today we would have docked in Mercia, been surrounded by metal and people and industry. Everything I hate. Instead, we're here. Alive. Free." She tilted her smile toward the patchy sunlight. "Can we go to Delford?"

Alonzo remained silent for a time. "'Tis not far out of our way, but such a destination is not prudent."

"Everyone who hunts us knows that Delford was my destination. Therefore, if we were smart, it would be the foremost place to avoid, correct?"

A hard crease deepened between his eyebrows. "You suggest we play fools and go there anyway?"

"Yes. It's what they would least suspect."

"True." Another long pause. "Your blessed supplies are low. You mentioned before that many in Delford are gravely ill."

"Hundreds, yes."

"You do not readily walk away from those in need. We cannot stay in Delford—you should not heal anyone at all and draw attention to yourself. I should not even be sighted, as my skin is far too memorable." He frowned, shaking his head. "What do you hope to gain from such a visit, beyond tormenting yourself?"

"I want . . . I want to know I made it there. Despite the attempts on my life, despite the plotting, the lies." She stared ahead. The mare's ears flicked as a red leaf spiraled to the forest floor. "You're right that it won't be easy for me. So many have suffered, are still suffering. If I can walk through Delford and offer a prayer and a silent apology, at the very least it means they are not ignored. Not forgotten."

"You cannot save everyone, Octavia. Not even the Lady can do such."

She nodded with the sway of her horse. "I know, and yet . . ."

"And yet." His smile was weary, resigned.

A few days together, and he knows me so well.

They rode on, hooves crunching on the duff. Octavia breathed as in her Al Cala and prayed for those left injured or dead during the past few days—the people on the *Argus,* the pox-stricken in Vorana, the gremlins in a burlap bag, the horses left kicking in the street, that boy and his grieving mother—even the puppy, who had likely succumbed to his fate days before.

As a nearby jay belted out a chorus in voice and body, she was reminded to add a prayer for the egrets.

Chapter 23

Delford was everything Octavia had hoped it would be. The hills were rolling and green, the trees lush. The place was fragrant with cow manure, not a pleasant smell, but one that evoked cozy memories and a sense of home.

Not home. Not for me.

The thought didn't grieve her as much as she expected.

She dismounted, ready to confront the place that had been her dream for so many months. Alonzo pulled a Waster's overcoat from his saddlebag and passed it down to her. She buttoned it up to cover the warded, pristine fabric of her uniform.

"From here, I will watch the road and the village," he said, nodding at the pastoral scene below. Smoke curled from chimneys and blended with a mottled sky. "If you take more than an hour, I will come into town."

"I shouldn't be long." She handed off her reins to him. Her hands glanced over her satchel, still tied to the saddle.

I am a visitor, that's all.

"Be careful." His tone of voice gave her pause. Black fuzz thickened the line of his jaw and his lips. Kissing him would feel different now—or would the increase in her magic pull her past the physical sensation completely?

She looked away. *I'll find my answers in the southern libraries. I must.*

"I'll be back soon," she said.

"I will be here."

She granted him a smile. As much as she dreaded whatever awaited her in the village, Alonzo would be waiting for her. She knew that as an absolute.

Octavia walked downhill. The road's ruts were deep enough to swallow her feet. In a nearby lot, a cow lowed. A flock of chickens scurried across a gap between the brown-tile-roofed buildings. A few other people milled about a well in the center of the square. The back of her neck prickled. Not with the sense of being watched, but with a sense of wrongness.

Everyone looks normal. Healthy. The village has none of the decay and disuse I was told of, with people too bed-bound to labor.

She followed the redolent scent of bread to a small shop just off the square. Cooling loaves lined a long windowpane.

"Greetings!" Octavia called.

In the kitchen, a white-scarved woman turned. Flour dusted her arms and the plump rounds of her cheeks. "Hey-o! Passing by, eh? Day-tripper to the Giant?"

"I am. The bread smells lovely."

"Shovel manure or stack wood for a loaf, or I'll take a coin, if you 'ave it."

Giggling children ran by dangling a fish on a rope, a

horde of delighted cats in their wake. Their bodies—all but the fish—rang with sound health.

"Tell me," Octavia said, slowly, "do you know of an Egan Covington?"

The baker's nose crinkled. "Can't say I do, 'n I know most everyone."

"What about a Des Murray or Wallo Rakely?"

She shook her head. "Nep."

The three men who came to the academy, who hired me for Delford—they don't exist, not by those names. Maybe they were Wasters, or hired actors.

Miss Percival concocted the perfect lie to lure me into their grasp.

"I've got a copper," Octavia said. "I see rolls back there."

"Aye. Solid coin'll get you a full dozen, plus cheese, if you'd like." She shuffled over and accepted the thin coin from Octavia's hand.

"Yes. Cheese would be grand." *If Leaf were here, it'd be all his.* She paused, looking around. "This is a fine village. With the mountains so close, have you had issues with the Waste?"

At that, the woman's face shifted to a grimace as she deftly folded the crusty rolls into a sheet of old newspaper. "No more'n most. Lost too many boys at the passes, my man included, but the village? It's a good one. If any Wasters dared to show 'ere . . ." She nodded to a rolling pin close by.

Octavia didn't doubt that she'd use it either. "My thanks, and my condolences." She pressed a fist to her chest.

The baker shrugged. "We get by." She handed over the makeshift bag of rolls and a hard cut of cheese.

Octavia walked away, burdened only by bread. The cheese fit in the wide pocket of the overcoat.

"You appear strangely happy," Alonzo said as she emerged from the brush. His horse grazed at the foot of a cottonwood.

"I suppose I am strangely happy. There's no sickness here. It was all a lie." She opened the parcel enough to pull out a few rolls of bread. Alonzo tucked the food into his coat as Octavia packed the rest away.

He studied her as he mounted. "I am glad. I was worried about your leaving this place behind, walking away from those in need. 'Tis green and beautiful here. Everything you hoped for."

"Not everything." She swung herself into the saddle.

He arched an eyebrow. "What is missing?"

"Well, it is green here, but I've seen many green places. What I wanted most of all was to belong, to be needed." She reined away as she flashed a grin at him. "Lady knows, you need someone to keep you alive and upright."

His chestnut stallion trotted alongside her. Alonzo's black plume of hair bounced on his shoulder. "I am delighted to oblige you, though 'tis my hope that your services are not often called upon in the future." They wound their way through the brush, forming their own trail. "I should also observe that the terrain will be much the same as this as we ride south."

"That's good. If we must ride for our lives, at least it will be beautiful."

"Yes. 'Tis ideal for wooing as well. Or so I hear."

They reached an open rise. His horse broke into a lope and surged past.

Octavia burst out in laughter as she rode in quick pursuit, ready to outpace—for a time—her guilt, her assassins, her concerns for tomorrow. Alonzo's resonant song kept perfect time with their hoofbeats.

Acknowledgments

At age four, I announced that I wanted to write books when I grew up. I also said I wanted to become Popeye. I think I made the right choice between those goals.

A lot of folks have helped me along the way. My gratitude to:

The gang at Codex Writers for the contests, camaraderie, and woots galore. Thanks to Luc Reid for creating a safe haven to keep me (mostly) sane. I'm grateful to early draft readers of *The Clockwork Dagger:* Pete Aldin, Rebecca Roland, Gary Kloster, Kenneth Kao, Vylar Kaftan, Rachael Marks, Steven R. Stewart, Jeff Lyman, Randy Henderson, and Michael R. Underwood. Special thanks to Elle Van Hensbergen and Anaea Lay for the full draft critiques!

Rachel Thompson, for coming up with the title and letting me rant and rave on occasion. Our friendship grew beneath the photograph of the Little Boy with the Big Loaf; let it forever live in infamy.

Rhonda Parrish, my dear friend, pen pal, and editor. You "get it." I'm honored to share my journey with you.

My super agent, Rebecca Strauss, for her ruthless revisions and constant support, and to everyone at DeFiore & Company.

The publishing team at Harper Voyager. I don't know all of your names, but I know you're all awesome. In particular, my thanks to my editor, Diana Gill, assistant editor Kelly O'Connor, and PR mastermind Caroline Perny.

Last but not least, my family. My parents, Larry and Lona Beth Davis, for unabashedly raising geeks. My grandma, Bonnie Nichols, to whom I dedicate Octavia's strategic use of undergarments. My brother, Scott, for reluctantly sharing the Nintendo and Super Nintendo. My husband, Jason, for his absolute support. And Nicholas, for being Nicholas.

ABOUT THE AUTHOR

Beth Cato lives near Phoenix, Arizona. Her husband Jason, son Nicholas, and crazy cat keep her busy, but she still manages to squeeze in time for writing and other activities that help preserve her sanity. She is originally from Hanford, California, a lovely city often pungent with cow manure.

Author website: www.BethCato.com and Twitter: @BethCato